Praise for Susan Stoker

"I will read anything Susan Stoker puts out . . . because I know it's going to be amazing!"

—Riley Edwards, *USA Today* bestselling author

"Susan Stoker never fails to pull me out of a reading slump. With heat, action, and suspense, she weaves an incredible tale that sucks me in and doesn't let go."

—Jessica Prince, *USA Today* bestselling author

"One thing I love about Susan Stoker's books is that she knows how to deliver a perfect HEA while still making sure the villain gets what he/she deserves!"

—T.M. Frazier, *New York Times* bestselling author

"Susan Stoker's characters come alive on the page!"

—Elle James, *New York Times* bestselling author

"When you pick up a Susan Stoker book, you know exactly what you're going to get . . . a hot alpha hero and a smart, sassy heroine. I can't get enough!"

—Jessica Hawkins, *USA Today* bestselling author

"Suspenseful storytelling with characters you want as friends!"

—Meli Raine, *USA Today* bestselling author

"Susan Stoker knows what women want. A hot hero who needs to save a damsel in distress . . . even if she can save herself."

—CD Reiss, *New York Times* bestselling author

T0120391

THE
Lumberjack

DISCOVER OTHER TITLES BY SUSAN STOKER

Game of Chance Series

Silverstone Series

Mountain Mercenaries Series

Ace Security Series

The Refuge

Deserving Alaska
Deserving Henley
Deserving Reese
Deserving Cora
Deserving Lara
Deserving Maisy (October 2024)
Deserving Ryleigh (January 2025)

SEAL of Protection: Alliance Series

Protecting Remi
Protecting Wren (November 2024)
Protecting Josie (March 2025)
Protecting Maggie (TBA)
Protecting Addison (TBA)
Protecting Kelli (TBA)
Protecting Bree (TBA)

SEAL Team Hawaii Series

Finding Elodie
Finding Lexie
Finding Kenna
Finding Monica
Finding Carly
Finding Ashlyn
Finding Jodelle

Eagle Point Search & Rescue

Searching for Lilly
Searching for Elsie
Searching for Bristol

THE
Lumberjack

SUSAN
STOKER

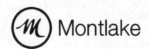

Montlake

Published by Montlake, Seattle

www.apub.com

Amazon, the Amazon logo, and Montlake are trademarks of Amazon.com, Inc., or its affiliates.

ISBN-13: 9781662509711 (paperback)
ISBN-13: 9781662509704 (digital)

Cover design by Hang Le
Cover photography by Wander Aguiar Photography
Back cover image: © Cavan Images / Getty

Printed in the United States of America

THE

Lumberjack

CHAPTER ONE

It took a few seconds after she woke up for April to realize where she was. What had happened. Well . . . what she'd been *told* had happened. She was in the hospital because her car had run off the road. She didn't remember any of it.

Actually, she didn't remember much of the last five years of her life.

The doctors told her that they had high hopes her loss of memory was a result of the bruising of her brain from the accident.

But "high hopes" wasn't super comforting. She would've preferred they told her in no uncertain terms that her amnesia was temporary. The thought of not ever remembering anything about her life of the last several years was terrifying.

She remembered who she was—April Hoffman. That she was forty-six and her mom was her only family left, and even everything about her childhood. But the hole in her memories about what she'd been doing for the last five years was, quite frankly, freaking her out.

Not because she thought she'd done anything horrible, but more because she'd had a steady stream of visitors who seemed to be really worried about her . . . and she couldn't remember any of them. She didn't like to see them upset, and it was clear they were extremely stressed out not only about her accident, but because she didn't know them.

Her head throbbed, and April kept her eyes closed. The light in the room exacerbated the headache she'd had since waking up in the emergency room. She heard shuffling from next to the bed and vaguely wondered who it was sitting with her this time.

From the moment she'd woken up in the hospital—in Bangor, Maine, she was told—April hadn't spent even one minute alone. It was disconcerting to realize the people who were sitting next to her bed were so loyal. She'd never had that many friends . . . that she could remember. And certainly none who would put their entire lives on hold to be bored out of their minds by sitting next to her hospital bed while she mostly slept.

The truth of the matter was, the April she remembered being was a loner. She'd always wanted to have friends she could hang out, shop, and laugh with. It seemed that whatever she'd been doing the last five years had resulted in just that . . . if only she could remember.

Her eyes finally opened when she heard a whispered argument nearby. April turned her head and saw the back of a man just outside her door. His legs were shoulder-width apart, and he was blocking access to the room. She could tell he had his arms crossed over his chest as he engaged in a very heated conversation with another man.

She stared at the man's back and desperately tried to remember something, anything, about him. His name was Jackson Justice, she'd learned, and he'd been a steady presence in her life ever since she'd woken up scared and hurting in the hospital.

She didn't know him, but something deep down inside made her immediately trust him. When the doctors told April that she had amnesia, he'd been the one she'd looked to for reassurance. When she'd woken up in the middle of the night with her head throbbing so badly she thought for sure she was dying, he'd been there, holding her hand and telling her she was going to be all right. He'd gotten her to slow her breathing and had stayed right by her side until she'd fallen asleep again.

Even when all the other people—her friends—streamed in and out of her room, he was the one she looked to when she got overwhelmed. He was the one who shooed everyone out at the exact moment she needed a little break from all their concern.

They all called him JJ, but for some reason, that name didn't feel right to April. When she admitted as much to him, he told her that she called him Jack. *That* had felt familiar. It was probably the first thing that felt right in the last week.

Jack had said they were friends, that she worked for the business he owned with the three other men who'd been visiting regularly over the last week with their wives, but he hadn't gone into any more detail than that. It felt as if she and Jack had more of a connection than simply boss and employee, but anytime she brought it up, he quickly changed the subject.

She was beginning to think that maybe they'd dated at one time and things hadn't ended well. Or perhaps they'd had a one-night stand. The not knowing was driving her crazy.

April watched as Jack's muscles tensed, then he consciously relaxed them slowly. He leaned toward the other man standing just out of sight, said something too softly for April to hear, then stepped aside. As he did, he looked into the room and saw she was awake.

She saw him tense up again, but he still allowed the other man into the room. As soon as April saw who it was, she understood the animosity in the air.

It was James Neal . . . her ex-husband.

Jack had also been with her the first time her ex arrived. He'd run into the room, gasped when he saw her, rushed to her side, grabbed her hand, and proceeded to fake cry all over it. April had been surprised, but not terribly worried. Jack, however, responded as if James was a serial killer. He'd grabbed and spun him around and slammed him into the wall on the other side of the room, as far away from her as he could get, and asked who the hell he was. James had sputtered a bit and said he was her husband.

That had caused Jack to nearly lose his mind.

Of course, April had been shocked herself, as she hadn't realized she'd remarried James after their divorce. But it wasn't long before he'd admitted that he was still an ex.

It wasn't an auspicious beginning for the men, and in the two days since, both had been on edge and, it seemed to April, on the verge of coming to blows every time they saw each other.

"I'll be down in the cafeteria if you need me," Jack told April from the doorway.

"She's not going to need you," James sneered.

Jack ignored her ex and held eye contact with her. "Okay?" he asked.

"Okay," April told him softly.

She wasn't sure how long they stared at each other—the connection she felt to this man was powerful—before he finally nodded and stepped out of sight.

"I can get him barred from your room if he's bothering you," James said immediately as he pulled a chair closer to the bed. The sound it made as it scraped along the tile floor made April wince.

"He's not bothering me," she told James.

Her ex huffed out an annoyed breath, then leaned back in the chair and put his feet up on the mattress next to her hips. "I hate hospitals. They smell funny, and everything is so depressing," he said.

April pressed her lips together and wondered why he was here at all. Her short-term memory was affected by the accident, but she also had a hard time remembering much about her marriage to this man. That had nothing to do with the knock to her head; rather, it was because they'd simply coexisted together for a long time prior to the divorce. Not talking or interacting much at all before calling it quits.

James was fairly good looking. He was around her height, five-nine or ten, and had dark-brown hair and hazel eyes. He wasn't fat and he wasn't skinny. Honestly, he was pretty average, much like April. Looks-wise, there was nothing objectionable about him.

Personality-wise . . .

He'd told her that her mom had called to let him know she'd been in an accident and asked him to come up to Maine and check on her since Mom couldn't travel. And after seeing for himself that she wasn't at death's door, he'd done nothing but complain about nearly everything. Bangor, the weather, the flight here, the expense of the rental car, the size of the hospital, the lack of his favorite restaurants . . . the list went on and on.

"You don't have to stay," she told him. "You've seen for yourself that I'm okay. You can go home."

At that, James dropped his feet from her bed and leaned forward.

April braced herself for whatever he was going to say next. He didn't make her wait.

"It was a mistake. Us getting divorced. We should give things another go. We were good together, Ape."

April wanted to roll her eyes at the nickname. She'd always hated it. Had told him more than once, but he ignored her and kept calling her that, thinking it was a cute way to shorten her name. It wasn't. It was annoying.

"We were once," she agreed. "But can you honestly say you were happy toward the end of our marriage?"

"Yes," he said without hesitation.

"I wasn't," April said.

That seemed to shock James.

"We never did anything together anymore. I could've put on a dinosaur suit and danced around the house, and I don't think you would've noticed."

"You're wrong."

"I appreciate you coming to check on me, I really do, but we're over," April said firmly, not wanting him to get any ideas in his head that maybe they could work things out and get back together.

James sighed. "I miss you," he whined.

"No, you miss not having to worry about anything having to do with normal life. Paying bills, being at the house when the exterminator showed up, cooking for yourself. You took me for granted, James. We weren't husband and wife, I was your live-in help. That's not a marriage."

5

"That's not true," he protested.

"It is. We grew apart. It happens," she insisted. "I appreciate you coming all this way to see me, but you hate it here. It's time you went home."

James studied her for a long moment. "I never understood . . . Why Maine? Why you'd come all the way up here? The winters are awful, and it's so isolated."

April shrugged. She wanted to confess that it was as far away from him as she could get at the time. And that she knew he'd never follow her. But she kept her mouth shut.

He sighed. "That JJ guy . . . he's not good for you."

April stiffened. There was no way she was going to discuss Jack with her ex. She had no idea where she stood with her boss, but James didn't get a say in anything she did now. "James, no—" she started, but he interrupted.

"Seriously, Ape, he'll run roughshod over you. He's bossy as hell. Shit, he's probably the reason you're here in the hospital in the first place! You shouldn't have been on that road. If he'd done his job instead of having his secretary do it for him, you wouldn't have been hurt."

"It's time for you to go," April said, her voice flat. "You don't know what you're talking about, and I won't have you bad-mouthing Jack."

"That's the problem—*you* don't know what you're talking about either," James fired back. "Because you can't remember. That guy can literally tell you anything right now. You aren't safe. Until you get your memory back, *if* you get it back, you're completely vulnerable. He could tell you that you're lovers and have you on your back with your legs spread, and you'd have no idea if he was lying or not!"

April saw red. She pushed with her arms until she was sitting more upright. "You're right, I don't know where my relationship with Jack stands, but he's been nothing but respectful. He's been a rock at my side ever since my accident. I trust him, James, more than I trust *you*, and I remember our marriage just fine . . . which is saying something, don't you think?" She sighed. Her head was throbbing even more now. "Go home, James. You've done your duty."

"You're making a mistake," he warned as he stood up, the chair making that horrible noise once more.

"Maybe so, but I've made a lot of mistakes in my life, including staying in a loveless marriage for way longer than I should have. But I know without a shred of doubt that the people who have rallied around me since I've been here aren't among those mistakes. Chappy, Carlise, Cal, June, Bob, and Marlowe have been better friends than any I've known, and I don't even remember them. And Jack? I don't know where we stand, but at least he doesn't come in here bitching about how much he hates hospitals and trying to make me feel guilty for being here in the first place."

April was breathing hard when she was done. It felt good to stand up to James. She hadn't done it much when they were married. It was easier to just go with the flow and not upset him. But she was done with that. She and James were divorced, and she wasn't going to let anything he said influence her ever again. She'd done that for way too long.

"Don't come running back to me when you realize the huge mistake you made moving to Maine," he growled.

April chuckled, even though it jostled her aching head. "It's been five years, James. I don't think I'll be running back to you anytime soon."

"Your mom is going to be disappointed," he retorted, clearly a last-ditch effort.

April shrugged. "She's always disappointed in me. She'll get over it."

With one last shake of his head, James turned and headed for the door.

April held her breath until he was gone, then scooted back down on the bed. The relief she felt in the ensuing silence was almost overwhelming. In that moment, it occurred to her that when Jack left her room, she felt anything *but* relief. And with that realization, a feeling almost like sadness coursed through her veins, for wasting years on a man she never should have married.

She'd made the right decision, sending him away. James was her ex for a reason. And while she could be thankful he was willing to do her mom a favor by coming to Maine to check on her, she was never, ever getting back together with him.

"April?" a woman's voice asked tentatively from the doorway. "Are you okay? I saw James leaving, and he didn't look happy."

Turning her head, April saw a very pregnant June peeking into the room. "Come in," she said, gesturing for the petite woman to enter.

June entered and pulled the chair James had been sitting in closer to the bed, being careful not to let the legs screech against the floor as she did so. She eased herself into it and leaned forward, putting her hand on April's forearm. "Are you okay?" she asked again.

"I'm fine. James won't be back . . . at least I hope not."

June smiled. "Really?"

"Really."

"Good! Oh—I mean, that was rude. Sorry. But he wasn't very considerate of you."

"Or of you and the others," April said with a small smile. She hadn't missed the way James had disregarded June, Carlise, and Marlowe. All three women were in various stages of pregnancy. June was about seven months along and definitely waddled when she walked. Carlise wasn't too far behind her, at around six months, but her baby didn't seem as big as June's; and Marlowe was only about four months along. Their men were always making sure they sat, had enough to eat or drink, and were comfortable when they visited.

It hadn't even seemed to cross James's mind that maybe the pregnant ladies might need or want to sit, so he never bothered giving up his seat.

June shrugged. "JJ will be glad he's gone too."

April's doctor had warned her not to push too hard to remember the last five years. He'd told her that he had every expectation her memories would return after her brain healed from the trauma it had experienced. But at that moment, April wished with all her might that she could remember her life. She wanted to know about the times she'd spent with June and the other women. Wanted to remember the stories of how they'd met their men. And she very much wanted to know why she felt so comfortable with Jack, and why she trusted him so easily.

"Why?" she blurted.

"Why what?" June asked with a tilt of her head.

"Why would Jack care?"

For the first time in her many visits, June looked uncomfortable. Which in turn made April tense.

"I'm not sure I'm supposed to talk about that with you."

"Please," April whispered. "I'm so confused. Were we lovers? Did we date? I don't understand why I'm so drawn to him and yet he treats me as if I'm his sister or something. He's protective and concerned about me, but he's keeping his distance. Did I do something to upset him? Was I a bitch to him or something?"

"No!" June exclaimed so vehemently, it made April feel a little better. "You haven't dated, and he *definitely* doesn't think of you as a sister," she added. "Things between you two have been . . . complicated. And that's all I'm going to say. I don't want to do or say anything that will hinder your healing. Besides"—her voice lowered a little—"I don't really know much about you and JJ, anyway. You guys are both super closemouthed about what's going on between you. But I'll tell you this—when JJ heard you were hurt, he didn't hesitate for even one second to get to you as fast as he could."

April's heart swelled at hearing that. She was still confused about where things stood between her and Jack, but with this new bit of info, she once again couldn't help comparing him to James.

Once during their marriage, she'd been rear-ended at a stoplight. It hadn't been that big of a deal, but she'd gone to the hospital just to be safe. She'd called James on the way, while she was in the ambulance, to let him know what was going on, and the first question he asked was how badly their car had been damaged. Then he said he was working late that night and asked if it would be okay for her to take a taxi home, where he'd see her later.

The difference between his reaction to her being in an accident and what Jack had apparently done was night and day. Maybe the two situations couldn't be compared, since they were so different in how badly she was hurt . . . but she had a feeling Jack would've reacted the same way if she'd only been in a minor fender bender.

June squeezed her arm, then drew in a surprised breath.

"What? What's wrong?" April asked in concern.

"Nothing, it's just the baby. He's kicking hard today. Wanna feel?" Without waiting for a response, June stood up and brought April's hand to her belly.

"It's a boy?"

"Oh . . . I forgot that you don't remember. We weren't going to find out, but the second Cal saw his little wiener on the ultrasound, he got so excited there was no way to keep him quiet." June chuckled. "You scolded him for like fifteen minutes, telling him that he shouldn't be so proud of a penis on a baby that hasn't even been born yet."

April smiled, just a little sad that she couldn't remember. She was happy, however, that June didn't feel weird about sharing the memory. She felt movement under her palm and gaped at June. "He's strong!"

"Yeah," the other woman said with pride.

It was obvious how happy June was to be pregnant, and April had no doubt she was going to make an amazing mother.

The doctor chose that moment to come into the room, along with the two interns who'd been glued to his heels every time he'd arrived to check on her.

"I'll leave you guys to chat," June said. "And I'll find JJ and let him know that James is gone," she told April with a wink before waddling toward the open door.

The doctor was all business as he checked her vital signs and asked the same questions he asked every time he came to see her.

"Any memory returning?"

"Not really," April told him. "I mean, everything that happened in my distant past is becoming clearer, but I still can't remember the accident or anything about my life in Newton."

"The results of the MRI you had last night are promising. The swelling in your brain has stopped, and has even shrunk a bit. I'm confident that with time, you'll regain most of your memory of your years here in Maine."

"How much time?" April asked with a frown. She was impatient to get her life back, and the fastest way for that to happen would be to get her memory back.

"There's no telling," the doctor said.

April sighed.

"I know it's frustrating, but you've made a very fast recovery so far, and I have no reason to think you've lost those memories forever. Just be patient. Take things at your leisure. Your memories could return slowly, one at a time in pieces, or they could snap back all at once. How's the pain today?"

"Around a five," April told him. If Jack had been there, she probably would've downplayed the throbbing in her head and said a three because she didn't like to see the worry on his face, but since she was alone with the doctor, she was more honest.

He nodded as if he'd expected that. "As your brain heals, you'll continue to experience some pain. Don't try to force your memories, that'll just make the pain worse. Wear sunglasses when you go outside and in bright light, and continue to get plenty of sleep and eat well-balanced, nutritious meals. I'm going to discharge you this afternoon . . . as long as you have someone who can stay with you for the next few days to keep an eye on you."

April smiled hugely. Oh, she so wanted to get out of this hospital room! But then reality crashed in on her. She had no idea what her living situation was. Did she have her own house? An apartment? She didn't know if any of her friends could stay with her, as the doctor wanted. Hell, she had no idea if she even had a guest room or a place for someone to sleep wherever she was living.

"She'll be staying with me," a deep voice said from the doorway.

CHAPTER TWO

It was almost comical how every head turned to look at him as JJ entered April's hospital room. The second June told him James had left, he'd hurried back upstairs to her side.

JJ *hated* her ex. He wanted nothing more than to shove his fist into the man's face, but he'd refrained . . . barely. He couldn't believe the guy had shown up and misrepresented himself, pretending to still be married to April. Taking advantage of the fact that she'd lost her memory.

April didn't really talk about her marriage, but from what he'd gathered from his friends, things between her and James hadn't ended badly, per se; it was just a very unhappy marriage there at the end. JJ wasn't sad about it. Anyone who couldn't see how amazing and wonderful April was, and didn't treat her as if she was the most important person in their world, didn't deserve her.

JJ knew without a doubt that *he* didn't deserve her either. But the accident had changed everything for him. It had brought the point home in a very painful way that life was short. He'd spent the last five years fighting his attraction to April. Making up every excuse under the sun as to why he should keep his distance. But the second he heard she'd been hurt, all those excuses fell away like dust.

He still didn't deserve her, but he'd decided to do everything in his power to be the kind of man she wanted and needed.

And then he found out about her amnesia.

It had almost taken his legs out from under him. She didn't remember him, or their friends, *at all*. She didn't remember Jack's Lumber, or how vital she was to their business. She didn't remember how each of their friends had met and fallen in love. Didn't recall anything about Newton . . . how much she loved Granny's Burgers, the first snowfall, the small-town atmosphere, or anything else about living in Maine.

He'd been ready to fall to his knees and tell April how big of an idiot he was, how much he admired and liked her, and to beg her to go on a date—but after learning about her injuries, he'd had second thoughts.

He didn't want to overwhelm her. Didn't want her to agree because she thought she had no choice. So he'd stuffed his feelings down deep, like he'd been doing for the last five years, and vowed to be a rock-solid friend. Someone she could rely on in what had to be an incredibly confusing time for her.

When her memories returned—and he had every reason to think they would, after talking with her doctor—he'd ask her out. Make sure she knew how important she was to him.

"I can't stay with you," April said in response to his offer to watch over her when she went back to Newton.

"Why not?"

"Well . . . *because*."

JJ smiled. It wasn't much of a protest. "There's more than enough room at my place. Your apartment only has one bedroom, and I'm too big to sleep on your dainty little couch."

"Oh," she said in a small voice.

JJ mentally kicked his own ass. She currently had no way of knowing where she lived or how big it was. He walked around the doctor and his interns to the side of the bed. April looked so lost lying on the white sheets. Her light-brown hair was lifeless against the pillow, needing a thorough washing. She was pale, with faint dark circles under her eyes, and her lips were chapped. But he'd *still* never seen a woman as beautiful as she was at that moment.

She was alive, and he was more than grateful that she'd escaped the horrifying wreck without more horrific injuries.

"I live not too far from the office in town. It's an older house, needs a lot of work, but I love it. The original wood floors creak with every step, and the kitchen was built sometime in the seventies, I think. But it's clean. And I have two bedrooms. You'll have privacy and time to heal, and you'll be safe. I give you my word," he said earnestly.

"I'm not worried about being safe with you," April told him, looking him in the eye. "You've been the one constant since I woke up. I just don't want to be a burden."

"You aren't. Not ever. It'll be my honor to help you get back on your feet."

"Because I work for you?" she asked.

JJ stared at her for a beat. He could do one of two things here. He could let her think that he was taking care of her like a boss would a valued employee. Keep things on a professional level. Or he could begin to let some of his feelings show.

He chose the latter.

"No. I mean, *yes*, I would want to help any of my employees. But not once have I moved a woman into my house simply because she's on my payroll. Or for any other reason, for that matter."

It was scary putting his heart on his sleeve, but JJ was done keeping his distance from April. He'd learned his lesson.

"Oh."

"Right, so . . . ," the doctor said, interrupting the moment. "If Mr. Justice will consent to look after you for a few days, I'll get that discharge paperwork started." The doctor smiled. "You'll need to check in with your local doctor daily for the next five days, and if anything changes—double vision, an increase in pain, your memories returning—contact him or her immediately. The last thing we want is you having an aneurysm and letting it go unchecked."

"Is that a possibility?" JJ asked in alarm.

"Her head hit that window extremely hard," the doctor said evenly. "Her brain rattled around in her skull, and while the airbags are meant to help, they jerked her around even more when they went off. Anything can happen; I'm just being cautious. If I thought she was in imminent danger, I wouldn't let her go home. She simply needs to take it easy and let the swelling in her head subside completely and not take any chances."

"She'll take it easy," JJ said firmly.

"Now you've done it," April said with a small laugh. "I'm gonna be wrapped in a bubble and not allowed to go anywhere or do anything."

"Damn straight," JJ muttered as the doctor laughed.

"You're a very lucky woman," the doctor told April. "And I think you're going to be just fine." He scribbled some things on a clipboard, then turned to leave, his minions doing the same.

As soon as they were gone, JJ leaned over April and fluffed her pillow. He fussed with the blankets and made sure she was comfortable. Then he picked up the chair and brought it closer to the bed. He sat and took her hand in his own.

"What?" she asked.

"What, what?" he countered.

"Why are you looking at me like that?"

"Like what?"

"As if you're trying to read my mind."

"Well . . . I'm trying to figure out how much pain you're in. If you're trying to hide how much your head hurts so I don't panic. I also want to know if you're upset that James left, and how you *really* feel about moving into my place. If you're uncomfortable with the idea and just agreed because you want to get out of this hospital, I can talk to the others, see if you can stay with June and Cal. Their house is huge. Or maybe even Bob and Marlowe's place; they just moved in, but they've got plenty of room too. It's quieter where they are, so that might be a better—"

April squeezed his hand. "Stop, Jack. I'm okay with going to your place . . . unless you've changed *your* mind."

"No!" he exclaimed. "Sorry," he added when she flinched. "I have no problem whatsoever with you being at my place. I'd prefer it, actually."

"Why?"

That was a loaded question. All JJ's good intentions of giving April some space, of letting her memories return before he pushed her, flew right out the window. "Because I've thought of having you in my home for longer than I'm comfortable admitting. And it sucks that you'll be there because you got hurt . . . but I can't say I'm upset about it."

She stared at him for a long moment. "What's going on between us?" she whispered.

"Nothing. And everything," he said honestly.

"That's clear as mud," she replied with a small chuckle.

"About as clear as our relationship has always been," JJ said with a shrug.

"I wish I could remember," she admitted. "But I knew something about you was different from the others from the second I first saw you."

"You mean when I was freaking the hell out because you had blood all over your clothes and dripping down your head?"

"Yeah," she agreed with a small laugh. "I don't remember the others, but I appreciate them being here. Taking turns sitting with me, keeping me company. But with you, it's . . . more. I feel safe when you're here. When I wake up in the night and look over and see you sleeping in that uncomfortable chair . . . it makes me feel as if there's more between us than boss and employee."

"There is. Always has been, even if we haven't wanted to admit it."

"So that's how it's been?" she asked.

"Yeah."

"Okay."

"Okay?" he questioned.

April nodded. "I feel as if I got a second chance at life. I don't remember the accident, but I've heard about it from the doctor, and Bob even showed me pictures of my car at the site."

JJ growled at that. He hadn't known his friend shared the pictures of her mangled car with April.

She smiled. "It's fine. I asked him about the accident, and he was very reluctant to show them to me, but I insisted."

JJ grinned at her. "That's because you've got us all wrapped around your little finger, and have since the day you started working for us," he said. "I swear, we're all a little afraid of you. It really should be called April's Lumber instead of Jack's Lumber."

The smile on her face faded.

"What? What's wrong?" JJ demanded.

"I don't remember anything about the business."

JJ leaned forward. "You will."

"You don't know that."

"I *do*," he insisted. "You just have to cut yourself some slack. No one expects you to get back to town and jump right back into everything. You heard the doc, you need to take it easy. Your brain is still swollen. Let yourself heal."

April sighed and nodded.

JJ could tell she was still worried about what would happen in the future, but they'd take things one day at a time.

"Can I ask you something?"

"You can ask me anything," he told her, reluctantly sitting back, giving her some space. He was an intense guy, and he knew it. He didn't want to overwhelm her.

"What really happened? With my wreck?"

JJ wasn't sure he wanted to talk about this; thinking about what happened to her made him feel helpless, and the terror and devastation he experienced the moment he heard about the accident were all too fresh in his mind. But if she wanted to know, he'd tell her.

"You got a call from one of the ski resorts about another tree that had fallen on one of the slopes. Chappy, Cal, Bob, and I were all at Bob's place, helping him and Marlowe move in, so you decided to head out to the resort on your own to check it out. See how big of a job it would be and, from what the employee who talked to you said, what mitigation efforts could be taken to keep any other trees from falling in the middle of the season. You were on your way when, the police assume, perhaps an animal crossed the road in front of you. By the look of the skid marks, you slammed on your breaks, then lost control of the car.

"There was a ditch alongside the road, and a pretty extreme drop-off beyond that. The car bounced out of the ditch and went down the hill, hit the bottom hard, and flipped. I'm not sure how long you were down there before a family drove by and saw the skid marks that disappeared over the edge. They called the police . . . and here you are."

April nodded. "It's weird. I mean, I know it happened to me, but since I can't remember any of it, it seems as if you're just reciting the plot to a TV show or something."

"I wish," JJ said. Then squeezed her hand. "But I always knew you had a hard head."

April chuckled, then winced. "Ow, don't make me laugh."

"Sorry," JJ said with a smile. "Why don't you close your eyes for a while. Rest before the doc comes back with your discharge papers."

"You'll stay?"

Her words warmed JJ's heart and made him feel as if maybe, just maybe, he'd actually have a chance with her. "Nothing could tear me away."

"Thanks. And for the record?"

JJ waited for her to finish her thought.

"I'm glad it's you here, and not James."

Damn. This woman slayed him.

"Although it *was* kind of funny to see how wary he was of you." April smiled even as she closed her eyes. "My mom never understood why we got divorced. I can't believe she sent him up here even after I spoke with her and told her I was fine."

JJ wasn't sure what to say in response to that.

"Although I think she regretted it after you talked to her that one afternoon. I swear, you had her in the palm of your hand after you listened to her talk about her latest crochet project for thirty minutes. Not even James had the patience to listen when she started in on her crocheting."

JJ chuckled. "I like her. Even if she did have bad judgment when it came to your ex."

April's eyes opened in slits, and she shrugged at him. "He wouldn't hurt me."

"He *did* hurt you," JJ countered. "He didn't see the treasure that was right in front of his face. Didn't treat you as if you were the most important thing in his world. But his mistake is my gain."

"Because of the business," she whispered.

JJ simply shook his head. He wanted to say so much more, but it was obvious April's head hurt, and again, this wasn't the time or place to tell her how much he loved her.

Yes, *loved* her. This woman had gotten so far under his skin it wasn't even funny. Physically, he'd never done anything more than hold her hand—and even that, only since her accident. But he still loved her with everything in him, and had for a long while now. He worried about her constantly, thought about her every day, and went out of his way to be around her as much as possible.

If she knew how madly in love he was, she'd probably freak out. He needed to tread carefully so as not to scare her.

"Jack . . . I don't . . . I can't . . ."

"Shhhh. You don't have to do a damn thing other than get better. You're safe with me. In every way. Understand?"

She nodded.

"Good. Now close your eyes and rest. I'll let June and Cal know they can head back to Newton, and I'll call Chappy and Carlise and tell them not to drive over today."

"Your friends have been amazing. Taking turns coming all the way out here to Bangor."

"*Our* friends," JJ countered. "And you would've done the same thing, and we all know it. Sleep, April. Soon you'll be home."

"Home," she whispered . . . then didn't say anything else.

It wasn't long before her breaths evened out and her muscles relaxed. JJ kept her hand in his and didn't move an inch. He'd always been the kind of man who was always on the go. Liked to be doing something. But there was nothing he could think of that he wanted more than to sit right where he was and watch the woman he loved sleep.

She'd scared the hell out of him, and he'd never take one day with her for granted again. She might never love him back, but he knew deep in his heart that he'd never love another woman. She was it for him. Even if it had taken way too long for him to get his head out of his ass, he'd spend the rest of his life making sure she knew how he felt.

CHAPTER THREE

April sighed in exhaustion when Jack gently lowered her to the sofa in his house. She shouldn't be so tired. She hadn't done anything. She'd been wheeled out to Jack's Bronco, waiting right outside the hospital, and then hadn't done more than sit next to him and talk as he'd driven them the couple of hours back to Newton. He'd told her all about the town during the drive, all the things she probably already knew but had forgotten.

He'd promised to get her a burger from Granny's Burgers as soon as possible, because apparently they were her favorite. He talked a little about Jack's Lumber and how it was formed when he and his friends were POWs in the Army and played rock paper scissors to determine where they'd settle down and what they'd do for a living once they were rescued. It seemed like a crazy thing to do, to base the rest of their lives on a game of chance, but since it had apparently worked out for them, she couldn't exactly protest.

Jack also told her how each of their friends had met. He talked about the snowstorm Chappy and Carlise had endured, up at Chappy's cabin in the mountains, and about her stalker. She'd been appalled to learn of June's family treating her like total crap, and the insane plan her stepsister came up with to try to get Cal to fall in love with her.

She was even more shocked to learn that Cal was a literal prince, mostly because he was so down to earth. He loved that no one in their circle treated him differently or cared about his royal lineage.

And when she heard that Marlowe had been imprisoned in Thailand with a life sentence, and Bob had actually broken her out of jail, April had been equally stunned.

The men and women who'd visited her in the hospital seemed so . . . *normal.* Not like people who'd been to hell and back. They were friendly and outgoing and welcoming. She was sure they all had to have their own brand of PTSD in one form or another, but they weren't letting their pasts beat them down. It made her admire them all the more.

"What are you thinking about?" Jack asked as he sat on the couch right next to her. She didn't mind his closeness. Not in the least.

"Your . . . *our* friends," she admitted. "They've been through so much, but they're all so happy now."

"Yeah," Jack agreed. "I can tell you that when Chappy, Cal, Bob, and I were sitting in that dark cell, hurting from the beatings and torture, the last thing we ever thought about was all this. No one thought they'd get married. And kids? No way."

"Why?"

Jack shrugged. "It's just . . . what we went through . . . it tends to strip away your humanity. We were on a precipice. Cal couldn't take much more torture, we all knew it. Our captors were getting bored with beating on us, and it was obvious our time was running out. I suggested that game of rock paper scissors out of desperation. We needed to think about something other than the pain. We needed something to live for, even if it ended up being a pipe dream. And it wasn't women. It wasn't children. It was something much simpler—freedom. The idea of being out of that cell, free to choose what we wanted to do with our lives, instead of being told where to go and who to kill by our government."

"I'm sorry," April said softly.

Jack shook his head. "I'm not explaining this well. I'm proud of serving my country. And I'd do it again, even knowing what the outcome might be. But things have worked out so much better than I ever thought they would, since the day we played that game. It's still hard for me to believe Chappy, Cal, and Bob are going to be dads." He smiled. "I never would've guessed things could turn out *this* great."

"What about you?" April asked.

"What *about* me?"

"You want kids?"

Jack shrugged. "Not especially. I mean, I like kids. I just never saw myself having them. Maybe I'm just selfish."

"Don't," April admonished. "That's society speaking. If you don't want kids, you don't want kids."

"What about you?" he asked.

April thought about it for a moment, then shook her head. "I don't think so."

"For the record . . . if I was with a woman who really wanted children, I wouldn't hesitate to give them to her. Even if that meant adoption, fostering, surrogate, or IVF. I'd do anything to make the woman I loved happy."

April stared at him for a moment. He sounded so . . . forthright. "I don't doubt that for a second," she finally said.

"Right. Enough of that. Our friends are happy, and so *I'm* happy. We're gonna be knee deep in babies soon, and I can't wait to laugh at Prince Redmon changing a dirty diaper."

April giggled, then winced.

"Shit, your head hurts. Hang on, hon, I'll get you a painkiller," Jack said as he stood.

"I'm okay."

"I saw the wince. You're not okay," he retorted as he rummaged through the bag from the hospital pharmacy.

"I don't want to get addicted to the pills," April admitted.

"I won't let you. The last one you had was this morning, hours and hours ago."

"They knock me out," she complained.

Jack chuckled. "Yeah, they do. But sleeping is better than wincing from every noise." He went into the kitchen, and she watched as he reached into a cupboard and got out a plastic cup. He filled it with water from the tap and walked back to her.

"You're right," she said.

"Of course I am. About what?"

April smiled. Jack certainly had a healthy self-esteem. "Your floors creak."

He sat beside her again, and the warmth from his body seemed to flow into hers from where they were touching. "You know, when I first moved in here, that drove me crazy. As a Special Forces soldier, I was used to being completely silent when I moved. So having my movements broadcast in such a loud way was unacceptable. But as the years went by, I got used to it . . . and as stupid as this might sound, it made me feel not as alone."

"It's not stupid," April reassured him as she reached for the cup and the pill he was holding out. He watched her carefully, in a way she wasn't used to, as she swallowed the medicine. "What?" she asked after a minute, when he didn't say anything and didn't get up.

"I'm glad you're here."

She wasn't sure what to say to that. "I appreciate you letting me stay for a few days."

It felt as if he was going to say something else, but then he just sighed and smiled at her. "Come on, scoot down, and I'll get a blanket and a pillow for you. You can sleep out here while I make sure your room is ready and maybe whip up something for dinner. Anything you're in the mood for?"

"Whatever you make is fine."

"I'll remember you said that when you see what an awful cook I am."

She smiled. "I'm guessing you probably cook as well as you do everything else, which means you're probably a closet gourmet chef."

"Guess you'll find out."

"I guess I will."

And for the first time since she'd woken up and realized she was missing huge chunks of her memory, April was looking forward to learning about this man all over again. She might already know everything, somewhere deep in her subconscious, but the rediscovery of his personality and quirks could be . . . fun.

∾

After getting April settled on the couch, JJ found himself perched on the coffee table, watching his woman sleep yet again. But this time it was almost surreal, because she was in *his* house, on *his* couch, under *his* blanket, using *his* pillow. Never in a million years would he have wished something bad would happen to April to get her in this position, but he couldn't deny how content he was, now that she was here.

Every time he thought about how close he'd come to losing her, it made his skin crawl. First with the accident. There was no reason she should've been on that road. It wasn't her responsibility to check out potential jobs. Besides, it was after hours. Somehow over the last few years, they'd all gotten complacent and taken April's penchant for working overtime for granted. That was going to stop now.

Jack's Lumber wasn't a twenty-four-hour service. If someone truly had an emergency, they could contact the police chief, and he'd get a hold of one of them if it was absolutely necessary. But April working past five o'clock and on the weekends was going to be a thing of the past . . . as was her driving out to check on jobs for impatient customers. Not only was it not in her job description, it wasn't safe. There were a lot of crazy people out there, even in small-town Maine, and JJ would never forgive himself if someone assaulted her or, God forbid, did something worse.

The day of the accident, April should've been at Marlowe and Bob's house, celebrating their move with everyone else. And that was on JJ's shoulders too. She'd skipped the gathering because she was avoiding *him*, because he hadn't been man enough to own up to his feelings. He'd made being around their friends awkward for her . . . another thing that was going to stop *now*.

The accident was bad enough, but then he'd worried about losing April to her dickwad ex. He'd had words with James more than once in the two days the guy was around—and the ass had stormed into the hospital ready to convince April they were still in love and their divorce was a mistake. The fucker had actually taken advantage of the fact she had amnesia!

If her brain injury had been severe enough that she'd lost more than just the last five years, there was a slightly better than average chance he might've succeeded.

The thought of April leaving Newton and going back to a man who never appreciated her wasn't something JJ could fathom. But . . . was he even any different? Letting her work way over her contracted hours? Not protesting when she checked out potential new clients?

He sighed. No, he wasn't. He'd taken advantage of April's work ethic, her desire to be helpful, and her need to please others. All traits he admired and loved about her, but not at her expense. From here on out, he'd be more cognizant of others taking advantage of her—including himself. And he'd make sure she knew exactly how much he and the others valued her as part of their team.

An idea formed in his head, and as soon as the notion hit, he knew it was the right thing to do. He should've proposed it to his friends long ago. He'd remedy that as soon as possible.

As he watched April, her eyes fluttered and her brow furrowed. He hated seeing evidence of the pain she was most likely still feeling. That sick churning in his gut returned. He couldn't think of her lying helpless in her wrecked car, injured and alone, without wanting to puke.

Without thought, he reached out and smoothed his fingers over her brow, then down her cheek. The touch was whisper-soft, a caress. Immediately, she sighed and turned her head into his palm.

Even in sleep, she was kind and loving. It was one of the things he liked best about this woman.

Hell, who was he kidding? JJ liked everything about her.

"Jack?" she whispered as her eyes opened to slits.

"Shhhh," he told her softly. "Everything's good. Close your eyes again, I've got you."

His belly flipped when she immediately did as he requested. One of her hands came up and loosely circled his wrist. She didn't pull his hand away from her face, simply held on to him as she leaned her head more heavily against his hand.

JJ knew this moment would forever be burned into his brain. He'd failed this woman in so many ways, and yet here she was, trusting him.

"What time is it?" she asked, eyes still closed.

JJ smiled. "Doesn't matter. You have nothing to do but sleep and heal, and nowhere to go."

She frowned a little at that. "I always have somewhere to go. Jack's Lumber won't run itself, you know."

JJ tilted his head and studied her. April's eyes were still closed, and he wasn't even sure she knew what she was saying. "You're right, it won't. But for now, Chappy, Cal, Bob, and I will run it."

"Don't mess up my files," April whispered, then her grip eased on his wrist, and JJ realized she'd fallen asleep once more.

He was buoyed by her words. She'd sounded like her old self, and it certainly seemed as if she was remembering. The doctor had said her memory would return, and JJ hoped her words while half-asleep were a sign he was right.

He ran his thumb over her cheek, then slowly slipped his hand away from her. She grumbled a little and turned onto her side. He lifted the blanket over her shoulders, tucking her in.

Forcing himself to walk away from her was difficult. He was relieved she was out of the hospital, and it felt right to have her in his house, but dinner wasn't going to make itself, and he needed to make sure she had healthy meals so she could continue to heal.

JJ headed into the kitchen and opened his pantry. He stared at the contents on the shelves before reaching for a box of noodles and some chicken stock. He'd make some homemade chicken noodle soup tonight. He had chicken in the freezer that he'd planned on baking at some point, but he figured soup might go down easier for April.

Making a mental note to go to the store for some fresh vegetables and other staples that he knew she would enjoy, including the brand of coffee creamer she preferred, JJ got to work cooking for the most important person in his life.

Two hours later, he walked back to the couch. April hadn't stirred, which told him more than anything else how tired she really was. Hospitals weren't very conducive to getting quality rest, and she'd had a big day, what with being discharged and traveling back to Newton.

Once more, he sat on the coffee table in front of the couch and simply watched her sleep for a few moments. She was adorable. Even with her hair in need of a good shampooing, and the bruises that could still be seen on her face, he'd never known anyone as pretty as this woman.

"April?" he asked softly. She didn't stir.

Smiling, loving that he'd learned something new about her—namely, that she was a deep sleeper—JJ put his hand on her shoulder and squeezed lightly. "April?" he tried again.

This time, she frowned in her sleep and shook her head. "Don't go . . . come back! Help me!" she mumbled.

"I'm right here," he whispered.

"Please!" she said, a little louder now. "Where are you going? Come back! Call 9-1-1!"

Alarmed now, JJ squeezed her shoulder a little harder and gave her a light shake. He wasn't sure what she was dreaming about, but the implication of her words made his stomach roil.

Had someone been there when she'd wrecked her car? The police said it looked as if she'd slammed on her brakes, most likely to keep from hitting an animal that had run into the road . . . but what if they were wrong? What if someone deliberately ran her off the road?

"April," he said loudly, hating that she was having even one moment of angst.

Her eyes popped open, and she stared sightlessly for a moment before focusing on him. "What?" she asked irritably, as if she hadn't just sounded completely panicked and freaked out.

"Are you awake?"

"I'm talking to you, aren't I?" she grumbled.

JJ couldn't help but grin. This was a first for him too. The April he knew was always chipper at the office. She usually got there before him or any of the others, looking well rested and happy when he strolled in shortly after. Realizing she woke up grumpy was . . . intimate. And he liked knowing that about her a hell of a lot.

"Dinner's ready if you think you can eat. How's your head feel?" JJ really wanted to ask her what she had been dreaming about, but the doctor had told him not to push her to try to remember anything. That her memories would come back when her brain healed, and if she tried too hard before then, it could do more harm than good. And JJ would rather flay himself alive than do anything that might hinder her healing.

"It hurts," she said softly. "But not more than before I lay down," she added as she began to push herself upright.

JJ moved quickly, helping her into a sitting position.

"How long did I sleep?"

"A couple of hours."

"Really? Wow, okay. I didn't realize I was that tired," she said sheepishly. "Sorry I wasn't better company."

"You're the best company I've had in years," JJ told her honestly. "Just having you in my space feels nice."

She stared at him for a long moment.

"What?" he asked.

April shook her head slightly. "I don't want to say or ask anything that might upset you."

"Say whatever's on your mind, April. I'm not going to get upset."

"Did we date?" she blurted. "I mean, I can't get a good read on where we stood before my accident."

JJ stalled, trying to think of what he could tell her about their relationship . . . or lack thereof. He'd already mentioned their attraction, but anything else felt like pushing.

"It's okay, you don't have to answer," she said when he paused too long, looking down at her hands in her lap.

JJ's hand moved without thought. He put a finger under her chin and gently lifted her head and turned it toward him. "I want to say that things between us were complicated, but that would be a lie. We haven't dated . . . but we wanted to."

She frowned in confusion. "We did?"

"We've been tiptoeing around our attraction for years, April."

"Oh."

JJ's lips twitched. "Yeah, oh." Then he sighed. "I've been an ass," he admitted. "I think you were worried because I'm younger than you, and I'm your boss. And I didn't want you to feel pressured into going out with me. You're a strong, confident woman, April, but when you first got here and took the job, you weren't like how you are now. You were starting over after your divorce, trying to find yourself. And I had my own demons I was fighting after being a POW, and it took all my energy to start Jack's Lumber.

"By the time things finally looked as if they would work out with the business and I noticed you as more than the woman who was working her ass off to help make us a success, we'd fallen into a routine. The last thing I wanted was to ask you out and, God forbid, make you feel like you had to quit if things didn't work out. And I think you had a similar concern. So, we simply . . . muddled along as we were. Then Chappy found Carlise, shit happened between Cal and June, Bob returned from Cambodia with Marlowe, and we were helping each of them deal with their situations, one after the other."

"It's weird," April said after a pause.

"What is?" JJ asked.

"To not remember any of that," she said.

"You will."

"What if I don't?" she asked, biting her lip.

JJ moved his hand from her chin to cradle the side of her head. "You *will*," he repeated.

"So . . . you want to date me now because I was in that accident?" she asked softly.

"No." He saw the instant hurt enter her eyes and hated that he'd done that. He hurried to explain. "I've *always* wanted to date you. Always wanted to bring you here, cook dinner for you. Laugh, watch TV, make love. But I've been a coward. And I've heard you talking to Carlise and the others. You always emphasized the difference in our ages. I guess . . . I guess I was afraid of rejection.

"And as I said before, I didn't want things between us to be weird, then have you leave. You're the heart and soul of Jack's Lumber, April. You keep us all on track. You've found us so many more customers than we could've gotten on our own. You're the reason people come back time and time again. The guys and I aren't exactly friendly and outgoing. But *you* are."

"So you didn't want me to quit," she said. It wasn't a question.

JJ shook his head. "No. I didn't want you to leave. Not seeing you every day would slowly kill me."

She stared at him for a long moment, and JJ had no idea what she was thinking.

Finally, she said, "When James came to the hospital and said he was my husband, I was so surprised. I mean, I was sure I remembered divorcing him, but I second-guessed myself, wondering if maybe divorce was something I'd *thought* about doing but hadn't gone through with, or maybe we'd gotten remarried or something."

JJ's jaw tightened. He remembered that moment as clear as day. It had taken every ounce of control he had not to punch the asshole. "When he lost you, he finally realized what he had, what he threw away. I can't blame him for trying to trick you into going back to him, but that doesn't mean I like it."

April gave him a small smile. "I remembered the divorce pretty quickly after he arrived. And I wouldn't have gone back to him. You want to know why?"

JJ nodded.

"Because even though I didn't remember *you*, I felt safer and more comfortable with you there in the room with me than I ever did during my marriage with James."

Her words hit JJ hard. He closed his eyes and inhaled deeply.

"I don't know why neither of us was strong or confident enough to admit that we wanted to date, but I'm not the woman I was even a week ago. Life is short, Jack, and I know how I feel *now*."

JJ waited, and when she didn't continue, he lifted a brow. "Yeah?"

She grinned. "Yeah. I want you to cook dinner for me. I want to sit here on this couch and watch TV with you. Laugh. Find out if you're as good a kisser as I suspect you probably are, and hopefully, in time, make love."

JJ's cock pressed painfully against the zipper of his jeans. This woman was so much braver than him. He wanted to push her backward and get to the kissing part of her statement right now, but the bruises were a glaring reminder of what she'd been through. And while he desperately wanted her, it wouldn't be fair to enter any kind of relationship until she remembered the last five years. It was possible that whatever she was feeling right now could disappear when her memory returned.

"You're thinking too hard," she scolded as she lifted her hands and placed them on his chest.

Her touch burned through his shirt as if she'd branded him. He reached for one hand and brought it up to his lips and kissed the palm. Then he did the same to the other one.

"If you don't want that . . . I understand," she said haltingly.

JJ realized he hadn't responded to her declaration.

"I want that. I want *you*," he rushed to say. "You have no idea how much. But I will *not* take advantage of you, April. I'm not your ex. I won't push you into anything before your memory returns."

"But what if it doesn't?"

"It will," JJ said without hesitation for what seemed like the hundredth time.

"How can you be so sure?"

"Because you're the strongest woman I know. And the most stubborn. There's no way you'll let your brain keep your past from you."

She smiled. "You make it sound as if I'm a tyrant," she teased.

"You are," JJ joked back. "You run Jack's Lumber like a little dictator. And we all do whatever you tell us because we're scared of the consequences if we don't."

She chuckled and shook her head. "Whatever."

"I'm not kidding. Like I told you at the hospital, you've got Chappy, Cal, Bob, and me wrapped around your little finger. You say jump, and we ask how high. But we do it because you're always right. You know just what to do to make our business successful, and we never could've created what we have here in Newton without you."

"Thanks," she whispered.

"You're welcome."

"So, what, I'm the den mother to a bunch of lumberjacks? Hey, wait. Jack's Lumber . . . lumberjack . . . that's funny!"

JJ threw his head back and guffawed. When he had himself under control, he looked at April and beamed. "That's exactly what you said the first time it occurred to you."

"It is?"

"Yup. And for the record, that's not what I wanted to name the tree business, but I was outvoted by the guys."

"Jack?"

"Yeah, hon?"

"Will you kiss me?"

JJ's heart felt as if it stopped beating in his chest for a moment before starting back up in overtime.

"Never mind," she said, shaking her head when, yet again, he let the silence between them go on too long.

JJ didn't think. He dropped her hands and reached up to cradle her cheeks in his palms. He felt her touch his chest once more, and he swore sparks shot from her fingertips straight through his bloodstream.

He didn't speak, simply leaned forward and brushed his lips against her own.

He'd meant to keep things light and easy. She'd just been hurt, and he didn't want to rush her. But he hadn't counted on April's determination. She wasn't content with a chaste touching of their lips. One of her hands moved to the back of his neck, and she tilted her head and parted her lips. Her tongue came out and brushed against the seam of his lips, and JJ was a goner.

He inhaled and acted before he thought about what he was doing. He loved this woman with every fiber of his being, and having her kiss him the way he'd always dreamed was too much for his self-control.

His tongue surged forward, and he took over. Showing April without words how much she meant to him. How relieved he was that she was all right. He wanted to brand her, ruin her for any other man. Make sure she never thought of her douchebag ex ever again.

Her fingernails dug into the sensitive skin at the nape of his neck, and JJ felt his nipples harden under his T-shirt. His cock pulsed in his pants. He'd gone from zero to sixty in less than five seconds.

April let out a sexy little moan that made him shiver. He wanted to devour her, but a part of him, deep down, knew he needed to treat her with care. Her head still ached. She was bruised all over from the accident.

How long they kissed, JJ had no idea. All he knew was that he couldn't get enough. But he finally forced himself to pull back, enough to rest his forehead on hers. They were both breathing hard, and he freaking loved the way April was gripping him, how her nails dug into his chest and she refused to let go of his neck.

"Holy crap," she breathed.

JJ couldn't stop the smile that formed on his lips. He licked them and tasted her there, which made him want to kiss her all over again.

"Best first kiss ever," he blurted.

She leaned back and stared at him. "Really? I figured my body remembered doing that sometime in the past, even if I didn't, and that's why it felt so natural."

"That was our first time," he repeated. "Although I've gotten off thinking about your mouth more times than I care to admit."

She smiled shyly. "I don't remember, but I'm guessing I probably did the same."

Thinking about her masturbating to the thought of him almost sent JJ over the edge. "Food," he barked.

April grinned.

"I need to feed you. And we need to stop talking about . . . you know."

"I'm thinking this isn't like you," she said with a huge smile. "You seem like the kind of man who's always in charge. Isn't afraid of any topic."

"You terrify me, April," JJ said without guile. "You have the power to break me more than any terrorist ever could."

She frowned at that. "Jack, I'm not . . . I'm harmless."

"You should know this about me before you decide whether or not you really want to date. I'm intense," JJ told her. "I've seen firsthand the evil that's in this world, and I'll do whatever it takes to keep it from touching you. You've been through enough shit in your life already.

"If you give yourself to me, I'll protect you from anything that might hurt you. It might make me seem controlling or overbearing, and others might frown on what our relationship looks like from the outside. I will never, ever hurt you. I won't tell you who to talk to, who to hang out with, or what to do with your life. But I *will* stand between you and the world. I'll be your champion and cheerleader, and the most intimidating bodyguard. No one touches you, April. Not without your consent. Not even me. But when we're here, behind closed doors, I'll be the fuzziest, gooiest, biggest pushover you've ever met."

JJ hadn't meant to spew all that out, but he meant every word. No one hurt the woman he loved. He'd burn the world down to protect her if that's what it took. He had enough contacts to do just that too.

After everything that had happened to Carlise, June, and Marlowe, he'd made it his business to foster relationships with other men like him, former Special Forces operatives around the country, who he could call on a moment's notice if needed. Just as he'd be available to help any of those men, they were willing to do whatever was required of them, if asked.

"You sound as if you think I'm going to protest," April said without inflection. "As if you think you're scaring me away."

"You *should* be scared," JJ said. "Because I meant every word."

"I may not remember the last five years, but everything before that is becoming more clear," she said. "I lived with a man who barely realized I was there. He planned work trips without consulting with me first. He went out to dinner on his way home from work and didn't let me know, so the meal I'd cooked for the two of us went to waste. He never called to check on me during the day, and when he *did* reach out, it was because he needed me to do something for him.

"He never thanked me for anything I did around the house, and when we had sex, it was all about his pleasure. I don't think, in all the years we'd been married, he ever made me orgasm. If you think I'm going to be upset that you want to know where I am, who I'm with, or when I'll be home, you're wrong. But I'm going to want the same in return."

"You're going to get sick of all the texts from me," JJ vowed.

"So we're doing this? Dating?" April asked.

JJ's heart thudded in his chest. Crap, hadn't he just said he was going to wait for her to regain her memory before getting in too deep with this woman?

Well, it was too late for that. Way too late. "Yes."

Her smile lit up her face.

"But I'm not going to make love to you until you remember."

Her smile died. "That's not fair. The doctor said it could be months before that happens."

"It won't be months," JJ said confidently.

April pouted.

He chuckled and leaned forward, doing his best to kiss the pout off her face.

"But we can kiss, right?" she asked against his lips.

"Yes."

"Good. There's lots of places I can kiss you."

JJ groaned. This woman was going to be the death of him.

April smiled again, then she got serious. "Is this weird?"

"Is what weird?"

"Me, coming on this strong? I mean, technically I just met you. I'm being kind of slutty."

JJ shook his head and frowned at her. "Don't. Don't denigrate yourself. I won't stand for it. And you know me. Maybe your conscious mind doesn't, but deep down, you *know* me. You said it yourself, you trusted me when you first saw me in your hospital room. Trust your instincts, hon. You've got really good ones. And trust me when I say there's a lot of unrequited lust built up in both of us that's dying to be released."

She nodded.

And just then, her stomach growled. Loudly.

JJ was moving before he thought about it. "Stay," he ordered as he stood.

"What am I, a dog?" April grumbled, but she was smiling as she said it.

JJ leaned over and kissed the top of her head. "No. You're my girlfriend who's hungry, and whose head hurts, and who deserves a little pampering after a hard week."

"Well, when you say it that way . . . ," April retorted. "I guess I'll stay right here and let you wait on me."

"Damn straight, you will," JJ told her. It was difficult to walk away from her, and not only because his cock was hard. Everything about April impressed him. Her resilience, her work ethic, her looks, her damn-the-consequences ability to go after what she wanted. While he hated what had happened to her, he couldn't be upset with the current situation between them. It was as if the shields they'd both had up had finally been lowered.

No, not lowered—obliterated.

She had a good point, though; in many ways, she'd just met him. She didn't know his history. The details about what had happened to him and his friends while they were POWs. She only knew his gentle side. He could be an ass, and he just had to hope that when she *did* see that side of him, she wouldn't change her mind about being with him.

Taking a deep breath, JJ grabbed a bowl and filled it halfway with hot chicken noodle soup. He didn't want to overfill the bowl and have it spill on her. He'd get up as many times as needed until she was no longer hungry.

He'd never had a woman of his own to take care of before, and he had to admit that it felt good. Really good. Some men would hate serving their women, but JJ loved it. It made him feel needed and useful. He wanted to cherish April, and he vowed right then and there to do whatever it took to make her happy . . . so she'd never want to leave him.

CHAPTER FOUR

The next morning, April lay in Jack's bed and stared up at the ceiling. She'd never felt so . . . cherished in her entire life. And she hadn't even been in Jack's home for twenty-four hours. Was she getting in over her head?

As advertised, he was intense—there was no getting around that. And she still felt a little weird about wanting to be with him as much as she did after essentially only knowing him for a week. But he was right; something deep down felt as if she'd known him forever.

And that kiss last night told her all she needed to know. She'd never felt as desperate to be with someone as she did when he gently touched his lips to hers. She'd made the first move to deepen the kiss and hadn't been disappointed in the outcome. Being with her ex had never made her feel the way she did when she was with Jack.

He told her that he could be an ass, and he wasn't lying. She'd seen him be rude to people in the hospital—anyone who upset her or made her uncomfortable—and when he was wheeling her out yesterday, he'd been kind of a dick to a man who dared walk in front of her while he was looking at his phone and not paying attention. He also swore under his breath at idiot drivers when they were on the highway, so she could see what he meant about being a little rough around the edges.

But the man she spent time with last night was everything she'd ever wanted in a partner. They'd laughed. He'd opened up about Jack's Lumber and the struggle it had been in the beginning, but swore none of them regretted it for a moment. He didn't go into detail about his time as a prisoner of war, and she didn't press, but she could tell it had shaped him into the man he was today.

And hearing him talk about protecting her, about standing between her and anyone who wanted to hurt her, made April tingle deep down inside.

For the most part, she'd been on her own her entire life. She hadn't been bullied or gone through anything traumatic while growing up, but that didn't mean people hadn't taken advantage of her simply because she was a woman. Then there was the typical disrespect women experienced every day. Her ex hadn't cared when men catcalled her or made suggestive remarks at the grocery store or while they were out and about. April had a feeling no one would get away with that when Jack was around.

When it had gotten late, Jack insisted on helping her to bed, and somehow she'd ended up in *his* bed rather than the guest room. The look in his eyes when he'd stood over her as she lay under his sheets made her want to throw the covers back and invite him to stay with her. But he'd turned and headed for the kitchen, then returned with one of her pain pills. He'd kissed her on the forehead, which was just as romantic as she'd always imagined it would be, and told her to sleep well. That he'd be out on the couch and he'd hear her if she called out and needed anything.

After dinner, she'd also talked him into taking her with him to Jack's Lumber today. She instinctively knew he had a lot of work to catch up on after staying with her at the hospital in Bangor for as long as he had. It hadn't been easy to convince him to let her tag along, and he'd made her promise to just sit and relax while he worked, but Jack's Lumber was apparently her home away from home, and April was looking forward to seeing the place she'd heard so much about.

Of course, she was also hoping that maybe being there would prompt some memories to return, but since Jack was so adamant about not pushing herself to remember, she wasn't going to mention that part.

Shortly before going to bed, she'd gotten a text message from the girls saying they would meet her at the office as well. Apparently there was a long-standing group text set up so they could all stay in touch. And it was very active, which April loved.

Everyone checked in on June and her quickly advancing pregnancy and congratulated Carlise on finishing another translation, and Cal had been updating everyone on his search for a replacement Forester for April's wrecked one. When April protested, it was Jack who'd gotten her to drop it, insisting that everyone felt the need to do something to help her as much as they'd always helped each other. And since her last Subaru had basically saved her life when she'd wrecked, she couldn't really complain about getting another vehicle that was the same make and model.

Cal was determined to get the best deal he could on principle, so he was wheeling and dealing with every Subaru dealer he could find. Not only that, but in a group on social media, he'd chatted with a guy who worked at the Subaru factory in Lafayette, Indiana, who could get him a friends and family discount.

It almost made April's head spin, how fast things were happening now that she was back in Newton, but she supposed she shouldn't be surprised. She'd known these people for months . . . in some cases, years. If something had happened to one of her longtime friends, she'd be doing the same thing. So even if it was a little uncomfortable and awkward for her, she still appreciated their support.

She was still lying in bed when the smell of bacon and cinnamon began to drift through the door. April scooted up and swung her legs over the side of the bed. She needed to figure out what she was going to wear, because the oversize T-shirt of Jack's that she'd worn home from the hospital wasn't going to cut it when she went out in public. She shuffled to the bathroom attached to the bedroom and winced when she turned on the light.

She'd hoped her headache would be gone by this morning, but that obviously wasn't the case. She stared at herself in the mirror and grimaced. Lord, she was a mess. She wasn't the most gorgeous woman in the first place, but her hair definitely needed washing, and she could use some lip balm and color in her cheeks. The bruises on her face were more yellow and green than purple and blue, which was good, but still not pretty.

Desperate now to get clean, April didn't hesitate to turn on the shower. While the water was warming up, she brushed her teeth with the toothbrush Jack had given her last night. Then she eased the shirt up and over her head, pushed her underwear over her hips, and stepped into the large space.

Moaning, she tilted her head back, closed her eyes, and let the hot water cascade over her body. This was literally the best shower she'd ever had in her life, and not only because she felt so dirty. The water pressure was strong, but not so hard that it hurt when it hit her skin. The showerhead was wide, one of those rain-type things. How long she stood there, April had no idea, but when she realized the water hitting her head was actually starting to make the ache worse, she figured she needed to move things along.

She used Jack's shampoo and washed her hair twice. He had no conditioner, which meant it would take a while to brush out the tangles, but she didn't care. She used his soap and couldn't stop herself from smiling as she realized she would smell like Jack all day.

It wasn't until she'd turned the water off and dried herself with a huge fluffy towel hanging by the shower that she realized she didn't have anything to put on. She could rifle through Jack's drawers and find another shirt, but she didn't want to snoop through his things.

She was still contemplating what to do when she heard Jack's voice from the bedroom.

"April?"

"Yeah?"

"Carlise stopped by your place and packed some clothes for you."

She was surprised, both by the kind gesture and because it was like he'd been reading her mind.

When she failed to respond, he explained, "She has a key, just as you have a key to her place, as well as June and Marlowe's houses. June actually had key chains made that say 'BFF,' and you all made copies of your keys for each other." She could hear the amusement in his voice at that detail. "Anyway, she brought the clothes by this morning, and I'm putting them out here. Okay?"

April's eyes welled up with tears. What she'd done to deserve such good friends as Carlise, June, and Marlowe, she didn't know. But she was grateful. "Okay," she called out.

"Are you all right?"

Figured Jack would pick up on the fact her voice was wobbly. "I'm good."

"April . . . I'm serious. What's wrong? Is it your head? Do I need to call the doctor? Shit, you did too much too soon, didn't you? That shower was too much. I should've offered to wash your hair for you. Are you decent? I'm coming in."

"No!" April said urgently. The towel she held in front of her was big enough to cover her from chest to feet, but she was still uneasy about Jack seeing her so vulnerable. "I'm okay. I promise. I just got a little teary at the thought of Carlise thinking about me so early in the morning."

Jack's voice sounded as if he was standing just on the other side of the door . . . and he probably was. "Are you sure?"

"I'm sure."

"All right. I've made some bacon, pancakes, and cinnamon rolls for breakfast. I also have coffee with your favorite creamer. Take your time getting dressed. I'll keep everything warm until you're ready."

April wasn't even sure what creamer she apparently liked so much. It was such a small, trivial thing . . . yet not being able to recall her favorite creamer suddenly felt overwhelming and a little disconcerting. But she took a deep breath. She just had to go with the flow. "Okay, thanks."

"You don't have to thank me, hon. It's my pleasure."

43

April heard his footsteps heading away from the bathroom, then the bedroom door closing behind him.

She cracked open the door and peeked out and saw a suitcase sitting nearby. She didn't recognize it but assumed it had to be hers. She pulled it into the bathroom and closed the door again. After placing it on the vanity, she unzipped it and smiled when she saw all the things Carlise had packed. Leggings, jeans, underwear, bras, T-shirts, sweatshirts, and a blouse or two. Along with shampoo, conditioner, a shower pouf, lotion, a toothbrush, toothpaste, and a little bag filled with things like tampons, nail clippers, aspirin, and other miscellaneous toiletries.

She got a little teary eyed all over again. Carlise had packed perfectly, and even though April didn't recognize the clothes as being hers, she figured by the sizes they had to be.

Picking out a T-shirt and a pair of leggings, April got dressed. She grabbed the brush that was in the suitcase but quickly gave up on getting the tangles out of her hair for the moment. It hurt her head too much to tug on her hair, so she simply piled her shoulder-length strands on top of her head with a scrunchie. She'd deal with her hair later. Right now, the scent of cinnamon and other food was making her stomach growl.

She pushed the suitcase out of the bathroom to deal with later and wandered out of the bedroom and into the living area. Jack had his back to her and was doing something in the kitchen. April took the time to study him for a long moment. Had James ever made her breakfast? She couldn't remember, and she didn't think it was because of the knock on the head making her forget.

James hadn't thought about anyone other than himself, and it probably never even crossed his mind to make her breakfast before he headed off to work.

She must've made a noise, because Jack abruptly turned and smiled at her. He reached for a mug that was sitting on the counter and filled it with coffee from the carafe warming on the coffee maker. He poured in a healthy dash of creamer, then brought it to the small table in the kitchen. "Come sit," he said, pulling out a chair.

April walked as if in a trance to where he indicated, and sat. Jack leaned down and kissed the top of her head. "Good morning."

"Morning," she mumbled, lifting the mug to her lips and inhaling deeply. She heard Jack chuckle but ignored him in favor of taking a sip. "Mmmmm," she sighed, before looking up at Jack. She froze when she saw his expression. "What? Do I have something on my face?" she asked self-consciously.

"No. I just . . . you're kind of out of it before you have coffee. I didn't realize that about you. Probably because I always saw you wide awake and ready to take on the day by the time I got to the office."

April shrugged. "This is good, thank you," she said, not sure what else to say in response to his comment.

"You're welcome. There's a coffee machine at the office, but you threatened us all that if you ever came into work and your creamer was empty, we'd pay dearly." He chuckled. "So we've all taken it upon ourselves to make sure you have plenty at all times."

April blushed, even though she wasn't sure why. "Well, it's good," she defended. "Although I have to admit, I don't know what it is."

"Southern butter pecan," Jack said, as if it was completely normal that she had no idea what kind of creamer she liked so much that she'd apparently threatened bodily harm if she didn't have it at the office. "It's too sweet for me. I'm more of a black coffee drinker, but I'm happy to be your creamer dealer."

April wasn't really surprised that Jack liked his coffee black. She took another sip as he turned back to the kitchen and began to fill two plates. The amount of food he put in front of her made April grin.

"I can't eat all that."

Jack simply shrugged. "Eat what you can. I'll either finish the rest or put it in the fridge for later. Oh, and here's your pain pill."

"I thought I'd just take an over-the-counter pill," she said.

But Jack shook his head. "Not today."

"Jack," April warned, but he held up a hand to stop her.

"This is your first full day out of the hospital. We're going to the office. You're going to be on your feet for longer today than you've been for an entire week. You're going to need it. I have no problem with you weaning yourself off the painkillers, but today isn't the day to start. I promised yesterday that I wouldn't let you get addicted, and I'm not going back on that promise. After I was rescued, I tried to deny the painkillers for the same reason. I didn't want to become reliant on them, but it was a mistake. I put myself through more pain than was necessary, and I don't want you to do the same."

In response, April reached for the pill he'd put on the table. She swallowed it down with her coffee and picked up her fork.

"Thank you for trusting me. I told you that I'd never hurt you, and I meant it. But I won't let you hurt yourself either, if I can help it."

This man. He was killing her. She also felt off kilter. She'd never been the recipient of this much . . . concern before. "Thanks," she said after a moment.

Jack nodded, then pointed at her plate with his fork. "Eat, before it gets cold."

She tilted her head. "You're bossy," she informed him, cutting off a piece of cinnamon roll nonetheless.

"Yup," he said without remorse. "I learned from the best . . . you."

"Me? I'm not bossy," April countered.

Jack laughed. Hard. "Um, I hate to be the one to tell you this, but you are. You boss me around all the time. And the rest of the guys. And the customers and our suppliers. Hell, you even boss Carlise, June, and Marlowe around. But it's part of your charm, and we love you for it."

April frowned. Was she really bossy? She wasn't sure what to think about that revelation.

"It's fine, hon. Promise. Now eat. We'll do something with your hair, then get going."

"My hair?"

"Yup."

Again, he sounded as if what he'd said was completely normal. In her experience—that she could remember, that is—men didn't concern themselves with a girlfriend's hair. Her ex only mentioned hers when it was messy.

But since the food in front of her smelled and tasted so good, she was momentarily distracted by shoveling it in as fast as she could. To her surprise, she ate most of what Jack had put on her plate.

He smiled at her with satisfaction as he picked up the nearly empty plate and brought it to the sink.

"I can help clean up," she told him.

But Jack merely shook his head and said, "I've got it. Why don't you go and get your brush or comb or whatever, then bring it out here and sit on the couch. I'll be there in a moment."

April was once again confused. "Why?"

"Why what?" Jack asked, pausing to look at her.

"Why would I come back out here? I'll just go brush it in the bathroom."

With that, Jack put down the plate he was holding and wiped his hands on a dish towel hanging on the fridge. He walked toward her and put his hand on her shoulder. "It looks tangled, probably because I didn't have the girly crap you needed for it in my shower. Sorry about that, by the way. I would've brought in your suitcase earlier, but I didn't want to disturb you, and by the time I heard the water turn on in the shower, it was too late. Anyway, I don't want you to hurt your head any more than necessary by tugging on those snarls, so I'll help you. I'll be gentle."

"I can do it," April whispered, once again overwhelmed by this man. She could hardly believe he was real.

"I know you can. But I can do it better," he said with a wink.

April rolled her eyes. "Cocky much?" she asked.

He chuckled. "When it comes to things that I know I'm good at, yes."

"So you've done this before? Brushed a woman's hair?"

"Nope. Never. But since I'd rather cut off my hand than hurt you, I know I'll figure it out. And I'll probably be gentler than you will, because you'll be impatient to get to the office, which means you'll probably just rip out the snarls rather than gently trying to get the brush through them."

Shoot, he wasn't wrong. "Whatever," she said with a roll of her eyes.

That only made Jack's smile bigger. "Go on, I'll meet you on the couch."

April headed toward the bedroom door, but turned at the last minute. "Jack?"

"Yeah, sweetheart?"

"I don't know what to do with this."

"With what?"

"You."

He nodded. "Just go with the flow, April."

"I can't help but wonder . . . have we only gotten to this point because I hurt myself? Because I can't remember the way things were between us?" she blurted.

His smile disappeared in a heartbeat. He still stood on the other side of the room, but the intimacy between them was just as thick as it was last night when they were side by side on the couch, touching each other.

"Partly, yes. The part about your accident, that is," he added quickly. "I realized what I'd almost lost. I was stupid not to act on my attraction to you before now. I don't know what I was waiting for, but your accident made me realize how short life really is, and I decided I don't want to waste any more time. But you temporarily losing your memory is *not* part of it. In fact, that part scares the crap out of me."

"Why?"

"Because I'm afraid when you do remember, there'll be an important reason why you didn't want to be with me. Why you kept your distance. That you'll resent me making a move when you were vulnerable."

April wasn't sure what to say to that. He had a point. Why *hadn't* she asked him out? Why hadn't she encouraged him to act on the obvious attraction they shared? Was there something she'd learned about him that she couldn't remember right now, something that made her keep her distance?

"Go get your brush, hon," Jack said.

Because she was so off kilter, she did as he asked, turning away from him. But not before she saw the look of hurt cross his face. She hated that she'd done that. He'd been nothing but gracious and kind, and she didn't want to make him feel as if she wasn't appreciative. Still . . . she couldn't help but wonder what might have kept them apart before now.

It didn't take long for her to grab the brush and head back out into the living room. Jack was waiting for her on the couch. He'd pushed the small coffee table out of the way, and now he gestured to the floor. "If you sit here, I can reach your hair easier," he said.

Nodding, April eased herself onto the floor between his feet and held the brush out for him. His fingers caressed hers as he took it, and April swore she felt tingles all the way to her toes at the innocent touch.

But that was nothing compared to the tingles she felt when he ran his hand over her hair and gently removed the scrunchie she'd put in earlier. Then he carefully sifted his fingers through the damp strands, and April closed her eyes. His touch felt so good. Too good. Was there such a thing?

No one else had brushed her hair beyond a hairstylist, and that didn't count because it never felt like *this*. Jack started at the ends, carefully brushing the strands before moving steadily toward her scalp. The rhythmic and gentle motions made her sigh in contentment. It was so relaxing, having his hands on her head.

She'd been worried that this would hurt, but she should've known better. Jack wouldn't hurt her. She knew that down to her soul. Whatever connection they had, it made her trust him.

Before long, she realized the snarls were gone and Jack was simply brushing her hair for the pleasure of it.

"Jack?" she whispered, not opening her eyes.

The brush paused midstroke. "Yeah?"

"Whatever reason I might've had for not encouraging you to ask me out . . . it won't matter. I know what I want *now*, and that's you."

She felt more than heard his exhalation.

"We'll revisit this conversation when your memory returns."

April shook her head and turned so her back was against one of his legs and looked up at him. "No, we won't."

He frowned.

"I'm not the same person I was before my accident."

"Of course you are," he said firmly.

"You said, and I quote, *I was stupid not to act on my attraction to you before now. Your accident made me realize how short life really is, and I decided I don't want to waste any more time.* I feel the same way. There's no way I would feel as close to you as I do, that I'd want you as much as I do, if I didn't already feel that way before the accident. Whatever reason I had for not letting you know I was interested was equally stupid. I'm guessing my memory returning will only make me want you more, not less."

Jack's eyes closed as he sat there with his hands resting on his thighs. She could feel how tense he was against her back as he struggled to get his emotions under control. When his eyes opened, his gaze burned into her. "You're too smart for your own good," he said after a moment. "You love to throw my own words back at me."

"Well, when you're right, you're right. And I'm guessing when you're wrong, I have no problem making sure you know it."

Jack smiled. "This is true. I hope to God you won't walk away when you remember."

"I won't." April was sure of that down to her toes. She'd be an idiot to walk away from this man. She'd been with him for less than a day, and he'd shown her more care and love than she'd ever received from anyone else. She desperately wanted to give him that care and love back tenfold.

"Right. How does your head feel? Still up for going into the office?" he asked.

"You trying to keep me from seeing how screwed up my domain has gotten in my absence?"

Jack burst out laughing. "Nope. You'll figure that out sooner or later. Might as well bite the bullet and get it done."

April smiled, then got serious. "I don't remember anything about what my job entails," she admitted nervously.

"You figured it out when you were first hired. I have no doubt you'll pick it up just as fast now," Jack said breezily, as if he didn't have any concerns about her going back to work. "But you aren't working today. You're still healing. Carlise, June, and Marlowe are meeting us there, so I asked them to keep you distracted."

"Distracted?"

"Yup. I know you. If you get behind that desk and the phone starts ringing, you'll insist on figuring everything out today, and you'll sit there as long as that takes. I want to ease you back into things."

April couldn't stop the small grin forming on her lips. Now that sounded more like her. "Okay."

"Why don't I trust that *okay* from you?" Jack asked.

"I don't know. I'm perfectly innocent," April sassed.

She loved the sound of Jack's laugh. She got the feeling he didn't do it enough. "Right. Up you go. Carlise put a pair of sneakers by the door. Find some socks and maybe a sweatshirt, because sometimes it gets cold in the office, and we'll head on out."

Jack pulled her upright but didn't let go of her once she was on her feet. He ran a hand through her smooth locks and said more to himself than her, "I love the feel of your hair." Then he gave her a sheepish grin and handed her the brush. "Go on, woman, stop wasting time."

April rolled her eyes. They both knew he was the one who was procrastinating. But she kept her mouth shut and headed for the bedroom. It was weird how normal this all seemed. Living with Jack. Bantering back and forth. She even loved the serious conversations they'd had. Being honest felt refreshing and comfortable.

As much as she was looking forward to seeing Jack's Lumber and hanging out with her friends, she couldn't help but be a little sad she wouldn't get to spend the day alone with Jack.

CHAPTER FIVE

Three hours later, JJ looked over at April and smiled. He couldn't keep his gaze from her for more than a few minutes at a time. When they'd first arrived at Jack's Lumber, he'd been worried seeing the office would somehow cause something to click in her brain and cause her pain. But she'd looked around without any kind of recognition and shrugged at him while saying, "It's nice."

He'd been both relieved and disappointed she hadn't immediately remembered everything, but he kept his emotions to himself as he'd shown her around.

The office wasn't fancy. There was a small reception area up front, then an interior door led to a larger space where JJ and the guys spent quite a bit of time and which, more recently, the girls had largely taken over for themselves. They'd made it more comfortable and homey with a couple of couches and some feminine touches, like pictures on the walls and pillows on the sofa, and every now and then, a bouquet of fresh flowers would appear. There was a full kitchen, and April had partitioned off a small portion of the room with curtains, to hide the boxes of supplies that had previously just been stacked in a corner.

Looking around, JJ realized he saw April in every nook and cranny of the place . . . which wasn't surprising, since she spent the most time here. He recognized her influence in the dishes in the kitchen, the flooring she'd picked out, even the way the boxes were stacked in the storage area behind the curtain.

She'd made Jack's Lumber her own, and no one would ever be able to fill her shoes if she decided not to stay. Even if she never regained her memory, he had no doubt she'd be able to find her place here again . . . if she wanted to. There was a possibility she might not take to Maine as quickly as she had the first time.

"Dude, you look like you just smelled Chappy's feet after he takes off his boots. What's up?" Bob asked as he nudged JJ with his shoulder.

"Hey! My feet aren't that bad," Chappy protested.

They were standing near the back door to the office, discussing the job that Bob and Chappy had just finished. Cal was across the room, making June more comfortable on the couch. The further along she got in her pregnancy, the more protective their friend became . . . not that anyone could blame him.

"I don't want April to leave," JJ blurted.

Chappy looked shocked. "Wait, she's *leaving*?"

"I don't know. It's possible. I mean, she could literally go anywhere and be an asset. Why would she stay here?" JJ asked. He was talking fast, and he realized he was starting to panic a bit, but couldn't make himself stop.

"Why *wouldn't* she stay?" Bob countered. "Did you say something boneheaded to her? Has she regained her memory and realized you refused to ask her out?"

"No, no, and no," JJ grumbled. "Being here, seeing how she's made this place hers . . . I just . . . I don't want her to leave."

"Sounds like someone's finally gotten their head out of their ass," Chappy said with a grin, lessening the harshness of his words.

JJ took a deep breath and turned to his friend. "I have. I love her. I don't know what I'd do if she left."

"She's not going to leave," Bob told him. "Look at her. She might not remember Carlise, June, or Marlowe, but she's already clicking with them again."

JJ looked back to the women and saw the smile on April's face. She was leaning toward Marlowe as if hanging on every word the other woman was saying.

He took a deep breath. The feeling of relief that swept through him was almost painful.

"You guys were stuck," Chappy said. "Stuck in a rut, in a routine. I think you were both scared to do or say anything that might change the status quo between the two of you. She probably worried because you're her boss, and she's older than you, and she didn't want to make the first move. And you—I'm not sure *what* your deal was, but I'm guessing maybe a fear that if things didn't go as you hoped, it would ruin your friendship."

JJ nodded, then mumbled, "It was stupid."

"I wouldn't say that," Bob said with a small shake of his head. "Maybe overly cautious."

Cal headed their way and, when he got close enough, asked, "What are we talking about so intently? World peace? The FBI's top ten wanted fugitives? Old man Smith?"

JJ's lips twitched.

"JJ's freaking out because he just realized he loves April, and he's afraid she's gonna leave when she gets her memory back."

"She won't," Cal said calmly, as if he could see into the future and knew without a doubt what he was saying was true.

"Still, I'm thinking it can't hurt to give her an incentive," Chappy added. "We all know she keeps this place running. That without her, Jack's Lumber probably would've folded long before now. Any objections to bringing her in as a partner?"

JJ's mouth fell open. He'd been thinking that exact thing. Had decided just yesterday to talk to the guys about making it happen. It was just another reminder of how he and his best friends were on the same wavelength.

"Absolutely."

"We should've done it before now."

His three friends looked at JJ.

"Well?" Chappy asked him.

"What if she thinks we're trying to bribe her to stay?" JJ asked. "Maybe we should wait until she gets her memory back. I mean, she's worked her ass off for this place. She might remember how much time she's spent here and decide she doesn't want to put in any more effort."

Cal rolled his eyes. "I think if she knows how much of her blood, sweat, and tears she's devoted to this place, she'll want to stay even more. She's stubborn like that."

"Right? Remember when she heard the city council was considering going with an out-of-town company to take care of the trees in the park, and she took it upon herself to go down to the mayor's office and give him a thirty-minute PowerPoint presentation on why Jack's Lumber would be the better choice?" Chappy asked with a laugh.

"Or when she volunteered us to play Santa and his elves for the annual holiday party, when the guy who normally played the part got food poisoning?" Bob added.

"You know her best, JJ. Do you honestly believe she'll think we're trying to manipulate her in any way if we let her know what we're planning? Or will she be flattered and appreciative that we've noticed how hard she's worked?" Cal asked.

JJ didn't even have to think about it. "She'd probably tell us that it's about time we realized how important she is to this place."

The guys all laughed.

"I'll get with our lawyer and have him start to work on it. What should the split be?" Cal asked.

Before JJ could speak, Bob said, "We each give her five of our quarter percentage, so we each own twenty."

"Sounds fair to me," Chappy said with a nod.

"I agree," Cal said.

"Me too," JJ piped in. They should've done this way before now. April was literally the glue that held Jack's Lumber together.

"I'm gonna go tell her now," Cal said, turning toward the women.

"Wait!" JJ exclaimed, grabbing his friend by the arm.

"Why?"

JJ racked his brain but couldn't come up with a reason that would sound rational.

"He's worried she's gonna think we're trying to bribe her to stay," Bob said with a smirk.

"We are!" Chappy said with a grin.

Cal turned to JJ. "Look, I get it. You've got all these emotions rolling around inside you about April. She was hurt. You're still freaked about what could've happened. I felt the same about June. Still do. Seeing her lying on the floor with all that blood pouring out of her was the scariest thing I've ever been through. I still have nightmares about it. But she's alive and pregnant with our son.

"Wasn't it you who said we couldn't live in the past after we were rescued? When we were trying to decide what to do with ourselves after we got out of the Army? The same thing applies here. What happened, happened. You have to look to the future. And from what I understand, you want April in your future. Right?"

JJ nodded.

"Then tie her to you, to us, to Newton, any way you can. It's not manipulative; it's going after what you want. And we all know you want April. Just as it's obvious she wants you too. We've watched the two of you tiptoe around each other for way too long now."

The other two men nodded their agreement.

JJ couldn't help but grin at his friends. "You guys are all so damn sappy. It's as if your wives' pregnancy hormones have infected you too."

"Damn straight," Chappy said with a huge grin.

"I won't deny it," Bob said. "Besides, sex lately has been even more amazing than before, and that's saying something."

Cal simply smiled.

"Fine. Go tell her," JJ told him.

"Was going to anyway," he retorted.

Susan Stoker

"He just wants an excuse to hover over his wife," Chappy said. "Which isn't a bad plan." He followed Cal toward the couches.

"Come on, time to join our women," Bob told JJ.

JJ had no problem with that.

His friends had claimed the spots next to their wives by the time he got there, and the only spot left was next to April. He didn't hesitate to sit next to her.

"You guys solving the world's problems over there?" Carlise asked with a grin. "You looked pretty intense."

"They always look that way," June countered. "They could be talking about the weather and they'd look as if they were planning a mission against a terrorist stronghold."

"Oh my God, you're totally right," Marlowe said with a giggle.

"Well, today we weren't discussing terrorists or the world's problems. Instead, we were talking about April," Cal told them.

Almost comically, everyone's gaze swung to the woman at JJ's side. He felt her stiffen, and he knew without a doubt she wasn't comfortable being the center of attention.

Turning so the bulk of his body blocked out the others, he took one of April's hands in his own. Cal would just blurt out that they were giving her part ownership of the company without any explanation, which would probably make April decline, because she'd feel as if they were pitying her or something.

"Breathe, hon," he said quietly when it looked as if April was thinking the worst. "We were just talking about something we should've done long before now. The timing for this might not seem right, but then again, maybe it's perfect."

"Spit it out, JJ!" Carlise said impatiently from the opposite couch.

His lips twitched, but he didn't take his gaze from April. "Do you like the office?" he asked.

Her brows furrowed, and she nodded.

"I'm not surprised, considering you picked out every piece of furniture in here and designed the space," JJ told her. "You've made Jack's

58

Lumber your own. You brought life to what started out as a cold, empty room. You've brought in half the clients we've ever had, and you make them feel as if they're part of a family when they choose us. Some of them are experiencing the worst days of their lives when trees fall on their houses or cars. You calm them down and go above and beyond simply arranging for us to remove the tree. You walk them through filing insurance claims, and you've even arranged for the community to help with food, money, transportation, and childcare, when needed. You are the heart and soul of Jack's Lumber, and you might not remember right now how integral you are to the success of this place . . . but *we* do."

"Please tell me you're changing the name to April's Lumber," Carlise teased.

Everyone laughed, and JJ saw April blush.

He smiled at Carlise. "No, but that's a thought." He turned back to April. "The guys and I are making you a partner. We're giving you an even stake in the ownership of Jack's Lumber. Twenty percent. Same as what we'll have. You've more than earned it. It's not a bribe to get you to stay. I mean, we hope you do—*I* want you to stay—but even if you don't, your stake in the company remains."

The other women clapped and gleefully congratulated April, saying how happy they were for her, but JJ only had eyes for the woman in front of him. He couldn't read the emotions flitting across her face.

"That's . . . I . . . I don't know what to say," she finally stammered.

"Say 'It's about time!'" Carlise said with a laugh. "JJ's not wrong. You work your butt off for this place. We've had to drag you out of here a time or two just to get you to come hang with us, and you definitely spend more than your fair share of overtime here."

"Carlise is right," Marlowe agreed. "I haven't been here as long as the others, but it's easy to see how much you love this place. And everyone around Newton loves you right back."

"I feel weird accepting this when I don't remember anything about the business," April said.

"Well, the good news is that you don't have to *accept* anything," Chappy told her. "It's happening no matter what."

"And you'll be back to bossing everyone around in no time," June said. "And I mean that in a good way," she tacked on in a rush.

The phone started ringing out in the front room, diverting attention away from April. Chappy stood to go answer it, then returned a minute later. "Looks like we have a job. Tree fell across the highway. The police chief asked if we could go out and assist the firefighters because of the size of the thing."

"I'm in," Cal said, then turned to JJ. "Can you get June home?"

"Of course," he told him.

"You should go too," Marlowe told Bob. "I'll hang out at June's until you guys get back."

"And I have a manuscript I need to work on," Carlise added. "Congrats, April, seriously. You deserve to own part of this business for sure."

The guys kissed their wives and headed out the back door. JJ knew they'd make quick work of the tree. "You want to stay here while I run everyone else home?" JJ asked April when the guys had left.

"Is that okay?" she asked tentatively.

"Of course. This is practically your second home. And before you feel weird about anything, feel free to snoop. Check out where everything is. Turn on the computer if you'd like. The password is on a piece of paper taped on the underside of the desk, inside the front drawer." He chuckled at the look on her face. "You insisted on keeping it there because you change it every three months and none of us can ever remember the new one."

As the other women collected their stuff and used the restroom, JJ leaned into April. "I don't know what's going on in that head of yours, but for the record, I didn't bring up the ownership thing. I mean, I had planned on it, but the guys beat me to it. You're important to us, sweetheart. And while I truly believe it's just a matter of time before your memory returns, if—and that's a big if—it never does, you'll figure out your place here again without any issue. And if Maine isn't where you want to stay, you'll always have the proceeds from this place to fall back on."

"That's too generous, Jack," she told him with a concerned look on her face.

JJ shook his head. "It's really not. And when you regain your memory, you'll probably demand *more* than twenty percent because of all you do around here." Not able to help himself, he leaned forward and kissed her forehead. "I'll be back in twenty minutes or less. Look around, refamiliarize yourself with the place. But don't overdo it. If your head starts to hurt, lie down and take a nap."

He knew she'd never do that, but he had to say it anyway.

"I think I can survive twenty minutes without you, Jack," she said.

He loved the sass she threw his way. She almost sounded like the April he knew before her accident.

"I know. You can survive anything." He forced himself to stand and turn to the others. Of course, they were all waiting by the door with huge smiles on their faces. They'd been not-so-covertly listening to his conversation with April.

They all called out their goodbyes and promised to be in touch soon. Jack took one last look behind him before he walked out the door, and saw April staring at him with a look he couldn't interpret. He lifted his chin at her, then made sure the door was locked before forcing himself to leave.

April let out the breath she'd been holding when the door shut behind Jack and the other women. She liked being around everyone. It truly felt as if she was part of a huge, happy family. But she couldn't deny the sound of silence was comforting. Her head was throbbing, even though she'd never admit it to Jack or anyone else, and the quiet felt amazing.

She remained on the couch for a few more minutes and looked around the space. To her surprise, she realized it *did* feel somewhat familiar. She wasn't sure if that was because some of her memory was returning or simply because it was a cozy room.

The couch she was sitting on was extremely comfortable, and she loved the suede material. She liked the color scheme of the space; it was calming but not boring. And the way the storage was set apart from the rest of the room felt natural.

She let out a small chuckle and shook her head. It probably wasn't surprising that she liked the room so much, if what the others said was true . . . that she'd picked out everything, from the paint to the flooring to the furniture. It was such a weird feeling to see firsthand things she'd supposedly done and not have any memory of doing them.

April couldn't help feeling overwhelmed with the guys' plan to make her part owner of Jack's Lumber. It was a little uncomfortable because she didn't feel as if she deserved it. How could she, when she didn't remember anything about the business? But she couldn't deny that, deep down, she also felt pride. Even if she couldn't remember her impact on the business, she'd been here for years. Why *shouldn't* she reap the rewards of her alleged hard work?

A determination rose within her. She had no idea if she'd regain the memories that had been lost in her accident, but even if she didn't, she wanted to stay. She really liked the men and women she was getting to know, and from what she'd seen of Newton, it was an adorable little town.

Then there was Jack. She'd never felt such a deep connection with a man, and she wanted to explore that further.

Excited to get to know Jack's Lumber again, April stood. She rummaged through the kitchen cabinets, then wandered over to the storage area. She looked into the various boxes and saw office supplies along with what had to be extra parts for chain saws and other mechanical materials that she wasn't sure about. When she'd looked over everything in the back room, she moved to the front reception area.

Glancing through the window, she saw the weather was overcast . . .

She had a sudden flash of Carlise complaining about the rain, and April remembered telling her friend that if she didn't like the weather, just wait five minutes and it'd change.

The memory startled April so much, she stopped in her tracks and stared into space. Had she really just remembered something, or was it just wishful thinking?

Taking a deep breath, April moved toward the desk. She sat in the chair, which was super comfortable. It was the perfect height for her, which wasn't surprising, considering how much time she supposedly spent here. She rolled up to the desk and automatically reached for the mouse to the right of the keyboard. She wiggled it, and the screen came to life. Then she giggled at the message that appeared on the screen saver.

> Do NOT mess with my files. Don't delete anything, don't move anything. Do so at your own risk!

It seemed that she was a little—okay, a lot—paranoid about anyone screwing up her organization. And definitely as bossy as Jack claimed.

Curious now, she opened the desk drawer and felt around for the paper Jack said would be taped inside. She found it and pulled it free and stared at the password she'd written. She recognized her writing, but it was bizarre that she had no memory of writing the word down. The password was fourteen letters long, both upper- and lowercase, with a few special characters and numbers mixed in.

April wasn't surprised she was vigilant about passwords. She remembered an office she'd worked in while she was married, where the computer system had been hacked because someone had a password that was easy to guess. She'd apparently learned her lesson.

She carefully typed in the password and held her breath as the operating system came to life. There were at least thirty different files on the desktop itself, and she read through the titles of each. Vendors, clients, donors, volunteers . . . the file names were all concise and clear.

Taking a deep breath, April clicked on the email icon.

Her mouth dropped open when she saw nearly two hundred unread messages. Hadn't anyone monitored the email while she'd been in the hospital? Leaning forward, she was surprised to see the dates on the unopened messages were all from the last two days! So it seemed someone *was* reading the messages; they just hadn't gotten to them in the last couple of days.

She couldn't resist clicking on the most recent email and reading it with a small smile on her face. It was from a customer, saying he'd just learned about her accident and he hoped she was feeling better soon.

The next email was from someone in Bangor—a vendor, from what April could tell—and she was sending get-well wishes too.

As she continued reading the emails, she was flabbergasted to learn the majority were to her specifically, wishing her a speedy recovery. There were a few requests for service and a couple of bills that needed to be paid, but for the most part, the messages were personal and heartfelt.

April sat back and stared at the screen in disbelief. For what felt like most of her life, she'd faded into the background. She'd done her job but never felt as if she was *seen*. Her husband certainly hadn't appreciated what she did for him, for their household, or for her job. But clearly, she wasn't just a secretary for Jack's Lumber.

Everything Jack had told her was true. She was valued here. A vital part of the business.

It felt good. *Really* good.

Suddenly there was a knock on the front door, scaring the crap out of April. She looked up from the desk to see a man standing there, smiling at her through the door's window.

She stood and walked toward the door, feeling nervous—before common sense dawned. This was a *business*. She had no reason to feel trepidatious, and the last thing she wanted was to turn away a paying customer. She unlocked the door and opened it, giving the man a polite smile. She didn't recognize him, which was expected, since she currently didn't know anyone from her life here in Maine.

He smiled back politely, and April relaxed a fraction. "Hi," she said. "Welcome to Jack's Lumber."

"Thanks."

When he didn't say anything else, just continued to simply stare, April invited him inside and walked back to the desk, feeling a little more comfortable with the piece of furniture between her and the stranger. As she sat, she asked, "Can I help you?"

"Maybe," he said. "I bought a piece of property near here, and I've been trying to get some estimates on how much it'll cost to clear the trees so I can build a house."

"We can do that," April said without thought. She felt a pang of guilt because she had no idea if Jack and the others actually *did* do that, but the words had fallen so easily from her tongue, she figured she'd probably said that exact thing many times. "How about if you write down your address and your name and number, and I'll have someone get back to you as soon as possible."

The man stared at her for longer than what felt polite, and April forced herself not to squirm.

"Are you all right?" he finally asked, without reaching for the pen or paper April had pushed across the desk.

"Of course. Why?" she asked a little defensively.

"I heard there'd been an accident," he said with a small shrug.

"Oh." Of course he'd heard. Newton was a small town, and by the number of emails in the inbox, everyone within a hundred square miles had heard about her accident. "I'm okay, thanks for asking."

"I've almost hit a moose myself. I mean, you'd think with them being so big, they'd be easy to see, but they appear out of nowhere. You're very lucky to not have been hurt worse."

For some reason, his words made April uneasy. Despite that, she nodded politely. "Yeah, I am." There wasn't anything about the man that should've made her feel unsafe. He was young and clean cut, with short, well-groomed black hair and an easy smile, and he wore an expensive-looking pressed shirt and tie. Even his slacks had creases down the front.

Nothing about him screamed danger . . . and yet she couldn't help but tense up as she waited for him to say or do something else.

"You look kind of pale," he said with a small tilt of his head. "And you're squinting. I bet your head hurts, doesn't it? How about I just come back later? I don't want to cause you any pain, April."

"It's okay," she said, but the man had already turned and was heading for the door. He opened it slowly, so as not to make the bell over the doorframe tinkle, looked back to wink at her, then walked outside, closing the door just as carefully.

April watched from behind the desk as he made his way toward a black pickup truck and climbed in. Without another glance, he pulled out of the parking lot and turned left onto Main Street and disappeared from view.

"That was weird," she said out loud. She'd just relocked the front door when she heard a noise from the back room and tensed up all over again. By the time she'd taken a few steps toward the other room, the door opened and Jack reappeared.

She was so relieved to see him, she almost crumpled where she stood.

"Hey, how are—what's wrong?" he asked.

"Nothing. You just scared me."

"I'm sorry," Jack said. "I parked in the back and used my key to come in that way. I see you've gotten into your computer."

She didn't miss the way he said it was her computer. "There were almost two hundred unread emails," she said, almost accusatory.

But Jack simply smiled. "I know. The guys have been keeping up with them for the most part, but obviously got behind. I'll get to them later."

"I went through them and moved the ones that were service requests or bills to the appropriate folders," she informed him.

Jack's smile widened. "Knew you'd get the hang of things fast," he said. "How many were from your fans, wishing you well?"

"Um . . . most of them?" she said uncertainly.

"Not surprised. The guys have been spending most of their time reassuring people that you'll be back soon and that you're on the mend. Come on, let's get you home. I'm thinking you could use some peace and quiet for a while."

April didn't even protest the home thing. Jack's house was the only home she currently knew. Her head did hurt, and she was weirdly tired even though she hadn't done much of anything today.

Jack walked to the front door, flipped the sign there so it said CLOSED, then came back toward her. He leaned down and logged out of the computer before wrapping an arm around her waist and leading her toward the back room.

"I can walk," April mumbled, even as she leaned into Jack.

"I know you can," he said without removing his arm.

April wasn't sure what was happening between her and Jack, but she liked it. A lot. As soon as she'd seen him, any fear she'd had about the man who'd stopped by had disappeared.

Her brow furrowed as Jack walked her to his Bronco. Something occurred to her suddenly—the man had used her name. How did he even know it?

Almost as soon as she had the thought, she dismissed it. Again, Newton was a small town, and she figured everyone knew everyone. Even newcomers like the potential customer had heard about her accident, how she'd swerved to miss hitting a moose—or whatever the animal was—and crashed.

"I was thinking chili for dinner. How's that sound?"

"Delicious," April told him as he held her elbow while she climbed into the passenger seat of his vehicle.

Instead of moving away from the door, he put a hand on her thigh and stood there staring at her.

"Jack?" she asked. "Are you okay?"

"No," he said flatly.

"What's wrong?" she asked, alarmed.

"I was an idiot."

April frowned. "What? When?"

"For the last five years. I was drawn to you from the moment we met, when you came into Jack's Lumber and practically demanded we hire you. I loved your confidence and your determination to make our business as good as it could be. Yes, maybe you were desperate for a job, but that didn't make me any less certain about your abilities to be exactly what we needed. And I wasn't wrong. But I was an idiot for not letting you know for five long damn years how much I cared about you."

"Jack," April whispered, overwhelmed.

"It's probably not fair of me to move so fast now, but I can't help it. As I told you before, I'm an intense guy. And I want you, April. All of you. Your hopes, your dreams, your fantasies, your worries and fears, your snarkiness, your bossiness, and your heart. I'm going to mess up, but you need to know from this point on, my only goal in life is to make you happy."

April's heart felt as if it was going to beat out of her chest.

"You don't have to say anything. I get it. I'm pushing. Probably too hard. But I want to make sure you know where I stand and that I'm not going to be that idiot anymore. When I want something, I go after it with everything I have. But I won't be *that* guy. If you get to know me and you don't like what you learn, I'm not going to be a stalker. I won't make things weird between us. I'll back off and let you live your life. But if you *do* decide you want to take a chance on me, I promise I won't let you down. I'll make it worth you putting up with my flaws and imperfections."

Then he leaned forward, kissed her on the lips hard and fast, and said, "Watch your feet" before closing the door.

April brought a hand up to her lips and watched with wide eyes as Jack walked around the front of the vehicle. He got in, and as if he hadn't just blown her mind, said, "We'll be home in a jiffy, and I'll get you settled so you can relax before dinner's ready." Then he turned the key in the ignition and headed down the road as if it was just an ordinary day.

But it was anything but ordinary for April. She was falling hard and fast for this guy . . . but she had a feeling she'd already been in love with him before her accident. How could she not? Even with him not making his intentions clear before, they were certainly clear now. Any girl would want to hear every single word he'd just said. She was no exception.

Closing her eyes, she leaned her head back on the seat behind her and smiled as Jack drove them back to his place.

~

Ryan Johnson watched from inside his pickup as Jackson Justice put April into his Bronco and drove out of the back parking lot of Jack's Lumber. Of course, Ryan Johnson wasn't the name he was given at birth, but at this point, names meant nothing. He'd picked the most mundane name he could think of. One that wouldn't stand out.

His entire goal for the last five years had been to blend into the background. He didn't want to be noticed. In order to get the revenge he longed for, he needed to be invisible. He'd kept his hair short, but not too short. He wore clothes that any other middle-class American male might wear. All while studying and honing his craft.

The craft that would help him take out Riggs "Chappy" Chapman, Callum "Cal" Redmon, Kendric "Bob" Evans, and Jackson "JJ" Justice.

He'd made it his mission in life to learn every little thing he could about the four men, including details about their families, who he'd always planned to use against them—until a different opportunity presented itself just in the last year. Namely, their women.

The fact that his enemies had each found women to love had changed his plan dramatically, but made it even more perfect.

Ryan wanted them to lose the most important people in their lives—just as they'd destroyed the one person Ryan loved the most.

His brother had been everything. Ryan idolized him. Yes, he'd gotten involved with a man in their hometown who was a bully . . . but he was a *charismatic* bully, able to convince a lot of young men to follow him and join his terrorist faction. And when he'd decided to kidnap some American soldiers—with no real idea of what to do with the men once they had them—Ryan's brother had obediently supported that choice.

Ryan had already taken care of that man. The asshole who'd convinced his brother to take part in the kidnapping. Made him suffer dearly for Ryan's loss.

Next, he would've gone after the men who rescued the prisoners—the men directly responsible for his brother's death—but the truth of the matter was, he didn't know who they were. He had no names for the Special Forces soldiers, no intel on how to find them.

But he *did* know the names of the four captives.

Ryan's brother had told him all about them. Bragged about the things he'd done to the filthy American prisoners. But even if he hadn't, there was plenty of video evidence available online, tapes the leader of the small faction had sent to the media.

Ryan might've been young, but he'd memorized his brother's every word and watched the clips again and again.

When he'd learned about the raid, about his brother's death, Ryan had been inconsolable—and furious. If it wasn't for those soldiers allowing themselves to be captured in the first place, his brother would still be alive! They'd be together, still in their hometown.

Instead, his brother was dead. The four men may not have fired the bullet that tore through his brother's heart, but Ryan still blamed them entirely. And he'd dedicated his life to making them pay for the death of the one person who'd actually given a shit about him.

Jackson Justice, the man who'd led the captured Delta Force team, had been the last to find a woman of his own—and she'd been right under Ryan's nose for years. He hadn't given their secretary, April Hoffman, a single thought . . . mostly because he'd seen no indication that Jackson himself cared about the woman.

Ryan hadn't caused the accident that had taken April's memories, but he'd been there when it happened. He'd seen it all go down. That moose coming out of nowhere—at that time, and in that place—was fate.

He'd been on the verge of rear-ending April's car to force her off the road himself when she swerved to avoid hitting the moose. He didn't have to do a thing. The animal was a sign from the universe that his plan was right and just.

He couldn't set the rest of it in motion yet. He had some things to take care of out in Colorado . . . and he wanted to mess with the rest of Jackson's team a little more. Wanted to scare them. Wanted them to face the obvious mortality of their loved ones before putting his final act of retribution into effect.

The fact that three of the women were pregnant was simply a bonus. Each of the men he hated more than anyone in the world wouldn't lose just one person they loved—but two. It was too perfect.

While there was no doubt that Ryan hated the former Special Forces team, the truth was, he hated everyone and everything. Hated America. Hated the food here. The cars. The superior attitudes of Americans. Hated the racism that infiltrated every nook and cranny, from the beaches to the mountains.

The urge to indulge in some sort of mass killing of Americans was strong. He had no problem with dying himself if it meant taking as many of the damn people in this country as he could with him. But his hatred of the men he blamed for his brother's death was stronger than the urge to kill a bunch of random strangers.

No, Ryan wasn't afraid of death. He welcomed it. But before he met his maker, he had some unfinished business to take care of.

He reached for the key in the ignition and started his truck with a smile on his face. His brain was teeming with ideas, ways to mess with the other men and their women . . . and very soon, he'd head out West to finish setting up the finale on the last five years of blood, sweat, and tears. After that, he'd return to Newton to set his plan in motion. To avenge his brother . . . and make the men who'd killed him pay.

CHAPTER SIX

A week had passed since April had first gone to Jack's Lumber, and she felt a hundred times better since that day. But to her dismay, even though the pain in her head had all but dissipated and the bruises on her face had disappeared, her memory still hadn't returned. She had flashes here and there of what she thought were recent memories from before her accident, but the last five years were still largely beyond her reach.

She was frustrated, but Jack had been her rock. No matter how upset she got, he stayed calm and positive that her memories would return, insisting she just couldn't rush things.

But with every hour that passed, April *wanted* to rush them. It was disconcerting to meet people around Newton who knew her and who she had no recollection of. Everyone was very understanding and patient, but April was nearing the end of her rope. She wanted her old life back.

Well, with one exception. Jack. She'd been told they'd both avoided their attraction before the accident, and she wanted no part of that old status quo.

Living with him was easy. They shared the cooking and chores, and he even insisted on going to the grocery store with her and taking an active role in deciding what they'd eat each day. It was a refreshing change from her previous relationship.

And there was no doubt that she and Jack were in a relationship. He kissed her all the time, touched her, told her how happy he was that she was with him. April always knew where she stood with him, which was another nice change.

The only problem was, he didn't seem eager to do anything too physical. Yes, the little kisses he gave her were nice, but he hadn't *really* kissed her since that first night in his home. Every day that went by made April feel more and more needy, especially since they spent nearly every moment together. If he really liked her as much as he claimed, why wasn't he moving their physical relationship forward?

She knew the answer to that, of course. He didn't want to have sex until her memory returned. He was still afraid she'd remember some reason why she didn't want to be with him, and he didn't want April to have any regrets. But she knew in her heart that wasn't going to happen. It felt as if she'd known Jack forever. She felt safe and protected in his presence. And more comfortable with him than anyone she'd ever been with.

Just a few nights ago, her cell phone had rung, and thinking it was her mother—who'd said she was going to call that night—April had answered without checking the display. To her dismay, it was James. He'd gotten the number from her mom and claimed he was just calling to check on her. Of course, after she said she was fine, he started in on how much he missed her and wanted another chance, how badly he regretted the divorce.

April tried to tell him, again, that they were never getting back together, and he'd continually cut in, not letting her talk . . . until Jack took the phone out of her hand. He told James in no uncertain terms that she didn't want anything to do with him, and if he ever called her again, he'd disappear and his body would never be found.

Then he'd hung up on James—who April could hear sputtering through the speaker—blocked his number, threw the phone on the coffee table, and said he was going for a walk.

When he'd returned a short time later, he apologized profusely. Explained that he couldn't stand James pretending to be someone he wasn't, making everything about him and not listening to a word April said. And he insisted that was still no excuse for stomping off or for grabbing her phone and threatening her ex.

The truth was, April was relieved. She didn't *want* to talk to James. Wasn't upset at all about what Jack had done. But she could tell his brief lack of control bothered him.

For the rest of the night, he wasn't as touchy-feely as usual, keeping a careful distance and speaking softly, as if he thought she was afraid of him after that confrontation with James. When it was time for bed, he kissed her almost distractedly before heading to the guest room, where he was still sleeping because he refused to let April move out of his bedroom.

He was still a little off the next morning, and it wasn't until April thanked him again for setting her ex straight that he'd finally started to relax.

Yes, Jack was a little rough around the edges. He probably shouldn't have threatened to make her ex disappear, but since he'd done it to protect her, she wasn't upset about it. Some people might've been worried about the violent tendencies that threat implied, but not April. She knew this man. Deep down, she had no doubt he wasn't inherently violent. Though she was just as positive that, if it came down to it, he'd use everything he'd learned in the Army to keep her safe.

So a week had gone by, and Jack hadn't done anything to move their relationship to the next level, not even so much as another deep, soulful kiss.

April was frustrated with the man, but more so with her memory, which still hadn't returned. She'd been to Jack's Lumber every day and was slowly learning more and more about operations. She'd started to schedule jobs for the guys, but only after promising each and every one of them that she'd never go out on her own to do the prechecks on a property. Since she'd gotten into the accident while doing just that, she didn't have a problem agreeing.

Carlise, June, and Marlowe were constantly dropping by to visit, and honestly, being at Jack's Lumber didn't feel much like a job. She loved what she did, and laughing and eating lunch with her girlfriends was one of the highlights of each day.

But the biggest highlight was spending time with Jack each morning before they headed to the office, and then when they got home. They cooked dinner together, went for walks, and argued good-naturedly about which shows to watch. One bonus of losing her memory was that she could watch shows she apparently loved for the first time all over again.

Another bonus was reading. She had a tablet full of electronic books that she'd read but didn't remember, so she got to read and enjoy the stories as if they were new.

But the frustration with her memory was growing . . . so she'd decided the time had come.

The time for her to go home.

She had an apartment that Jack had been visiting to bring her clothes and other things, like her reading tablet, but he hadn't found the time to bring April there herself. She had a feeling it wasn't that he didn't have time but rather, he didn't want her to leave.

Honestly, she didn't want to leave either, but she couldn't continue living in this limbo. She wanted Jack. Wanted a *real* relationship with the man—including all the physical perks.

Yes, she'd only been living with him for a week, and it was just two weeks since her accident, but memories aside, she felt pretty great. Jack had flat-out sworn he wouldn't move their physical relationship forward until she remembered everything, and that sucked, but she had to respect his decision. That was Jack—honorable to the core. He'd never take advantage of her situation.

So if their relationship couldn't grow until her memory returned, April would do whatever she could to facilitate that. Namely, go back to her own place. Try to force her brain to remember the recent past. She had a feeling Jack wasn't going to like it. At all.

They'd gotten home from the office around six, made homemade au gratin potatoes, steak, and corn on the cob for dinner. They ate at their leisure, talking about their day and their friends between bites, then cleaned up the kitchen and, as was quickly becoming their routine, sat down to find something to watch together on the TV.

Jack had just grabbed the remote when April blurted, "It's time for me to go home."

Okay, she hadn't meant to be so blunt.

His head whipped around, and he stared at her with an expression she couldn't read. She hurried to fill the awkward silence.

"My head doesn't hurt anymore, and thanks to you and Cal, I have transportation again."

Cal had pulled up in front of Jack's Lumber two days ago in a brand-new red Subaru Forester exactly like the one she'd totaled, thrown the keys on the desk in front of her, and said, "Sorry it took so long."

April had been baffled, but no matter how much she protested or how many times she'd tried to explain that it wasn't in her nature to accept such an extravagant gift, the guys wouldn't give in. Cal finally huffed out a breath and explained that the cost was nothing to him and he'd gotten it for her partially because June spent so much time at Jack's Lumber, and if she went into labor, he wanted April to have reliable transportation to get her to the doctor without having to wait for someone to come get his wife.

She'd finally given in. Although it still didn't sit well with her, deep down, she loved the little car.

She continued speaking because Jack was still just staring. "It's weird that I'm living here, Jack. I'm in your room, and you're in the guest room. I don't like taking your bed. It's not fair. And it's not like we're a real couple," she ended, kind of under her breath, feeling petty even as the words came out.

"Not a real couple?" Jack finally broke his silence to ask incredulously.

"You haven't kissed me since that first night . . . not a *real* kiss . . . and I basically forced that one on you," she told him.

He snorted. "You didn't force me to do anything. And you know why I'm waiting."

April nodded slowly. "I do. And it actually makes me want you more. How many men would do that? Turn down a sure thing because you think it's what's best for me? You're an honorable man, Jack, from the top of your head to the tips of your toes. And I appreciate it. Appreciate *you*."

She shrugged one shoulder as she added, "I want more. I want a real relationship. But I refuse to put pressure on you, so I'm done waiting passively for my brain to get its shit together. I want to go back to my place. Not only to see if I can jump-start my memories, but also . . . being here with you, and not *being with* you . . . it hurts, Jack."

He frowned. "I have to make sure this is what you want. That you aren't going to regret being with me once your memories return."

"I know," April insisted. "I also know I had some reticence about getting involved before my accident, so the not-dating thing isn't just on you. After talking to the girls, I also know you were right about the things you suspected. I was worried because you were my boss, because things could get weird. Worried that I'm older than you. Apparently, I even had some concerns about ever getting serious with a man again, after James. But you aren't him. And I'm over the age gap.

"I just want to be with you, Jack. And I think you want the same thing . . . but you're holding back. Again, it hurts being so close to you but feeling so far away. So I'm going to do what I can to get my memories back, so we can *both* be sure of each other."

She stared at him, hoping against hope that he'd agree. It wasn't that she wanted to move out of his place, but she definitely wanted a real relationship with this man. She wanted him to pick her up and carry her into his room, put her down on the bed she'd been fantasizing about sharing with him for the last week, and make long, slow love to her.

She had no doubt he'd be amazing. That he'd rock her world. There was no way he'd be as selfish as her ex in bed. But if he needed her to get her memories back first, she'd do whatever it took, even if it meant leaving him to make that happen.

April sighed when he remained silent. "And I . . . I think maybe it's best we take a break too. I've been with you nonstop since my accident. You've felt responsible for me. I don't want to be someone you think is fragile, someone you have to keep in a protective bubble. As much as I love knowing you're there if I need you, I need to figure out how to be myself."

"You haven't felt like you can be yourself here?" Jack asked.

It was the first time April had heard hurt in his voice. She hated that, she truly did. But she wanted more from this man, and the only way to get it was for her damn memories to return.

"I've been more myself since the accident than I think I have in a long time. I love being here with you. You have no idea how much I enjoy spending time doing mundane things like shopping, cooking, and cleaning with you. But I want more. I want *you*, Jack."

"I don't want you to resent me," he said softly.

"I won't," April said fervently.

"I can't take the chance. If you end up hating me for making love to you, it would kill me." He raked a hand down his face, suddenly looking tired. "I'll take you to your apartment, but if you change your mind, all you have to do is call me. I'll be there in a heartbeat."

April was glad that he wasn't fighting her too hard on this decision, even as sadness filled her. She loved being with Jack. She felt safe with him. And despite still thinking this was the right choice, she couldn't help feeling like moving out of his home was a huge step back. "Thank you, Jack. I'm doing this for us, you know."

"I *do* know. And it just proves to me that you're the stronger person in this relationship."

April couldn't stop the smile that spread across her face at hearing that. "Whatever," she said with a roll of her eyes. "You could crush me like a bug."

She was relieved to see Jack's lips twitch in return. But then he said in a serious tone, "You and I both know I'm completely harmless when it comes to you." He leaned toward her a fraction. "I'm serious, April. If you feel even the smallest bit of unease, you call me. You can come back here, or I can take you to one of the girls' houses. I just want you to feel comfortable and safe."

April nodded, and they stared at each other for a beat. Then she stood and walked into his bedroom to start packing. As she did so, her emotions ran the gamut, but by the time she was done, she was more determined than ever to prove to Jack that her lack of memory had nothing to do with how she felt about him, now or in the future. She'd go back to her apartment and hopefully remember at least some of the last few years, then she could come home.

Home.

Anywhere Jack was already felt like home to her.

"I'm ready," April said quietly after she walked out of the bedroom.

Jack turned from where he was standing in the kitchen, and the look of misery on his face was nearly her undoing. She almost told him she'd changed her mind, that she'd stay. But she needed to do this. For both of them.

"I'll follow you to your place," he told her.

"That's not necessary. It's not that far away," she protested.

"I'll follow you," he repeated firmly.

There. That. His protectiveness was both a blessing and an irritant. But April couldn't say that he hadn't warned her.

She nodded and led the way out the door. His headlights shone in her rearview mirror during the four-minute trip to her apartment complex.

When they got there, he walked her up to the second floor, all the way to her door.

"Do you want to come in?" she asked.

He shook his head. "If your head hurts, don't be stubborn, take a pill," he said.

April sighed. "It hasn't hurt for a few days now. At least not bad enough that I need to take something."

"Still. Don't overdo anything. No staying up late cleaning or trying to refamiliarize yourself with your place. There's time for that later. Are you coming into work tomorrow?"

This man knew her so well. It was uncanny and comforting at the same time. She was itching to explore her apartment. It was as if she was moving into a stranger's place, and yet it was her own. She hoped to get more insight into her life here in Maine by looking at her belongings.

"April?"

"Oh, sorry. Of course I'm coming into work. Why wouldn't I?"

"Just checking. I'll see you there. Oh, shit. I bet you don't have anything to eat here. I'll bring your creamer to the office. I'll also make a breakfast sandwich for you."

"You don't have to do that," she told him softly. She hadn't even thought about the state of her pantry and fridge when she'd decided to go to her apartment.

"I know. But I am. If you need anything, don't hesitate to reach out."

"I'll be fine," she said.

"I sure you will, but still, I don't care what time it is. If you need me, call. Okay?"

"Okay."

They stood there in her doorway, staring at each other, before Jack brought a hand to the back of his neck and rubbed while looking down at the ground and sighing. "I hate this," he muttered.

"Jack—" April started, but straightened and took a step back.

"No, this is good. You need to figure out who you are without me hovering. But just because you've moved back here doesn't mean we're going back to the way things were," he said almost fiercely.

"I don't remember how things were," April reminded him. "And I don't mind you hovering," she couldn't help but say.

He pressed his lips together, then took a step toward her. One of his hands held her nape, and the other snaked around her waist. He pulled her against him roughly as he lowered his head, kissing her hard and almost desperately.

April immediately opened her mouth and grabbed his waist. She'd wanted this kind of kiss from him for the last week. Passion bloomed between them, and April felt her nipples harden under her bra and goose bumps break out on her arms. She moaned low in her throat at the feel of his tongue stroking her own.

As if the small sound brought him to his senses, he lifted his head. Thankfully, he didn't move away from her. He kept his hands clasped around her almost painfully.

"Jack?" she whispered when he didn't say anything.

"My place is gonna seem so empty without you there," he finally said.

April's determination wavered. What was she doing? This man wanted her to stay with him. Why was she being so stubborn? Was it so bad that he wanted to wait for her memory to return before he'd touch her intimately?

Actually, yes. Because as sure as he was that she'd remember him and everything else from the last five years, she wasn't as confident. It could be months before she remembered. Months of being near him but unable to have him.

"But you'll get to sleep in your own bed tonight," she told him.

He snorted. "As if I want to be there without you."

April rolled her eyes. "You know as well as I do that I wouldn't have minded if you'd climbed in next to me. In fact, I invited you to do just that, and you were the one who refused."

"You're killin' me, April. Just so you know."

Amazingly, April realized she was smiling. "You'll live."

"At least my sheets will smell like you."

April pouted. "And mine *won't* smell like you."

"Nope," he agreed. Then sighed. "Right, I'm leaving now, while I still can. Again, don't worry about breakfast. I'll take care of it."

"Thanks."

"You don't have to thank me for making sure you eat," Jack said, shaking his head. Then his hands dropped, and April didn't have a choice but to let go of him in return.

He backed up slowly. Not taking his gaze from her own. "Get inside," he ordered.

"Bossy," April mock complained.

"When it comes to your safety, yes," he agreed.

"I'll see you tomorrow."

"You will."

April hesitated, then sighed and reached for the door. She slowly shut it, then locked the knob and the dead bolt. She turned and rested her back against the door and closed her eyes for a moment before taking a deep breath and opening them again.

As she looked around, it felt as if she was in a hotel room of sorts. A somewhat familiar one, but a strange place regardless.

She picked up the suitcase Jack had carried for her and wandered around looking for her bedroom. It seemed as if she was fairly neat, which wasn't a surprise, as she remembered that from her past. Some of the items around the apartment were familiar, but others were new and interesting. There were shells on a shelf, some driftwood on the wall . . . but it was the pictures that fascinated her the most.

At least a dozen of them sat on a tall, skinny bookshelf in the corner of the room. Looking closer, she saw the photos were of all the people she'd gotten to know during the last week. April standing in the middle of Chappy, Cal, Bob, and Jack, in front of Jack's Lumber. Shots of her with Carlise and the other women. One of April standing on a beach with her hair blowing in her face as she laughed. Then in front of a huge tree with Jack at her side, a chain saw resting on his shoulder.

Picking up the photo, she brought it closer to examine it. Jack was so damn handsome, and whoever had taken the picture had caught her looking at him with an expression of adoration on her face.

Seeing that picture was absolute proof that what she felt for Jack wasn't a product of him spending so much time with her in the hospital or taking care of her since she'd come back to Newton. The feelings she'd had for him were deep seated and not new.

The pictures were an interesting glimpse into the life she'd led over the last few years. April realized that she looked happy in every image, which reinforced that she enjoyed her life in Newton and this was her home now.

Determination rose within her yet again. Jack might think she didn't know her own mind, but he was wrong. Maybe her brain being sloshed around in her head was making her act differently than she might otherwise, but she was done tiptoeing around their attraction.

She wanted Jack. Period.

April replaced the picture on the bookshelf and went into her bedroom. She put her suitcase on the floor, not bothering to unpack because hopefully, she'd be back in Jack's house sooner rather than later.

It was still somewhat early, but she was mentally exhausted, so she grabbed her toiletry bag and went into the attached bathroom to get ready for bed. She took in every tiny detail of each new room, hints into her life before the accident.

It was surprising how she seemed to know where stuff was, despite not recognizing most things. In the bathroom, she unerringly found her toothbrush and toothpaste and the lotion she used on her face before bed. Back in the room, she went to her dresser and opened the correct drawer on the first try. Muscle memory, perhaps.

She grabbed a silk nightgown and stripped off her clothes and tugged the nightie over her head. Then she crawled under the comforter and sheet . . . and stared at the ceiling.

It was dark, but there was a light outside that threw shadows around the room. Turning her head, April saw the curtains on the window were open, letting in the light. Annoyance swept through her as she stared at that window. *That* felt familiar. She climbed out of bed and shut the curtains, the feeling of déjà vu almost overwhelming. How many times had she gone to bed and forgotten to close the curtains and gotten annoyed by the light?

She returned to the bed and turned onto her side with her back to the window. April now stared sightlessly into the dark. She felt . . . weird. The bed felt cold. Too small. She was already used to Jack's king-size bed, so this full-size mattress wasn't cutting it anymore. Not only that, but the sheets weren't as soft and, as she'd warned, didn't smell like him.

Not liking the way her head was beginning to throb, April closed her eyes.

She was fine. She'd been the one who insisted on going home. She couldn't call him and tell him she'd changed her mind. That would make her seem weak, and one thing she knew for certain she *wasn't* was weak.

Ignoring the little voice in her head that insisted while she might not be weak, she was certainly extremely stubborn, April sighed.

Her last thought before sleep overtook her was she didn't like being here. Which sucked, because this was her home. Her space. But it felt empty. And lonely. And maybe a little bit scary. The sounds were different from those in Jack's house. She could hear music from her neighbor's place on the other side of the wall, cars on the street outside.

It was all so . . . unfamiliar.

CHAPTER SEVEN

JJ wasn't sleeping. He couldn't. He felt as if he'd lost the most important thing in his life. His house was empty. Soulless. He should've done what April wanted—hell, it was what *he* wanted—but he couldn't touch her, sleep with her, until she remembered everything.

He had a deep-seated fear that she'd remember some huge reason why she wouldn't date him before the accident—aside from the fact he'd never expressed his interest. And how could she *not* resent him if he took advantage of her? So when she'd said she was returning to her apartment, he didn't feel he had a choice but to let her go.

He hated it. Didn't like that she wasn't here in his bed. It smelled like her, which was almost more than he could stand. More than once he'd almost gotten up and gone into the guest room where he'd spent the last week, but he couldn't make himself move.

Jack hadn't ever been a coward. He'd always met whatever life dished out head on. But he had no idea what the right thing might be when it came to April. He'd decided he was done holding back with her, yet knew he couldn't be with her, completely, then lose her. Knew without a shadow of a doubt that losing her would send him into a downward spiral he'd never recover from.

It was better not to have had her at all, never taste her, never feel her pussy clamped around his cock, never watch her orgasm under him or hold her all night long, than to experience all that and more, only to lose it.

Turning onto his side, JJ punched the pillow under his head—and instantly groaned. All that did was make her scent waft up into his nostrils even more. His cock was hard as a pike, but he refused to touch himself. Didn't feel as if he deserved to get off when he'd chased April away.

He wondered for the hundredth time what she was doing. Had she let her curiosity get the better of her and explored her apartment? Was she sleeping? Going through the photo album he knew she had on a shelf under her TV? Found her stash of Girl Scout cookies she kept in her freezer because she was addicted to the things and wanted to be able to indulge in them all year?

Shit, JJ knew her apartment better than *she* did at this point, and he hadn't even been inside that often. But he'd memorized everything about her space the few times he'd been there. It was homey. Comfortable. It was no wonder she wanted to go back. Even without her memories, she must've unconsciously known it was a place she loved.

Sighing, JJ closed his eyes and willed his brain to stop. To shut down.

What seemed like hours later, he turned over and looked at the clock. Shit. Only ten minutes had passed since the last time he'd checked. It was three twenty-two in the morning, and he hadn't slept at all. How could he, knowing April wasn't on the other side of the door?

It had taken one week. One measly week for him to become addicted to her. His psyche needed to know she was safe. That she wasn't hurting. And when she was in his bed, he could check on her in the middle of the night. Make sure her brow wasn't all scrunched up in pain as she slept. Could make sure she was warm enough.

He'd gone years without needing her in the other room. But after her accident, after feeling so helpless watching her in that hospital bed, he knew his body had somehow rewired itself to be completely tuned in to the woman. It was an odd feeling, but it felt right.

"She's fine," JJ said out loud. "She's an adult who's lived on her own for a very long time now. She doesn't need you hovering."

His words seemed to echo back in the empty room. Mocking him.

He really should get up. Do something productive, since he was awake. But he didn't know what to do. It wasn't as if he could go and start chopping down trees or anything at this time of the morning.

Just when he'd decided to get up and take a shower, to try to wash away the cobwebs in his head, his cell phone rang from the bedside table.

Instantly, JJ was wide awake. He lunged for the phone, and his heart almost stopped beating in his chest when he saw April's name on the screen.

"What's wrong?" he barked as he answered.

"Jack?"

God. Her voice sounded all wrong. Tiny and scared.

He was already on the move. He didn't need to know what was happening with April to instinctually understand he had to get to her as fast as possible. But he asked again anyway. "It's me. What's wrong?"

Without pause, he rushed toward the front door, grabbing his keys along the way.

"I don't know . . . my head . . . it *hurts*. So bad!"

Fear coursed through Jack's entire body as he ran to his truck. His hands were shaking when he shoved the key into the ignition. He didn't remember if he'd locked or even closed his front door; all that mattered was getting to April. "Are you at home?"

"Yeah. I woke up, and it feels as if my head is going to explode."

"I'm coming, hon. Hear me? I'll be there in two minutes." Jack knew he should tell her to hang up and call 9-1-1, but he couldn't bear to lose their connection. He'd call when he reached her apartment.

"I'm scared," she whispered.

"I know, but I'm almost there."

"I feel nauseous. And Jack?"

"Yeah, baby?" JJ had never felt this kind of fear before. Not even when he and his team had been held captive. Not when his captors tortured him. Not when he thought he might die at their hands.

He shouldn't have let her go back to the apartment. This was his fault, and if anything happened to April, he'd never forgive himself.

"I remember."

"You remember what?" he asked as he pulled into the parking lot of her complex.

"Everything."

If possible, that one word made JJ's fear ramp up even higher. "It's okay. You're okay. I'm here, and I'm coming up."

A whimper was her only response, and the sound tore his heart in two.

Thankful that he'd forgotten to give her the spare keys to her apartment that he'd been using to collect some of her things, JJ took the stairs two at a time. He was inside a moment later and running toward her room.

It was dark, but he didn't need a light to get to her. He unerringly headed to the side of the mattress she was lying on. She whimpered again, and Jack reacted instinctively. He climbed under the covers, took the phone away from her ear and threw it and his own on the side table, then pulled her against him. One hand went to the back of her head, holding her close, and the other went around her waist.

She immediately curled into him, pressing her nose to his chest. Her arms were folded in front of her, and he felt her fingers against his bare skin.

"Jack," she whispered, and he felt the warm air from that one word against his heart.

"I'm here," he soothed. "I've got you, I'm here."

She was shaking now, little sobs escaping her mouth. It was the most gut-wrenching sound he'd ever heard.

"I need to call 9-1-1," he told her.

"No!" she begged. "It's less painful already. Just hold me. Please?"

Everything within JJ told him to turn over and grab his phone, but he felt frozen. He couldn't let go. Literally couldn't make his muscles unclench from around her.

How long they lay like that, he had no idea, but eventually he felt her relax bit by bit. He'd never been as relieved as he was when she finally melted against him fully.

"Sweetheart?" he whispered.

"It's better," she told him, but JJ had a feeling she wasn't being completely honest.

"What happened?" he asked. "Can you talk without pain?"

"I woke up, and . . . it all just came back! It felt as if an avalanche of memories were pounding on my brain."

"You really do remember *everything*?"

"Yes."

He stiffened. But his grip on her didn't loosen.

"I remember the accident. It was an animal, just like the police thought. A moose. I swerved so I didn't hit it. Everything was so loud when I crashed, and I was so scared. I knew you'd be mad at me for going out there without telling you first."

"I'm just glad you're okay," JJ told her.

"I remember my interview with you. Meeting the guys. How Carlise and Chappy met. How each of the girls were forced to share beds with their guys, and the next thing they knew, they were in love. How Bob lied about visiting some nonexistent aunt and snuck off to another country to free Marlowe. The pregnancies, the lunches, our clients—all of it. But most of all . . . I remember lying in this bed, wondering what I was doing wrong. Why you weren't interested in asking me out."

"Oh, hon," JJ said, closing his eyes and holding her even more tightly.

"I didn't know what to do differently. How to be the kind of woman you'd want, especially since I figured I was too old for you. I remember all the times I masturbated in this bed, thinking about you. I started avoiding get-togethers with our friends because it was getting so hard to be near you." She paused. "And I . . . I was going to leave. I'd started looking online for jobs in Bangor and Portland."

"No!" JJ burst out, shaking his head. "You can't leave me. I won't allow it. I need you! And you're *exactly* the woman I want. But I was terrified I wasn't good enough for you."

"You're everything I've ever wanted," she mumbled into his chest. "Stubborn, intense, bossy, protective. I've watched you for years. You'd do anything for your friends. *Anything.* That kind of loyalty . . . it's so sexy, Jack. And I wanted it for myself."

"You've got it. Got *me*," he told her.

"Do I?" she asked.

"Yes."

He felt her sigh against him.

"How's the head now?"

"Fucking hurts," she told him.

JJ smiled, even though the situation was anything but humorous. "I'm calling 9-1-1," he said as he began to turn. But she made a small sound of distress and seemed to burrow deeper into him.

"No, please! I'm okay. I just . . . I think it's because of the memories. I just need to lie here. If the ambulance comes, they're going to make me move. Shine bright lights into my eyes, which will make my head hurt more. I just need the dark and silence . . . and you."

Fuck. She was killing him. It was the wrong thing to do, but Jack couldn't deny her anything. It didn't bode well for the future. She could totally use his reluctance to say no to her advantage. But hell if he even cared at the moment.

"Twenty minutes, then I'm calling if the pain hasn't lessened," he told her firmly.

He felt her nod against him.

They lay there in silence, JJ holding her in an iron-tight grip and April snuggled into his chest as if she never wanted to leave, and a sudden thought hit JJ.

She remembered everything—and she wasn't pushing him away. When she'd been scared and in pain, she'd called *him*.

For the first time since she'd decided to go back to her apartment, hope bloomed. Maybe, just maybe, she really could be his.

He had every intention of calling for an ambulance in twenty minutes, but as the burst of adrenaline waned, the sleepless night caught up to him. The scent of the woman he loved seeped into his consciousness as he held her in his arms. His eyes closed, and JJ fell into a deep sleep.

April lay in Jack's arms and couldn't remember ever feeling safer. Her head was throbbing miserably, and every movement sent spikes of pain shooting through her. But pressed against Jack's body, feeling his heartbeat under her cheek, knowing he hadn't hesitated to come as soon as she'd called, she had no desire to move.

Memories continued to flood her mind. The frustration she felt when Jack treated her like just another friend—or worse, merely an employee. The joy at knowing her friends had fallen in love. The terror when they'd each been hurt or in danger. The anticipation of June, Carlise, and Marlowe giving birth. The sorrow she'd felt at making the decision to move on with her life somewhere else once the babies were born.

The love she felt for Jack that she didn't think would ever be returned.

It was all so overwhelming.

When she'd first woken from her fitful sleep, her head feeling as if it was literally going to explode, the only person she'd thought to call for help was Jack. And he'd come. Immediately. The second he'd gathered her into his arms, the pain lessened. It didn't disappear, but knowing he was there was a massive relief.

Suddenly her bed didn't seem so lonely. She'd fantasized about him holding her this way more than once over the years. The stories she'd woven in her head about how he'd feel against her body were nothing compared to reality. She didn't want to move. Didn't want morning to come. Because with the sun would come changes. She knew that as well as she knew her name.

Would Jack insist on keeping his distance, even after she'd remembered everything? Would he try to be noble and give her space to decide what she wanted?

Screw that. She didn't need space. She knew what she wanted, and that was Jack. She loved him. Had for years. And if he changed *his* mind about being with her, she'd have no choice but to leave. Immediately.

Now that she knew what she'd be missing, the feel of his arms around her, the way her entire body tingled when he kissed her, Jack calling her *hon* and *sweetheart* in that deep voice of his . . . she couldn't continue to live in Newton and not have it all.

Thankfully, the nausea eventually subsided, and the throbbing in her head lessened a bit as well. She discovered she loved watching Jack as he slept. It was as if she was getting a chance to see a part of him not many people did. His guard was down, and he trusted her enough to sleep in her presence. But it was the strength of his arms, never waning, that had her tearing up. Even in sleep, he was protective.

Light had just started to creep in around the curtains when he stirred against her. He didn't wake up like most people. He didn't gradually come back to consciousness. One second he was breathing deeply, still asleep, and the next he was fully awake.

"April?" he murmured.

"I'm here," she said with a small smile.

"Shit, I fell asleep, and I was going to call for help. How's your head?"

"It's okay," she told him.

He made a skeptical noise in the back of his throat.

"I am. I mean, I still have a headache, but nothing like last night." She felt him shifting, and she responded by getting impossibly closer.

He chuckled, and the sound rumbled through her entire body since she was plastered to him from head to toe. "You're like an ostrich or something, refusing to take your head out of the sand."

"I'm scared."

All humor was gone from his tone when he asked, "Of me?"

"No, of course not. Of how things might be different, now that my memory is back," she admitted softly.

Jack's arms tightened around her, and the hand that had been tangled in her hair all night began to massage her head gently as he held her close. "They *will* be different."

April's entire body stilled. Tears filled her eyes.

"You're mine," Jack added, and April could barely breathe as he continued. "You remember our past. How I was a jackass and didn't man up and ask you out like we both know I wanted to. I made you question your appeal and had you thinking about leaving. That's done. You remember all my flaws and negative personality traits. And yet, you still called me when you were in pain and needed help. I'm not letting you go, April. As long as you want me, I'm yours."

She closed her eyes to try to stop the tears.

"April?" Jack asked after a moment. "I can feel your tears on my skin. Please tell me those aren't freaked-out, scared, I-don't-know-how-to-get-out-of-this-situation tears."

She shook her head. "They're relieved tears. I-can't-believe-he's-saying-the-things-I've-longed-to-hear-for-years tears."

Jack shifted, and for the first time in hours, he loosened his hold. Using the hand in her hair, he gently tilted her head back so he could see her face.

April felt her cheeks heat. She probably looked like a complete mess. Blotchy skin, red eyes, hair in disarray . . . but the emotion she saw in his eyes was anything but disgust.

He slowly lowered his head and brushed his lips against hers. "Today's the first day of the rest of our lives."

She smiled at him.

"Jeez, sorry, that was so damn cheesy," he said with a roll of his eyes.

It was, but April didn't care. She rested her cheek against his chest once more and sighed in contentment.

"We need to see your doc today," he said.

April frowned. "No, we don't. I'm okay."

"We do and we are," he said firmly. "You scared me last night, hon. I don't like that you were in so much pain. You could barely talk on the phone. We'll go to the doc, get you checked out. You know he wanted to see you the second you remembered anything."

April sighed. "Fine."

"Good. We also need to let the others know. They'll be thrilled."

They would. The girls would squeal in excitement, and the guys would give her chin lifts and tell her it was about time. She loved her friends, and it was a relief to be able to remember their shared histories.

Neither she nor Jack attempted to get out of bed. He stroked her hair gently, and she idly traced circles on his chest. Several minutes went by before something occurred to April. She lifted her head and looked at him. The sun had risen far enough now that the light coming through the curtains allowed her to look him in the eye. "Um, Jack?"

"Yeah?"

"You're naked."

He chuckled. "Not quite. I've got my briefs on."

"You took off your clothes before getting into bed with me?" she asked.

To her amazement, his cheeks turned pink. "Not exactly . . ."

She frowned in confusion.

"I was in bed when you called, obviously, and I didn't want to take the time to get dressed. My only concern was getting to you."

She stared at him in disbelief, mouth gaping. "You came over here in nothing but your underwear?"

He shrugged. "Yup."

As his words sank in, April's eyes filled with tears once more.

"Shit, what's wrong?" he asked anxiously.

"I . . . you . . . no one's *ever* done anything like that for me before."

He relaxed. "It's a good thing I didn't get pulled over. I wasn't exactly going the speed limit," he joked.

April couldn't wrap her mind around the fact that he'd been in such a hurry to get to her, he hadn't even stopped to put on a pair of pants. Or shoes. Then she thought of something else. "I don't really have anything that will fit that you can borrow to wear home."

Jack shrugged nonchalantly. "I'll call one of the guys to bring me something. I need them to check on my house anyway. I'm not sure if I shut my front door when I left."

That had April rising on an elbow. "What? Jack, that's crazy! I mean, Newton isn't exactly crime central, but what if someone went in and stole stuff?"

"Then I'll replace it. You're much more important than any material crap I own."

Gah. This man. He was killing her. "Okay, you need to stop," she told him.

He frowned. "Stop what?"

"Being so awesome. I can't handle it. I'm not a crier, and you've had me crying twice this morning already. You need to go back to being annoying and bossy."

He chuckled, and the sound went straight between her legs. He rolled until she was under him. April could feel his skin against her own, and even though the nightgown she'd put on the night before had ridden up, which was thrilling enough, she wished she could feel his skin against hers *everywhere*.

"No can do," he said with a shake of his head. "You need to get used to this. You come first, April. From here on out. I don't care what it is, your well-being and wants and desires will always come first for me. I'll never be ashamed to admit you've got me wrapped around your little finger. You want something? I'll bend over backward to give it to you."

"All I want is you," she admitted. "Your attention, your time, your affection. I spent so much of my marriage coming in second, I don't ever want to be in that situation again."

"You won't," Jack vowed.

"But the same goes for me. I want to make you happy too."

"You already do."

April shook her head. "You know what I mean. I don't want you to do stuff you hate just because I want to do them."

"Not possible."

"Jack," April whispered, feeling overwhelmed.

"This is who I am," he told her. "I warned you. This is why I wanted to wait for your memories to return. So you'd remember how focused I get. How stubborn I am. How I'm kind of a dick sometimes. I wanted you to truly know what you were getting into when you decided to be mine."

Oh, April knew, and she wanted to pinch herself to make sure she wasn't dreaming. "I know who you are, and I want every inch of that man, Jackson Justice."

She jerked in surprise when she felt one of his hands on her outer thigh. He caressed her briefly before moving that hand upward.

"Good. Because I want you too, April Hoffman." His hand came to rest on her belly, and she inhaled sharply as his thumb brushed against the cotton of her panties while his pinky teased her belly button.

This was happening, and she was ready. More than ready. She'd dreamed about this moment for years and could hardly believe Jack was here, in bed with her. Practically naked, touching her.

Just as his head started to lower, his phone rang from the nightstand.

April winced at the loud sound, and Jack swore.

He rolled over and grabbed the phone. April could hear the conversation easily in the silence of the morning and because Jack was so close.

"Yo."

"JJ? It's Bob. Why the hell is your front door open? Are you all right?"

"I'm good. I'm not there."

"So I've discovered. What's going on?"

"I'm at April's apartment. I need a favor. Can you bring me some shoes, socks, jeans, and a T-shirt?"

"Um, sure, but . . . I have questions."

"I bet. I need to take April to the doc, so we'll be late getting to the office. I think we only had that one small residential job this morning. Can you and the others take care of it?"

"Of course. Is April all right?"

"Her memories returned."

"*What?* That's awesome!" Bob exclaimed.

April smiled at hearing the genuine happiness in his voice.

"Yeah, although it came with a killer headache, so we're going to go and get her checked out."

"Right, of course. But your door? And the clothes?" Bob asked.

Jack chuckled. "She called in the middle of the night. I rushed over here without stopping to do much of anything else."

"Like get dressed or shut your door. Got it. I'll be over in ten or fifteen."

"Thanks. I appreciate it."

"Can I tell Marlowe?"

"About April's memories returning? Sure."

"No, about you running around butt-ass naked in the middle of the night," Bob said with a laugh.

"You're an ass," Jack told him.

"Whatever. See you soon."

Jack clicked off the connection and shook his head. "I don't know why I put up with him."

"Sure you do. He's your friend," April said.

The expression on Jack's face turned serious. "Are you really feeling okay this morning?"

"Yeah. Again, I have a headache, but it's nothing like last night. And the pain is fading."

"You aren't just saying that so I don't freak out?" Jack asked.

April smiled. "No."

"Okay. Let's sit you up and see if the pain comes back," Jack said as he shifted so his legs were hanging off the side of the bed.

April put a hand on his arm, making him stop and turn to look at her.

"I . . ." Shoot. She wasn't good at this kind of thing. But she needed to be better at saying what she wanted. She'd wasted a lot of years by not speaking up when it came to Jack.

"What? You can talk to me about anything," Jack told her.

"I want to stay at your house tonight. In your bed. With you," she blurted.

The intensity on Jack's face would've been frightening if she didn't want him so much.

"Was already planning on it, sweetheart. As long as the doc gives his blessing, and you feel up to it, you're mine tonight. In every way."

"I'm already yours," she whispered.

Jack closed his eyes for a moment before pressing his lips together and standing. "Go on and sit up, hon. See how you feel before you stand."

She scooted up on the mattress and couldn't help but stare at the man next to her bed. She'd lusted over him in jeans and a T-shirt while wielding a chain saw, but practically naked? He was irresistible. Surprisingly, he had a small pooch on his belly, but his thigh muscles rippled as he moved, and his arms were just as strong. In short, he was perfect—and he was *hers*.

"You look at me like that any longer, and we're gonna have problems," Jack said.

April raised a brow. "I'll risk it," she retorted.

Jack laughed. "Spunky. I like it a hell of a lot better than you whimpering in pain. Come on, let's get you up and dressed. As much as I like Bob and know that he's madly in love with his wife, I don't want him seeing you in that sexy nightie."

April wanted to argue. Point out the cellulite dotting her thighs and how her upper arms were getting saggy and how she could never lose the extra weight she carried around her middle . . . but she resisted the urge. If Jack thought she was sexy, she wasn't going to complain.

She smiled as she took his hand and let him help her out of bed. The look of satisfaction and lust in his eyes was such a change from how she was used to him looking at her that she blushed.

"I'm going to go wait for Bob in the other room. Take your time getting ready," Jack said as he took a step away from her. His fist clenched at his side, as if it was taking all his control not to grab hold of her.

When he'd gotten to the door, April said, "Jack?"

"Yeah?"

"Thanks for coming over. I didn't want to call anyone else."

"If you ever feel scared, or unsure, or in pain, you call me," he ordered. "No matter what time it is or what we're doing. You call."

"I will," April agreed.

Jack nodded, then abruptly turned and exited the room.

Taking a deep breath and wincing at the pain it caused her head, April headed for the closet. She grabbed some clothes before going to the bathroom. Her life had taken a weird turn in the last couple of weeks, but she couldn't be upset. How could she, when she had what she'd wanted for years?

Jack said she was his, and he was hers right back. She was going to do everything in her power to keep him. Smiling, she started to get ready for the day.

CHAPTER EIGHT

JJ grinned as April greeted Marlowe. Carlise and June had already been by Jack's Lumber to visit their friend and tell her how happy they were that she'd regained her memories. Bob mentioned Marlowe had some morning sickness and was resting, so she'd arrived later than the other women.

April's visit with the doctor had gone well. He said the headache from the return of her memories was fairly normal and should dissipate as the day went on. He told them to call if it didn't fade or the pain got worse and recommended over-the-counter pills to manage it in the meantime, and they'd scheduled another appointment for next week.

Relieved that the doctor wasn't alarmed by April's pain level, JJ didn't object when she insisted on going to the office. He stopped at the local diner first and made sure she had a big breakfast before heading to Jack's Lumber.

Not much work had gotten done so far because Carlise and June had arrived minutes after him and April, then the three women had reminisced about what seemed like every memory they'd ever had together.

Chappy and Cal also told April how happy they were that she was on the mend, then proceeded to spend plenty of time giving JJ shit about wandering around Newton in the middle of the night practically naked. JJ didn't care about their teasing because he knew they would've done the same thing if it had been their woman who'd called them in distress.

"Is she really all right? The visit with the doctor went okay?" Bob asked JJ as they watched April and Marlowe chatting happily.

"Yeah, although she scared the shit out of me," he admitted.

Bob nodded. "I can imagine. When we heard the audio of what Marlowe was going through with that asshole in his car and I wasn't there, I felt completely helpless."

JJ had also been worried and scared when Marlowe's whole situation with her coworker went down, but he felt as if he understood his friend even better now.

"So . . . she remembers everything?" Bob asked.

"Apparently."

"And she's okay with the two of you?"

JJ pulled his gaze from April and looked at his friend. "She says she is, but . . . I know I was a jerk. I was holding back for no good reason, acting like a coward. I feel like a total ass that I waited until she was hurt to admit how deep my feelings for her ran. I'm scared to death she's going to internalize my reticence and talk herself into thinking that I don't really care about her. That the only reason I finally acted on my feelings was because of her accident."

Bob shrugged. "Wasn't it?"

JJ clenched his teeth and looked back to Marlowe and April. They were laughing about something, and seeing the smile on April's face made him relax in a way he didn't understand.

"Look, I'm not an idiot. I've been your friend for a long time, JJ. We've been to hell and back together. If you think any of us missed the looks you've given her when you thought no one was watching, or how you were extra grumpy because you couldn't articulate your feelings and that's why you were being such an ass, you're wrong. We all just assumed you two would eventually work out whatever was holding you back, and you'd end up together."

"I just don't want this to be one-sided," he admitted.

Bob chuckled and smacked the back of JJ's head.

"Ow! What the hell?" he complained as he glared at Bob.

"Just as we noticed the looks you were giving her, we saw the looks she gave *you* when your back was turned. Not to mention the way she worried about you when you were working too hard or when you got hurt. Remember that time a few years ago when that tree fell the wrong way and almost cracked your head open like an egg? She was a basket case, JJ. You didn't see it because she hid it so well, but she couldn't sleep for worrying about you, she harassed the rest of us about being safer on the job, and she even asked Chappy to look out for you when you returned to work."

"She did?" JJ asked in surprise. As far as he knew, she'd taken the incident with a grain of salt, acting just as even-keeled as she always had.

"Yes. That woman has loved you for years. Do I think it's stupid that you waited so long to let her know you're interested? Of course. But *she* waited too. You both had baggage you were trying to work through. So what if it took her getting hurt for you to overcome those demons in your head insisting you weren't good enough, or whatever other bullshit you were thinking. You're together now . . . and you need to make the most of it."

JJ looked back at April and nodded. Hell yeah, they were together now. His hands itched to touch her. He longed to see her looking up at him from his bed. "You're right," he belatedly said.

"Damn straight I am," Bob said with a grin.

JJ rolled his eyes.

"Come on. I want to check on Marlowe. She was puking her guts out this morning, and I want to make sure she's feeling all right."

She looked as if she was feeling fine to JJ, but since he wanted to check on April and see how her head was doing, he didn't argue. The two men wandered over to the couch where the ladies were sitting. Bob went straight to Marlowe and, without a word, pulled her to her feet, sat, then settled her onto his lap.

"I was sitting there!" Marlowe exclaimed with a laugh.

"And you're still sitting here," Bob said calmly.

"He's so annoying," Marlowe told April, not hesitating to snuggle into her husband as she got comfortable.

JJ didn't copy his friend's maneuver, but he did set himself next to April on the couch so closely her entire thigh was touching his. He wrapped an arm around her shoulders, and to his delight, she leaned into him, giving him her weight.

"Oh yeah, I can see how annoying he is," April told Marlowe.

They both grinned.

"What were you guys talking about before we so rudely interrupted?" Bob asked.

"Now that April has her memories back, we were just talking about some of the better ones we have together," Marlowe said.

"Like?" Bob asked.

"There's so many," April said with another grin. "The lunches we've had while you men were out slaving away, how much we cried when June asked all of us to go to Liechtenstein whenever she and Cal get around to having their royal marriage ceremony, and some of our crazier girls' nights out."

"I do have a question for you," Marlowe said to April. "I've wondered about this forever and for some reason never asked, but it's okay if you want to wait to answer until we're alone."

"Oh, this I want to hear," JJ said with a grin.

"Yeah, that wasn't the best intro if you wanted to keep whatever it is between us," April told her friend with a small smile.

"Sorry. I mean, I don't think it's a huge deal, but it was back when Kendric and I were in Cambodia. I called here, to Jack's Lumber, because it was the only number I knew. You answered, April, and rounded up the guys to talk to me."

"I remember," she said softly. "You sounded so scared."

"That's because I was. Kendric was unconscious and hurting, and I had no idea what to do. Anyway, at one point in the conversation,

JJ, you wanted to talk to the others without me hearing, so you asked April to mute the phone."

"I did," JJ said. "And for the record, it wasn't because I was trying to keep things from you, I just needed to talk through options with my team."

"I understand. I mean, I was a stranger, and for all you knew I was lying my ass off and was planning on hurting you guys, or Kendric, if you showed up," Marlowe said.

JJ huffed out a breath. "We didn't think that at all," he told her with a small shake of his head. "Honestly, I just didn't want to stress you out further by talking about retrieving Bob and not you. At least, not at the same time. Before learning you'd married Bob, we thought we had no legitimate way to get you on a plane."

Marlowe nodded, then turned her gaze back to April. "I heard the phone beep, but the speaker wasn't muted. So my question is—did you do that on purpose?"

JJ looked at April and wasn't surprised at all to see the sly expression on her face. "Yup. If it had been me in that situation, I wouldn't have wanted people talking about me, deciding my fate, without my input. I figured you had every right to hear what was being said about you."

"But I told you to mute it," JJ scolded.

She shrugged. "I know."

He growled low in his throat. "How come you never do what I tell you to?" he complained. "I can't count how many times I've told you to stay put, only to see you on a worksite. Or I say we can't take a job, and you schedule it anyway."

"I do the things you ask that make *sense*," April said without hesitation. "When you tell me to do stupid things, I ignore you."

JJ sighed. "You're a pain in the ass."

April smiled. "Yup."

Honestly, JJ had absolutely no problem with the way April was running Jack's Lumber. In most cases, she was right in the decisions she made, which was why he'd never really taken her to task for disobeying him.

"And for the record, I was absolutely right in letting Marlowe hear that conversation, because if she hadn't, you guys wouldn't have known she and Bob were married," April said with a smug smile.

She wasn't wrong.

"Thank you," Bob told her. "Seriously. I would've been furious if I'd woken up on that plane and found out Marlowe had been left behind."

Marlowe turned to Bob and said something so low, JJ couldn't hear, but he took the opportunity to lean into April. "I love how you always think about other people and what they need."

April gave him a small smile. "I know what it's like to feel as if no one cares what happens to you. To be going through the motions of life without anyone seeing you. I knew there was a chance you'd get really upset at me for not muting the phone, but I trusted you guys; you weren't going to say anything bad about Marlowe, and it was important to me that she not be left out of whatever decision was going to be made about her future."

JJ lifted a hand and palmed her cheek. This woman constantly surprised him. Made him want to be a better person. "You'll never again know what it's like to feel as if no one cares what happens to you. I see you, April. Don't ever doubt that. And while I might not have shown it, I've seen you for the last five years."

She stared at him for a long moment before lifting a hand, covering his own on her cheek, then turning her head and kissing his palm.

JJ wanted nothing more than to pull her up, tow her to the parking lot, stuff her into his Bronco, and take her home. But he was interrupted by Marlowe saying, "Well, for the record, thank you. I was very relieved I didn't have to be separated from Kendric."

JJ's palm tingled where April had kissed it, but he forced himself to focus on their friends. Difficult, when he couldn't stop thinking about April's words from earlier. How she'd come right out and said she wanted to be with him tonight . . . in his bed. She was braver than he'd ever been since they'd met.

Conversation turned to work, as it usually did, and the four of them talked about the job they'd yet to do for the ski resort, the same one April had been going to scope out when she'd had her accident.

"Oh! I didn't tell you what happened yesterday!" Marlowe exclaimed.

JJ felt unease creep up his spine when a frown appeared on Bob's face. Whatever she was about to share, his friend didn't like it.

"What?" April asked.

"Kendric and I were in that new furniture store that opened in Rumford . . . you know, the one that's in that huge warehouse? I think they're trying to be like IKEA, but trust me, they aren't anything similar. Anyway, we'd decided to start looking for baby furniture, because this little nugget is going to be here before we know it." Marlowe put her hand on her belly, and JJ smiled a little when Bob's hand covered hers.

"Kendric went to look at bookcases or something, and I was in the baby aisle. There are huge shelving units, like floor to ceiling, and I'd stopped to check out one of the cribs. The employees have put together one of everything they sell in the store, and the crib was displayed on a shelf at eye level, so you can see what it'll look like when it's assembled. They have boxes piled up both above and below the put-together piece. So . . . I looked at the crib and decided I didn't really like it and had just moved when one of the boxes from the top shelf fell! It landed *right* where I'd been standing not two seconds earlier!"

"Holy crap," April breathed.

"Right? Scared the hell out of me," Marlowe said with a nod.

"What happened?" JJ asked.

"I have no idea. But the box burst open, and the wood from the crib went flying everywhere. One small piece hit my leg, but thankfully nothing else got me."

"Trust me, I gave the management a piece of my mind," Bob growled. "I don't know how that box managed to fall from where it was sitting, but that's the last time we'll set foot in that place, I can tell you that."

"It wasn't that big of a deal," Marlowe said, patting Bob's leg.

"Not a big deal?" Bob asked incredulously. "That box was heavy, and it fell from several feet up. If it had landed on you, you could've been seriously hurt."

"But I wasn't," Marlowe soothed.

"That's crazy," April said with a shake of her head.

"Yeah. As much as I don't like to admit it, it rattled me," Marlowe said.

"Scared the shit out of *me*," Bob said in a low, hard voice. "I was across the store and heard the huge crash, and for some reason, I just knew Marlowe was in danger."

"Because you're paranoid," she said without heat.

"Yup," Bob agreed.

"Well, I'm glad you're okay, but did you find the furniture you wanted?" April asked with a small smile, clearly trying to lighten the mood.

Marlowe giggled. "No. But now I'm thinking Kendric would be okay with making a nest of blankets on the floor instead of getting any baby stuff at all."

"Damn straight," Bob mumbled as the women laughed.

JJ felt bad for his friend. If that had happened to April, he'd be freaking out. And the management would be hearing from his lawyer for sure. The thought of innocently shopping and almost having a box full of heavy wood fall on April's head made him want to lock her in his house and never let her out again. Online shopping wasn't his favorite, but that story was enough to give him second thoughts.

"And no, I refuse to buy our groceries online," Marlowe said, as if she could hear what JJ was thinking. "I mean, there's a lot of things we kind of have to get online, living out here in such a small town, but I draw the line at letting someone else pick out my bananas or touch my meat."

"No one's touching your meat but you," Bob muttered.

April giggled as Marlowe rolled her eyes at her husband.

"With that, I think I need to get some work done," April said with a shake of her head.

"No," JJ told her.

She turned to him. "What?"

"No. I need to get you home so you can rest."

"I don't want to rest," she protested.

"April, not twelve hours ago, you called me with your head hurting so bad you couldn't even open your eyes. You went from not remembering the last five years to all the memories coming back at once, making you incapable of doing anything but moan in my arms. I'm not going to let you overdo it today. The doctor said you needed to rest, and you aren't going to do that if you're sitting at the front desk, looking through your files and trying to see what we might've messed up while you weren't working."

She glared at him. "One hour," she cajoled.

"No," JJ said with a shake of his head.

"Thirty minutes."

"No."

"Jack!" she protested.

"April!" he echoed.

She turned to Bob and Marlowe. "Tell him he's being unreasonable," she begged.

"Actually, I think he was remarkably lenient, letting you come here after the doctor's visit," Bob said with a shrug.

"Who asked you?" April grumbled.

He chuckled. "You did."

"Marlowe?" April pleaded.

But her friend gave her a sympathetic look. "I think he's right. You've got a furrow in your brow, as if your head hurts, and a nap couldn't hurt after all you've been through. The last thing you want is to have a relapse, for your memories to go away again if you try to do too much, too soon."

April sighed, sat quietly for a moment . . . then admitted softly, "I'm afraid if I go to sleep, the memories will disappear."

"They won't," JJ told her firmly. "How about this—you come to my place now and take a nap, and I'll go out and get us Granny's Burgers for dinner."

April turned to him. "Are you trying to bribe me?"

"Yup," JJ admitted without reservation.

"Dang it. It's working," she grumbled.

Everyone laughed.

Marlowe stood, with Bob's help, and held out a hand to April. She took it without hesitation, and Marlowe pulled her to her feet. Then she wrapped her arms around her. "I'm glad you're okay. I was so worried about you."

"Thanks," April whispered as she hugged her friend back.

As soon as Marlowe let go, JJ wrapped his arm around April's waist and pulled her against his side. It would be a long time before he forgot how much pain she was in when he'd gotten to her the night before. The way she'd burrowed into him as if he could take away the throbbing in her head. He'd felt so helpless when all he could do was hold her.

"What about the office?" April asked as JJ steered her toward the back door, where they'd left their jackets. Winter hadn't settled in yet, but it would be here soon. The weather had gotten colder, and JJ was well aware that April wouldn't miss the hot summer temperatures. He'd learned over the years that she much preferred to be cold than hot. He hadn't even noticed the cold weather when he'd been running around in nothing but his briefs the night before. All he'd been thinking about was getting to April.

"I'm going to come back after getting Marlowe settled at home," Bob said. "Chappy and Cal are out on a job, and I'll wait for them to get back before I head out for the day. Besides, everyone around here knows our hours are wonky since you've been hurt. They'll leave a voicemail or email us if they can't get a hold of anyone. It's fine."

April sighed. "All right. But I don't like it."

JJ chuckled. "Noted. Come on, time to go."

They all walked outside, and JJ locked up the office before putting a hand on the small of April's back and steering her toward his SUV.

Marlowe called out another goodbye from Bob's pickup, and April waved at her. Then she turned to look at JJ. "Jack?"

"Yeah, hon?"

"Thank you."

"For what?"

"Everything. For staying with me in the hospital. For driving me home. For helping to arrange for me to have a car. For letting me stay with you. Not making me feel weird about being in your house instead of my apartment. For coming over last night. For being practical . . . all of it."

JJ stopped on the passenger side of the car and slid his fingers into April's hair. He brushed his thumb against her cheek for a moment. "You don't have to thank me, April."

"I do, I—"

"No, you don't," he interrupted. "Because if you think there's anywhere I would've rather been than at your side, you haven't been paying attention. If you think I would've let you convalesce in your apartment, by yourself, you don't know me. But you will. From this point on . . . everything I do is for you. Even making you go home and take a nap when you don't want to."

"I'm not a kid," April said seriously.

"No, you're not. You're a mature adult who's lived a life without someone at her side who gives a shit. I give a shit, April. Yes, you can make your own decisions, and if you really wanted to stay here and fiddle on the damn computer, I wouldn't have stopped you. But you've been through hell in the last couple of weeks, and your head *does* hurt.

Marlowe didn't need to tell me that. I can see it for myself, and it kills me. Let me take care of you, sweetheart. Let me spoil you. Please."

"I'm not used to being spoiled," she told him.

As if JJ needed her to admit it. "I know," he said simply. "I warned you. I'm intense. And bossy. And I'll scorch the earth to make sure you're safe. If that had been you in the store, and that box had fallen off a shelf and almost hit you . . ." He shuddered before continuing. "Let's just say I would've made a scene that the manager wouldn't soon forget. No one hurts you, including yourself.

"I need you to understand that you have a champion now, April. And while that might sound cool, there will be times you'll get pissed at me because of it. I'll annoy you, and you'll call up one of the other girls and bitch about me being overprotective and smothering, and you'll wonder what the hell you've gotten yourself into. But then I'll bring you a cup of coffee with your favorite creamer and let you watch those stupid home-improvement shows you like, and I'll make love to you, and you'll understand that I've got your back at all times.

"When the shit hits the fan, I'll stand in front of you and protect you with everything I have. When necessary, I'll stand behind you and let you shine and do your thing. And I'll be at your side when we need to face our demons together."

JJ knew he was being over the top and probably a little aggressive in his desire to make her understand what she was getting into. But he needed her to hear this *now*, because once she gave herself to him, it would literally kill him to let her go.

"Okay," she whispered.

"Okay?" he asked.

"Yes. I've never had a champion before. I think I'll like it. And so you know, there will be times when I need my space. I'm used to doing things without consulting anyone because there's never been anyone who's given a shit *what* I do. It'll take some getting used to, I think.

"And I'm going to need you to cut me some slack when I do something you don't like. I can be moody and bitchy. And while I've loved being around you this past week, I don't think I can be the kind of girlfriend who likes to be attached at the hip with her man. I can drive myself places and go shopping and hang out at the house by myself. There will be times when I just want a bowl of cereal for dinner or won't feel like talking about anything. I tend to leave my shoes in every room, and I hate doing dishes. I love taking pictures, so you'll need to get used to being in them more than you have in the past. And . . . as much as I love the thought that you want to protect me, you aren't allowed to put yourself in danger to save me. Got it?"

"Everything but that last part, yes," JJ told her.

April scowled. "I mean it, Jack. You've been through enough hell already. How do you think I'd feel if you were hurt protecting me? It would kill me. The guilt would eat me alive."

"How about we both do everything in our power to lead boring lives here in Newton, so it's not an issue?" JJ asked, trying to distract her. There was no way in hell he would ever agree to let her get hurt if he could do something to prevent it.

"Sounds good to me," she said with a smile. Then she leaned her head into his hand and closed her eyes. "Take me home?"

"Yes," he said.

Her eyes opened. "Nap, food, TV . . . and no, I won't make you watch one of my horrible home-improvement shows," she teased, then got serious once more. "Then bed. Together."

JJ's cock twitched in his jeans.

"I mean, we slept with each other last night, but I don't think that counted."

"It counted," JJ said with a nod. "I got to hold you, feel your heart beat against mine, and smell you on my skin."

"You know what I mean," she protested. "I want you, Jack. I have for years. I *need* you."

"I need you too," he said. "But we'll see how your head feels."

April rolled her eyes. "Is this one of the times you're making decisions for me for my own good?"

"Yup."

"Fine. But I'm telling you, I'm feeling okay. Yes, my head hurts a little right now, but the doc said that was normal. And it's nothing like it was when I woke up last night. I'm thinking an orgasm would get the blood flowing and actually help more than hurt."

JJ shifted, his cock pressing uncomfortably against his zipper now. "Damn, woman," he complained.

April grinned. "Take me home, Jack."

JJ had a feeling that for all his tough words about doing what was best for her, they would amount to nothing when she got an idea in her head. It wasn't as if he could deny her anything. And since he wanted her as much as she apparently wanted him, he was a total goner.

Leaning down, JJ kissed her. It started out as a mere touch of lips, but she was having none of that. She gripped his neck and held him against her as she opened her mouth and her tongue sought entry to his mouth.

Again, realizing that he couldn't deny her anything, JJ opened for her. They made out in the parking lot of Jack's Lumber for several minutes, until he finally pulled back and realized he was panting.

"Why did we wait so long to do this?" she asked with a sparkle in her eye.

"Because we're stupid?" JJ answered.

"Pretty much. Take me home," she ordered again, running a hand down his chest.

"Yes, ma'am," he said obediently. He reluctantly slid his hand out of her hair.

"I guess I know how to get you to do what I want," she said with a sly smile.

"Guess you do," JJ agreed. Then he kissed her again, hard and fast, not letting her coax him into more this time before helping her into the vehicle, handing her the seat belt, and waiting until she'd fastened it. He closed her door, took a deep breath, then headed around the SUV to the driver's side.

The Lumberjack

〜

Ryan Johnson watched from the trees at the back of the parking area behind Jack's Lumber. He'd spent many hours sitting there, plotting and planning. He watched Marlowe and Kendric Evans drive away and April and Jackson talk forever before making out. He scowled furiously as they kissed. "Enjoy it while you can, asshole."

Ryan had spent so many years planning his revenge, nothing would stop him now.

He was leaving for Colorado tonight to prepare for the final show-down between him and the four men. He'd been there several times in the last year, getting certain things ready, so it should only take him a day or two to finish. Then he'd come straight back to Newton—and kick off the beginning of the end.

At one point in his life, he would've felt bad about the women get-ting caught in the middle of his revenge . . . but Ryan had stopped feel-ing much of anything beyond hate long ago. The women had become necessary for him to reach his end goal. That they would die was now icing on the cake.

Riggs, Callum, Kendric, and Jackson would suffer just as much as he had. They'd feel the same pain Ryan had suffered after learning of his brother's death.

His brother, the person he'd loved above all others, ruthlessly killed and thrown away as if he was nothing but a piece of trash.

But he wasn't. He'd been doing as ordered while attempting to make a better life for himself and Ryan. He was only fourteen when his brother was killed . . . when the four Americans had been held hostage . . . but he now felt far older than his years.

He'd begged his brother to let him join him in the mountains. To participate in the interrogation of the American soldiers and do his part to secure the life they both sought. But he wasn't allowed. He was told to stay home. To wait for instructions.

So he had. And he'd never seen his brother again.

His father didn't care, and his mother was equally useless. Only Ryan had vowed to make the Americans suffer. He wouldn't rest until they felt the same despair and anguish Ryan still endured.

And the time was approaching. Meanwhile, he was having more fun than he'd anticipated. Making that box fall off the shelf at exactly the right moment had been tricky, and while he'd missed hitting Marlowe, seeing how upset Kendric became was worth it. He'd wanted to injure the bitch, maybe even cause her to lose the brat she carried. *That* would've tortured her husband. But now that he'd thought about it, it was better she'd only had a close call.

He had two more incidents planned before he moved on to the main event. He'd fully intended to send the other two women to the hospital, like April, but with time to consider, he realized three "accidents" resulting in hospitalization would only make the men suspicious. If they thought the women could be in danger, they'd close ranks, and he'd never be able to get to them.

No. It was better to scare them. Engineer random freak events that wouldn't cause the men to think twice, wouldn't have them putting two and two together and realizing an enemy was out there, watching and waiting.

Ryan chuckled. A low, terrifying sound. He watched as Jackson scanned the parking area, but he wasn't worried that he'd be spotted. He was deep in the woods, and he'd sat there many times without being seen. The soldiers thought they were safe here in middle-of-nowhere, Maine. Didn't sense the danger that was right in front of their faces.

He couldn't wait to mess with their heads. It would be so much fun! They'd be scared out of their minds, and he'd enjoy every second. They'd watch their women and unborn children die, unable to do a damn thing about it.

They'd deeply regret their part in what had happened five years ago—then the men themselves would die. Ryan would get justice for his brother and the satisfaction of knowing the soldiers had died with the failure to protect their loved ones weighing on their useless souls.

He wanted to get on with it. Put his final plans into action immediately. But he needed to be patient. First up—two more accidents. Then he'd make his move.

Shifting to his feet, Ryan walked through the woods, away from Jack's Lumber, to exit on a quiet residential street where he'd left his black pickup. He got behind the wheel and headed for the run-down house he'd been renting. It was fine in the summer, but with winter approaching, it was more obvious what a piece of shit the place was, with cold seeping into every crack.

"I fucking hate Maine. Snow. America. This fucking town!" Ryan mumbled as he pulled into the small garage and closed the door behind his truck. If he had more time, he'd also turn his hatred toward the man who owned the piece-of-crap rental. Make him suffer slowly. Instead, he'd simply burn the place down before he left.

Smiling, feeling anticipation build within him, Ryan entered the house and went straight to the bedroom he'd turned into a workspace. Most of the explosives had already been moved to Colorado and were in place, but he figured . . . the more, the better. And making the IEDs, land mines, and other surprises the soldiers would find when they tried to rescue their women kept Ryan busy while he struggled to be patient.

Food held no appeal. Neither did sleep. All Ryan wanted to do was make more and more weapons to bring down the four men who'd taken away his brother. Time was ticking, just like the explosives he was making, and soon, he'd hit start on the timers.

CHAPTER NINE

April thought she should be nervous, but for some reason, she wasn't at all. She'd waited for this moment for years, and the fact that it was finally here made her tingle with anticipation. Her memory coming back was a miracle. And for a moment, when she'd been in Jack's arms in her apartment, all the worries she'd had for years almost overwhelmed her.

But she'd pushed them aside. They were bullshit. Her age, the fact that Jack was her boss . . . they were just excuses. She wanted him, and it was obvious he wanted her too. She didn't want to wait any longer. Yes, Jack was intense. And he wasn't wrong, she'd probably get irritated with him more often than not when he got all heavy handed.

But she'd spent too many years with a man who barely noticed her existence. She probably could've announced to her ex that she was going to walk across a tightrope stretched over the Grand Canyon and he wouldn't even have looked up from whatever he was doing.

If April told Jack that she wanted to go skydiving, or bungee jumping, or any of the other things she'd once wanted to do in her lifetime, she knew without a doubt he'd veto each and every one of them. But if she insisted, he'd give in—after personally inspecting all the gear, interrogating whoever would be assisting her, and probably doing a very thorough background check on the company. Even then, he'd most likely insist on doing everything with her. Be the man she was strapped to when she jumped out of a plane or tandem bungee with her.

And that didn't turn her off. Not at all. Why would it?

Smiling to herself, April stared into the mirror in Jack's bathroom. He'd brought her back to his place and tucked her in to bed, and she'd slept like a log for two hours straight. When she'd gotten up, he had a delicious turkey soup in the slow cooker. While eating, they'd laughed about things that had happened at the office over the years, then watched a paranormal show about finding Bigfoot somewhere in Southwest Virginia.

When it was over, she'd excused herself to get ready for bed . . . and now she was staring at herself, letting the anticipation of what she hoped was about to happen sweep over her. She studied her face, trying not to let the wrinkles around her eyes and the way her skin sagged a bit more each year bother her.

Instead, she focused on what she liked about herself. She was tall for a woman, at five-nine, and average size, not skinny or overweight. Her breasts weren't as perky as they used to be, but they were full and perfectly round. She had good hair . . . had always loved the brown color with the natural streaks of blonde thrown in, giving it depth.

Squinting, she could see a few sprinkles of gray beginning to grow in, but she wasn't overly concerned about them. She was almost fifty, after all. Okay, she still had a few years before she hit that milestone, but either way, fifty was just a number. She had roughly half her life left. And if she could spend those years with Jack, she'd be a very lucky woman.

Her blue eyes sparkled with anticipation, and while she kind of wished she had her nightie from the night before rather than the over-size T-shirt of Jack's she'd borrowed, she dismissed the thought. It wasn't as if she'd be wearing anything at all for long . . . she hoped.

A smile crept over her lips at the thought of waking up that morning to Jack in nothing but his briefs. The man had run out into the cold night with almost no clothes on because he was desperate to get to her. Yeah, she might get annoyed with him in the future, but all she had to do was remember last night and she had a feeling any annoyance would fade. He hadn't even paused to put on pants or shoes. He'd raced to her side simply because she'd needed him.

Closing her eyes, April took a deep breath. Jack was overwhelming, but in the best way.

"April?" His deep voice came from the bedroom.

Her eyes opened, and she smiled again. Turning, she opened the door without hesitation.

Jack was standing in the middle of the room, looking a bit unsure about what he should do next. It was almost . . . cute. Jackson Justice wasn't a man who was unsure about *anything*. He was used to making decisions about the business, as the leader of his Delta Force team, in emergencies. So seeing him standing in his own bedroom, looking vulnerable, made April love him all the more.

Yes, she loved this man. Now that her memories were back, she knew that without a doubt. She knew everything there was to know about him. And she admired all of it. The reason she'd felt so safe with him, despite having no memory of the man, made perfect sense now. Deep down, her unquestionable love for Jack made her yearn to be near him, stranger or no.

"You okay?" he asked when she simply stood in the bathroom doorway, staring at him.

"I'm perfect," she said, feeling calm. She wanted this. Him.

She walked toward him slowly and didn't stop until she was plastered against his front and her arms were around his neck. His own arms automatically wrapped around her waist, holding her tightly.

"Are *you* okay?" she asked.

His lips twitched. "Yeah. But I'm not the one who's had the headaches."

"Well, my head feels fine right now."

"You sure?"

April could tell he was asking about more than just how her head felt. "I'm more sure about being here, about making love with you, than anything I've ever done in my life. To be honest, I never thought we'd get here. I want to be with you, Jack. I've always wanted this. Always wanted *you*."

She saw and felt the relief sweep through him. His arms tightened even as the rest of him relaxed. Well, all except for the part pressing against her belly. His cock was hard, and the thought of finally seeing it, touching it, having him inside her, made April squirm in his grip.

Without hesitation, he grabbed the bottom of the T-shirt she wore and pulled it up and over her head in a move that underscored his decisiveness. He wasn't waiting. Wasn't moving slowly. Now that they were here, about to make love, he wasn't wasting another second.

April blushed as she forced herself to stand still under his intense gaze. She wasn't wearing anything under his shirt, and it took every ounce of strength she had to let Jack look his fill.

The overhead light was still on, and every one of her flaws was on full display.

"Damn, woman . . . you're so beautiful," Jack breathed, before reaching for his own shirt. Within seconds, he was standing just as naked as she was. So handsome, it took April's breath away.

They stood there inches apart, breathing hard, each taking in the other.

Then Jack blew her mind by lifting a hand and holding it near her face . . . but not touching. "May I?" he asked, seeking permission to touch her.

Any other man would've been on her by now. Would've grabbed her boob. Would've stuck his hand between her legs. But not Jack. He wanted to be sure she wanted this.

In response, April took his hand in hers and placed it on her cheek. "Yes. Please, Jack. I need you."

He took a step forward, bringing his body flush with hers. She felt his hard cock against her belly, skin to skin now, and inhaled deeply. His other hand rested at the small of her back, and he roughly yanked her closer.

That small loss of control made April smile. That's how she wanted this man. Not controlled and methodical but out of his mind with lust for her. Because that's how she felt about him.

"I'm terrified of doing something to scare you. To turn you off," he said in a low, almost tortured tone.

"You don't scare me, and you definitely don't turn me off," she reassured him. "Make me yours, Jack."

"You *are* mine," he returned. "Have been for years, even if I was too chickenshit to admit it."

God, April loved hearing that. She snaked one hand to his butt, the other clenching against his back. She squeezed his ass and smiled up at him. "I've wanted to do that forever. You have the best ass."

He grinned. In turn, his hand went to her breast and squeezed. "I've wanted to do *this* for years. You have the best tits."

April laughed. When she'd imagined how things would be if she and Jack ever got together, she'd never suspected they'd laugh together like they were, not with his focused, almost surly demeanor.

His fingers rolled her nipple and pinched gently. The slight pain went straight between her legs, and she could feel herself cream for him. April arched her back into his touch, and her fingernails dug into his butt cheek. "Please, Jack . . . please."

"You don't have to beg for anything, sweetheart," he told her, his gaze glued to her chest where he was playing with her nipple. He began to walk them backward toward the bed. "I'm gonna love you so hard," he promised, "you're never going to want another man. You won't even be able to *think* about anyone else."

Goose bumps broke out on her arms. If any other man spoke to her that way, she'd probably roll her eyes and tell him he had an overinflated ego. But this was Jack, and she had a suspicion he was right.

The back of her knees touched the mattress, and Jack dropped his hands from her and motioned to the bed. "Scoot up."

Keeping her gaze locked on his face, she did as he requested, quickly moving backward until she was sitting in the middle of his king-size bed. The same bed she'd slept on for the last week and dreamed about him joining her under the covers on.

Jack moved like a panther, sleek and smooth. He put one knee on the bed, then the other as he crawled closer. When he loomed over her, April lay back. He caged her in, lowering his naked body to hers. His cock brushed her thigh, branding her with his heat as it came to rest against her belly.

She grabbed hold of his biceps, which rippled as he stared down at her with his weight on his forearms. He didn't say anything for a long moment.

"Jack?" she asked tentatively, not sure what he was waiting for.

"I've got condoms," he said, seemingly out of the blue. "But I haven't been with a woman in years. Not since I met you."

The implication of that sank in, making April love him all the more.

"It's always been you," he went on. "Even when I didn't want to admit it. Even when I told myself that nothing could happen because I'd break if you walked away. I was still yours."

"My ex was the second man I'd ever been with, and we hadn't made love for over a year before calling it quits."

Jack blinked at her. "Seriously?"

April nodded. "Yeah."

He took a deep breath and closed his eyes. Then they opened, and April swore they were even darker than they'd been a moment ago. "I can't believe there weren't scores of men who wanted in there."

It was a crude statement, but April didn't take offense. "I'm not exactly a Kardashian," she said with a shrug.

"No, you're a Marilyn Monroe." He shifted, and one of his hands slowly caressed down the length of her body. "You're curvy, and mysterious, and gorgeous . . . and all mine."

April shivered and gripped his biceps harder. "If you stopped talking and started some action, I would be," she sassed, her body practically vibrating from waiting.

He grinned, then got serious. "Where do we stand on pregnancy?"

April gaped. Was he really asking her if she wanted kids? *Now?* Besides, she thought they'd already talked about this. "What?"

"How do I protect you?"

Oh! He wasn't literally asking her about future plans for children. Thank God. He was being a responsible adult, having the birth control talk.

"I had an ovarian cyst . . . when I was in my twenties," she explained haltingly. "I had to have it removed, along with my ovary and fallopian tube. Only on that one side, but as a result of another cyst found the next year on my remaining ovary, my doctor put me on the pill. I've been on it for over twenty years now. It's highly unlikely that I can get pregnant anyway, because of my age and all the other factors." She was babbling now, but this was a little awkward. She'd never had the birth control talk with a man because she'd been married and James had known all about her medical history.

"You okay? Those cysts won't come back?"

Her heart melted. Figured that he was lying on top of her, naked, anticipating what she hoped would be the best sex of her life, and the second he heard she'd had some sort of medical issue, all his attention was on her well-being. "I'm good."

Jack nodded. "As I said before, I've got condoms."

"Latex bothers me," she blurted. "I don't know if I'm allergic or what, but every time I've had sex with one—which was only with one guy, but still—I got a UTI. If you trust me, I'd prefer to go without. If that's okay," she added at the end, because she was nervous and couldn't read the look on Jack's face.

"Are you seriously asking me if it's *okay* if I take you bare?" he asked.

"Um . . . yes?" April said uncertainly.

"Not only is it okay, it's a fucking dream come true," Jack rumbled. "Can I come inside you?"

April licked her lips and nodded, his words making her ridiculously hot.

Jack leaned down and put his forehead against hers. And he didn't move for long seconds.

"Jack?"

"Give me a minute," he whispered.

April wasn't sure what was going on with him, but she did as he asked, running her hands up and down his back soothingly. After a moment, he lifted up and braced his hands on the mattress on either side of her. His gaze went down her body. He looked at her so adoringly, April squirmed beneath him.

"I never knew all those years ago that a simple game of chance would bring me the most important thing in my life. Would turn out to be such a gift."

April's eyes teared up at his words. He didn't give her time to respond.

"I'm going to love every inch of your body tonight, April. Worship you. Show you how much you mean to me. I don't deserve you, but I'm damn sure going to ruin you for any other man."

"I'm okay with that, as long as I can do the same," she retorted.

He grinned then. "This is gonna be fun," he said—before he lowered himself quickly and latched his lips around one of her nipples.

April squealed and arched into him. He didn't ease into his caress. He sucked hard on the stiff peak and shifted so he could take hold of her breast with his hand.

"Jack!" she exclaimed as she writhed beneath him.

His lips made a popping sound as he let go of her nipple, and he grinned at her. His fingers went to the nipple he'd just been feasting on, rolling it and pinching slightly. Again, electricity shot to the aching spot between her legs.

Jack didn't speak, simply turned his attention to her other nipple and lowered his head.

How long he spent worshipping her breasts, April had no idea. She'd also had no idea she was so sensitive! She'd never had a man pay as much attention to her chest as Jack. Her pussy was dripping, and he hadn't even touched her there.

"Jack, please," she moaned as she grabbed a handful of his hair.

"Please what?" he asked, blowing across her stiff nipple.

"Touch me!"

"I am," he reasoned, sounding very satisfied with himself as he played with both nipples now.

April let out a small growl and tried to push him onto his back. But of course she couldn't move him. When she let out a dissatisfied grumble, he acquiesced and rolled them.

But as soon as she was on top, Jack's hands went to her hips, and he pulled her up his chest.

April was embarrassed. She knew he could feel how drenched she was, since her legs were spread so wide over his chest she was leaving a trail of wetness on his skin. She wasn't sure what he was doing when he continued to pull her forward, his intention not dawning on her until she was hovering over his face.

In her defense, she'd never had a man do this before. Yes, her ex had gone down on her, mostly at the beginning of their marriage, but it was obvious he'd never enjoyed the act, so she didn't push for him to do it.

The way Jack stared and licked his lips made her thighs clench in anticipation. He grabbed a pillow and shoved it under his head, bringing his mouth closer to her pussy.

"I've dreamed about this moment forever. You like oral, hon?"

She shrugged and stared down at him, his gaze like a brand.

He grinned. "Guess we'll find out." And with that, he lifted his head, not taking his gaze from hers as he licked the slit between her legs.

April jerked in his grasp and braced herself on the headboard.

"Yeah, hang on, sweetheart."

Then there was no more talking as Jack began to eat her out in earnest.

Dear Lord, April had never experienced anything like it. His hands on her thighs, holding her open to him; his tongue licking slow at first, then faster; the way he sucked on her clit; the sounds he made as he feasted on her.

Before long, her thighs shook from holding her own weight. April was terrified she'd somehow smother him, so she tried to keep herself way above his face. But he was having none of that. He growled, and the sound reverberated through her pussy, up her entire body, as he pulled her down roughly, making her widen her stance.

All thoughts of trying to protect Jack flew from her mind as she neared orgasm. She barely realized she'd started to undulate, searching for more direct stimulation on her clit. A frustrated sound escaped her lips when she wasn't getting what she needed to come. His tongue felt amazing, but she needed more.

"Show me," Jack ordered. "Touch yourself. Show me what you need to come."

If April hadn't been so turned on, so lost in the pleasure Jack was giving her, there was no way she'd have had the guts to touch herself. But she wanted to come so badly and was completely uninhibited at this point.

One of her hands unclenched painfully from the headboard, and she snaked it down her body. She frantically strummed her clit in the way she liked best as she chased the orgasm, which felt just out of reach.

"Holy hell, that's hot," Jack said. His hands were clamped around her thighs, basically holding her up, and she felt his tongue against her folds as she stroked herself. Her inner muscles clenched against nothing as she neared her peak, and April whimpered. She wanted to be filled, but there was no stopping her orgasm at this point.

She continued to rub herself as Jack licked and sucked at the juices dripping out of her body. Every last one of her muscles clenched as she stood at the precipice.

"Come for me, hon. I want to see it. Drench my face," Jack ordered.

April barely heard the words as she was already flying over the edge.

She shook and trembled and felt Jack desperately licking her flesh as she orgasmed, his moans loud and deep. She lifted her hand from between her legs, and Jack immediately latched onto her clit. She shrieked and tried to pull away, but he had a firm grip on her legs and she couldn't move.

What had been an amazing orgasm turned into something almost painful, in a good way, as Jack continued to stimulate her overly sensitive bundle of nerves.

She almost blacked out and could've sworn she felt the world sway around her, until she realized that was Jack sitting up and throwing her backward in one smooth motion. Then he was between her legs, and she could feel his cock notched against her extremely sensitive folds.

"I need you," he growled.

April wondered what the hell he was waiting for, because she wanted him inside her more than she wanted to breathe—then she realized he was waiting for permission once more.

"Yes! Please, Jack. Inside me. Now!"

That was all he needed to hear. One second she was empty, and the next, she was so full it was almost painful.

Jack's head lowered, and he kissed her. Hard and deep, almost desperately, as he held still inside her body, letting her adjust. April could taste herself on his lips and feel her juices all over his face. Sex had never been like this for her. Desperate, messy, and so damn passionate, she felt as if she was burning up from the inside out.

JJ felt as if he was going to combust. He'd always loved giving oral, but with April, it was a whole new experience. Seeing her masturbate inches from his face, feeling her fingers brush against his tongue as he licked her while she stroked her clit . . . it was hotter and more intimate than anything he'd ever experienced before.

When she'd come, he could literally see her inner muscles clenching, since she was spread open so wide right in front of his face. Seeing her juices seep out of her cunt, knowing her body was wet and ready for him, made him lose all control.

He'd thrown her to her back even as she was still coming and had his dick notched at her opening before he'd come to his senses at the last second. He'd never taken a woman without her consent, and he wouldn't start now.

When she'd told him yes, JJ's hips pushed forward without any input from his brain. One second he was panting with need, then he was buried inside the hottest, wettest, tightest pussy he'd ever had.

His nipples were hard against his chest, he could smell her juices all over his face and neck, and he still needed more. Cognizant that it had been a long time for her—even more so than it had for him—he continued to kiss April, trying to distract himself from the need to thrust.

It didn't work. Feeling her tongue duel with his made him even more desperate.

JJ lifted his head and stared down at the woman he couldn't live without, couldn't imagine going a day without seeing for the rest of his life, and willed himself to calm down. To make this good for her.

To his amazement, April smiled. Her hands went from his neck to his chest, where they ran up and down, catching on his nipples and making him shudder.

"You're big," she whispered.

JJ smiled at that but couldn't unclench his teeth enough to respond.

Then she moved her hips. It was just a tiny motion but enough to make his cock twitch deep inside her body. He knew he'd let loose a spurt of precome, and the image in his mind of coating her channel with his essence was so erotic, he was amazed he didn't blow his load right then and there.

"Move, Jack. I need more!"

Slowly, he lifted his hips. The loss of her warmth around his cock was almost painful. Desperate not to hurt her, he slowly sank back inside her welcoming sheath.

"More," April moaned again, trying to thrust up into him.

JJ took a deep breath. "I'm trying to go slow," he managed to get out.

"Well, stop it!" she scolded. "I don't want slow. I want *you*. Unrestrained. Wild. I want you to want me as much as I want you."

A harsh snort left JJ as he stared down at April. "Impossible," he said. Then added, "Hang on."

April grinned.

If she wanted him out of control, she was about to get her wish.

JJ scooted his knees up a little on the mattress and hooked her knees in his elbows before resting his palms on the mattress. She was spread wide open for him now, and JJ couldn't help but look down to where they were connected. His cock was buried so far inside her, all he could see was their pubic hair meshed together. He shifted his hips and was rewarded with the sight of his dick, covered in her juices, appearing from between her folds.

It was carnal, and erotic, and broke the last of JJ's control.

He slammed back into her and barely registered their twin moans. He couldn't stop now. She'd unleashed the beast, and his only goal was to fuck her hard and fast.

His hips flew, his cock thrusting in and out of her pussy. The sounds of their bodies smacking together as he entered and retreated turned him on even more. He never wanted this to end. Wanted to make love to her for hours.

Her hips attempted to meet his when he thrust inside her, but with the way he was holding her legs open, she didn't have much leverage. April's hands went to her tits, and she began to pinch her nipples. That made him even harder. She was so damn sexy, he couldn't stand it.

"Touch yourself," he ordered.

"What?" she gasped, her gaze unfocused.

"I want to feel you come on my cock. Touch yourself," he repeated.

Without hesitation, one of her hands went between her legs.

"Watch me take you," he told her. JJ knew he was being bossy, but he couldn't help it. He wanted her to see how beautiful they were together.

She reached for a pillow with her free hand and stuffed it under her head, giving her the height advantage she needed to see where they were joined.

Her fingers moved on her clit, brushing against his cock every time he pulled out, and it was all JJ could do not to come right then and there. But he gritted his teeth and held on. He really did want to feel her come on his dick.

Plunging into her body felt amazing, and as she pleasured herself, her inner muscles tightened around him, so JJ paused when he was as deep inside her as he could get. He looked down at the woman under him, and love almost overwhelmed him.

She wasn't afraid of her sexuality. She touched herself in front of him with a total lack of restraint. There wasn't an ounce of shyness in her when they were together like this, and he fucking loved it.

As they'd done when she was straddling his face, her muscles began to twitch violently as she neared her peak. He experienced her orgasm as her inner muscles squeezed and flexed around his cock. It was something he'd never felt before, and it was as fascinating as it was a turn-on.

His body once again moved without conscious thought. JJ fucked her harder, loving the way he had to fight to push through the spasming muscles of her pussy as she continued to orgasm.

"Yes, Jack! Oh yes!" she panted as she thrashed beneath him, pushing him closer and closer to the edge. April would never be the kind of lover who lay under him limply as he got off. No, she gave as good as she got; even now, she was grabbing at his ass, urging him to take her even harder and faster.

His orgasm came upon him without warning. One second he was enjoying the way her body felt around his dick, and the next, he'd slammed inside her and released his load.

He groaned, and the world went dark as he came. Spurt after spurt erupted from his dick as he orgasmed inside a woman without protection for the first time in his life. He actually felt the warmth of his own release surround his cock as he filled her. The strength in his arms gave way, and he collapsed on top of April, stopping himself from crushing her at the last second.

He lay there panting, trying to regain his equilibrium. His orgasm had turned him inside out, but almost as soon as he came back to himself, he wanted to do it again.

Lifting his head, he peered down at April.

She had a satisfied smile on her face and was grinning up at him. "Hey," she said lazily.

JJ didn't bother to answer; his head dropped, and he kissed her. This time it was a slow, intense meeting of lips and tongues. He wanted to thank her. Let her know how much he loved her. Worshipped her.

When he finally lifted his head, she licked her lips, and he felt her inner muscles tighten around his cock, which was still buried inside her.

"Am I crushing you?"

"No," she said, even as she nodded.

JJ put a hand on her ass, holding her against him, then rolled until she was on top. To his immense relief, she wiggled a little, getting comfortable, then rested her head on his shoulder. He could feel their combined juices leaking out from where they were connected, onto his balls and sheets, but he didn't care. Nothing mattered but holding his woman.

"How's your head?" he asked after a moment.

"What head?" she mumbled.

JJ chuckled. Then sobered. Jesus, he'd been so rough with her. It hadn't been that long ago that she'd been in the hospital.

"No," April said in that same lazy tone.

"No what?" JJ asked.

"No, you aren't allowed to second-guess the best sex I've ever had in my life."

He relaxed. "How'd you know what I was thinking?"

"Because I know you, Jackson Justice. You're a worrywart. You worry about your friends, about the business, and now you're worrying that what we just did was too rough. For the record, it wasn't." Her head lifted, and she stared at him. "Unless you're regretting it. Unless I was too . . . uninhibited."

JJ couldn't help it; he laughed. "The only thing I regret is that it's over. You were perfect, sweetheart."

She sighed in relief and lowered her head back to his shoulder. "Whew! I don't know where all that came from. I've never been like that before. But you didn't seem to mind, so I just did what felt good."

"I always want you to be that way with me," JJ told her.

"I will. And same goes for you. You are so unbelievably sexy. I'm still pinching myself that you're with me. I do have one complaint, though . . ." Her words trailed off.

JJ stiffened. "What's that?"

"I didn't get to explore you. Taste you."

Now his body stiffened for a different reason. "You want that?"

"Duh," she said, and he felt her smile against his skin.

"As soon as I get the strength to pull out of your warm, soft body, maybe I'll give you a chance."

She laughed, and he felt it in his cock. "You can't stay in there forever."

"Wanna bet?" he retorted. It was a stupid argument, but he didn't care, and it seemed as if April didn't either, since her inner muscles clenched around him.

"Careful, love," he whispered, just as he felt his softened cock slip out of her pussy.

"Shoot," she mumbled.

JJ grinned and shook his head.

"Jack?"

"Yeah?"

"I love you."

JJ swore his heart stopped beating at hearing those words.

"I'm not saying it to pressure you into anything. But life is short. I've learned that the hard way, and I didn't want to go one more day without telling you. Nothing has to change, I just—"

JJ rolled once more. He took her head in his hands and stared down at her. "You're wrong. Everything's changed."

She bit her lip as she stared at him.

"Because I love you too. You're braver than I'll *ever* be for saying it first."

"Whatever," she whispered, but he saw tears form in her eyes.

"And as I said, this changes everything. I warned you before that if we did this, I'd become even more protective and overbearing. And now it's a done deal. Knowing you love me? I've never wished for anything more in my life than to hear those words. I'm gonna swaddle you in Bubble Wrap and keep you in an orgasm haze, right here in my bed, so nothing can hurt you ever again."

JJ was being ridiculous, but he couldn't help it.

April simply rolled her eyes. "I don't mind you being protective, but holding me hostage in your bed seems a little extreme, don't you think?"

"No."

She giggled, but the sound died when JJ moved and she felt his hardening cock against her thigh.

"Again?" she asked, one brow raised in surprise.

"Yes," he said, as he reached down and took hold of his cock and fed it back into her body.

April moaned and arched her back, but her legs opened wider, welcoming him.

This time their lovemaking was slow and sweet . . . for the most part. It wasn't until JJ sat back on his heels and held April on his lap, stroking her clit and feeling her explode around him once more, that he lost control.

After he'd filled her with his come for a second time, he shuffled them around so they were lying properly on the bed, and she fell asleep on his chest.

Still awake, JJ took a deep breath. She probably thought he was kidding about the protective thing, but he'd been through enough hell to understand how precarious life was. He couldn't lose her. It would literally kill him.

Turning his head, JJ kissed April's forehead. She mumbled in her sleep and clutched him tighter as she shifted against him. The overhead light was still on, the sheet was bunched under his ass, April was hogging the blanket, and he could feel the stickiness from their releases between his legs, on his face, and in the wet spot beneath him. But JJ had never been more comfortable.

It would be the most difficult thing he'd ever done, not locking April in his house like he'd threatened. He didn't want to stifle her, and hell, Jack's Lumber needed her. But she'd simply have to get used to having him hover from here on out. She was like a precious glass flower in the middle of a field of boulders. He'd be her force field, making sure nothing and no one touched her. And God help anyone who tried to hurt what he'd searched for his entire life.

CHAPTER TEN

"I've never seen JJ acting so . . . weird," Carlise said as she took a sip of her orange juice.

April nodded. "I know, it's ridiculous." But she smiled as she said it. She and the other women were at Marlowe and Bob's house, having a girls' night in. A week and a half had passed since she and Jack had slept together, and it had been an amazing ten days.

Every night, they made dinner together . . . laughed, talked, sometimes watched TV. Then he made love to her. Often fast and hard, other times slow, with Jack teasing her mercilessly before letting her come. She'd finally convinced him to let her go down on him just a few days ago, and they'd both been turned inside out by the time they fell asleep.

And the overprotectiveness had officially begun. The women had originally planned on going to the Sunday River Brewing Company, which was about ten miles south of Newton, for their girl time. And even though Cal had offered to drive them there and pick them up, Jack vetoed the idea. He'd said it was too far away, the women were too pregnant, and there could be "nefarious sorts of people" there.

It was ridiculous, and Jack was being way too over the top, but since April didn't really care where she spent time with her friends, she let herself be persuaded to hang out at Marlowe's house. But she'd put her foot down when Jack told her that he and the rest of the guys would be there too.

"I told him it wasn't a girls' night if the guys were here," April said to her friends.

"It's kind of cute, though," June replied with a shrug.

"Right? I mean, we all knew you and JJ liked each other, but I don't think any of us expected him to be so . . ." Marlowe's voice trailed off as she tried to think of an appropriate word.

"Concerned?" Carlise offered.

"Protective?" June said.

"Pussy-whipped," Marlowe said with a grin.

Everyone laughed.

"I mean, Cal's been over-the-top watchful, especially the further I get into my pregnancy, but JJ makes him seem like the most neglectful husband in the world in comparison," June said with a grin.

"Does it bother you?" Carlise asked. "I mean, the other day, when you left the office to get lunch at Granny's Burgers, he came back while you were gone and freaked out because he didn't know where you were."

April shrugged. "Honestly? No. I figure things are still new between us, he'll calm down before too long."

"I wouldn't be so sure of that," Marlowe warned. "He's the most intense of all the guys. And I think he feels responsible for all of us. Which makes sense; he was the team leader when they were in the Army, and I have a feeling he blames himself for their capture and everyone's subsequent torture. But he *loves* you, so it's only natural that he's extra cautious."

"I still can't believe you guys are finally together," June said with a sigh. "We were beginning to think it wasn't going to happen."

"Yeah. Carlise was totally ready to lock you guys in a room and force you to share a bed . . . you know, because all of us basically did that and ended up married," Marlowe said with a grin.

"There was no forcing involved," April informed her friends as she sipped her glass of wine. She was the only one drinking alcohol, for obvious reasons. "And I *was* in his bed when we came home from the hospital. That has to count. Kind of."

Everyone chuckled.

"Well, I'm happy for you," Marlowe said. "I haven't known you and JJ for as long as everyone else, but it's obvious you love each other, and you're perfect for one another as well. You take his protectiveness in stride, and when he's being ridiculous, you have no problem calling him on it. I think you guys are going to be just fine. Besides, there's something to be said for having a protective guy at your side."

"Agreed," Carlise said.

"Same," June added.

"Speaking of protective," Carlise said, "did I tell you guys what happened two days ago?"

"Oh Lord, what now?" June asked with a laugh.

"I was coming back from Rumford after stocking up on some stuff from the discount bulk store. I was minding my own business, singing Cyndi Lauper's 'Girls Just Want to Have Fun' at the top of my lungs, when I felt something brush against my arm. I nonchalantly looked down—and there was a freaking *tarantula* crawling on me!"

"What?"

"Holy shit!"

"Are you kidding!?"

All three of the other women spoke at once.

"No! I'm not kidding! I literally freaked out. I was lucky there wasn't anyone coming in the other lane. I swerved all the way across the yellow line before getting back to my side. I swear my Jeep went up on two wheels, with the erratic way I was driving. I stopped in the middle of the freaking highway and leaped out of the car, shrieking like a loon. I couldn't get rid of the feeling of that thing crawling on me."

"Holy crap, how'd it get there? Wait, does Maine even *have* tarantulas? I thought there weren't any venomous spiders in the state at all," Marlowe said.

"No, that's snakes," Carlise told her. "Although tarantulas are usually found in the desert, and we all know that Maine is *not* the desert."

"So what happened? And how the heck did one get in your car?" April asked with a frown.

"Well, some older guy who stopped when I was dancing in the middle of the road, screaming my head off, got me calmed down and actually found the thing in my car. He said it seemed pretty docile. The police showed up, which was embarrassing, and they said it had to be someone's pet that had escaped. Probably crawled in my car because it was warm in there from the sun," Carlise explained.

"What did Chappy do when he heard about what happened?" June asked.

"That's where the protective bit comes in—he literally didn't talk to me for five hours. Not because he was mad but because he was so freaked out and distraught that something could've happened to me. If there had been a car in the other lane, I could've hit them head on. Or I could've ended up in a ditch on the other side of the road.

"Anyway, he went outside and detailed my Jeep from top to bottom, even using some kind of foam crap to seal practically nonexistent holes so no more critters could get in. And as of now, he told me that if I want to go to Rumford—or anywhere else, for that matter—he'd drive me. It's a tad annoying, but since I'm almost in my third trimester and don't fit well behind the wheel anyway, I don't really care."

"Wow, you were lucky," Marlowe said.

"Almost as lucky as you, when that box didn't land on your head," Carlise agreed.

"Almost as lucky as *me* that my memory returned," April threw in.

"We're a bunch of lucky bitches for sure," Carlise said. "We have healthy babies on the way, except for you, April, but since you don't want any, that's cool, and we have men who would do anything for us."

"I'll drink to that," Marlowe said, holding up her cup of apple juice.

April raised her glass to the others and smiled as they clinked.

They each took a swallow, and talk turned to business and pregnancy and plans for the guys taking time off from work when their children were born. April listened to the others chat and laugh, and couldn't help but think how blessed she was. She had great friends and was soon going to be an honorary aunt, and she finally had the man she loved.

"April's over there smiling like she's plotting something evil," Carlise commented after a while.

"No plotting, just grateful for all I have. You guys, a job I love, and a man who actually gives a crap about what I'm thinking and doing."

"You don't talk much about your ex," June said tentatively. "Was your marriage awful?"

April thought about the question for a moment, then shrugged. She'd never really talked to *anyone* about James. Not because she was traumatized but more because she was embarrassed. Maybe it was the alcohol, maybe it was because of all the orgasms she'd had recently; whatever it was, she opened up for the first time.

"It wasn't awful," she said. "It was just kind of . . . there. We were simply coexisting. Going through the motions. James didn't care what I was doing, where I was, how I was feeling. And honestly, by the end, I didn't really care about him either. We saw each other in passing, and that was about it. I'm kind of ashamed that I let our relationship get to that point before ending it."

Carlise held up a hand and shook her head. "No, you don't get to think that way."

April frowned. "What way?"

"Like it was your fault. There were two of you in that marriage, and your ex could've tried harder to connect with you."

"Just as I could've tried harder to connect with him," April countered.

"Maybe," Carlise conceded. "But marriage is a lot of work. It's not all sunshine, roses, and orgasms."

For some reason, April blushed at that.

The other women all grinned.

"Okay, the orgasms are great, and I'm all for them," Carlise backpedaled. "But seriously. There are disagreements, rough patches to get through, all that."

"But that's the thing. We *didn't* disagree. We didn't have any rough patches. We were just coasting along," April insisted.

"Which was boring as hell," Marlowe said gently. "Right?"

April nodded.

"And I'm thinking JJ is never going to be boring. I've only been around for a little bit, but I've heard you guys really go at it when you disagree."

"Which isn't a bad thing," June interjected. "I mean, you guys disagree about stuff, but you're always respectful when you argue, and you always seem to be able to come to an understanding."

"That's what a marriage should be like," Carlise said with a nod. "Full of passion, and laughter, and truly caring about the other person. What would your ex have done if you came home and said you almost wrecked your car because there was a venomous duck inside that scared you?"

"Venomous duck?" April asked, laughing.

The others laughed as well, and Carlise said, "Whatever. Something unexpected that shouldn't have been there that scared you."

April shrugged. "He probably would've asked what was for dinner."

Carlise looked smug. "And JJ? If that was you in the Jeep with the spider, what would he have done?"

"Sold the Jeep, forced me to go to the doctor to make sure I didn't get bitten, and start a campaign to kill all tarantulas left in the world," April said without hesitation.

"Exactly. You have no reason to feel embarrassed by your marriage. You got out. You did the right thing," Carlise said firmly.

"And now you're here with JJ," June added.

"And deliriously happy," Marlowe said.

April smiled. "I am. But—"

"No buts!" Carlise exclaimed.

The others giggled.

"Except for our husbands' butts. Can we talk about those?" June asked. "Cal's got a butt to die for."

"Sorry, I love ya, but it doesn't compare to Riggs's ass," Carlise said smugly.

"Wait a minute, Kendric's ass puts *all* your guys' butts to shame," Marlowe argued.

April listened to her friends argue about which of their husbands had the best ass and wasn't prepared when Carlise turned to her. "Well?" she huffed.

"Well what?" April asked.

"Aren't you going to pipe up and tell us that we're all wrong? That JJ has the best butt?"

"Nope," April said, doing her best to hide her smile as she took another sip of her wine.

"Wow, that's surprising," June said, a brow raised.

"No point in arguing something with someone who's wrong," April added, almost as an aside.

April wasn't sure who threw the first pillow, but the next thing she knew, the four of them were having a huge pillow fight. No one hit very hard, very aware that there were three precious babies that had to be protected, and April wasn't very coordinated since she had the handicap of being tipsy, but by the time they were done, all four were breathing hard, and their stomachs hurt from laughing so hard.

"Point for JJ for insisting we have our girls' night here," June said as she reclined in her chair. "We wouldn't have been able to have a pillow fight at the bar."

April grinned at everyone and blurted, "I love you guys."

Everyone turned to her.

"I mean it. When my memory was gone, you guys were so nice to me. You took turns coming up to Bangor. You didn't treat me any differently, even though I couldn't remember you. And you had no doubt that my memory would return. You don't know how much that means to me."

"Well, honestly, you're the glue that holds us all together," Carlise told her. "When I first met you, when I was up at the cabin in the mountains, I was scared to death about what you'd think of me, considering JJ suspected I'd drugged Riggs or something. But you were kind and motherly, and it was obvious to me even then how much the guys respected you and looked to you for guidance."

April winced. "Yeah, motherly, that's what I want to be."

"I didn't mean that in a bad way. It's just that it was obvious you're kind and nurturing. Chappy told me later that you were the one who made Jack's Lumber a success. That without you, he was sure they would've gone out of business within two years."

"Cal says the same thing," June agreed. "And you have no idea what *you* mean to *us*. I'm scared to death to have this baby. I don't know anything about being a mom, but I know with you to help me, I'll be able to muddle through."

"And I was afraid *all* of you guys would think I'd done what I was accused of back in Thailand," Marlowe admitted. "That you wouldn't accept me. But April, you were the first person to welcome me and make me feel at home. It wasn't a hardship to take turns visiting when you were in the hospital."

"I'll take it one step further and say this," Carlise said, leaning forward and pinning April in place with her gaze. "If you didn't regain your memory and never remembered us, or the good *and* bad times we'd had together in the past, it wouldn't have mattered. You'd still be our friend and our mentor in a lot of ways, and we'd just have new memories to replace the ones you didn't have anymore."

April's eyes filled with tears. She didn't know what she'd done in her life to deserve these women. Or Jack. Or the other guys. "We're going to raise some kick-ass girls and boys," April managed to say.

"Hell yeah, we are," Carlise agreed.

"Strong little girls who speak their minds and don't take crap from anyone," June said.

"Protective boys who respect girls and don't think they're any weaker than they are," Marlowe added.

April smiled at everyone, then sighed and closed her eyes. The room was spinning, in a good way. It had been a long time since she'd let down her guard like she had tonight, and it felt great. She heard the others whispering, but she was feeling too mellow to open her eyes and join the conversation.

It wasn't until she jerked at the sound of a door closing that she realized she'd actually dozed off.

Sitting up, April looked around. The girls weren't in the room—but Jack was. He was leaning against a doorjamb, staring at her with a small smile.

He was as gorgeous as ever, and April once again had to pinch herself to remember that he was hers.

When he saw she was awake, he pushed off the door and came toward her. He knelt down in front of the sofa and put a hand on her knee. "Hey."

"Hi," she said with a small smile.

"Ready to go home?"

April frowned and looked around again. "What time is it? Where is everyone else?"

"When you fell asleep on them, Carlise called Chappy. Since he was with me and the other guys, we all came to collect our women."

"I wasn't done girl bonding," April said with a pout.

Jack chuckled. "Well, if it makes you feel better, the pregnant women were just as tired as you. Marlowe was already up in bed snoring when we got here, and Carlise and June were dozing themselves."

"Oh, okay," April said with a nod, as if falling asleep at the end of their girls' night was perfectly normal.

Jack smiled again, then stood and held out a hand for her. April took it without hesitation and sighed happily when he pulled her against his side and wrapped an arm around her waist.

When she stumbled as they walked to the door, he asked, "How much did you have to drink?"

April shrugged. "A couple of glasses."

"How big were the glasses?" Jack teased.

April grinned.

Bob appeared from the stairs and gave her a quick hug. "Thanks for coming over and keeping Marlowe company," he told her.

April rolled her eyes. "You say that as if we had a choice. I mean, we wanted to go to a bar."

"Uh-huh," Bob said with a grin.

"You guys were all in on it, weren't you?" she asked suspiciously. "You just let Jack be the bad guy, and once I said it was okay, you knew the other women would go along with the plan."

"Always knew you were smart," Bob said, still smiling.

"Whatever," she said, although there was no heat to the word. Honestly, she enjoyed being able to wear elastic pants and a T-shirt instead of dressing up to go to a bar.

"Thanks, Bob. I'll see you at the office tomorrow," JJ said.

"Yeah, you guys have that job at the new housing development," April said with a nod. "Lots of trees to take down."

"Ma'am, yes, ma'am," Bob said with a small salute.

"Shut up," April told him.

"Come on, let's get you home and get some aspirin in you so you don't wake up with a headache tomorrow."

Jack led her outside, and she turned and waved at Bob once more. Then called out for him to tell Marlowe thanks for the night and she'd see her later. She turned, was surprised to see the other two ladies still getting bundled into cars by their husbands, and yelled the same thing to Carlise and June. They each waved back at her, and seconds later, April was smiling at Jack as he got her snapped into the seat belt in the front of his Bronco.

When they were on the way to his house, she turned her head lazily and stared at him.

"What?" he asked after a moment.

"Nothing. I just think you're really handsome."

His lips twitched.

"And your ass is the best, no matter what the other girls say."

He flat-out laughed at that. "You had a good time tonight, I take it."

"Yup," she said, popping the *p* sound.

"Good."

"You were right."

"About what?" he asked.

"About not going to the bar. It would've been loud, and the girls can't drink anyway, and we wouldn't have been able to have our pillow fight."

"You had a pillow fight?" Jack asked, his brow raised.

"Uh-huh. Over whose man had the best ass."

Jack shook his head with a grin. "I'll never understand women."

"Good. We like to have some secrets," April told him.

Jack reached over and took her hand in his. She closed her eyes as they drove. After a minute, she opened her eyes again and asked, "What would you have done if I'd never regained my memory?"

"You did, so it's a moot point."

"But what if I didn't?"

"April, you *did*."

"Humor me, Jack. Would you have loved me?"

When he turned to look at her, April sucked in a breath at the emotion in his eyes. "I already loved you, April. I would've given you time to get to know me, and somehow, someway, made you love me back. I wasn't going to lose you, not when I'd already been an idiot and screwed up my chance in the first place."

April smiled and squeezed his hand. "Okay."

"Okay?" he asked.

"Uh-huh. And for the record . . . you wouldn't have had to work too hard to get me to love you back. My brain might've forgotten, but my heart didn't. It's always been yours."

They didn't speak again until Jack had parked the car, come around to her side, and taken her hand, then led her into the house. He escorted her straight to the bedroom, where he said, "You have three minutes to get ready for bed. I'm going to get you a glass of water and aspirin. Then I'm going to show you how much your words mean to me."

April smiled. "I've always wanted to have drunk sex."

Jack's smile was downright dirty. "You're about to get your wish, sweetheart."

"Yay," she whispered.

"Two and a half minutes," he warned as he backed toward the door.

Then April was rushing, fumbling with her pants. She almost tripped over them as she shoved them down her hips as she entered the bathroom. She needed to pee, brush her teeth, and undress before he got back.

She didn't quite make it in time, but Jack didn't seem to mind being the one to strip her shirt off over her head and remove her lingerie. He waited until she'd taken the pills he'd brought before he pushed her back on the bed and proceeded to show her the perks of drunk sex.

As she lay boneless on top of him a good while later, with his cock still buried deep inside her body, April thought she heard him whisper "My heart's always been yours too" before she fell into a deep, satisfied sleep.

CHAPTER ELEVEN

JJ hid a grin when he saw April wince as the bell over the front door tinkled at his entrance. She'd woken up that morning with a hangover, despite the aspirin. She bitched that she *never* got hungover, and when JJ asked how many times she'd gotten drunk lately, she'd mumbled under her breath that she couldn't remember the last time, maybe when she was in college.

His woman was adorable when she had a headache because of too many glasses of wine. He didn't like when she was hurting from the accident, but this? It was a little funny. Especially because she was grumpy and out of sorts, and yet when he kissed her goodbye before heading out to the worksite for the new housing development, she melted in his arms.

He and the rest of the guys had worked hard plotting out which trees needed to come down and when, in accordance with the building needs of the houses that were scheduled to go up. It was a big job but one Jack was proud to be working on. They'd talked the developer into saving as many trees as possible, to give the neighborhood an older feel, instead of just razing all the trees on the entire acreage.

He would've been back to the office earlier, but Marlowe had called Bob and said she was at the library with two flat tires. JJ gave his friend a ride into town, and they'd discovered two huge nails in the back two tires of Bob's pickup. It was annoying, but luckily Marlowe had only borrowed her husband's truck to go to the library that day instead of heading to Bangor to go furniture shopping with June, as had been her original plan.

June had woken up with odd cramps, and Cal put his foot down and refused to let her risk her health, or their child's, on something as trivial as shopping. So Marlowe had gone over to visit her friend, then to the library to check out some books.

Getting new tires was a minor pain, but it would've been a disaster if the women had been on the interstate when the tires deflated or, worse, had come apart.

"How's the truck?" April asked when the door closed behind JJ. He'd called her and let her know he was running late and coming back to the office for lunch.

"Two flat tires. It'll be fine."

She wrinkled her nose. "Ugh, that stinks."

JJ shrugged, then walked around the desk and pushed her chair back before leaning against the desk in front of her.

"Um, you're in my way," she said with a smile.

"I know. It's time for lunch."

April looked at her watch. "Actually, it's past time for lunch."

"You already eat?" he asked, knowing the answer.

"No. But I could've."

"I know. And I don't expect you to wait for me when I'm late, hon. If you're hungry, you eat."

"Honestly, I had zero appetite until just before you got here. I need to remember that I'm not twenty-two anymore and apparently can't handle my liquor like I used to."

"I think you handled it, and me, just fine last night," he said, not able to resist the innuendo.

She did her best to hold back her smile but failed. "That *was* fun, wasn't it?"

Fun wasn't the word JJ would've used. His woman was always passionate and sexual, but last night, with her inhibitions lowered even further because of the alcohol, she had been insatiable.

"Yeah, it was," he agreed without hesitation. "Although I don't want you getting drunk on a regular basis just for the sex," he said.

April shrugged. "Ditto. I mean, I liked last night, but I like *everything* we do together. There's something to be said for simply snuggling, or slow, easy lovemaking instead of . . . you know."

"Instead of you trying to swallow me whole and then fucking me into oblivion before insisting I do the same to you like you're the best porn star there is?"

He loved the blush that spread across her cheeks. "Yeah, that."

"Damn, I love teasing you. But now I need to feed you. How'd the morning go?" he asked.

"Good. I got two new signed contracts back, put out feelers for the ropes course Bob wants to run, and connected with the Maine Forest Service to tell them we'd be interested in training with them for search and rescues."

JJ shook his head. April never ceased to impress him. If she could do all that while hungover, there was no telling what else she could accomplish.

"Right, so you must be starved after all that. You want to go out or head home?"

"Home," she said without hesitation. "We have leftovers we can eat."

And she was sensible too. He wanted to spoil her and had a feeling she would make that hard to do. She was practical and down to earth and so much more. Frankly, everything he'd ever wanted in a partner. Why it had taken him so long to get his head out of his butt and ask her out, he'd never know. He'd been afraid of nothing.

"But I need you to move so I can shut down the computer," she told him with a smirk.

JJ leaned down and kissed her before standing up and stepping out of her way. He watched as she efficiently did what she needed to do in order to secure the computer and the files she'd been working on, before standing to face him.

"I'm ready."

It took everything in JJ not to pull her into the back room and throw her down on the couch. Two things stopped him—one, she'd probably pitch a fit about getting one of the couches dirty and be embarrassed about others sitting on it after they'd had sex; and two, he really did want to feed her. It would make her feel better if she put something in her belly besides the crackers she'd choked down that morning.

So, instead, JJ took her hand and led her from the building. He'd parked out front, and now he waited patiently as she locked the office before walking her to his Bronco.

~

It was time.

Ryan had been patient long enough.

He'd messed with the other women a bit. He was a little disappointed that they hadn't been hurt because of his tricks but, in the end, was glad he hadn't alarmed their men. If they thought for even a moment that someone was out there purposely trying to harm their women, he could be found out, making it next to impossible to get to the soldiers.

But he'd had his fun, at least. Now it was time for the main show to begin. And he knew exactly how he was going to get all the women together.

By the time the soldiers realized their women were gone, it would be too late. The game would be on. And it *was* a game. At least for Ryan. A deadly one. A game that would end his years of plotting and planning. A game that would end in the deaths of the four men he hated with every fiber of his being . . . and the women they loved.

A game that would put an end to his grief.

After he took the lives of those responsible for the death of his brother, Ryan would join him in the afterlife. There was nothing keeping him here on earth.

CHAPTER TWELVE

The next afternoon, April hung up the phone and sat back in her office chair with a sigh. Jack had called to let her know the meeting he and the other guys were attending with the town council, their attorney, and the insurance company about the ropes course they wanted to build on the outskirts of town was running late, so he might not make it back to the office before five.

Jack's Lumber had bought a parcel of land not too far from Newton, and they had big plans to make it a recreational destination for tourists and locals and also a retreat for businesses where they would emphasize teamwork and trust. And the best part, at least in April's eyes, was that in the winter, it could be transformed into a play area. With sledding hills, tubing runs, and even an area where handicapped children—and adults, for that matter—could get in on the fun in a safe, friendly environment.

April was incredibly proud of Riggs, Chappy, and Jack. Instead of dismissing Bob's need for excitement—the reason he'd been working with the FBI on very dangerous rescue missions behind everyone's backs—they'd embraced it, working with him to come up with ways he could be content here in Newton and still get the adrenaline rush he craved every now and then.

Jack had sounded tired on the phone, but also excited about the opportunities. Jack's Lumber was doing well financially, but there were only so many trees they could remove for developers and only so far they could go as a business with smaller jobs. The course was a great way to build a legacy for the children of their friends and keep the guys involved in the community.

It had been four weeks since April's accident, and while she'd hated what happened to her and it had been extremely scary, she was more than thrilled with how it had jump-started her and Jack's relationship. She was a bit worried that they'd jumped into being together *too* quickly. April hadn't gone back to her apartment since the fateful night she'd gotten her memory back . . . but she didn't miss it.

How could she when Jack had moved practically all her stuff to his house? She was making plans with her landlord to break the lease and didn't feel even a twinge of concern about moving in with the man she'd loved secretly for years.

He was everything she'd ever wanted in a relationship. No, things weren't always smooth, they were two adults who were used to living on their own, but there was no comparing her relationship with Jack to what she'd had when she was married.

For one, Jack always seemed excited to see her, whether they'd been apart for two minutes or ten hours. They shared the responsibilities around the house. He didn't expect her to do all the cooking, cleaning, laundry, and everything else typically thought of as "women's work." Just as she didn't expect him to always deal with garbage or the yard or any other male-associated tasks. They were a team, working together to get things done, and it felt amazing.

But it wasn't just that, of course. It was how Jack made her feel. As if she was the most important person in his life. When she talked, he looked her in the eye and *listened*, and they could talk about everything from intellectual subjects like space travel and what it might look like in the future to ridiculous topics . . . such as whether the spider who'd made a home on their front porch would like the name Eric or Thomas better.

He made her laugh, and she couldn't wait to see him at the end of every day, something she couldn't have said about James toward the end of their marriage. He also took care of her better than she took care of herself, paying attention to the smallest details.

April had no clue why she'd ever thought she and Jack wouldn't be a good idea. Of course, things were still new, and there was a possibility they wouldn't work out in the end, but she worried less about that with each passing day. Now that they'd both admitted their feelings for one another, she was confident they'd be together for the long haul.

And then there was the sex.

She'd be the first person to claim there was more to a successful relationship than sex. But *Lord*, Jack was good at it. He always made sure she came first. He made her feel like the most beautiful woman in the world in bed, when she knew that definitely wasn't the case. And he had the ability to turn her into someone she didn't even recognize. Someone passionate, almost desperately so at times.

She loved Jack so much and couldn't imagine her life without him. He was smart, extremely loyal to those he cared about, intense, protective, very hardworking, sometimes absent minded when he was involved in a task, kind of messy, and a cautious driver, and when he did let himself go, his laugh was contagious.

In short, Jackson Justice was even better than April could've imagined, and she felt like the luckiest woman alive. She'd do everything in her power to be someone he could rely on and be proud of.

The buzzer on the back door made April jump in surprise, tearing her out of her inner musings. She snort-laughed under her breath. She'd been so lost in her head, thinking about Jack, that a UFO could've landed outside the front door and she probably wouldn't have noticed.

She wasn't sure who was out back, as they weren't expecting any deliveries today, but she pushed her chair away from the desk to go greet whoever it was anyway.

As April unlocked the back door, she had an easy smile on her face.

That smile died when the man standing there—holding on to June's upper arm—pointed a pistol in her face and growled, "Back up. Now."

Surprised, April quickly did as ordered, stumbling backward, her brain trying to comprehend what was happening. The man entered Jack's Lumber and slammed the door behind him. He smiled then, a scary, evil twisting of his lips, as he said, "Hello, April. I'm glad to see you doing so well after your *accident.*"

His words were polite, but the insinuation behind them made her skin crawl.

April tilted her head and tried to place where she'd seen the guy. Then it hit her. "You've been here before. You came in, inquiring about hiring Jack's Lumber for a job."

"Yes," he said without seeming concerned that she recognized him.

Even though April's memory had mostly returned a couple of weeks ago, she still got flashes of things that had happened in the past five years now and then, things she hadn't immediately recalled. Most of them were trivial, and the doctor said her brain was still healing, so he wouldn't be surprised if she continued to have small flashbacks for weeks to come.

She had one that very moment, as she stared at the man who seemed familiar for more than one reason.

Gasping, April said, "You were there."

His eyes gleamed at her words. "At your accident? I was."

"The black truck," April whispered. "You saw it all but drove away without helping me."

"Why would I help you? I didn't cause your accident, but it made me happy all the same."

April's stomach lurched. Who said things like that?

"Here's the thing . . . I've been waiting a very long time for this day. Years, in fact."

"I don't understand," April whispered, terror making her mind feel sluggish, in turn making it difficult to think.

"You will in time."

"Who are you? What do you want? We don't keep money here."

He chuckled. "I don't want money," he informed her. Then he shook the pistol he hadn't stopped pointing at her and said, "I want you to text Carlise and Marlowe. Tell them you need them to come here."

Horror made April recoil. "No!" she exclaimed. There was no way she was going to get her friends involved in whatever was happening here. It was bad enough seeing June's pale face and the tears in her eyes.

The man with the gun tsked in his throat and shrugged. Then he turned toward June, who'd been silent the entire time, and jammed the pistol into her belly, making her grunt with pain. "You want to reconsider?" he asked with narrowed eyes.

Nausea churned in April's stomach. She swallowed the bile that made its way up her throat. She could handle violence toward herself. But even not knowing this man or what he wanted, she had no doubt he'd do what he threatened. He'd shoot June in the stomach and kill her unborn child. The evil and emptiness in his eyes confirmed that without a doubt.

"Please don't hurt her," she whispered, hating how helpless she felt.

"Text them," the man said in a low, menacing tone as he gestured to her hand with his head.

It wasn't until right that second that April realized she had her cell phone in her grip. Hope soared briefly. Maybe she could pretend to be texting one of the other women and she could call 9-1-1 instead.

But the man got close enough to see the phone in her hand, yanking June along with him. "Hold it out so I can see what you're typing," he told her.

With the man so close, there was no way she could do anything but what he ordered. For a second, she thought about trying to overpower him. There were two of them, she and June, and only one of him. He wasn't very tall, only around five-eight or so, but he was fairly muscular. And he had crazy on his side.

At a loss as to the best course of action, April hesitated. Chappy and Bob would never forgive her for getting their wives involved in whatever was happening, but she didn't know what else to do! According to Jack, the guys would be tied up with their meeting for a couple more hours yet. She wasn't expecting anyone to stop by. She couldn't stall for hours, not with the look of determination in the man's eyes. Whatever he was planning, he'd come here obviously knowing he had time to get it done.

She hesitated too long. The guy swung his hand and hit June in the face with the gun.

She cried out and fell to the floor like a stone. The man didn't let her stay there. He hauled her up with one hand and hit her again. This time, he left her crumpled on the floor, holding her face with one hand and her pregnant belly with the other.

April was horrified for a single moment . . . then she was outraged. This man *dared* to touch her friend. Hit her *twice*!

Clarity struck. He wasn't bluffing. He'd kill June without a second thought—but he hadn't yet.

That meant he needed them. As long as they did what he said, he'd keep them alive. And the longer they were breathing, the more time Jack and the others would have to save them.

April had lived through her friends' worst days. June being shot, Carlise being buried underground in an avalanche, and Marlowe almost dying of strangulation. She'd always wondered how she'd react if she were in a similar situation and had figured she'd be a basket case. Would cry and fall apart completely.

But no. At this moment, determination swam in her veins. No one had the right to do what this man was doing. She didn't know what his endgame was, but she'd play along and not give him the satisfaction of knowing she was afraid. That deep inside, she was screaming and crying and curled into a useless little ball.

"Don't hit her again," she said in an even tone she barely recognized. "I'll text Carlise and Marlowe."

"Do it," the man growled, pointing the gun down at June's stomach. The bastard was holding all the cards at the moment. And he knew it.

She quickly sent a separate text to her friends. She kept it short, saying she needed them at Jack's Lumber and to come to the back door as fast as they could get here.

April wasn't surprised when both women immediately said they were on their way. That was the kind of friends they were. If someone needed something, they'd all drop everything to get to them.

Her nausea hadn't dissipated. If anything, it was worse now than before. But April stood tall and glared at the man as he smirked at her and pocketed her cell phone.

Time seemed to crawl as they waited for Carlise and Marlowe to arrive. April had never hoped for a flat tire, or one of their cars to be out of gas, or *something*, more in all her life.

But when the first knock came on the back door, she knew her prayers had been for nothing.

"Open it," the man ordered. When April hesitated, he pulled back his foot as if to kick June, and April quickly said, "I'm going! Don't hurt her."

Feeling as if her shoes were filled with concrete, she walked to the door and opened it. Carlise was there with a worried look on her face. "Are you all right? I came as soon as I could."

April stepped back—and saw the moment Carlise spotted the man with the gun. "What the heck?"

"Come in and join the party," the man said, again with that disgusting smile on his face.

For a moment, Carlise looked as if she was going to turn and run—but the man simply turned to June and fired the gun.

To April's surprise, it wasn't that loud, and only then did she realize he had some sort of silencer on the end of the weapon.

Carlise screeched in surprise, and April's heart nearly stopped.

But he hadn't hit June. He'd fired into the floor right next to her.

"Get in here or the next bullet goes into her belly," the man threatened.

Carlise stepped inside the door, and April shut it behind her.

"I'm so sorry," she whispered to her friend.

But Carlise didn't seem to hear. Her eyes were fixated on the small hole in the floor the bullet had created.

"Now we wait for the last one to arrive, and we can go."

Go? Go where? But April didn't ask. She didn't think the man would answer her anyway.

"Please, can Carlise go to June?" April asked instead.

"No."

"She's bleeding. It's not going to change anything that's going to happen if you let her help her," April cajoled.

The man stared at her for a beat before nodding once. "All right. But no funny business. Otherwise, the next bullet goes through a baby's head."

April hated this man more with every word out of his mouth, but she didn't let any of her feelings show on her face. "Go on," she told Carlise, nudging her. "Go check on June."

Carlise was nearly as far along as June, only a month or so behind in her pregnancy, and she was at the point where her belly seemed to protrude more with every day that passed. She also had started to waddle a bit when she walked. Just the other day, the two women were making fun of their awkward movements.

But now, when Carlise walked with her head held high toward June, April couldn't have been more proud. Carlise was obviously scared and confused. She'd walked into a situation in which she had no idea what was happening, but she was doing her best to hold on to her composure.

April watched as she managed to get to her knees next to June, pulling her into a long hug. Then she used the sleeve of her shirt to dab at the blood on June's forehead from where she'd been struck.

"What's your name?" April asked quietly, still standing by the door. If she could get this man to see her and the others as humans, not as objects for whatever nefarious plans he'd concocted, maybe she could squeeze an ounce of compassion out of him.

"Ryan Johnson."

April blinked. The name was so . . . ordinary. She wasn't sure what kind of name she'd expected from someone so evil, but it wasn't that.

"It's nice to meet you, Ryan," she said from lips that felt numb.

He laughed. Loudly. A sound that grated on April's nerves. "No, it's not. You don't mean a word of that. And I know what you're doing. It won't work. Your path is set. Nothing you say or do will change the outcome. No matter how hard you try to humanize yourself and your friends, you're all just pawns in this game."

"Does that mean you'll let us go?"

He smiled, and it was anything but comforting. "If you do what I tell you and don't cause me problems, you and the brats you carry in your wombs will live to get to our next destination."

That didn't sound good to April. She swallowed her fear and asked, "And where's that?"

But a knock on the door sounded before Ryan could answer . . . not that April thought he'd really tell her where he was planning on taking them.

"Let her in," Ryan said, turning and pointing the gun at June and now Carlise, who were huddled together on the floor.

Taking a deep breath, April reluctantly opened the door for Marlowe.

"Hey, girl, what's up?"

And just like Carlise, Marlowe saw Ryan in the room and the other two girls on the floor, and her eyes got huge.

"Get in here," Ryan told her in a harsh tone.

This time, it was April who considered running out the open door. She could move much faster than her pregnant friends. She could get help. But almost as soon as she had the thought, she dismissed it. Ryan might very likely shoot someone in retaliation if she left. She couldn't live with herself if that happened.

So she calmly shut the door behind Marlowe and waited to see what he did next.

It didn't take long. Ryan leaned down and grabbed June by the arm once more. She whimpered as he hauled her to her feet. Carlise awkwardly managed to get to her feet as well. Ryan jammed the barrel of the gun back into June's belly and said, "This is what's going to happen now. You're going to give me your cell phones, and then you're all going to walk outside, nice and calm, and get into my vehicle. If you speak, or scream, or do anything to draw any attention to yourselves, I'll shoot the fetus. Understand?"

Everyone stared at him, unmoving.

"*Understand?*" he yelled.

Quickly, everyone nodded.

"Good," he said in a normal tone once more.

The man was unhinged, and April realized once again how much trouble they were all in.

"If you do what I tell you, you'll be fine," he said in an almost gentle voice. "You aren't my concern. You're all just a means to an end. So be good girls, and you and your unborn brats will stay alive. Defy me, try to escape, or be a pain in my ass, and I'll use your bellies for target practice. You might live, but your babies will not. Got it?"

Everyone nodded once more.

Marlowe and Carlise handed over their phones, and April assumed Ryan had already confiscated June's. She prayed that he didn't understand the phones could be tracked and he'd leave them on, but she had a feeling he was way ahead of them where that was concerned. That the phones wouldn't help their men, or the police, find them.

April hated the looks of fear on her friends' faces. There was nothing she could do to help them. They were all equally helpless.

"Open the door, April," Ryan said.

She wondered how in the hell this man knew her name, and the names of her friends, but supposed it didn't matter at the moment.

She opened the door and watched as her three friends shuffled through.

"Lock it behind us," Ryan told her, and April did as requested. She knew the front door was still open, and if anyone came by and found the place unlocked and empty, maybe they'd notify the police or call one of the guys. She had to hold on to that hope.

Ryan led them over to a black pickup truck, the same one April had finally remembered driving off from the scene of her accident. This time, there was an enclosed trailer attached to the back.

"No," Carlise whispered in horror.

"Open it," Ryan ordered April.

She knew Carlise was remembering the hole in the ground where she'd taken refuge when the avalanche had almost buried her alive. She still struggled with small, dark spaces as a result. But again, none of them had any choice at the moment.

She opened the back of the trailer and peered inside. It was completely empty except for a bucket in one corner. The ramifications of what that bucket was for made her previous resolve to be strong waver.

"Get in," Ryan ordered.

April saw the defiance spark in both Marlowe and Carlise. And it scared the hell out of her. She and June had already witnessed the violence their kidnapper was capable of.

Even as April shook her head subtly at her friends, Marlowe suddenly went flying forward. She fell to her knees right behind the trailer, her head whipping forward with the momentum and smacking the metal floor of the oversize box.

April turned in time to see Ryan's foot lowering to the ground. The monster had kicked Marlowe in the back! Quickly moving to help her friend, April couldn't help but wince at the scrape marks on Marlowe's pants and the huge bump that was already forming on her forehead.

"Get in," Ryan ordered again.

Without a choice, the women did as they were told.

The sound of the doors closing behind them echoed in April's head. They all heard the unmistakable sound of a lock being clicked shut, and the pitch dark seemed to close in like a malevolent fog.

Someone whimpered, and it snapped April away from the pit of despair she'd been in danger of tumbling into.

"Come here, you guys," she said softly, bracing herself on the side of the trailer. She heard shuffling as the others moved. The second she felt someone brush against her, she gently grabbed hold of an arm. Within seconds, the four of them were standing in a huddle, their arms around each other and their bodies shaking with fear and shock.

The sudden movement of the trailer almost sent them all to the ground. "Sit, everyone, so we don't fall."

They moved as one, not willing to let go of each other.

"I'm sorry! I'm so sorry!" April said as the trailer began to move faster.

"No, *I'm* sorry," June sniffed. "He came to my house, and I opened the door. I knew better! After everything that happened to me, I shouldn't have answered the door when Cal wasn't there, especially when I wasn't expecting anyone."

"It's not your fault," April soothed. "How could you know an insane asshole would kidnap you?"

"June, are you all right?" Carlise asked.

"I think so," June answered. "It hurts."

"What does?" Marlowe asked.

"Everything. My arm where he grabbed me and hauled me around. My head where he pistol-whipped me. My hip where I fell."

April closed her eyes, which was stupid, as it was just as black whether they were open or shut, but somehow she felt that by closing her eyes, she could block out the pain she heard in her friend's voice.

"What the hell is happening?" Marlowe whispered.

"The buzzer on the back door sounded, and when I went to answer it, the guy was there with his gun on June. I never would've done what he asked and texted you guys if he hadn't struck June and pointed his gun at her belly," April told her friends.

"We know," Carlise said, and April felt an arm tighten around her waist. "But where is he taking us? Why?"

"I have no idea," April admitted. "But I've seen him before. He came into Jack's Lumber before I got my memories back."

Before anyone could reply, the trailer bounced as they picked up speed, and April winced as she thought about how June might be feeling as they were all jostled about.

The longer they drove, the colder it got inside the uninsulated trailer. The floor was uncomfortable, and April knew the three pregnant women would be even more miserable than she was herself.

As they drove toward an uncertain fate, one by one, the women around April broke down. They began to cry and tremble even harder. But April's eyes were dry. She was just as scared as the others. Just as freaked out. But she was also furious. This Ryan guy had no right to do what he was doing! She had no idea what his problem was, but taking them, threatening her friends' unborn children, was downright sadistic, and April was going to do everything in her power to screw with Ryan's plan—whatever it was.

"Listen, ladies. Listen hard. We're going to get out of this."

"You don't know that," Marlowe whispered.

"I do," April said, her confidence and anger rising with every word that came out of her mouth.

"How?" June asked.

"Carlise, when you were missing in that avalanche, Chappy wouldn't stop until he found you. He dug through that snow with his bare hands, ripping them to shreds and not caring one bit about his own pain. His only goal was to get to you.

"And June, when you were shot, I'd never seen a man so determined to make the people who'd ordered that hit pay dearly. When he wasn't at your side at the hospital, he was on the phone, using every contact at his disposal to make sure you got justice.

"Marlowe, Bob broke you out of a *freaking prison*. You told us all about how he refused to let your body touch that nasty drainage water, and how he slept in dirty straw, despite the gouges on his back, so you wouldn't have to. Do you guys really think our men will sit back and wait for someone else to find us? Do you think they'll not do *everything* in their power to get us back?"

"But *how*?" Carlise asked, repeating June's question in a quivering tone.

"I don't know. But they'll do it. Jack told me he'd never let anyone hurt me. I believe him. We just have to stay strong," she said firmly. "We can't fall apart. We have to stay alert, observe what's going on around us, catalog it all, so when the time comes we'll have the information we need to either save ourselves or help our men save us. Understand?"

There were sniffs from the women still huddled together around her, but they all agreed.

"And we have to take care of each other. No keeping secrets. If you're hurting, speak up. If you're about to lose it, let us know, and we'll hold you until you feel strong enough to keep going. We need to keep each other warm, comfortable, and calm. We need to trust each other," April went on.

"Ryan's going to want us to fall apart. I have a feeling he'll delight in scaring us and seeing our tears. We can't let him get to us. But we can't do anything stupid either. We have to do what he tells us to do, to protect ourselves and our babies."

April heard someone take a deep breath, then Carlise said, "You're right. We can do this. We're tough bitches. Look what we've already lived through."

"Yeah," Marlowe agreed.

April waited for June to speak, and when she didn't, she prompted, "June?"

"I'm scared," the other woman whispered.

"I know. I am too," April told her.

"You don't sound like it," she argued.

April let out a snort. "I'm terrified, but at the moment, I'm more mad. Mad at this jerk who used my love for my friends against me. Against all of us. Mad that a psychopath was able to get a gun. Mad at lawmakers, mad at the people who made the stupid door at Jack's

Lumber without a peephole. I'm even a little mad at our guys for being in a meeting when we needed them most, however irrational that sounds. I'm mad at the entire freaking world—and right now, that anger is getting me through. Have no doubt that I'm scared, June, but I'm trying to channel what I know our guys will be thinking and feeling. They're going to turn over every rock to find us. And they'll make this Ryan asshole pay."

"What if he's got people helping him?" Carlise asked.

"Then our guys will make them pay too," April said without hesitation.

"I'm having cramps," June said in a voice so soft, it was almost inaudible.

"What?" Marlowe asked.

"I think they're cramps . . . but what if they're not? What if I'm losing the baby? Or . . . going into labor?"

For the first time, April's bubble of anger deflated slightly, and she almost panicked. First, it was a little too soon for June's baby to be here, but second . . . she couldn't have a baby in the middle of whatever fucked-up situation this was. They didn't have any drugs or doctors, nothing to make sure her little boy was born healthy.

She took a breath. No. She couldn't panic. Her friends were relying on her to be the strong one. She was the den mother; she had to act like it.

"Take a deep breath," April ordered June. "Now another. Good. You have to stay calm. You're here with us. We aren't going to let anything happen to you or your baby."

"I think I'm having contractions. What if I go into labor?" June asked.

"Then we deal with it," April said matter-of-factly, while inside, she was freaking out.

"We've got this," Carlise agreed.

"Yeah, who better to help you give birth than two women pregnant with their own kids?" Marlowe said a little shakily.

"Two pregnant women and a badass warrior woman," Carlise said with a small laugh.

April was flattered they thought of her that way, but it also scared her. Put a lot of pressure on her. She pushed those feelings aside for now.

"Come on, let's get more comfortable. Lie down. We can share body heat easier that way," April said.

Everyone shifted, and April made sure to put herself against the side of the trailer. The wall rattled and was cold at her back as she curled herself around June. She placed a hand on her friend's extended belly and swallowed hard when June covered her hand with her own. The other two women were cuddled into them as well, and as the miles passed beneath them, toward whatever destination Ryan had in mind, April closed her eyes and thought about Jack.

Find us, she thought. *Please, I need you to be the badass, pissed-off boyfriend you told me you'd be if anyone ever put their hands on me.*

Just thinking about Jack made her relax a little. She had no doubt, not one, that when Jack found out she and the others were missing, he'd move heaven and earth to find them. And Lord help Ryan when he did. Jack wouldn't have any mercy . . . and since she was feeling a little bloodthirsty right about now, April was glad.

CHAPTER THIRTEEN

JJ clicked the phone off without leaving another message for April. He'd called her twice, but she hadn't picked up, which wasn't like her. Unease swam through his belly. His rational side said she was probably busy with a customer, but she'd never *not* called him back after getting a message. Even before they were dating, she was conscientious about returning his calls.

And it wasn't as if Jack's Lumber was all that busy with walk-in traffic. Yes, she got a steady stream of emails and phone calls from current and prospective customers, but that wouldn't prevent her from returning his call.

"What's up?" Bob asked as he came up next to JJ. They were still in their meeting, on a short break, and JJ was more than ready to be done. Bob looked energized and excited about the opportunities they were on the verge of nailing down, and JJ was glad. But he still couldn't stop worrying.

"April's not answering her phone, and she hasn't called me back or texted after I left a message," JJ told his friend.

"I'm sure she's just busy," Bob said with a shrug.

"I don't know . . . ," JJ admitted.

"You want me to call Marlowe and see if she can get a hold of her?" Bob asked.

"Do you mind?"

"Of course not." Bob reached for his phone and clicked on his wife's name. He frowned after several seconds went by and she didn't pick up. "Huh," he said. "She didn't answer."

JJ's oh-shit meter went on high alert. He turned toward Chappy and Cal, who were talking to the mayor of Newton, and whistled.

Both men immediately turned their heads and started in his direction. Without explaining, when they got close enough, JJ said, "Call Carlise and June. See if you can get a hold of them."

The hair on the back of his neck was standing straight up, and JJ already knew down to his bones that something was wrong. He didn't know *how* he knew, he just did. Others might accuse him of being paranoid, insist his time in the Army had made him overly cautious—but they'd be wrong.

Both Chappy and Cal pulled out their cells without question.

And when neither woman answered, JJ felt sick, knowing his gut feeling had been correct.

"What the hell's happening?" Chappy asked as JJ immediately turned for the door, his friends on his heels.

"I don't know. But April didn't answer either and hasn't returned my previous call," JJ said as he walked.

"They could be together, having some sort of girls' spa day or something," Bob said.

But it was Cal who shook his head and said, "No way. June wouldn't do that to me. She knows that the closer she is to her due date, the more worried I get about her. She would never forget her phone or turn it off."

"Same with Carlise," Chappy agreed.

"So . . . what? How could all four of our women be out of contact at the same time?" Bob asked.

Acid swam in JJ's gut. He didn't know the answer to his friend's question, but the what-ifs were killing him. They could've all been visiting at the office and overcome by carbon monoxide. Maybe there was a fire. Maybe they'd all gone out to eat together and had a car accident.

He didn't know. Just knew in his gut that April was in trouble.

In the parking lot, Chappy got into Cal's SUV, while Bob got into the passenger seat of JJ's Bronco. They drove way too fast through town and toward Jack's Lumber.

Seeing all four of the women's cars in the back lot should've made JJ feel better, but instead, it made his dread exponentially worse. He didn't bother turning off the ignition before tearing out of his car and heading for the back door. When he turned the knob, it was locked. Which made him feel a teensy bit better, since he'd lectured April time and time again to make sure the doors were locked when she was there alone.

Chappy was there with a key before JJ could run back to his car and grab his key chain. He pushed the door open, and JJ honestly expected to see the worst.

To his surprise, they were greeted by silence. No one was there.

Cal strode to the door that led to the front part of the office and was back in a heartbeat, shaking his head.

"Where are they?" Bob asked rhetorically.

"All their cars are here. If they went somewhere, someone would've had to be driving," Chappy agreed.

JJ's senses were still on high alert. The hair on the back of his neck hadn't subsided. He was just as tense now as he'd been when he first couldn't get a hold of April. "Everyone stop. Don't move," he ordered as he scanned the area.

At first glance, everything looked normal. Nothing was out of place. The coffeepot on the counter was half full; the pillows on the couch were perfectly placed where April liked them to be. Everything looked as it always did.

Then JJ's nostrils flared as he inhaled deeply. "Does anyone else smell that?" he asked.

His friends immediately tensed, and he saw their heads lift a fraction as they sniffed the air.

"Fuck—is that *gunpowder*?" Bob asked.

JJ's gaze dropped to the floor. If someone had been wounded, there'd be evidence. But the floor was just as clean as it always was. There were no bloodstains, nothing to indicate anything nefarious had taken place. Regardless, JJ knew as well as he knew his name that something had happened here. Something awful.

"Has that hole in the bloody floor always been there?" Cal asked, pointing to a small round blemish in the floor.

JJ strode over to where Cal was pointing and crouched down. He reached out and fingered the small hole. "No," he said, not recognizing the sound of his own voice.

"Shit! This looks like blood," Chappy said, inspecting a dark smear on the floor not far from the hole. JJ had missed it because it blended in so well with the dark wood.

Without a word, he strode to the back door. His attention was hyperfocused now, as it used to be when he was on a mission. He hadn't felt like this in years, had almost forgotten the feeling entirely. But all his senses were instantly honed.

His life, the lives of his teammates, and the lives of their women depended on him not missing one single thing.

He studied the small parking lot behind the office. The women's vehicles were all there, as was his Bronco and Cal's Rolls. His eyes scanned the gravel-and-dirt lot carefully until he saw what he was looking for. "There," he said, using his chin to indicate the back part of the lot, near the trees. Tire tracks from what looked like a smaller SUV or pickup . . . and some sort of trailer. The set of tracks behind those of the vehicle were closer together and didn't have much tread.

"Bloody fucking hell!" Cal swore.

"Are you kidding me?" Chappy exclaimed.

"If one hair on my wife's head is hurt, someone's gonna die," Bob said in a vicious tone.

JJ didn't say a word. His teeth were clenched together so hard, he was sure to crack a tooth at some point. He took a deep breath as his friends continued to swear.

"Enough," he ordered firmly. "Being pissed off isn't helping."

"How can you be so bloody calm?" Cal barked.

"Evidence is indicating that someone kidnapped our fucking wives, and you're telling us *not* to be pissed?" Chappy ranted.

"Fuck that," Bob muttered.

"I'm pissed," JJ told his teammates. "But being angry isn't going to do them any good. Strap on your boots, Deltas—we have work to do."

His words sank in immediately, and his friends instantly focused like the well-trained soldiers they were. Then each man nodded and looked to JJ for guidance.

"What's the plan?" Chappy asked.

"Call the police. Track their cells, see if we can pinpoint exactly when something went down," JJ said.

"Then what?" Cal asked.

JJ smiled. The kind of smile April had never seen on his face. A calculating, deadly, determined grin that his teammates recognized. "Then we go hunting," he said.

His declaration seemed to calm the others even more.

"And I'll tell you right now, I'm calling in every marker we've got. Starting with Tex. We know people," JJ said. "We need to use every single connection we've ever made. Former Deltas, Special Forces . . . hell, even civilians. Someone's got our women, and I don't care why, but they'll regret touching them. Mark my words."

"I'll call the police chief," Bob said.

"I'll call Tex," Chappy added.

"And I'll call the phone company, see if I can sweet-talk them into pinging the cells," Cal said. "Then I'll get in touch with my parents."

JJ nodded. He had no idea how the Liechtenstein royal family might be able to help, but he had no problem using their connections if it meant finding April and the others. Fear churned in his gut, but he'd learned long ago to channel that fear into action. This was the most important mission of his life, and he wouldn't fail. Not when his future depended on it.

~

April didn't know how much time had passed; it was hard to tell when you were inside a pitch-black box, but eventually it felt as if they were slowing down. They'd stopped a couple of times now, actually, and each time, April wondered if they should pound on the side of the trailer, try to get someone's attention.

But after discussing it with the others, they all decided their best bet was to be compliant . . . for now. It wasn't until Ryan didn't get what he wanted that he'd hit June. And no one wanted to see if he would follow through on his threats if they pissed him off. So they sat tight, huddled together, waiting to see what would happen.

Each time they stopped, they headed out again within a few minutes. Ryan hadn't opened the door to the trailer, and he hadn't communicated with them in any way. Eventually, they'd had to resort to using the bucket in the corner to do their business. It was difficult and embarrassing, but as April reminded everyone, they had to do whatever was necessary, and there was nothing embarrassing when it came to survival.

When they stopped this time, something seemed different. For one, they didn't immediately leave again.

"Where do you think we are?" Carlise whispered.

"No clue," April said. "But I think we were on the interstate. With the way this trailer was rattling and being buffeted by the wind, we were driving pretty fast."

"He has to sleep at some point, right?" Marlowe asked.

April nodded. "Yeah, you're right. Maybe he's doing that now. Stopping to sleep for a while. How're you doing, June? Are you still having contractions?"

There was a small pause before June sighed. "Yeah."

"Are they closer together?" Carlise asked.

"A little."

"Shit," Marlowe swore softly.

"It's fine. If June has her baby, we can handle it," April said firmly.

No one replied. Until Carlise said wryly, "I know we're supposed to be positive, and April, we've always looked to you for guidance, but I have to say it . . . you're talking out your ass."

April blinked in surprise—then she smiled. Then she actually laughed out loud. "Right, let's get it all out. Who else wants to bitch?"

"My back is killing me," June said. "This floor is so hard."

"I like roughing it at Riggs's cabin, but peeing in a bucket sucks," Carlise added.

"And it stinks in here," Marlowe said. "It reminds me too much of that prison in Thailand."

"I'm scared," June admitted softly.

"Me too," Carlise agreed.

"Terrified," Marlowe said. "We don't know what this guy wants or what he's going to do to us when we get to wherever we're going."

"Not to mention we're locked in here. What if he wrecks? What if he decides to just leave this trailer somewhere?" Carlise asked.

"And he hasn't given us any water or food or anything," June griped.

"I'm worried about what our guys are thinking and doing. They have to be freaking out by now," Carlise said softly.

When they stopped talking, April asked, "Is that it? Come on, now's the time to say what you're thinking."

It remained quiet in the trailer, and April took a deep breath. It was her turn. "I'm scared you guys hate me for getting you into this. I'm terrified that June is gonna have her baby, and I have no clue what to do. I don't want any of you to get hurt, and I'm so hungry I'm dizzy. But you know what? Things could be worse."

Someone snorted.

"I mean it," April insisted. "That asshole Ryan could've shot June back in the office. Or we could be alone. Having you guys here makes this somehow better. Not easy, but easier. We're smart women. We can figure out how to survive this."

"There's four of us. What if we jump him the next time he opens the back?" Carlise asked.

"Or maybe we can find some rusted-out spot or something that leads to the outside and we can stick a piece of fabric out of the hole to try to signal someone?" Marlowe added.

"And we've all read enough baby books about what to expect. If I do have this kid, I trust you guys to help me. We can do this," June said in a firmer voice.

April wanted to cry, she was so grateful her friends were working hard to overcome their fear.

"Who *is* this guy?" Marlowe asked. "Why us?"

"From the little I got from him, I'm thinking taking us has more to do with our guys," April said.

"I agree," June said. "He could've shot us all by now. Raped us. Done more than just shove us into this box and start driving."

"It makes no sense, though," Carlise said in exasperation.

"It does if he set something up ahead of time," June said. "Something to lure our guys in?"

"Oh shit," April muttered. June was right. That *did* make sense. But the question was . . . where?

"Why, though?" Marlowe mused.

"Does it matter?" Carlise said matter-of-factly. "Maybe Riggs looked at him wrong. Maybe he hates the Liechtenstein royal family. Or Bob said something sarcastic, or he's after JJ because he's got a rival tree business that isn't doing well because of Jack's Lumber. Kidnapping four women is extreme, so whatever his reason, he's obviously justified it in his own head."

She wasn't wrong. April nodded to herself. "We need to get him to open this door," she said firmly.

"I'm not sure that's the best idea," Marlowe said with a tremble in her voice.

"When he first came to the office, he liked when I begged him. When I gave in to whatever he told me to do. I can try the same thing. See if begging him helps."

"Like, to let us go?" June asked.

175

"I don't think he's ever going to do that," April said with a sigh. "But you guys weren't wrong. It's awful in here. Cold. The floor is way too hard, and that bucket *is* disgusting. Do you guys trust me?"

All three of her friends answered in the affirmative immediately, which made April's heart swell and her eyes fill with tears. "Right, so I'll be our spokesperson. He's arrogant and thinks he's got everything worked out. I'll talk to him and see if I can convince him to help us."

"Be careful, April," Carlise said. "We can't do this without you."

April reached over and blindly patted what she thought was her friend's leg. "Yes, you can, and you will. Your husbands are counting on you all being strong and hanging on until they can get here."

"You really think they'll find us?" June asked.

"Yes." It was Marlowe who answered. "Kendric managed to break me out of a Thai prison. Finding us and making this Ryan guy pay? Piece of cake, especially since all four of our guys will be working together."

"You're right," June said in a tone that sounded stronger than a moment ago.

"Hell yes, they're going to find us," Carlise agreed.

April thought back to when Jack was reciting some of his so-called faults. How he'd sworn to scorch the earth to keep her safe. It had seemed over the top at the time, but now? Imagining him in soldier mode and making that asshole Ryan regret ever touching her sounded pretty damn awesome.

"We've got this, girls," April said, relieved that her friends had somehow shaken themselves out of their backslide into hopelessness.

CHAPTER FOURTEEN

JJ was as focused as he'd ever been. "Sitrep," he barked as he entered the back room of Jack's Lumber. They'd decided to use it as home base. They all felt closer to their women there, since that's where they'd last known them to be.

It was well into the evening now, dark outside, but no one was tired. Not even close.

"The police chief has organized some search parties, but we all know they aren't going to find anything around here. Whoever took our women is long gone," Bob said.

"My parents have gotten in touch with the king and queen, and their best tech experts are on it, seeing if they can find any digital trace of who might've done this," Cal said. "But more importantly, thanks to Chief Rutkey's help, the phone company is finally working on pinging their phones. They should be getting back to me anytime now."

"I talked to Tex. He's pissed. Like, *really* pissed. He's contacting a group of men he knows who live in Indianapolis," Chappy informed them.

"Who are they, and how can they help?" JJ asked.

"I'm not sure. All I know is that they have a towing company called Silverstone."

Irritation swamped JJ. The last thing they needed was some random guys without resources. Just bringing them up to date was precious time they needed to find their women.

"Holy shit! Silverstone?" Bob asked.

"You know them?" JJ asked, a little harsher than intended.

"They worked with Willis, the FBI contact I also worked with on my missions. He didn't mention the name of their business, just said he worked with a group of former Special Forces soldiers who ran a towing business in Indiana. They took contract jobs to . . . eliminate bad guys."

"Assassins?" Cal asked with both brows raised.

"Apparently," Bob said with a nod. "I've heard nothing but amazing things. Willis was super upset to lose them. They stopped contracting after getting married and starting families. They're completely legit now, running Silverstone, but they're the real deal."

JJ nodded reluctantly. Another former Special Forces team on their side *would* be great.

"Do we have any clue who the perp is?" Bob asked. "Who has our women and why?"

"Unknown at this time, but Tex is working on it," Chappy said.

Given some of the violent things they'd done in the course of serving their country, Tex was literally the only person who JJ *wasn't* worried about digging into their backgrounds.

Just then, Cal's phone rang, and he answered it and put it on speaker. "Callum Redmon," he said.

"Mr. Redmon, this is Alice from the phone company, returning your call."

"What did you find out? Where is she?" he asked without beating around the bush.

"Well, it looks like your wife's phone is in Canada."

The four men exchanged confused looks.

"Excuse me?" Cal asked the woman.

"It's currently pinging off a tower in Montreal. And for the record, she doesn't have the international plan, which I can help you activate. Trust me, it'll save you hundreds of dollars."

"What about the others?" Cal barked, obviously not interested in a sales pitch. "Are they in Montreal too?"

JJ tensed as he heard the woman's fingers clicking on a keyboard. "No. The other three numbers you gave me are in three different places. One's in Boston, the other is in Portland. Maine, that is, not Oregon." The woman laughed at her own joke, but when Cal didn't seem to appreciate her humor, she continued quickly. "And the last number is no longer transmitting, but the last ping was near Albany, New York."

JJ's mind spun. All the reasons he could think of for their phones ending up in different places weren't good. Not at all.

"Sir?" Alice asked. "Are you still there? Do you want me to activate the international plan on your wife's phone? It's only ten dollars a day, and trust me, that's way cheaper than what accessing Canadian cell towers in roaming mode is costing now."

"Shut it down. Deactivate the phone," Cal said, then hung up without another word, cutting off the poor woman.

"So whoever took them either gave their phones away, or they were stolen," Chappy said.

"Looks that way," Bob said tightly.

JJ pressed his lips together. The possibility of tracking the women via phone was out. Unless . . . "They could've been taken by traffickers," he said. "Heading to different places."

Cal shook his head. "No, I don't think so."

"Why not?" JJ asked, wanting desperately to agree with his friend. Fear rolled in his gut at the thought of April being in the hands of anyone in the trafficking industry.

"Whoever took them took them *together*. Yes, it's possible that he or she stopped somewhere and split them up, but I'm thinking two obviously very pregnant ladies and—no offense, JJ—an older woman like April aren't exactly the usual suspects when it comes to the sex trade."

He wasn't wrong. JJ nodded.

"Then who? And why?" Bob asked.

"At this point, it doesn't matter. Whoever took them is dead," JJ growled. "What else do we have? Video?"

"Nothing I've found yet," Chappy said. "Our inside camera is pointed at the front door, and the one outside catches the street directly in front of Jack's Lumber. If the vehicle pulled around to the street, it must've turned right, out of frame, because no truck with a trailer passed in front of our camera."

"Shit," JJ said, running a hand through his hair. Living in Newton had made him complacent. Crime rarely happened in the small town, but he should've known better—especially after shit *had* happened. To his own friends' women. He blamed himself for not having a camera on the back door. It was stupid, and possibly the worst mistake he'd ever made.

"What about other businesses?" Cal asked.

"The police chief is checking with them."

"We don't have time for that," JJ said, knowing down to his bones that time was ticking. They needed to figure out where their women were *now*.

The gazes of his best friends were locked on him. Looking to him for direction. But for the first time in his life, JJ was at a loss.

He always had a plan. Was the team leader, the man the others turned to when missions were FUBAR. But he had nothing right now. It was as if their women had disappeared without a trace.

His heart raced, and inside, he panicked. Outwardly, he remained as calm as ever.

"You got nothin'?" Bob finally asked. "How can you be so relaxed right now?" he barked harshly. "Oh, because April's not your wife? Because she's not pregnant?"

Anger rose hard and fast within JJ, but he didn't lash out. Didn't respond in any way. He understood where his friend's anger was coming from.

"Seriously, JJ, are you made of fucking ice?" Chappy asked. "*April's* out there! Maybe hurt. Definitely scared. We thought you two finally admitted how much you meant to each other. Were we wrong?"

Again, JJ knew their anger was coming from a place of fear and helplessness and despair—all the things JJ felt inside himself. And

Chappy wasn't wrong—he *was* encased in ice. It was the only way to keep all those emotions inside. He knew himself too well. If he let them out, he wouldn't be able to think. Wouldn't be able to help April and the others at all.

"June's about ready to have our son," Cal said in the most tortured voice JJ had ever heard. "Stress isn't good for her or our child. What if she goes into labor while we're standing around twiddling our thumbs? For God's sake, *help us!*" He was practically yelling by the time he was done.

JJ straightened. His hands shook with the adrenaline coursing through his bloodstream. He didn't hate his friends for turning their fear and frustration on him. That had always been his job as team leader. To stay stoic, to make decisions that were best for everyone . . . and yes, to be a punching bag when needed.

"We're going to find them," he said in a voice he didn't recognize. It was full of venom, and hate, and determination. "Cal, your wife and son will be fine. The others will take care of her. Chappy, Carlise is smart and steady. Bob, Marlowe's been to hell, and she still had your back when things seemed hopeless. And my April is the glue that will hold them all together.

"They're holding on. For *us*. And we will *not* let them down. Whoever has them made the worst mistake of his life. No matter what his beef with us might be, he should've let it go. Because now he's going to die a very painful death. Mark my words, we're going to find them. And when we do, anyone and everyone who had a hand in taking them will pay.

"As for not caring . . . I care," JJ said. "You know I do. But I'm keeping it locked down. I can't lose myself to my fear. I can't think about how scared April is. How worried she has to be. Whether or not she's hurt. Whose blood that is on the floor. If I do, I'll lose it, and I won't be able to help them at all.

"So you guys can be pissed. You can rant and rave, punch shit, throw stuff. I don't care if you destroy this office and everything in it.

Susan Stoker

I'll continue to keep it together for us all. Hate me if you want, but that won't change a goddamn thing. I'm still going to find my woman and tear apart anyone who's hurt one hair on her head."

His teammates had gone still at his first words. Now, they stared at him with a mixture of appreciation and guilt. Finally, Chappy spoke quietly. "I'm sorry for doubting you, even for a second. We all know who you are. You've saved our lives more than once and gotten us through situations no one should've lived through."

"I'm sorry too," Cal told him. "I just . . . I'm so damn worried for June, I can't think straight!"

"You're right. Our women are stronger than we're giving them credit for. We just need one fucking clue! Even the smallest scrap, and we'll be on them," Bob said.

"Damn straight," JJ said with a nod.

Chappy came over and put a hand on his shoulder. The weight of his friend's hand was negligible, but the support and meaning behind it were immeasurable. Cal approached and rested a hand on his other shoulder. Then Bob advanced from the front, wrapping his arms around Chappy and Cal's shoulders, engulfing them all in one large embrace.

No one said a word, but the support the men had for each other invigorated them. Gave them strength.

JJ loved these men. He'd literally die for them, just as he'd die for their wives. He prayed long and hard it wouldn't come to that. That they'd somehow luck out and find the women safe and sound and without a scratch on them.

But he knew deep down, instinctively, the fight of their lives was upon them. What they'd experienced as POWs would seem like a walk in the park compared to getting their women back. That didn't matter. They hadn't trained so long and so hard, hadn't seen and done what they had, hadn't experienced hell, only to lose the people who'd made it all worthwhile.

Stay strong, April. We're coming for you.

The words were silent, in his head, but JJ didn't need to say them out loud. He knew without a doubt that April knew he'd find her.

CHAPTER FIFTEEN

The women had been huddled together for probably another hour when they heard scraping on the back side of the trailer.

April sat up and whispered, "Remember, let me take the lead."

"Good luck," Carlise told her softly.

"You can do it," Marlowe encouraged.

"We trust you," June added.

April's heart was beating triple time in her chest. She had no idea what was about to happen. The person about to open the door could be Ryan. Or it could be someone he'd sold them to. Yes, she'd absolutely thought of all the scenarios that they could find themselves in, and one was being sold into the sex trade.

Whoever was out there was going to find four women who seemed to be completely cowed and docile. Fighting wasn't in their best interest, not if they had no weapon. And even though April really, *really* wanted to scratch the eyes out of anyone who appeared at the door, she took a deep breath and told herself to be patient. To do whatever she could to outsmart their kidnapper.

The door opened, and even though it was dark outside, a streetlight in the distance was still too much for April's sensitive eyes. They'd all been in complete darkness for so long, even the smallest light made her wince.

Squinting, April saw that it was indeed Ryan who'd opened the door to the trailer. All she could see behind him were trees. Wherever he'd stopped, he'd backed the trailer up so no one would see what was inside if he opened the door.

"Please," April pleaded in the most pathetic voice she could muster. "Do you have any water?"

"Why should I give you anything?" Ryan asked.

Now she really wanted to punch him in the nose, but she forced herself to keep her head down and her tone neutral. "We've been good. Haven't made any noise. All we want is something to drink. *Please*." She was laying it on thick, but she hoped it would work.

To her surprise, Ryan said, "Get over here."

Looking up, April saw he was pointing at her. Reluctantly, she scooted forward on the cold floor of the trailer, staying several feet shy of the door.

"Here," Ryan ordered as he pointed to the edge of the trailer.

For a moment, April hesitated. She didn't want to get any closer to this asshole. She looked at him, trying to stall, really studying him for the first time. He was much younger than she'd first realized. At the oldest, he couldn't be more than twenty-one or twenty-two, but it was also possible he was still a teenager. He had dark hair and a five-o'clock shadow. In the dim light, his eyes looked like empty black orbs. In his current jeans and T-shirt, he could blend in just about anywhere, except . . .

April didn't think he was American. He'd cut his hair to resemble a lot of other young men, and the clothes were age appropriate. But as much as he tried to hide it, his words were slightly accented.

"I said, come *here*, April," Ryan repeated, sounding irritated.

She moved without thought, scooting forward.

"You want water?" he asked.

"Yes. Please."

"And food?"

"That would be appreciated," she told him.

"It stinks in here," Ryan said.

"If you let me empty the bucket, it'll smell better," April said.

"Fine. Do it."

April stared at him for a minute, shocked that he'd agreed without any fuss. She was also very wary. What would he want in return for his supposed acts of kindness?

"No funny business. I'll still shoot someone without hesitation if you do anything stupid," he said.

It was then April saw the familiar gun in his hand. She'd missed it before. She nodded quickly. "No funny business. Promise."

She turned and crawled back toward the others and the bucket, which had been secured to the back corner of the trailer. She unhooked the bungee cord holding it in place, having brief visions of using it to wrap around Ryan's throat and strangle him.

She scooted to the edge of the trailer, and Ryan took a step back. Not a big one; just enough for April to put her legs out and stand. It felt so damn good to stretch, to be upright, but she quickly moved to the tree nearest the trailer and emptied the waste bucket.

Without moving her head, April looked around and saw they were at what looked like a rest stop. She was right that they'd probably traveled on the interstate. Ryan had parked at the back of the lot with all the semis. The loud ruckus of truck generators would mask a lot of noise, and if the truckers were asleep, it was possible no one would hear them yelling anyway.

She quickly moved back to the trailer and climbed inside without waiting for orders. She pushed the bucket toward the other women and turned back to face their kidnapper. "Thank you," she said, even though the words felt like acid on her tongue.

"So compliant," Ryan drawled smugly. Then he surprised her by quickly leaning into the trailer and grabbing her wrist, yanking her toward him.

It took everything within April not to recoil. Not to punch him in the face. Instead, she let him drag her back out of the trailer. He slammed the doors shut with one hand and locked her friends back inside. Not for the first time, true fear swam through her veins. What was he going to do with her now? Was he going to kill her? Give her to some serial killer he'd contacted to meet them at the back corner of this truck stop?

She tried to pull her arm from his hold, but he simply tightened his fingers around her wrist. He dragged her to the passenger side of the black truck and ordered, "Get in."

He didn't let go of her wrist, and April slowly did as he said.

She sat in the seat and watched in dismay as Ryan pulled out a set of handcuffs and quickly attached one end to her wrist and the other to the handle. Then he smiled. A satisfied grin that scared April to her toes. He slammed the door, walked around to the driver's side, got in, and turned the key. He quickly pulled out of the parking spot and headed for the exit, back to the interstate.

April's head spun. She had no idea what was happening. She felt guilty for the comfortable seat when her friends were still in the back on that unforgiving steel floor, probably freezing. Ryan also had the heat on low, so it was toasty warm in the cab.

"Thank you for letting me sit up here," she muttered after a moment.

"I like how polite you are," Ryan said.

April knew she needed to get this man talking. Try to figure out where he was taking them and why he'd kidnapped them in the first place, but her mind was suddenly blank. She wasn't sure what to say or ask.

She watched as they approached a green sign. It informed drivers that they were about a hundred and twenty miles from Syracuse. She blinked in surprise. It was about five hours from Newton to Albany, and since they were on the interstate, they had to be headed toward the big city, but it felt as if they'd been locked in that trailer for a lot longer. And they probably had, actually. Ryan had made several stops.

So they were headed west. Being polite and docile had gotten her some useful information after all. It was a start.

"You want food and water?" Ryan asked again out of the blue, scaring April.

"Yes, please." She didn't have to fake the quiver in her voice.

He nodded to a bag between them. "I stopped and got dinner a while ago. You can have what I didn't eat."

April wanted to gag, but she controlled herself and pulled the fast-food bag over and peered inside. There were a few bites of a hamburger in a wrapper and a couple of french fries at the bottom of the bag. They were cold and soggy, but April reached in and grabbed them anyway. She choked them down and asked, "And water?"

Ryan nodded to a drink in the cup holder. "There's some ice."

This guy was an ass. Making her eat his leftovers as if she was some kind of dog. But she didn't let any of what she was thinking show on her face.

She ate the rest of his hamburger and tipped the cup up to slurp down the melted water in the bottom. No way was she using the same straw he had. She drew the line at that.

She sucked a cube into her mouth, and it was almost sad how good the melted ice felt going down her throat.

"My friends are thirsty and hungry too," she said softly. "And cold. Do you happen to have a blanket or something?"

"Just like a woman. You give them a mile, and they want an inch."

April stared down at her hands in her lap and refused to smile at how he'd messed up the familiar saying. It was one more thing that made her think he wasn't originally from the US.

"I suppose you want to call Jackson too, don't you?"

April's head whipped up, and she stared at Ryan. Was this a trap? Was he just torturing her with the possibility of being able to talk to Jack? Probably. But she couldn't stop herself from whispering, "Oh, God. Yes. Please!"

"Which do you want more? To talk to Jackson? Or food, water, and blankets for your friends?"

April's mind spun. Shit, she wanted to talk to Jack more than she wanted just about anything in the world right now. If she did, she might be able to give him some clues as to where they were. Like the fact they were headed west, or that Ryan's truck was black, or that he was pulling a trailer.

But Ryan was probably just fucking with her. He wasn't going to let her call Jack. He wasn't *that* dumb. And ultimately, she couldn't deny her friends' needs.

As much as it hurt, she finally said, "Food, water, and blankets."

Ryan laughed. Cackled, really. "So loyal," he taunted. "I was looking forward to telling the other bitches that you chose dick over them."

April sat as still as possible. "So you'll stop and get them food and stuff?" she asked tentatively.

"Don't need to stop. It's in the back," Ryan said, pointing over his shoulder.

Turning, April looked in the back seat and saw a large cardboard box. She only got glimpses of what was inside from the streetlights they passed, and anger threatened to overwhelm her. He'd had provisions all along. He could've put them in the trailer to begin with! Instead, he was delighting in torturing her and her friends.

She hated this man. *Hated* him.

It didn't matter. She had to play his game. Had to be smart.

"Thank you so much," she breathed, trying to sound both awed and submissive.

They drove in silence for a few minutes, and April was dying to ask him when they could stop and transfer the stuff to the trailer, but she kept her lips pressed together.

"There's a white bag on the back seat. Grab it."

Turning again, April spotted the small bag. She reached for it, but because her right wrist was cuffed to the door, she couldn't stretch far enough. "I can't."

Ryan shrugged. "Oh well. There's a phone in there that I was going to let you use to call Jackson. But if you can't reach it . . ." His voice trailed off.

April was pretty sure he was lying—but what if he wasn't? He was acting . . . weird. She had a feeling everything he was doing was all part of his plan. She was just a pawn in the cruel game he was playing with the men. But so be it. If she was a pawn, she'd do what was expected of her—for now.

She lifted her ass off the seat and once more reached for the white bag. The handcuff pulled painfully at her wrist, but the fingers of her left hand brushed against the bag. She almost had it.

Ryan suddenly swerved to the left, making April cry out in pain as the cuff dug into her wrist. The bag fell off the seat and onto the floor.

Ryan laughed uproariously. "Whoops, sorry," he said insincerely. "You almost had it too, didn't you?"

She *almost* told him to fuck off but stopped herself at the last minute. It was almost scary how much hatred she had in her heart for the man next to her. She tried to live her life being kind. People had stuff going on that no one knew about. So she tried to give everyone the benefit of the doubt. But she couldn't find one redeeming thing about Ryan. He'd struck June twice and kicked Marlowe. He'd given April something to eat and drink, but it was his castoffs. And he'd bought blankets and food for her and the other women but had withheld them for reasons only he knew.

And now he was taunting her with being able to talk to Jack. Torturing her.

Determination rose within April. He wasn't going to win. Wasn't going to get the satisfaction of seeing her cry.

She stretched her arm out as far as it could go and nearly whimpered at the pain in her right wrist, but it was worth it when her fingers actually got hold of the white bag. She gripped it firmly and sat back down in the seat.

"You got it. Good job," Ryan deadpanned. He still had a smirk on his face.

April looked at her right wrist and winced. She was bleeding. The steel had cut into her skin, but she'd done it. Gotten the stupid bag.

"Such control," Ryan drawled. "Not even a single tear. Go on, look inside. I know you're dying to."

She opened the white bag—and blinked in disbelief at the small black flip phone sitting on the bottom. Holy crap, was he *really* going to let her call Jack?

"Yes, it's a phone," he said, as if he could read her mind. "And since you've been a good girl, I'll let you call Jackson. But you only have two minutes. Understand?"

"Yes, sir," she said, the polite term popping out without thought. She was still afraid he was going to yank the bag from her hand and throw it out the window or something, laughing at her naivete in thinking he was actually going to let her call for help.

"And there are rules," Ryan went on. "You aren't allowed to tell him what I'm driving. Or about the trailer. You can give him any other clues you'd like. Let's see if he's smart enough to figure them out."

April's mind spun. Clues? She wasn't good at word games. And she and Jack hadn't been together long enough for them to have any private jokes or innuendos. *Crap crap crap!* "Can I tell him your name?"

"Sure," Ryan said with a shrug.

April was still suspicious, but the thought of talking to Jack was too overwhelming for her to wonder why Ryan was being so generous.

"About the girls? Can I talk about them?" she asked, not wanting to risk saying anything that might piss Ryan off.

"Yes."

"Can I tell him where you're taking us?" she asked.

Ryan's smile grew. "Where am I taking you?"

"I don't know. I was hoping you'd tell me so I could tell Jack."

Ryan threw his head back and laughed yet again. "Not so broken after all, huh?" he asked rhetorically, still laughing. "Colorado. We're going to Colorado," he said when he had control over himself.

April was shocked to her core that he'd actually told her. Of course, he could be lying and probably was. Any moment, he could turn south and head for Mexico or something . . . but for some reason she believed him. Maybe because he was enjoying this game so much.

"What was it Einstein said? Every action has an opposite and equal reaction? Actions have consequences. This is his. And his team's."

She had no idea what Ryan was referring to. Her first inane thought was he'd just recited Newton's third law, not something Einstein came up with. On the heels of that—it was obvious, just as she'd thought, that this kidnapping wasn't about her or the other women. It was about Jack and his team.

Her heart thumped hard in her chest. Suddenly, she didn't want to call Jack. Didn't want to involve him in whatever Ryan had planned.

"We're bait," she whispered, horrified.

Ryan glanced at her. "I knew you were smart," he said. Then his face got hard. "Two minutes. And remember the rules. If you break them, no one eats or drinks until we're in Colorado, and you can all freeze to death for all I care."

April could tell he was done fucking around. Colorado was his endgame. Messing with her was just part of the fun.

Her hand shook as she reached into the bag and pulled out the cell phone. She was extremely grateful her memory had returned, and along with it, Jack's phone number. Most people didn't bother to memorize their loved ones' numbers any longer; there was no need when you could just click on a button to call them. But she'd always been a little old school and was very thankful for it now.

She flipped open the phone and realized it was probably one of those untraceable things. The kind drug dealers and other criminals seemed to have in abundance. Taking a deep breath, she slowly dialed Jack's number and prayed harder than she could remember praying in a very long time that she didn't mess this up. That Jack answered. That he'd figure out what was happening and where they were. And that her phone call wouldn't get him and the others killed.

CHAPTER SIXTEEN

They had nothing.

No clues.

No hints.

No footage.

Nothing that would lead them to the women.

JJ's skin crawled. The hair on the back of his neck stood up. Something had to break. It always did. April and the others would *not* be tragic statistics. Women who disappeared into thin air with no suspects, their bodies never found.

No, four women weren't just snatched up without the kidnapper wanting something. Money, revenge, sex, power—*something*.

He stilled. Revenge . . .

They hadn't gotten a ransom call in the hours since they'd discovered the women missing, so perhaps that could be taken off the table. It was possible whoever had kidnapped the women wanted sex, or wanted to sell them for sex, but three pregnant ladies weren't exactly the ideal targets. Power was still an option . . . but most likely in conjunction with something else. Like revenge.

That had to be it. Someone from their past *was* trying to prove a point. Get back at them. Lure them into a trap.

JJ spun and blurted, "Revenge."

The other guys looked up from what they were doing—pacing, searching the internet for any kind of information that might help, staring helplessly into space.

"What?" Chappy asked.

"Revenge. Whoever took them did so to get back at us for something."

Bob snorted. "That doesn't exactly narrow down the suspects," he said gravely. "We've pissed off a lot of terrorists and other bad guys."

"But why now? It's been years since we've been active," Cal argued.

JJ opened his mouth to respond when his phone rang. It was sitting on the table near him, and he picked it up.

The caller was "unknown."

His adrenaline spiked. He hit a button on the phone to record the call and answered. "Hello?"

"Jack? It's me."

JJ felt as if he'd entered a long, dark tunnel. His vision got hazy on the sides, and he fell into the chair he'd been standing in front of while racking his brain about what to do next.

"April?" he asked, unsure if that brain was now playing tricks on him.

"It's me. I'm okay," she said quickly. "I only have two minutes, so you need to listen. Are you listening?"

"Yes, baby. I'm listening."

He heard her breath hitch at the endearment, but she took a deep breath and continued. "We're okay. All of us. We're all together. We're going to get food and water, so tell the guys not to worry."

"You know as well as I do that's impossible," JJ said.

"I know, but we're together and hanging in there. Remember that sunset we watched together? How pretty it was and how fast the sun seemed to disappear?"

JJ had no idea what she was talking about, but he immediately said, "Yes."

"Good. His name is Ryan. Ryan Johnson. He said I could tell you."

JJ looked up at the others, who'd all gathered around him since his phone was on speaker. The confusion in their eyes made it clear they didn't recognize the name either. "Where are you? Where is he taking you?" JJ didn't think she'd be able to tell him, but he couldn't not ask.

"He said Colorado," April said. "Remember that time we went fishing? You laughed when I refused to touch the worms? I didn't like the way they squirmed. It felt wrong to put that hook through their bodies. You said without the worms, there would be no fish. It didn't make me feel any better."

He was sure she was trying to give him some sort of clue. He struggled to figure out what it meant. "You were adorable," JJ muttered. He knew as well as she did that they'd *never* been fishing together.

"Promise me that we'll take that vacation when I get home," she said urgently.

"Which one?" JJ asked anxiously.

"The one overseas. You promised to take me to see the Great Pyramid of Egypt. I want to ride a camel. Remember?"

"Yes."

"I love you, Jack. I can't wait to go home. To cuddle with you again, eat Fig Newtons while watching TV. And remember, it's a law that I get the third one, no matter what."

A deep voice said something in the background, and JJ thought it sounded like "Time's up."

"April?" JJ asked. "We're coming for you! Hang in there."

But there was no response. The line was silent. She'd either hung up or someone had taken the phone away.

JJ squeezed his phone so hard, his knuckles turned white. He wanted to stand up and throw it across the room, but if he did that, April wouldn't be able to get a hold of him again.

"Breathe, JJ," Cal said, putting a hand on his shoulder.

JJ's first urge was to fling it off. He wanted to beat the shit out of someone. But instead, he took a deep breath and reached for the calm he needed in order to figure out what the hell his woman was trying to tell him.

"April is a bloody genius," Cal said.

JJ whipped his head up to look at him.

"She just gave us a bunch of clues."

"You know what she meant?" JJ asked urgently.

"No idea. But I know that's what she was doing. Everything she said was too random *not* to be clues. We just have to decipher them."

JJ took another breath. His friend was right. He didn't understand half the things she told him: they hadn't gone fishing or discussed a trip overseas, so they had to be clues. And if they were going to find the women, they needed to figure them out. The sooner the better.

"Ryan Johnson," Chappy said. "Do we think that's really the guy's name?"

"No way in hell," Bob said with a shake of his head as he sat next to JJ. "It's too common. It's got to be made up."

Cal nodded. "Which is why he probably didn't have a problem with her telling us."

"So a dead end. Moving on," JJ said, pulling a piece of paper over from the coffee table and writing the name Ryan Johnson at the top, then putting a line through it.

"Knowing they're headed to Colorado is good. Really good, but can we trust that's actually their destination?" Cal asked.

JJ ground his teeth in frustration. "No clue."

"Why would he let her tell us that?" Bob asked.

"Because he wants us to know. Wants us to follow him," Chappy guessed.

JJ thought about that, reluctantly agreeing it was probably the case.

"Can we catch them on the road before they get there? I mean, there aren't a whole lot of ways to get to Colorado from here," Bob said.

"Are you kidding? We don't know *where* in Colorado they're going, and he could take Interstate 90 and cut down, or 80, or 70, or hell, he could go south and jump on 40 and go north when he gets to New Mexico," Chappy said in disgust.

JJ did his best not to panic. He didn't want to think about April and the others being in their kidnapper's clutches for a second longer than necessary, but he wasn't sure how to find them amid the vast interstate network.

"Bloody hell!" Cal swore, kicking a nearby folding chair. It went flying backward, sounding obscenely loud in the otherwise quiet office.

"Replay the call," Chappy said grimly. "April said a bunch of other stuff. If she was giving us clues, we just have to figure them out."

JJ clicked a button, and soon April's stressed-out voice once again filled the air around them. It physically hurt him to hear how scared she was, but he was also as proud as he could be that she was obviously trying to stay calm.

"What's with the fishing thing?" Bob asked, his brows furrowed as he stared intently at the phone, as if that alone would help him understand what April was trying to convey.

"Worms? Is there a fishing spot around here that she knows about?" Chappy asked.

"Hook?" Bob added.

JJ closed his eyes and concentrated. He thought about the last time he went fishing, how he chose each worm, got them on the hook properly so they didn't come off each time the line was cast—then it hit him.

"She's talking about *baiting* a hook," JJ blurted. "Worms are bait."

Chappy nodded. "She's warning us that whoever took them is using the women as bait."

For the first time since he found out that April was gone, hope began to blossom in JJ. No, April telling him the women were bait wasn't exactly anything they could use to find them, but it meant their kidnapper might not have taken them for a more nefarious purpose, such as selling them, or raping and torturing them . . . he hoped.

"So they're going to Colorado, and this Ryan Johnson guy wants us to follow . . . ," Bob mused.

"Egypt?" Cal asked. "Was she trying to tell us that she thinks he's Egyptian?"

JJ thought that one over for a moment. "Maybe," he hedged. "It's possible she was simply trying to let us know that she doesn't think he's American. I'm not sure how much experience she has in determining nationality."

"Unless he told her something," Bob challenged.

"So Ryan Johnson is a made-up name, and he's possibly from Egypt," Chappy said. "We had a few missions in Egypt."

"Yeah, but they were mostly reconnaissance," JJ said. "We didn't engage with anyone while we were there. Why the hell would someone be pissed at us for that?"

Frustration was clear on his team's faces.

"And *camel*? Was she trying to let us know something about hills, mountain, humps?" Cal asked.

The four men threw ideas out but couldn't think of anything April might have been trying to tell them with that particular clue.

"So that leaves the sunset comment and the Fig Newtons. JJ, have you guys watched a sunset together?" Chappy asked.

JJ shook his head. "Not really. I mean, maybe when we were in the car together coming back from a jobsite or something. But not, like, sitting down purposefully to watch it."

"The sun sets in the west," Cal commented. "Maybe she was telling us that's the direction they're going."

"But she came right out and told us they're going to Colorado," Bob countered. "Why would she bother with the cloak-and-dagger shit if she was just going to come right out and tell us the destination?"

"I don't know. But she said that the sun had set fast. Maybe she was telling us that her kidnapper wasn't taking any breaks, or not that many, and they'd be there sooner rather than later," Cal offered.

JJ's head hurt. He hated this. Despised it. He was proud of April for doing her best to give them clues, but trying to decipher them felt nearly impossible.

"Fig Newtons. Law. Third. That one is easy. Newton's third law," Bob said confidently.

"When two bodies interact, they apply forces on each other, so there's an equal and opposite reaction," Chappy recited.

"Which goes back to the bait thing . . . I think," Cal said.

"Damn. Which goes back to something we did or didn't do," Bob finished.

JJ sighed, and his shoulders slumped. Without more to go on, they were still flying pretty blind. Over the years, he and his team had completed jobs that meant hundreds, even thousands, of people might be unhappy with them as a result. From Benghazi, Tunisia, Iraq and Iran, India, Ireland, the Philippines, Uzbekistan, Palestine, China, Russia, Colombia, Africa . . . the list of places they'd been in was never ending.

He was on the verge of feeling hopeless again, but that wasn't an option. Not even close. "Right, until this Ryan Johnson guy wants to give us more information, until he lets April call back, we have to go with the little we have. Ryan Johnson, made-up name, from our past, took our women as bait, wants us to follow him to Colorado. And until we find out exactly where he's going, we need to plan for every contingency. It's likely he's been planning this for a while. Which means he has a very specific location in mind. Somewhere he can draw us in and take us out."

"The mountains," Chappy said firmly.

"That's what I was thinking," JJ said. "Some area he's familiar with. He's not going to go to Denver or Colorado Springs or any other city. He most likely wants to kill us, which means he needs privacy. No one around to see what he's doing."

"There's a lot of wilderness in Colorado," Bob said skeptically. "How do we figure out where he's going?"

"We don't. Not yet," JJ said. "But he'll let us know when he's ready to play. Until then, we need to prepare. I'm going to make some calls. I know some people who live in Colorado who'll absolutely help us."

"Who?" Bob asked.

"Rex and his team, for one," JJ replied.

"The Mountain Mercenaries," Chappy said.

"Who are they?" Cal asked, looking from one friend to another. "Can we trust them? How do you know they'll help?"

"They'll help," JJ said without hesitation. "They live in the Colorado Springs area and, like the Silverstone team, used to be Special Forces. SEALs, SAS, Marines, Coast Guard."

"Wait—Ronan Cross, right?" Cal asked. "He's the Brit?"

"I'm not one hundred percent sure, but maybe," JJ said.

"I've heard of him and some of the stuff he's done. He's kind of legendary," Cal said, clearly impressed.

"Rex is their leader. He was in the Army. He got the team together after they were discharged from their respective military units, and for years they hunted down women and children who'd been taken in the sex trade," JJ told his team.

"Wait, I've heard of that guy," Chappy said. "Wasn't he the one whose wife was taken, and he found her ten years later in South America?"

"That's him," JJ agreed with a nod.

"Holy crap, he's a badass!" Chappy said in awe.

"They retired from international work, but they still take the occasional job here in the States. I have no doubt they'll help us when they hear what's going on, especially since the women are heading to their own backyard, so to speak," JJ added. "And they're tight with another group of men who live south of Denver. I've crossed paths with Logan and Blake Anderson, from Ace Security. He and his team will help."

"How can you be sure?"

"Because I helped track down one of Logan's twins when he was kidnapped," JJ told his friends.

"What? How come we didn't know about this?" Chappy asked, eyes narrowed.

"I've done a lot of things you guys don't know about. Both before and after the team was formed," JJ admitted. "It doesn't matter. All that matters is finding our women. I'll turn in every marker I've ever collected, call in every contact I've made over the years, do whatever it takes to find them safe and sound."

"So we've got Silverstone, Mountain Mercenaries, Ace Security, and Tex," Bob said. "That's a lot of boots on the ground, plus Tex, and Cal's royal family behind the scenes. When can we head to Colorado?"

"Tomorrow. I need to make calls tonight," JJ said. "We don't know what we're walking into, but since this asshole expects us to come running, he's gonna be ready for us. It's been a long time since we've been on a mission, and we'll have a bunch of men we've never worked with at our sides too. This isn't going to be easy," he felt compelled to warn.

"Didn't expect it would be," Bob answered. "But I didn't get Marlowe out of that shithole prison to lose her now."

"Carlise should've died in that storm. It was fate that led her to my doorstep . . . that and Baxter," Chappy added.

"And June never knew what family was until she came here," Cal said quietly. "She's been so excited about our son, and now she's probably scared out of her mind. I'll do whatever it takes to bring her home."

JJ nodded. The four of them certainly had the motivation to find their women. He just hoped that would be enough. "Tomorrow," he repeated. "Go home, get some sleep if you can. In the morning we'll start planning for every contingency we can think of. No one touches our women and lives. *No one.*"

His friends all nodded grimly.

After the others had left and he was alone in the office, JJ studied the space. Everywhere he looked, he saw April. Every piece of furniture. Every item in the kitchen. A sweatshirt thrown over a chair. The pen lying on top of a stack of boxes that she'd left there after inventory. If he opened the fridge, he'd see the cans of Sprite she loved to drink. Her favorite creamer. Hell, the place even smelled like the beachy lotion she loved so much.

Alone, surrounded by April, JJ's legs collapsed under him, and he went to his knees on the hard floor. His head bowed, and he closed his eyes as he desperately tried to retain his composure. She'd sounded so scared but so determined to tell him as much as she could. He couldn't imagine what she was going through, what *any* of the women were experiencing.

No, that was a lie. He'd been a prisoner. He knew. She was terrified. Confused. Maybe cold and in pain. Trying to get through one minute at a time and having no idea what was going to happen next.

The thought of April being in that situation made him want to kill someone. JJ hadn't enjoyed some aspects of being a Special Forces soldier. Taking a life wasn't something he'd ever done lightly. But at this moment, he yearned to end the man who'd dared touch April. JJ had been a dumbass and waited way too long to let her know how he felt, and now she could be taken from him before they'd barely had a chance at happiness.

No. He wasn't going to allow that to happen.

Looking down, JJ saw he was still clutching his phone. Feeling as if he was in a fog, he clicked the replay button on the call he'd recorded. He needed to hear April's voice again. Get another confirmation that she was alive.

He played it again. Then again. Over and over. Her terrified voice echoed around him, and with each replaying, JJ's determination and anger increased. He'd once told her that he'd scorch the earth to protect her from anyone who dared try to hurt her. Well, it was time for that to happen.

"I love you, April," he said out loud, his voice breaking. "I'm coming for you. Just hang on a little longer."

Then he clicked on Tex's name in his contact list. When the other man answered, JJ didn't beat around the bush. "I need Rex's number," he said gruffly.

Tex didn't ask questions. He rattled off the digits, then asked, "What do you need from me?"

Operation Scorch the Earth was on.

CHAPTER SEVENTEEN

April's entire body shook as she held a hand to her face. Ryan couldn't have just jerked the phone from her hand to stop the call. No, that would be too reasonable. Instead, he'd punched her. It hurt. A lot. Then he'd laughed, turned off the phone after she'd dropped it in shock, and thrown it out the window.

They drove in silence for another twenty miles or so before Ryan pulled off the highway on what looked like a completely desolate exit. He steered the truck to the side of the road and got out without another word.

April's heart thumped hard in her chest. There was no telling what he had planned next. Now that she'd called Jack, he could kill her and dump her body in the miles of wilderness around them. Or he could kill the other girls and leave their bodies to rot. He could rape them, separate them by giving them to other people . . . her mind spun with the possibilities, and none of them were good.

He wrenched open her door, making her cry out in surprise as her wrist was still connected to the handle. She almost fell onto the dirt-packed ground, and Ryan laughed again, as if her body being jerked around was the funniest thing he'd ever seen.

He grabbed her wrist in a grip so hard, April winced in pain. This man might not be tall, but he was still way stronger than she'd ever be. He unlocked the handcuff from around the door handle but left the other end around her wrist. Then he stared at her for a long moment.

April held her breath. This was it. She was going to die. Right here and now. Her only solace was that she'd been able to tell Jack she loved him one more time, during their call.

But instead of pulling out that damn gun of his and shooting her, Ryan pointed to the back door. "If you want that shit for your friends, get it now. You have ten seconds."

April was moving before he'd even stopped talking. She wanted those blankets. And food and water.

She threw two comforters over her shoulder and grabbed a pillow. She shoved a twelve-pack of water into the pillowcase and hugged it to her chest. Then she reached into the box again and picked up several plastic bags, draping them around her wrist and arm. She had a feeling it had already been more than ten seconds, so she was reluctantly grateful to Ryan for letting her grab as much as she did. Of course, he didn't bother to carry any of the stuff, just left her to shuffle along in front of him as he pushed her toward the back of the trailer.

As he used a small key to unlock the padlock on the door, once again April had a wild urge to drop everything and run. She could disappear into the woods around them and wait for someone else to stop so she could call for help. She could tell the police what the truck and trailer looked like. They could track down Ryan and rescue Carlise, June, and Marlowe.

But she wouldn't leave her friends to an uncertain fate. No way. They were in this together, and somehow, someway, they'd get through it.

The trailer door creaked as it opened, and April's heart sank at seeing her friends. They were huddled in the back corner of the space. Carlise and Marlowe had June between them, and they were all clutching each other as if they were sure they were about to die.

Anger once more swelled up inside April. Ryan was inhuman for what he was doing.

"Well?" he barked as he looked at her. "Get in!"

She moved then, awkwardly climbing back into the trailer and going to her knees to scoot toward her friends. The door slammed behind her, loud enough to make April's ears ring, and the darkness seemed even blacker now that she'd been out of the trailer for so long.

"It's okay," she said quietly. "I've got blankets. And food and water. We're going to be all right."

"Water?" June croaked.

April swallowed hard and nodded. No one could see her, so she forced herself to sound more cheerful than she felt. "Yes." She leaned over, and the pressure on her arm was immediately lessened as the bags came to rest on the floor of the trailer. The handcuff dangling from her wrist jingled as she reached into the pillowcase and pulled out three waters.

"There's only twelve bottles, so we need to conserve them as much as we can," she warned as she shuffled her way over to where she'd last seen her friends. She touched a foot first, then suddenly she was yanked into the huddle.

"We were so scared for you!" Carlise admitted.

"We thought maybe he was hurting you. That he'd killed you and was planning on doing the same to us. Are you okay?" Marlowe asked in a shaky voice.

"I'm all right," April reassured them. "I have a lot to tell you, but not yet. Drink," she said as she sat back, blinking away tears she was grateful her friends couldn't see. She felt overly emotional. She should feel better, since she'd been able to talk to Jack and give him some information and because they now had blankets to keep them warm and food and water to fill their bellies. But for some reason, after talking with Ryan, she was even more scared than she'd been before.

Whatever Ryan had planned, it wasn't good. Not for them, and not for their men. She trusted Jack and his team, but Ryan had obviously planned this revenge for a very long time. Revenge for what, she had no idea—but his goal was death. For all of them.

A hand brushed against hers, and she released the bottle of water she'd been gripping. The other two were taken from her, and she heard the crack of the plastic tops being opened.

April was thirsty herself. She'd only had a few ice cubes to tide her over, but she wasn't pregnant. Her friends needed the water more than she did.

"Oh my God, that's the best water I've ever had in my life," June exclaimed with a small laugh. "Even warm, I've never tasted anything better."

The others agreed, then Marlowe asked, "What in the world happened while you were out there?"

For some reason, April didn't want to talk about it yet. Didn't want to scare her friends more than they already were. "First, blankets. And I have a pillow! Only one, so we'll have to share, but it should make it a little more comfortable in here."

She scooted back toward the mound of supplies she'd brought and separated the blankets from the bags. She tried to fluff up the pathetic pillow Ryan had provided, refusing to think of where he'd gotten it and whose head might have been on it last.

She brought the items over to her friends, then she was rummaging blindly through the bags, trying to remember what she'd seen before looping the handles over her arm.

Her hand touched on something long and skinny and obviously metal. Excitement rose within her as she fumbled with the object for a moment before saying, "Everyone close your eyes for a second."

"What's the point? We can't see anything anyway," Carlise grumbled.

"I know, but trust me, do it," April cajoled.

She waited a beat, then clicked the small button on the side of the flashlight she'd found with the food. Immediately, a bright light filled the trailer, illuminating every dent in the metal, every piece of dirt on the floor, the bucket in the corner . . . and her three friends.

"Holy crap, is that what I think it is?" June asked. Her eyes were still scrunched closed, but it was obvious she and the others could see the change in light through their eyelids.

"Yes. It's really bright in here now, though, so open your eyes slowly," she warned.

Within a minute, all the girls were huddled around her, peering into the bags, exclaiming excitedly over the food. Crackers, meat sticks, potato chips, and other snacks. It looked like Ryan had raided a convenience store for the crap in the bags, but it was food, so no one was complaining.

"Wait," Carlise barked, startling everyone. "What did you have to do in order to get this stuff?" she asked. "And don't lie. Did he hurt you? Your eye is swollen." Her eyes suddenly widened in alarm. "And are those *handcuffs* on your wrist?"

April had hoped the food would distract everyone a little longer and give her more time to come up with something to tell them that wouldn't completely freak them out. But then again, these women were some of the strongest people she'd ever met. They'd already been to hell and back, and no matter how much she wanted to shield them, they deserved to know what Ryan had planned. Or at least what he'd told her.

"I'm okay," she reassured them quickly. "He cuffed me to the door, probably so I wouldn't try to jump out while he was driving. And mostly, Ryan just liked messing with me. Making me feel stupid. But I didn't have to do anything repulsive to get this stuff. Though I would have," she admitted. "I would've done just about anything he wanted if it meant ensuring you guys were more comfortable."

"No," June said with a scowl, obviously angry. "Absolutely not. And this goes for the rest of you too," she said as she eyed the other women. "No one willingly does *anything* that will get them hurt, physically or mentally, just to spare anyone else. That's how kidnappers operate. They use one person against another. Those bastards tried to do that with Cal and the guys when they were prisoners. He told me about it one night, after he'd had a nightmare. I know he didn't really want to, but I was hoping talking would help.

"He said the terrorists constantly said they'd stop hurting them if they gave up information. They'd told one of the guys they'd stop hurting Callum, specifically, if they outlined the details of their mission.

They tried to use the men's loyalty against them. We have to stay strong. Together. Got it?"

Everyone nodded, and for the first time April realized they *were* experiencing something akin to what their men had suffered, in some ways. Not nearly on the same level, as they weren't being beaten or carved up with knives, but the emotions were similar.

"Carlise is right. Your eye is swollen. Did he hit you?" Marlowe asked April.

She nodded. "Yeah. You know, I've seen countless movies where people are hit, and they shake it off and continue with whatever it was they were doing. But I have to say . . . it hurt. I literally couldn't breathe for a moment, and I couldn't have fought back if I'd wanted to," April admitted.

"Right?" June said. "That shit hurts!"

Before she knew it, Marlowe had moved next to her and wrapped an arm around her waist, June had moved to her other side and done the same, and Carlise had scooted forward so her knees were touching April's, and she lifted a hand to her face. Her fingers barely skimmed over the skin there, and she frowned as she examined her. "I wish we had some ice," she muttered.

April couldn't help but smile at that. "While we're wishing, I could use a Sprite," she whispered.

The others chuckled around her before the mood turned serious once more. "Talk to us," Carlise said urgently. "What happened, and don't leave anything out."

So April told her friends everything. About her feelings, what Ryan had said, every time he taunted her, about the phone call with Jack, about the leftover fries and hamburger . . . and her suspicions about what might happen when they arrived in Colorado.

"I tried to give Jack clues, but they were awful. There's no way he'll be able to make heads or tails of them. I'm not that good at thinking on my feet, and it's harder than you think to come up with anything useful when the pressure's on."

"I'm sure you did fine, and JJ and our guys are smart. They'll understand," Carlise soothed.

"Colorado is a long way away," June fretted. She had one hand on her belly and was staring off into space.

"We've only stopped for short periods of time since we started," April tried to reassure her. "Ryan's not messing around. He wants to get there as fast as he can."

"The cramps or contractions or whatever they are haven't stopped," June admitted. "They're getting stronger."

Fear almost overwhelmed April, but she locked it down. "Maybe you having that baby in here will gross Ryan out and make him think twice about what he's doing," she said lamely.

"No, it'll give him someone else to threaten," June said, a tear falling down her face. "And someone else to use to hurt Cal."

"Or maybe it'll give Cal more incentive to kill him," Carlise said firmly.

"Exactly. And I know you and Cal have already been considering names, but I'm thinking maybe Trail," Marlowe joked. "Short for Trailer."

June snorted.

"Or Truckee," Marlowe added.

"Maybe Royce . . . you know, after Cal's SUV," Carlise suggested with a grin.

"Cooper, Aston, Lincoln," Marlowe continued.

"Buck," Carlise said, motioning toward the bucket in the corner with her head.

June was giggling now. "Um, love you guys, but no. *Hell* no."

"Ford? I know—Cruz, since we're cruisin' down the road," April said, grateful that Marlowe had changed the mood in the trailer.

They continued to suggest names based on vehicles and on their situation.

When they seemed to run out of steam, June said quietly, "Maximilian. Max for short. We talked about it a little bit. It's a name that runs in Cal's family."

"It's awesome," April said sincerely.

"I love it," Marlowe told her.

"Max and Bax . . . they'll be brothers," Carlise said.

Everyone laughed. Baxter, the dog who'd saved Carlise from a snowstorm and led her to Chappy's cabin, was definitely always going to be the Chapmans' firstborn.

June took a deep breath, then turned to April. "So . . . he's taking us to Colorado. Then what? How will our guys find us? And what do you think he has planned for them?"

"I don't know, but I'm guessing he'll either let me call Jack again and tell him where we are, or he's got something else up his sleeve. As far as what he has planned . . . it won't be good."

"Then we'll have to do what we can to help," Marlowe said firmly. "We aren't helpless. Even if we're pregnant and not as strong as Ryan, there's four of us and one of him."

"We've been in tough spots before. We can outsmart this asshole," Carlise agreed.

"Maybe me having this baby *will* rattle him. He can order us to be quiet, but a newborn can't exactly be threatened into silence," June said.

April shivered. Babies couldn't be threatened, but they could be silenced . . . permanently. She made the decision right then and there: if June had her baby before they were rescued—and they *would* be rescued, she refused to think otherwise—she'd do whatever it took to keep Ryan from ever touching little Max.

"Right, so . . . for now, we need to get some calories in us, even if they're junk calories, get some rest, and wait for whatever happens next," April said firmly. "I suggest we spread one of the comforters on the floor to protect from the cold seeping through the metal, and use the other as a blanket. You three can probably fit under it together."

"What about you?" Carlise asked with a frown.

"I'll be okay. I'm not pregnant like the rest of you."

"Nope, not happening. We share," Marlowe said firmly. "We're pregnant, not invalids."

"I know, but . . . please," April begged. "I'll be okay. I'm not even cold." That was a small lie, but she didn't feel the least bit guilty about it. "I can snuggle up against whoever's on the end. How about that?"

It took a while, but finally the others agreed. After using the bucket once more and eating some of the junk food, they put June in the middle, Carlise against the side of the trailer, and Marlowe on the other side. April lay down in front of Marlowe and clicked off the flashlight. They knew they needed to preserve the batteries, but the dark made their situation feel that much more scary.

"They're coming," she whispered after a moment. "You should've heard Jack. He was so pissed, but controlled. They're going to find us, and it'll be okay. I know it."

The others murmured their agreement and fell silent, each lost in her own thoughts.

It was hard to believe that just that morning, April had been lying next to Jack, replete from his latest bout of lovemaking, warm and safe.

She'd be there again. She wouldn't allow herself to think otherwise.

CHAPTER EIGHTEEN

Two days later, JJ stood in the middle of the Pit . . . the bar-slash-pool-hall that Rex owned with his wife in Colorado Springs. It looked run down and like a dive from the outside, but inside was surprisingly clean and trendy. Pool tables were in a back room, spread far enough apart that people had plenty of room to play but close enough for the space to feel cozy. The bar was in the main room, where a jukebox stood in the corner.

But it was silent and empty now. Rex had closed it for the night so they could use the space for planning. The Mountain Mercenaries were all there—Gray, Ro, Arrow, Black, Ball, Meat, and, of course, Rex. Not only that, the Ace Security guys were also in attendance—Logan, Blake, Nathan, Ryder, and Cole.

The Silverstone team had arrived in town the day before, and Bull, Eagle, Smoke, and Gramps were ready and willing to do whatever was necessary to help.

In any other situation, JJ might have been overwhelmed by the amount of testosterone in the room. With the anger that simmered just beneath the surface. But right now, he gloried in it. Knowing he had so much experience and deadly skill behind him was reassuring.

As if it wasn't even a question, he'd found himself in the role of team leader. He was used to leading his small team of Delta operatives, so having nineteen pairs of eyes trained on him, waiting for his direction, would've been overwhelming. But because this was the most important mission of his life, he actually wished for twenty more men.

Rex was sitting at a large oval table in the back room, his focus alternating between JJ and the screen in front of him. He and Tex had been in constant communication and were doing what they could to track Ryan Johnson electronically.

They'd already found the three cell phones belonging to Carlise, Marlowe, and June. They had been wiped of any fingerprints and found in three different vehicles, and the owners had no idea the phones had even been in their cars. One was in the bed of a truck, another was under the passenger seat of a car, and the last had been found on the floorboard of a semi. It was likely Ryan had hidden them in the other vehicles while at a rest area or gas station.

They had to assume the fourth phone, which had stopped transmitting around Albany, was April's, but they hadn't actually found it. Tex had also done his best to track the number April had called from, but it was a burner and couldn't be traced.

Frustrated that the phones were a dead end, Tex switched his focus to Ryan Johnson. But because the name was so common and they had literally no details about the man, identifying him was turning out to be a near-impossible task.

Rex was working on locating the truck and trailer. They didn't have the make or model, or even the color, but because of the tire tracks behind Jack's Lumber, they knew it was a smaller pickup. Maybe a Toyota Tacoma or Ford Ranger. So Rex was looking through hours and hours of traffic cams on the interstates around Albany to see if he could spot any kind of truck with a trailer. Of course there were plenty, so he was pretty overwhelmed trying to narrow down the field.

The rest of the men were basically dead in the water without knowing exactly where the women were being taken. They'd gone over their respective skills—everything from marksmanship, explosives, engineering, interrogation, and negotiation to mountaineering and swimming. Collectively, they had all their bases covered for wherever Ryan might lead them . . . but for now, they could only wait. And it turned out none of them were big fans of waiting.

"Tell us about your women," Gray said into the tense silence.

Thinking about Carlise, Marlowe, June, and April, wondering what they might be enduring, was almost too painful to bear . . . but the men didn't hesitate to talk.

"June, Marlowe, and Carlise are all pregnant," Cal told the others. "But my wife, June, is closest to her due date. She actually told me the morning before they were taken that she felt funny. Not in a bad way, but she was sure our son would be making his appearance soon.

"June was shot by a man her stepmother hired to pretend to stalk her. He pocketed the money they gave him instead of actually doing any of the things he promised. I almost wish he hadn't, because then I would've been on alert. Could've protected her. Instead, he just entered her place of work one day and shot her. No warning. She almost died. It was the worst day of my life . . . until now. At least then I could sit with her, tell her I was there, that I loved her. I feel completely helpless."

"Do you have a name picked out?" Logan asked.

"Maximilian," Cal said. "It's a family name. Max for short."

"We're going to get June, and Max, back safely," Logan said in a rough tone. "My child was taken too, and trust me when I say I know what you're feeling. What you're all feeling," he said, looking at Chappy and Bob in turn.

"Marlowe was an archaeologist. She was arrested and sentenced to life in prison in Thailand after a coworker called in a bogus tip that she had drugs. Drugs he'd planted in her stuff. I broke her out of jail, we fled across Thailand into Cambodia, and she literally saved my life when I almost died because of a damn infection. We were married while on the run, and I swore to always protect her. I failed."

"Bullshit," Eagle said. He was one of the Silverstone guys. "If you were sitting at home twiddling your thumbs, you'd be failing her. You're here, doing everything you can to find her. That's not failing."

The men looked to Chappy next.

"Carlise got lost in a snowstorm, and with help from a stray dog, she found me and my cabin. Of course, I was so sick when she arrived, I

213

passed out on her for three days. But she was levelheaded and calm, and even without knowing the stove used gas and not electricity—which we didn't have because of the storm—she wasn't fazed."

He paused, then sighed before continuing. "She had a stalker who tracked her down and forced her to run straight into the path of an avalanche. She hid in an underground bunker, was buried alive until we could find her. She's strong . . . but this is too much to ask of her, of *any* of the women," Chappy said in a tortured tone.

"Your women sound a lot like ours," Meat said. "They're all survivors. They aren't going to wither away and die while waiting for you to find them. They're going to fight back with everything they have. And you know what? If we can't find them? They're still going to win. You know why?"

Chappy lifted a brow.

"Because they love you, and they'll fight to get back to you, just as you'll fight to get to them."

JJ nodded. He'd heard stories about a few of these men's wives. The things they'd survived had been horrific and would've broken most women. But they'd not only survived, they'd blossomed in the years since. They'd had children, made families, and gone on with their lives. Not as victims but as survivors.

"What about April?" Gramps asked. "She's the one who made the phone call, right?"

JJ nodded. "Yeah. She and I aren't married. She isn't pregnant. But I'd die for her without a single regret. I wanted her for years, but it took me way too long to get my head out of my ass. Took a car accident, some short-term amnesia, the fear she might choose her ex over me, and a frightened phone call in the middle of the night . . . but I finally got smart. The entire time I was fighting my attraction to her, it felt like I was dying inside. She's my everything. And without her, Jack's Lumber wouldn't exist today. We would've gone under. She's smart, loyal, funny, and so damn beautiful it makes my heart hurt to look at her. To know she's mine.

"I don't know who we pissed off to put my April in this situation, but they're going to die for touching her."

The room was silent for a beat before Rex pushed his chair back from the table and strode over to JJ. It wasn't obvious he'd been listening to the conversations going on around him, but apparently he had been.

He put a hand on JJ's shoulder. Rex was taller by a few inches and more muscular. He had a lot more silver in his hair and more wrinkles around his eyes. But the intense look on his face matched the emotion JJ had seen in his own mirror that morning.

"My wife was gone for ten years. Ten of the longest goddamn years of my life. But not once did I give up hope that she was out there somewhere. Finding her was a miracle. And lucky as shit. She was bent but not broken. Even after the hell she'd been through, she was still my Raven. We're going to find April and the rest of the women. We're going to make this Ryan guy pay. Mark my words, this is going to end sooner rather than later."

JJ nodded. He couldn't speak through the lump in his throat. He'd been operating on pure adrenaline for the last few days. Every minute that passed without knowing where the women had been taken ate at his soul. He didn't know what April was thinking, if she was hurt, if her kidnapper had tortured them.

The not knowing was almost worse than knowing what she was going through. Worse because of all the scenarios that flickered through his head. He'd seen enough death and destruction, and abuse against women, in his life that the thought of any of those things happening to April was agony.

And that's what Ryan wanted. JJ knew that down to his soul. The man hated him and his team for some reason and wanted them to suffer. He was playing a game with them, a game that would end with his long, slow death.

JJ didn't like killing. Never had. But ending Ryan Johnson was going to be a pleasure. A warning for anyone else stupid enough to use his woman to try to get to him.

Some people would look at him and just see a lumberjack, a backwoods hick who couldn't string two words together properly while he swung an axe—or rather, a chain saw—for a living, but after this was over, no one would doubt he was a man who could, and would, protect those he loved.

"Um, Rex, you might want to get over here," Bull said as he hovered over Rex's laptop. "Tex is trying to get a hold of you, and he's not being patient about it."

Rex hurried back to the table, followed closely by JJ and several of the other men. It was a tight squeeze, but JJ was quick to get a front-row seat to whatever was happening. Chappy and Cal elbowed in next to them, and Bob stood right behind them.

"Tex, I'm here, what's up?" Rex said, after clicking on the video-chat program.

Tex appeared on the screen. He stared at the camera and said, "April's phone pinged."

JJ froze. Every muscle in his body tensed. "Where?" he barked.

They'd thought her phone was gone. Destroyed, run over, thrown away, whatever. But apparently it was still part of Ryan's game. And the men standing in the Pit were more than ready to play.

Tex's gaze left the camera and went to the screens in front of him. They could hear his fingers clicking on the keys as he worked to pull up the information they all were desperate for.

"South of Bailey, Colorado. It's a small town west of Denver."

"Off 285, right?" Ryder asked.

"Yup. It's rugged out that way. Miles and miles of wilderness surrounded on all sides by Buffalo Peak, Green Mountain, Topaz Mountain, and North Tarryall Peak."

"Shit, if he's out there, it'll make finding him much harder," Smoke grumbled.

"Not necessarily," Arrow said. "No, there's not a lot out there, but that makes the people who live in the area very observant."

"So if there's anyone around who isn't supposed to be there, they'll know. Especially someone who isn't a local," Chappy mused.

"Exactly," Arrow said with a nod.

"And we can use drones and even a chopper to help search," Ball added.

"This asshole *wants* to be found," Bob growled. "He wants to lure us to his playing field."

"Where he feels he has the upper hand," Cal agreed.

"He's gonna be surprised when it's not just the four of you who come crawling out of the woods but all of us too," Gray said with a somewhat bloodthirsty smile.

"We can't show our hand, though," JJ warned. "If he realizes we're not alone, he could hurt the women. Or run and live to play this game another day."

"Not happening," Chappy said with a shake of his head.

"We know how to be stealthy," Bull told him. "We aren't going to screw this up for you."

"This guy's going down," Cole agreed.

"I've been doing tons of digging, and I might've found something else," Tex said.

All eyes went back to the screen.

"On a hunch, I hacked into the Social Security database and searched for any obvious red flags. Tax returns being filed for deceased people, or years where there was no activity on a number and then all of a sudden it's in use again, babies who have bank accounts, et cetera. Things like that. Guess what I found?"

When the pause dragged out, JJ growled in annoyance. They needed to get moving. Set up camp in Bailey and start looking from there. He didn't have time for Tex's guessing games.

Thankfully, Tex quickly went on, "Seven years ago, a two-year-old named Ryan Johnson drowned in the backyard pool of his home. But lo and behold, his Social Security number pinged on a credit report three years ago."

JJ's heart rate sped up as Tex continued.

"Looks as if the account was opened in New York City, with regular deposits coming from overseas . . . bouncing from Israel, Johannesburg, and Dubai."

JJ turned to meet Chappy's gaze, then Cal's.

"What if this has to do with our last mission," JJ said quietly. "Where we were POWs."

"What do any of those cities have to do with that?" Cal asked.

"I'm not sure. But terrorists always have connections. And if I was hell bent on revenge or making an escaped POW's life miserable, I might need to rely on others in my network helping to finance my plans."

"Wait, you think that particular mission is coming back to haunt us? Haven't we suffered enough?" Bob bit out.

JJ kept his gaze glued to his teammates as he racked his brain, trying to figure out who this Ryan Johnson could be. "The rescue teams killed all of our captors, didn't they?"

"That's what we were told," Cal agreed.

"But could they really have gotten them all?" Chappy asked.

"We all know how terrorist cells work. There are layers and layers. Those on top don't get their hands dirty, and they order the people lower on the totem pole to do the frontline work," Cal agreed.

"Well, in this case, *all* of you are right," Tex went on.

Looking back at the screen, JJ saw a satisfied smirk on Tex's face. "From the classified documents I've been able to dig up on that rescue mission, the teams that went in cleaned up extremely well. And after you left, the Army concentrated on that area for several months. There were additional missions to hunt down and eradicate every member of that especially nasty group."

When he paused, JJ asked impatiently. "So . . . ? This isn't related?"

"I didn't say that. And funny you should use that word," Tex replied. "Related. *Relatives.* Our government had no problem taking out the people they knew were terrorists . . . but they didn't kill their family members."

JJ blinked. "Ryan's related to one of our captors?"

"Bingo," Tex said with a nod. "That's my best theory, at least. It's been nearly six years since you were POWs. Ryan Johnson didn't appear on the radar until three years ago. From what I've been able to dig up on the person using infant Ryan Johnson's Social Security number, he's male, twenty years old, has signed rental agreements—two where credit checks were completed, in both New York and Denver. In the last year, he gave up the New York apartment but continued to use the bank account there. He's got charges from motels, rental-car agencies, and an ongoing charge for an online porn site."

JJ swallowed hard. He wished Tex would hurry up and get to the fucking point. Despite that, he was soaking up every scrap of information in morbid fascination.

"To hurry this along," Tex said as if he could sense the impatience of his audience, "if our Ryan Johnson is twenty, that means he was in his early teens when you were POWs. That's a good age to be influenced by outside forces. And if he had a male relative who happened to be one of your captors, and that man was killed, Ryan certainly could've felt a deep sense of hatred for the men he decided were responsible.

"I know it sounds warped and fucked up, but it's possible he blamed the four of you for his relative's death. Forget about the fact that his brother or father or uncle, whoever, made the decision to become a terrorist and was torturing innocent men. That wouldn't matter to our kidnapper. The hatred probably festered, and if more of his neighbors and friends were killed in the following months with the Army's crackdown, he probably made plans.

"Plans that included getting money from the terrorist network, learning English, moving to New York, getting an illegal Social Security number, and learning to blend in. For whatever reason, he decided the mountains of Colorado would be where he made his stand and exacted his revenge on the four of you."

It was an outlandish and improbable story. But if Tex had done the research . . . it was most likely true.

"So what will we be walking into?" Gray asked.

JJ forced himself to concentrate. He should've been the one to ask that question.

"Nothing good," Tex said with a worried frown. "The terrorists who held you guys captive were an offshoot of a much larger group, but still well funded. They were also experts in IEDs and other explosives."

JJ pressed his lips together. *Shit.*

"There's no telling what our Ryan has come up with, but if he's using the women as bait, he's confident in whatever he's prepared. Booby traps, IEDs, pits with spikes at the bottom . . . it could be anything."

"Stop calling him 'our Ryan'!" Chappy said in a ferocious tone. "He's not *our fucking Ryan.*"

"Sorry," Tex said immediately. "You're right. All I'm saying is . . . you need to be careful. All of you. I haven't spent my life watching over you and yours to lose you now."

"You aren't losing anyone," Rex said gruffly. "We're smarter than this kid. He doesn't know who he's dealing with. He might get lucky and outmaneuver Chappy, Bob, JJ, and Cal, only because they'll be concentrating on their women. But with the Mountain Mercenaries, Ace Security, and Silverstone at their backs? He's as good as dead."

Tex nodded. "I'll be watching," he said unnecessarily. "If you need anything, you call. Hear me? I've got teams of SEALs and Delta Force men I can get there in hours if need be. And there's a group of men not far from you, in northern New Mexico, who are former Special Forces as well. No one messes with our women and lives. Over and out."

The screen went blank, and the room was silent for a moment as everyone digested what they'd just learned.

JJ turned to the others. "No matter what happens, I'll never forget that you all dropped everything to join us."

"No," Gray said with a shake of his head.

Rex nodded in agreement, as did everyone in the room.

"You're us, and we're you. We've been where you are, and there are no markers taken or given today. We're doing the right thing. The thing we've been trained to do. Protect others. Keep evil from winning. No thanking us. Ever."

JJ felt overwhelmed, and he knew his team probably did too. This was why they'd joined the Army. The camaraderie. The teamwork. They were a part of a huge family network and hadn't really appreciated it. Not completely.

"Let's go get your women," Nathan said quietly. He hadn't said much up to this point, but he was just as invested as everyone else. It was easy to see.

They all headed for the door, and JJ realized he and his team were hanging behind.

"Are you guys all right?" he asked softly.

"No," they all said at the same time.

Chappy added, "But we will be. I honestly wasn't sure we would find them. But now? I have no doubt."

"Same," Bob said with a nod.

"I'm not doing so good," Cal said, taking a deep breath. "But I trust you guys and our new teammates with not only my life but June and Max's as well."

"We're going to get our women home," JJ said firmly. "They may not like how we lock them in our houses and never let them outside on their own again . . . but we're getting them home."

The others chuckled, but they understood what he meant. If their women thought they had protective husbands before, they hadn't seen anything yet.

"Come on. We've got a terrorist to track down," JJ said.

He'd said those words many times over the years, but never had they felt as heavy as they did today.

The four men followed the others out of the Pit and to their vehicles. They needed to get to Bailey and find their women.

CHAPTER NINETEEN

The trailer had stopped and started so many times, April and the others barely even noticed it much anymore. They had no idea if Ryan was screwing with their heads with so many stops. No clue how much time had passed since April had been taken out of the trailer, then returned with the food and blankets.

By April's estimation, it had been at least two days. They were out of water once more, and the food that was left held no appeal. The women were exhausted, cold, and scared out of their minds.

But none of that really mattered—because June was definitely in labor. Her contractions had increased in intensity and number, and there was no denying that baby Max was determined to come into the world, whether they were ready or not.

"Breathe, June. That's it. You're doing so good," April said from behind her. She was leaning against the side of the trailer with June using her as a backrest. Carlise was next to her, holding one of her hands in a death grip, and Marlowe was kneeling between her legs, occasionally checking to see how far along she was.

Thank goodness they had the flashlight. Without it, this experience would be utterly terrifying and far more difficult than it was already.

No one was prepared for the trailer door to open. The sun wasn't shining. The overcast day looked extremely gloomy and depressing.

"Out," Ryan ordered.

"June can't walk. She's having her baby!" April barked, way more harshly than she might've if she wasn't so worried about her friend.

"If she doesn't walk, I'll shoot her right now," Ryan said, lifting his hand and pointing that fucking gun right at June's midsection.

April had a few choice words for the man she hated more than she could remember hating anyone in her entire life. She was hungry, stressed, thirsty, sick of peeing in a bucket, and so freaking worried about June having her baby in such unsanitary, remote, and unsafe conditions.

"Please! June needs a doctor. She's in labor," April tried again.

"I don't care. No, strike that. I *do* care. I'm glad. It makes everything about my plan even better. I bet Prettymon will be reduced to a sniveling child when he learns what's happening. Get out. *Now!*"

April turned to her friends, trying to ignore the man still holding the weapon pointed at June. "Girls . . . let's do this. Marlowe, you scoot down to the end first. Carlise, you help hold June up. I'll get her to the opening, and we'll all help her walk."

No one moved.

"Please, Marlowe," April whispered.

"We've got this," June said weakly, surprising April. "Just think of the story I'll have for Max."

"Right, okay," Carlise said as she lowered the blanket back over June's lap. It was the only usable blanket they had left. When June's water broke, they'd used the other one to soak up the liquid, and it was currently under her.

Ryan had watched without comment as they'd had their discussion, and now he took a step back as Marlowe scooted toward him and slowly got out of the trailer. She swayed on her feet, and a look of pain crossed her face as she stood fully upright for the first time in days.

Carlise held June as she helped her move toward the opening. April hovered behind them with a hand on June's back and one on Carlise's arm.

When all four of them were standing behind the trailer, April looked around. All she could see were trees. The truck and trailer were backed up near a dilapidated cabin. There were no other houses in sight, and only the sound of the wind in the trees and the occasional bird.

Surprisingly, they were quite a distance from the cabin. Maybe about thirty yards, despite a trail leading right beside it, easily wide enough for the truck. April figured it was Ryan's petty way of torturing them just a little more.

"Here's what's going to happen," he said as if he was talking about the weather and not pointing a gun in their faces and threatening all of them. "You're going to walk in a straight line toward the door. If you take one step to the left or the right . . . let's just say getting shot will be the least of your worries."

April tilted her head as she studied him, even as a sick feeling made her stomach cramp. "Why?" she blurted before she thought better of it.

"Glad you asked," Ryan said gleefully. "Because every inch of the ground around that cabin is rigged with explosives. Trip wires, IEDs, land mines . . . you name it, it's there. If you don't walk exactly where I tell you, if you lose your balance, if you try to run . . . KABOOM!" he yelled.

All four women jerked in fright at his exclamation.

"So *you*," he said, jabbing his gun in June's direction. "You'll walk, by yourself, or you and that brat will die. There will be arms and legs raining down like confetti. How do you think your precious prince will like *that*?"

April felt June shaking. But she couldn't have been more proud of her when she straightened her spine and said, "I think Cal is gonna kill you slowly and painfully, until you're begging him to put you out of your misery." Her menacing tone was even more impressive, knowing how much pain she was in.

Instead of getting mad or looking concerned, Ryan simply laughed. "The only ones begging will be the soldiers. Now get going. Time is ticking."

Despite knowing she and the others were bait, April had still prayed that Jack and the guys would find them. That they'd figure out her lame clues and swoop in like the heroes they were. Now, for the first time, she actually didn't *want* to be found.

She had no idea if Ryan was lying about the explosives or not, but it was obvious he had something horrible planned. Whatever sick game he was playing, the women weren't his focus. He'd used them, and would continue to use them, to hurt the guys.

She wouldn't let that happen. She didn't know what she could do to prevent it, but she'd rather die herself than sit back and watch Jack walk into an ambush.

"See those pink circles on the ground?" Ryan asked as he motioned toward the cabin with his head.

April and the others turned to see what he was talking about. Sure enough, there were circles on the ground, about two inches wide, bright pink, leading from the back of the trailer to the front door of the cabin.

"If you step precisely on each of those, you won't blow up. But if you miss, or try to be a hero and run, you'll die. There are explosives to each side and *between* the marks. And to show you that I'm not bluffing, that I've rigged this entire area with enough charges to blow up anyone and anything that steps in the wrong place, let me give you a little demonstration."

April held her breath as Ryan bent down to pick up a fairly large rock on the ground. For the third time, she wanted desperately to run. She was the only one who had even a remote chance of outrunning this asshole. But she wouldn't. Because Ryan would shoot her, or shoot one of the women out of spite.

And it didn't look as if anything was in the immediate area. She'd probably have to go miles to find help, and she wasn't exactly a good outdoorswoman. Oh, she could camp, and didn't mind hiking, but cutting through the woods without a trail and with no idea where she was or where she was going didn't sound like the smartest idea.

Not to mention, June was having a baby. She needed all the help and support she could get.

Ryan grinned at them before he heaved the rock to their right.

All four women let out various sounds of shock and fright when the rock landed near the tree line to their right—and the earth around it immediately exploded with a loud and scary boom.

Ryan laughed maniacally. "And that was a small charge," he told them. "Not enough to set off the others . . . but just think what that could do to a leg or foot. It would blow it clean off, that's what! There would be blood and guts everywhere."

April turned her back on the rocks and dirt still settling and stared at the pink circles on the ground. As he'd said, they were in a straight line to the cabin door.

She had the terrifying thought that maybe Ryan was messing with them, that the pink circles actually represented bombs, and as soon as they stepped on one, they'd be blown to bits.

So she blurted, "I'll go first."

Ryan chuckled. "So noble. And such a fucking martyr. Go right ahead."

She wanted to reach back and grab hold of Marlowe's hand, but if she was about to die, she didn't want any of the others to be anywhere close to her.

Taking a deep breath, she walked toward the first circle. Her mind cataloged everything about those pink marks, embedding every detail into her consciousness. She counted her steps—it was eight from the back of the trailer, which was backed up precisely between two large trees—to the first circle.

Her gaze shot up, and she paused just long enough to quickly count the pink marks. Twenty-five, each an average step apart.

Her gaze lifted to the cabin, then went back to the circles. There was very little grass around the circles Ryan had placed on the ground. The soil was also loose and uneven, as if the ground all around the cabin had been dug up . . . probably to bury the explosives, just as he'd claimed.

With her gut roiling, April fully understood how meticulously Ryan had planned everything. It had to have taken him months. She turned her head and looked back at their kidnapper, the truck, and trailer. "How long did this take you?" she blurted.

He smiled and looked pleased at her question. "Years," he said with a shrug. "Although the last few weeks have been the most fun. Watching my targets. Fucking with them . . . and you."

"In what way?" April asked, curiosity getting the better of her.

"Well, first was your accident. The amnesia was a bonus. I was going to fuck with your tires when you got to that ski resort so you'd have an accident on the way back, but the moose did all the hard work for me."

"You were there?" Carlise asked in shock.

"Yes. I watched her car flip, then left her to suffer," Ryan said without any trace of remorse.

"Oh my God," Marlowe gasped.

"And the spider? The nails in the tires? The box falling off the shelf? All me," Ryan boasted. "I wanted to scare you but not necessarily kill you. That would take all the fun out of my plan. Besides . . . I didn't want to alarm the soldiers. I needed them unsuspecting. And it worked." Ryan cackled in glee.

"Why?" Marlowe whispered.

"Because they killed my brother!" Ryan screamed abruptly, his face a sudden mask of rage, making April and the rest of the women jump in surprise.

"When they were rescued, my brother and his friends were slaughtered. They didn't stand a chance. And it's all *their* fault!"

April's mind spun. Jack didn't like to talk about his time as a POW, but he'd told her a little bit about that awful experience. How helpless he'd felt when they sliced into Cal's body. How they all had to watch each other get tortured over and over. About the rock paper scissors game that decided their move to Maine and the decision to start Jack's Lumber. How weak they all were when they were finally rescued. How frustrated he was that he couldn't help the Navy SEAL and Delta Force teams take out the terrorists.

"But they didn't kill anyone," April couldn't stop herself from saying. "They were too injured. All they could do was lie there and listen to the fighting around them."

Ryan stalked toward her. Before she could do more than blink, he backhanded her.

She fell to the ground with a hard thump, actually surprised when she didn't set off any explosives. Ryan leaned down and jerked her up by her shirt. April heard some of the seams tear, but she grabbed his wrist and otherwise stayed as limp as she could.

He held the gun to her head, and his voice trembled as he spoke.

"My brother was my entire world. The only person who gave a shit about me! We were poor. So fucking poor, we sometimes added dirt to our soup to thicken it. He always gave me the bigger portions, made sure I had clothes on my back, and he was trying to build us a better life. And if it wasn't for Jackson fucking Justice and his three friends, he'd still be alive today! He has to *pay*. Has to lose the thing he loves most in this world. As do the others. You and your friends are gonna die. Mark my words—your men will feel their hearts bleed just as I did that day."

April's mouth had gone dry as dust. She didn't dare breathe. Didn't move. All she could do was pray his hand shaking in rage didn't make him accidentally squeeze the trigger of the gun pressed against her temple.

She didn't want to die. Not today, and definitely not at this psycho's hands. But she was oddly satisfied to finally understand why they were there. He couldn't have been more than a young teenager when his brother was killed. Young enough to have trouble coping, to let anger fester inside him.

Ryan glared at her for a moment longer before shoving her away from him. Once again, April fell to the ground. Her face throbbed where he'd hit her, but she didn't dare take her gaze from him or even reach up to touch her cheek.

"Get up," he said, before spitting on her.

His spittle landed on her jeans, but April ignored it. She slowly got to her feet, not wanting to make any quick moves around their captor. He was on edge, and she didn't want to test his control any more than she had already.

"Walk, bitch. And make every step count . . . or don't. I don't give a shit."

Very slowly and carefully, April turned and stepped on the first pink circle.

When nothing happened, when she didn't blow up, she released the breath she hadn't known she was holding . . . and took another step. Even though it was cold outside, a bead of sweat rolled down her temple. She ignored it as she concentrated on stepping on each of those damn pink circles.

She was vaguely aware of some of her friends starting their journey toward the cabin behind her, but she kept her eyes trained on the ground. She counted the circles as she went. Fifteen, sixteen, seventeen. They seemed to go on forever. Twenty-three, twenty-four, twenty-five . . .

She'd arrived at the single doorstep of the cabin. She reached for the doorknob and turned it, pulling the door open. It almost knocked her off her feet as it swung toward her. The inside of the cabin looked just as bad as the outside. The floorboards were broken in places and covered in dirt and debris. Looking up, she saw a small hole in the roof in one corner, and a mouse scurried away into another hole in the floor.

Her nose wrinkled in disgust, but she was honestly surprised to also see two plastic tubs in the room. She could see water bottles and cans of food inside one of them.

The sound of someone swearing behind her made April turn. She held her breath as Marlowe neared. She had her arms out to her sides for balance and was biting her lip as she did her best to step exactly on the pink circles. When she got close enough, April reached out and grabbed her wrist, pulling her into the relative safety of the cabin.

The two watched June's every step as she slowly and painfully made her way toward them. She stopped after every other circle to pant. One hand was on her belly, and she had a look of agony on her face.

"That's it, June. Slow and steady. You're doing great," April encouraged softly.

"You're almost here. You've got this," Marlowe added.

April's gaze went past her friend to Carlise, who was currently still standing next to the trailer. For a moment, she was afraid Ryan was going to snatch her up and drive off with her or something. They seemed to be having a very intense conversation, with Ryan doing most of the talking. But then their kidnapper handed something to her and shoved Carlise toward the circles.

April's gaze once more swept the area carefully. She studied where the pink circles were in relation to the trees and other landmarks. She supposed somewhere in the recesses of her brain, she was trying to memorize where to step in case they needed to flee from the cabin. She wasn't sure what Ryan was going to do once they were inside, but if he left them alone, she was sure as hell going to make a run for it . . . miles of wilderness be damned.

Marlowe grabbed June as soon as she got close, and April helped her mostly carry June into the cabin. They got her to the floor in one of the few unbroken places, then April turned back to the door. Carlise had arrived while they'd been moving June, but to April's surprise, Ryan was also closing in. He walked much faster than they had, obviously sure about the placement of his explosives.

When he neared the door, April instinctively backed away, grabbing Carlise's arm as she went. They stood between June and Marlowe and their kidnapper. But Ryan didn't say a word, simply slammed the door shut.

It felt as if the entire cabin shook when the door closed—but it was the sound of hammering that surprised April.

"Stay here," she ordered Carlise as she crept toward the door. There was a hole in the door about waist high, and she leaned over to peer through it. She could see Ryan's hips, and that was about it. But it was clear what he was doing. April had seen the long boards propped up next to the cabin when she'd approached but had been too busy worrying about where she was putting her feet to do more than absently note their presence.

Without thought, she reached for the door and tried to push it open. As expected, the boards Ryan was hammering across the doorway kept it from opening.

She heard him chuckling from the other side. "Don't want my little birdies fleeing their cage," he told her as he continued to hammer. "And don't bother trying to get out any other way, because, remember . . . explosives," Ryan said. "They're all around the cabin. There's nowhere you can go to escape. So just sit tight and relax. I'm sure the soldiers will be here soon. No matter what you tell them, they aren't going to survive.

"And when I detonate the huge bomb I've put under the cabin and they realize all their efforts have been wasted and you are dead anyway—including the new brat, if you've managed not to kill it—I'll end them too. I'd say it was nice knowing you, but I'd be lying," Ryan finished.

He pounded on the boards for a few more minutes before silence filled the cabin.

April risked peeking through the hole in the door, devastated when she saw Ryan walking away from the cabin—picking up the pink circles as he went. He even had a small hand rake, which he used to carefully brush away the footprints from their trek to the cabin, leaving the path looking almost the same as its surroundings.

"April?" Carlise said tentatively.

Wanting to cry, but forcing the tears back since crying wouldn't help their situation, April turned.

Carlise was still standing in front of Marlowe, who was kneeling on the floor holding June's hand. They were both staring at her with wide eyes, as if waiting for her to tell them what to do. As if she could magically save them from this messed-up situation.

"Are you all right?" Carlise asked. "He hit you pretty hard."

"I'm okay," April said, even though her cheek throbbed and she could still feel the barrel of that gun against her temple.

"He told me to give this to you," Carlise said, holding something toward her.

Looking down, April blinked in disbelief. "That's my phone," she whispered.

"I know. He was adamant that I give it to you as soon as we got in here. I'm sure it's part of his game."

April nodded. She was sure too. Ryan hadn't done anything without a good reason. The food, letting her call Jack while they were on the road, the pink circles. Everything had been devised down to the smallest detail.

This was just another part of his master plan, but April couldn't have stopped herself from reaching for the phone in Carlise's hand if her life depended on it. And the shitty thing was, it probably did.

She expected this to be another trick. For the battery to have been removed or the phone to have very little charge. To her surprise, the cell looked exactly as it had when she'd last seen it. She unlocked it with her thumb, and the main screen appeared, the battery still three-quarters charged. He'd either plugged it in at some point or it had been off for most of the drive.

The latter guess clicked in April's brain. Yes. He'd turned it off so it couldn't be traced, but now that he had his bait where he wanted it, he'd turned it back on and didn't care if she called Jack, because he needed the guys to come. *Wanted* them to race in like the honorable men they were.

For a second, she wanted to turn off the phone again, bury it. Anything to keep Jack from coming here to save them. But it was too late. Ryan had already turned it on, and if she knew Jack and his friends like she thought she did, they'd already picked up their location. *Not* calling Jack would be stupid at this point. She needed to warn him. Tell him about the explosives.

Again, she had no doubt that was all part of Ryan's plan. He wanted them to know everything, because she had a feeling it would make killing them all the more satisfying.

June let out a half groan, half scream, taking April's attention away from the phone. Turning, she saw her friend grimacing, tears streaming down her face.

Her own pain disappeared in a flash. April glanced to Carlise. "Check those bins in the corner, see what we've got. Marlowe, get behind June to support her back, like I was before. June, you're doing great. We're going to be fine."

"How . . . can . . . you . . . say . . . that?" June asked between breaths.

"Because compared to what we've already been through, this is child's play. We have a roof over our heads, that asshole is gone, and we've got each other. And women have been giving birth like this, with nothing but their friends around them, for thousands of years. Piece of cake."

"Easy . . . for . . . you . . . to say . . . ," June said with a small grin.

April went over to June and knelt down. She grabbed one of her hands and squeezed hard. "I promise you, June, you're going to see Cal again. And when you do, you'll get to introduce him to his son. His healthy and beautiful baby, Max. Prince Maximilian, heir to the Liechtenstein throne."

June laughed, but it turned into a grimace as she bore down as another contraction hit. When it passed, she looked up at April. "Max doesn't have a chance in hell of being king."

"Doesn't matter, he's still royalty, and so are you." April leaned down and got into June's face. "Whatever happens, don't you give up. Understand? You fight. For Max. For Cal. For us. For *you*."

June took a deep breath, and the look of determination that came over her made April relax a fraction. "I won't."

"Good." April turned to the other two women. "You guys either. We're gonna get through this. Ryan won't win. *Love* wins. Always."

Carlise and Marlowe nodded.

"What did you find?" April asked Carlise.

She turned back to the plastic tub she'd been poking through and pulled out a sheet and a cheap, threadbare blanket.

"Perfect," April said as if she'd shown her a fully loaded first aid kit. "Bring the blanket over, and we'll put it under June." She took the sheet from Carlise and wondered how they could cut it up to use as swaddling for Max and to clean him.

"There's also water and some cans of tuna, green beans, and some other veggies," Carlise said.

"Please tell me there's a can opener too," Marlowe said dryly. "I wouldn't put it past that jerk to give us food but no way to open it."

Everyone laughed a little at that. It was a good way to release some of the tension that was thick in the room.

"Right? But they're pop-tops, so no can opener needed," Carlise said.

"I think we could all use some water right about now. You too, June. Even if you don't feel like it, you and Max need it," April said firmly.

June nodded, and soon they were all gulping down the water, trying to slake their thirst. April wanted nothing more than to sit and snarf down one of the cans of food, but there wasn't time. Not only was June going to have her baby sooner rather than later, but she needed to call Jack.

It was weird to want to hear his voice so badly while dreading it at the same time. Ryan was out there waiting and watching, and she hated to do anything that might play right into his plan. But hearing Jack's voice would go a long way toward soothing her nerves. And the others needed to talk to their husbands as well. They all needed the boost.

After checking on how far June's labor had progressed and feeling slightly alarmed that she seemed to be way more dilated than the last time she'd checked while in the trailer, April knew she'd run out of time. She needed to talk to Jack, warn him, tell him everything she knew. The sooner she did, the sooner they could get out of here.

CHAPTER TWENTY

"JJ, get over here! April's phone was turned back on," Rex said urgently.

The entire team—minus Eagle, Cole, and Meat, who were up in a helicopter searching from the sky for any sign of where Ryan might've holed up—was just south of Bailey, Colorado, in a cabin that Tex had procured for their use. They were antsy and amped up, waiting for the smallest clue as to where to start looking for the man who'd kidnapped the women.

Since April's phone last pinged, they hadn't had any further indicators. While they thought Ryan might've gone into the mountains, they didn't have a good place to start looking, as the wilderness stretched for hundreds of miles in every direction.

"Where?" JJ asked impatiently as he watched Rex click on his keyboard. "Here in Bailey?"

"No, a tower about twenty miles south of us. There are a few towers between here and there, but her phone is pinging off the last one before cell service is lost because of the mountains," Rex said. He pulled up a map and turned his computer toward the other men, who'd quickly gathered around him. He pointed at a spot on the map that was literally completely green.

"Let's go," JJ said, standing up straight.

"Hold on," Gray said urgently with a shake of his head. "We need a plan. We can't just rush into the jungle like greenhorns."

"Our women have been gone for three days!" Chappy snapped. "Probably scared out of their minds. We need to go get them *now!*"

"I know, but seriously, we've lived in Colorado for years. There's nothing out there but steep ravines that're easy to fall into and tons of wilderness. As far as we've been able to find out, there aren't even any trails."

"He had to have gotten them there somehow," Bob said. "He couldn't have force marched three pregnant women through the wilderness."

"Good point," Blake said.

"Let's get in touch with the guys in the helo and let them know. They can tell us what they see from the air," Ro suggested.

"And while we're waiting, we can head in that direction. Go as far as we can in the vehicles before we need to hike," Smoke agreed.

"The more I think about Bob's point, the more I agree," Cal said. "There's no way June could hike very far in her condition. And I'm guessing none of the women have proper shoes on to be walking around the forest."

"You think this asshole cares about any of that?" JJ asked.

"No. But he has a plan. And if he's too far off the beaten path, he wouldn't be able to execute said plan as well."

JJ's head spun. Cal and Bob were both right. They were thinking much clearer than he was. He needed to start behaving like a Delta, a team leader, and less like a man who was desperately worried about the woman he loved.

"Right. So turning the phone on wasn't a mistake," JJ said. "He turned it on wanting us to know where he is."

"Definitely," Chappy said with a nod.

"Call it," Rex ordered. "The phone. See if you can talk to this Ryan guy. See what he wants."

JJ immediately reached for the phone in his back pocket—and it scared the shit out of him when it started vibrating in his hand before he could even unlock it.

Looking down, he saw April's name on the screen.

Adrenaline shot through his system as he took a deep breath. He activated the recording app before answering the call.

"Justice here," he barked.

"Jack? It's me."

The sound of April's voice nearly brought him to his knees. As it was, he sank into the chair someone shoved at him.

"Are you all right? Are you hurt?"

"We're okay. But Jack, I need to tell you—"

He interrupted her, wanting to make sure she was truly all right before going any further. "No, love, *are you all right?* Did he touch you? Hurt you? It's been three days . . . I . . ." His voice cracked, and JJ did his best to gain control. "Talk to me, sweetheart."

"I'm okay. We were in the trailer for nearly all of that time. He took me out just once to let me call you, but we've all been in the trailer since. We had some food and water. It wasn't until we stopped for the last time that we even saw him again."

"Did he touch you?"

April hesitated—and a red haze fell over JJ's vision. He didn't need to hear the words. He knew the asshole had put his hands on his woman.

"I'm okay," she insisted. "But you need to listen. Please!"

"He's dead," JJ told her. "I told you what would happen to anyone who dared put their hands on you."

"Fine, Jack, but can you shut up and listen to me already!?"

JJ heard someone snicker, and remarkably, his own lips twitched. His April was fierce. And he couldn't love her more. "Sorry. I'm listening."

"Right, so he drove a black pickup. A smaller one. I'm sorry, I don't know what kind it was or the license plate, but he had a white trailer hooked to it, one that opened in the back. He had it locked while we were in there, so we couldn't get out. We didn't stop much, and never for longer than it might take to get gas, so I think he's probably loopy from lack of sleep. I didn't see anyone he might be working with, only him."

Rex's fingers were flying over his keyboard, typing all the information April was giving them, either to pass it on to someone or so they could review it without replaying the recording.

"That's good," he told her.

"Yeah, but it's not," she went on. "We're in a cabin. I have no idea where. There are trees all around it, and he nailed the door shut, so we can't get out."

"What about windows? Can you get out that way?" JJ asked, interrupting her.

"There are two, but they've got boards over them as well. I'm guessing he probably nailed them up before we got here."

"What about peeling up the floorboards?" he asked.

"Jack!" she exclaimed in irritation.

"What?"

"We can't get out," she said firmly. "One, because June is having her baby. Like, *right now*. And secondly, because he told us he's surrounded the place with explosives."

The room around JJ was so silent, he could hear the blood rushing in his ears. "What?"

"Bombs. IEDs. Things that go boom. We had to walk on a very specific path to even get to the cabin. He'd marked it with pink circles, but he picked them up after he nailed the door shut. And that's not all," April said.

"What else?" JJ asked, his mind churning, trying to come up with a plan to rescue April and the others.

"He said he put a big bomb under the cabin itself," she admitted, her voice quiet now. "That he would blow it up if you guys got anywhere close."

"*Fuck!*" someone said behind him.

"He could be bluffing," JJ said almost desperately.

"I know. But he did throw a rock to prove that he wasn't lying about the stuff around the cabin," April said. "The rock wasn't even very big, and it still detonated something in the ground."

"All right. What else?" JJ didn't feel like himself. He felt as if he were floating, watching himself talk on the phone from high above.

"He blames you guys for the death of his brother in the raid, when you were rescued. I tried to tell him that you guys couldn't have killed him because you were in no shape to do much at all, given how badly you were tortured, but he kind of lost it and wouldn't listen. He's been planning this for years," April told him urgently. "He wants you to watch *us* die, then he plans to kill you."

JJ wasn't surprised at her words. He and the others had already pretty much decided that whoever this Ryan person was, he had to be connected to one of their missions, and Tex had hit the nail on the head with the male-relative scenario. Irrationally, he thought it was unfair that it turned out to be something they hadn't even done themselves, but that didn't matter.

"That's not going to happen."

"I'm scared," April admitted in a barely there whisper.

"I know, but you're doing so good," JJ soothed. "How'd you get your phone back?"

"He gave it to me," she admitted. "He wanted me to call and warn you."

JJ's back straightened. Whoever Ryan was, he was conceited as hell, and it would be his downfall.

"I didn't want to call," April admitted, voice shaking now. "I didn't want to lure you to your death."

"No one's dying," he told her firmly. "Trust me."

"I do."

"Good." He heard one of the other women speaking in the background, and then April said, "The others need to talk to their husbands."

JJ didn't want to hand his phone over, but his friends deserved to talk to their wives. "Okay, but don't hang up when they're done. Come back to me."

"I will."

When JJ heard Marlowe's voice on the other end of the line, he handed his phone to Bob.

He tuned out his friend as he tried to figure out how to manage this impossible situation.

"You think he's still there?" Gray asked quietly from next to him.

"Absolutely. He's desperate for revenge. He's gonna want to see his hard work and plans to fruition."

"I agree," Gramps said.

"But . . . he still doesn't know about us," Black said with a small grin.

"That's right," Nathan agreed. "He's expecting the four of you, and that's it. Maybe some local cops or something. He's not expecting sixteen additional well-trained men . . . I mean, I'm not exactly in the same league as most of you, but I can hold my own," the tall, almost nerdy-looking man said with a shrug.

"Stop, Nathan," Blake scolded. "I'd choose you over any ole former SEAL."

"Hey, careful," Black bitched.

JJ let them blow off steam with their banter for a moment before getting serious. "You're right, Nathan. You guys are our best advantage. Chappy, Cal, Bob, and I can go in, make sure his attention is on us, before you take him out."

"You don't want to be the one who ends him?" Bull asked with a raised eyebrow.

"I don't give a fuck about him now. He's nothing. A coward who's deflecting blame for his brother's actions onto us. Hear me clearly—all I care about is my woman's life. And Carlise, Marlowe, and June. They're my priority. As long as they're safe, I don't give a shit who kills Ryan. I just want him gone."

Everyone around him nodded in satisfaction.

"I'm thinking we can take out this asshole without too much issue, especially since he's not expecting us, but how are we getting to the women?" Smoke asked.

"Before he's able to blow the cabin—that is, if it's even on a remote," Ball said.

"It could be on a timer," Ryder agreed.

"If that's the case, we need to stop messing around and get to that cabin," Bull said.

JJ was glad to hear the concern in the other men's voices.

"April did say that they were in that trailer, and when they were let out, they were at the cabin, so that tells us we were right, Ryan did drive pretty much straight to it," Ro said.

"Which means there are roads. That will make it quicker to get there," Ball agreed.

"But what road? What cabin?" Smoke asked.

The back-and-forth between all the men felt useful. Familiar. It was what he and his team did when they were on a mission. And since JJ knew without a doubt that the four of them weren't on top of their game, were more worried about their women than anything else, it was a relief to have these men at their backs.

"June?" Cal said in such a broken, tortured voice, everyone turned to look at him. He was holding JJ's phone and had it on speaker. His knuckles were white, his hand was shaking, and his eyes were shut as he spoke to his wife.

"I'm . . . okay . . . the girls . . . are here . . . Max is gonna . . . be okay too . . ."

It was obvious June was in a lot of pain and it was taking effort for her to talk.

"I love you guys. So much," Cal said.

"We . . . know . . . just think . . . when you get . . . here . . . you'll get to meet . . . your son."

"June, I'm sorry! I'm so sorry I'm not there! I just—"

"No!" June barked firmly, cutting him off. "Why would I . . . want you . . . here . . . looking at my . . . stretched out . . . hoohah? Besides . . . you'd . . . probably pass out. April's . . . got this . . . under . . . control. If you . . . think she's . . . gonna let anything . . . happen . . . to her nephew . . . you don't . . . know her."

Cal let out a pained half sob, half chuckle. "Right. You've got the best support group I could want around you right now."

"Damn . . . straight . . . I . . . do. I think . . . I'm gonna go . . . have a baby . . . now. Don't get killed, Cal. I'll be pissed . . . if you . . . do."

"I love you, Juniper."

"I love you too. Go . . . kick . . . some ass."

They all heard a thunk, as if June had dropped the phone, then an anguished, muted scream echoed throughout the room.

Every single man froze at hearing the pain in June's tone as she struggled to have her baby.

Cal was shaking even harder when Chappy took the phone from him and handed it back to JJ.

Feeling sick, JJ brought it up to his mouth. "April?" he asked.

"Hey, I'm sorry, but I can't talk. I need to . . . June . . ."

"It's okay. I understand. You've got this, April."

"I don't have a choice," she said, and JJ hated hearing the fear in her voice.

"I'm gonna deliver Max," April went on. "Then I'll help you guys as much as I can. There's a hole in the door, and I can be a lookout or something."

It was so like his mother hen to want to be everything to everyone. "We've got this."

"Jack, I can help," April insisted.

"I know you can. And I'll call when we get there. Okay?" JJ said, wanting to soothe the terror underlying the forced calm she was trying to project. If looking out that damn hole in the door would make her feel as if she was helping, he'd gladly let her.

"Okay. Be safe, Jack. You have to make an honest woman out of me."

JJ stilled. "You want to marry me?" he asked.

"Duh," she said with a small huff.

"You're taking my name," he informed her.

She laughed, and the sound was a little less forced this time. "I am?"

"Yup."

"Hoffman is my maiden name. It's not *his*."

"Don't care. You'll be April Justice before the week is out."

"Kill Ryan, don't die, get us out of here, and I'll be April Justice before *tomorrow* is gone if you want," she vowed.

"Done. Now go deliver our nephew. I'll see you soon."

"Love you, Jack."

"I love you too, April."

The phone went silent as she clicked off the connection.

"Smooth, man," Rex said with a grin on his face. "I never would've thought *insisting* she take your name would work in a million years, but damn if it didn't."

JJ's fingers tingled. He wasn't sure if it was because he was holding his breath or because of the surplus of adrenaline coursing through his veins, but it didn't really matter. He was going to marry his woman. Sooner than later.

"Meanwhile, I was transmitting info to Meat in the chopper, and he's already found the cabin," Rex said.

"What?" Chappy gasped.

"Where?" Bob barked.

"How does he know it's the right one?" Cal asked, a bit more composed after his emotional conversation with June.

"He said there's a black truck connected to a trailer sitting on a dirt road less than a mile from the cabin. He thinks April was right and this guy's not bluffing. The dirt around the cabin is disturbed, as if he'd been digging in it," Rex said.

"Burying mines and IEDs," Gray said grimly.

"Looks like it," Rex agreed. "I've got the coordinates. There's no sign of the Tango, but he's there, I'd bet my life on it. I'm thinking we can get within two miles or so of the cabin, then go in on foot from there. We can split up, surround the area. You four can act all incompetent and get his attention. Once the rat comes out of his hole, we'll take him out, then figure out how to get the women to safety."

JJ's stomach rolled at that. If the cabin was surrounded by explosives, and if there really was a bomb under the cabin itself, there was no telling how much time they had. And with every tick of the second hand, JJ felt the urgency ramp up more and more.

"Let's go," he said firmly.

The Ace Security crew, Silverstone, and the Mountain Mercenaries all headed for the door. Everyone had looks of concentration on their faces, aware of what was at stake.

JJ turned to his team and took a deep breath.

But it was Cal who spoke. "June's having my baby. She went into labor in a bloody *trailer*. Not in a sterile hospital surrounded by doctors and nurses, and without the damn epidural we'd planned so she wouldn't be in pain. And it's too early. Max isn't supposed to be born for another few weeks."

"He'll be okay," JJ told him.

"I know," Cal said in a surprisingly firm tone. "Because she's got Carlise, Marlowe, and April with her. But that doesn't mean I'm not mad as all bloody hell. He's *stolen* this from us. Sharing the experience of our first child being born. Something we can never get back."

"I don't mean to eavesdrop," Rex said from the door. Everyone else had left, but he'd lingered, obviously overhearing their conversation. "I'll personally kill him for you. Slowly. Painfully."

Cal studied the man. From what they understood from the others, Rex wasn't Special Forces. He'd been in the Army, but only for a short time. He wasn't the first person JJ would guess was willing and eager to kill in a roomful of men who'd done just that in the past. Then again, he'd been through more pain than any one man should ever have to

245

cope with. Not knowing where his wife was, or even if she was alive, for ten long years. He now had her back, along with a son he didn't know she'd had while in captivity, and both were thriving.

"I'd be much obliged," Cal said formally. "As would the royal family."

Rex smirked. "I don't want anything to do with that, no offense."

"None taken. There are many days when I feel the same," Cal told him.

The two men nodded at each other, then Rex disappeared through the door.

"While we'll always be Delta, today, we're just four men who will do anything to get back the women we love," Chappy said quietly.

"The protector, the royal, the hero, and the lumberjack," Bob agreed. "I've heard our women call us that more than once. And I want to be my wife's hero . . . again."

"You already are," JJ told him. "And you're definitely a protector," he told Chappy. "Cal will always be June's royal prince. And I'm happy to be a simple lumberjack," JJ said, feeling prouder at that moment to be exactly who he was than he could remember in a very long time. "We've got sixteen badass men on our side; let them do the hard work. Our only priority is that cabin. Understood?"

"Ten-four."

"Yes."

"Absolutely."

JJ didn't think he even needed to say that, but the last thing he wanted was one of them to get lost in their anger toward Ryan. He needed their focus on the cabin. On figuring out how to reach the women and get them out safely.

He had a feeling that was going to be the hardest part of this mission. Not neutralizing the kidnapper. Not figuring out where he was hiding or waiting for him to show himself. Not worrying about whether he planned to take them out with a sniper rifle—which JJ doubted, because that would be too fast, and this asshole wanted to see their faces. Wanted to see their pain when they thought their women would die.

No, those explosives worried JJ more than anything else. One wrong step, one wrong move . . . hell, with some bombs, just disturbing the ground too much could make everything blow. They needed to be calm and methodical. Let the men they'd called for help take out Ryan.

"Let's go get our women," JJ said.

Without another word, the four men turned for the door.

CHAPTER
TWENTY-ONE

Bull stopped the truck, and JJ and his team, along with Eagle, Smoke, and Gramps, hopped out of the back. It had been a tight fit, but they'd wanted to take as few vehicles to the area as possible. Once they got the women out of the cabin safe and sound, they'd call in the chopper to take them to the nearest hospital.

They'd stopped and picked up Eagle, Cole, and Meat on their way, who hadn't wanted to be up in a helicopter while the takedown was happening, and right now there were twenty deadly, well-trained men ready and willing to do whatever it took to neutralize the enemy and rescue the hostages.

The remaining men were in the two trucks behind Bull's, and they all convened at the edge of the woods.

"It's a mile-and-a-half straight-line distance northeast to the cabin," Rex said, pointing in the proper direction. "We know Ryan's truck is farther out, but we *also* know he's going to want to be within eyesight of that cabin. I'm not too concerned about running into him before that. So we'll stick together if we can until we get within a half mile. Our team will head to the west, while Logan's crew will head around south. Bull, you and your guys go north. We'll surround the cabin and let JJ and his men walk straight in along the road. *Everyone* keep your eyes peeled for this asshole. If you find him, let the rest of us know, and we'll converge on your location."

Everyone nodded, and they all did radio checks. The small transmitters in their ears would let each of them stay in contact.

"Keep your eyes in the air as well as on the ground," Logan reminded them. "The trees around here are big enough to hold an adult, but considering the amount of time he's spent in these woods setting those explosives, he could've also built some sort of underground bunker."

"It's possible he's set up cameras too," Bull added. "I wouldn't put it past him."

JJ's blood ran cold. If he had, and Ryan realized it was more than just the four of them, their entire plan could blow up around them . . . literally.

"Just stay alert," Gray told them. "Let's not give this guy any more credit than he deserves. If anyone sees any kind of trail cam or gets a sense that they're being watched, inform the rest of us, and we'll go to plan B."

They had no plan B, as far as JJ knew, but he nodded anyway. They were all very aware that their time was ticking, just like the bomb that may or may not be under the cabin.

The men made quick work of the first mile before the groups separated, disappearing into the wilderness around JJ and his team. As they continued on alone, he could feel the thumping of his heart, and every step he took sounded loud in the silent woods. None of the men spoke, each lost in his thoughts about the love of his life and what she might be going through.

"We're getting close," someone said through the transmitter several minutes later.

JJ held up a closed fist, indicating his men should stop. He turned to his friends. "Whatever happens, get to the women. They're our objective."

Chappy, Cal, and Bob all nodded without hesitation.

"You talk to him," Chappy said quietly. "When he makes himself seen, I mean."

"Agreed," Bob said. "You've always been the best at talking Tangos down, or at least distracting them."

"I can't think about anything other than June and the pain she's in," Cal said in a shaky voice. "I've been perfectly fine in much more dangerous situations, but I literally can't think straight at the moment."

The trust his men were showing him was almost overwhelming, but JJ nodded. He had no problem talking to this Ryan guy. Ever since he'd learned April had been kidnapped, he'd been on edge. Furious, but mostly controlled. Losing it now wouldn't help his woman, and that was all that mattered.

Taking a deep breath, JJ continued toward the coordinates of the cabin the men in the chopper had given them. The other teams were comforting background noise in his head, talking quietly through the radios, informing the others of their locations.

"I've got the cabin in sight," someone said.

"Same with us."

"No sign of our target yet."

One second, JJ and his team were walking along the dirt tracks that passed for a road, and the next, they'd stepped into a clearing. As their eyes in the sky had said, the ground was mostly dirt in a wide perimeter around the small cabin, with very little vegetation. As for the structure itself, it looked as if one strong gust of wind would take the thing to the ground.

JJ fought the temptation to run to the door. Knowing April and the others were right there, so close and yet so far, made him desperate to get inside and see for himself that they were okay. Unhurt. But he forced himself to stand still.

"What now?" Bob asked quietly.

Looking around, JJ didn't see any sign of Ryan, but he knew he was near. The hair on the back of his neck was sticking straight up, and his sixth sense told him that the man was watching them carefully.

"Ryan Johnson?" he called out, careful not to speak too loudly, because he had no idea if the explosives the asshole had planted were sound activated or not. April told him Ryan had already detonated a bomb, so probably not . . . but he still wasn't willing to take chances.

"You wanted us to find you, so here we are!" he announced.

He could hear Gray and the others checking in, letting him know they didn't have eyes on the man either.

"Maybe he left," Chappy suggested.

But JJ shook his head. "No, he's here. He's meticulously planned this for years."

Just then, a new sound echoed in the quiet around them.

The cry of a very unhappy baby erupted from inside the cabin.

JJ automatically reached out and grabbed Cal's arm, keeping him from taking more than a single step toward the sound.

"Easy, Cal," he told him.

"That's my son," Cal said quietly, sounding as if he was in a trance.

"Crying is good," Chappy soothed. "Means he's breathing. And I have to say, he sounds like he's breathing *really* well."

Prince Maximilian Redmon did not sound happy, but JJ couldn't keep the small smile from forming on his face. April had done it. She'd successfully brought June's baby into the world. He knew Carlise and Marlowe had undoubtedly helped too, but he was certain his mother hen had taken the lead role.

Then . . . a slow, methodical clapping sounded from behind them.

All four men spun to face the threat at the same time Bull's voice echoed in their ears. "Target located. Repeat, target located."

JJ had a second to think to himself "No shit, Sherlock" before all his attention was centered on the man coming out from behind a large tree. He had no idea where the man had been hiding or how sixteen men failed to spot him before he simply waltzed into the clearing, but at the moment, nothing mattered but ending the threat to the women and to all their futures.

Studying Ryan, JJ realized he looked nothing like he'd pictured in his head when he thought about April's kidnapper. First of all, he looked so damn young. Even younger than the twenty years Tex had mentioned.

Secondly, he looked . . . normal. From his haircut to his clothes, he in no way looked like a terrorist. Which was a stupid notion, because JJ knew more than most that there was no stereotypical "look" for terrorists. They blended into whatever environment they inhabited, just as Ryan had done.

"Congrats on being a daddy," Ryan told Cal in only slightly accented English.

JJ had the brief, irrational thought that it was almost a shame this man was going to die. Because he was obviously very talented, very smart. He could've done a lot of good in the world, but instead he'd let hatred fill his heart and his head.

"Another royal Redmon, how exciting," Ryan said as he lifted a hand and pointed a pistol at Cal. "Too bad he won't meet his dad."

For a second, JJ thought Ryan was going to pull the trigger, just shoot Cal right then and there, but he kept talking.

"I've waited for this moment for longer than you know," Ryan growled.

Grateful the idiot wanted to talk, JJ stayed silent, letting him say what he felt he needed to say. All the while, he could hear the men around them, their backup, talking to each other through the radios and quickly and silently moving into position to surround Ryan before making their move.

"You killed my brother!" Ryan accused dramatically.

"Which one was he?" JJ asked in a bored tone, as if he was talking about something as inconsequential as the weather.

As expected, Ryan's anger was instant.

"He was *innocent!*" Ryan spat. "He was there to carry water, to bring you assholes food. He wasn't involved in the kidnapping."

JJ's eyes narrowed as his gaze ran over the kid in front of them. When Ryan's head tilted defiantly, as if asking JJ what he was looking at, a memory of another man doing the same thing exploded in his head.

Except back then, the man had tilted his head to study JJ, just like that, before using a knife to carve into his skin.

"I remember your brother," JJ said as he straightened, no longer looking or sounding bored. "He was about your height, smelled like body odor, and always wore black pants and an old T-shirt with a picture of the Twin Towers in New York before they were taken down by terrorists."

Ryan's mouth dropped open in shock. He immediately regained his composure, but the lapse was enough to tell JJ that he was right.

He felt his teammates shift next to him, as if they'd remembered the especially sadistic man who'd tortured them as well.

"And you're wrong about him being innocent. He was involved in every step of our captivity and torture," JJ said.

"No, he wasn't!" Ryan insisted. "He told me that he was just there to earn money, to buy food and clothes for our family—"

"He lied!" JJ yelled harshly, wanting to shake Ryan so badly, he'd let down his guard. He just needed him distracted enough that Rex or one of the other men could get to him. "Your brother was a *terrorist*. He hurt people. Probably raped women, hit little kids, and spat on every tradition you and your countrymen ever held dear!"

"No," Ryan said, shaking his head. "He was saving money to get us out! To bring us to the city where I could go to school."

JJ laughed. It was a mean sound. "He was *never* leaving. He wanted to work his way up the organization. He craved attention. Notoriety. Wanted to be in charge. Eventually, he would've sucked you into that life with him."

Ryan stared at him for a beat, then shook his head. "You're lying to try to save yourself. It won't work."

JJ crossed his arms over his chest, curling his lip in disgust. "And you're a bitter asshole who's more like your brother than you know. You kidnapped four innocent, defenseless women, delighted in their terror." He heard Rex telling the others to stand back, that he was moving in.

"Thank you for the compliment," Ryan said almost calmly, clearly not as rattled as JJ had hoped. "I've spent my life learning everything there is to know about explosives, to avenge my brother and make him proud. I've rigged the cabin and everything around it with every different type of bomb there is. You might be able to beat one, but you'll *never* get around them all.

"Your women are going to die," he said flatly, as if killing four women and a baby was nothing to him. "And you're going to watch. Then I'm going to kill you too. Finish what my brother apparently started all those years ago. If you say he was part of the group that tortured you, then he had a reason. And I say good for him. I will complete his mission . . . and join him in the afterworld."

"Oh, you'll do that all right," JJ said—before Rex exploded out of the trees behind Ryan.

The young man spun, but it was too late. Rex hit him dead on with a powerful punch, knocking him flat on his back.

The weapon he'd been holding went off, and JJ jerked, praying neither Rex nor anyone else had been hit. In seconds, Rex easily disarmed and subdued the smaller man. And from behind him, Ro, Arrow, Logan, Blake, and Bull appeared.

To JJ's surprise, Ryan laughed. It was a maniacal sound, almost unhinged.

"You think you've won. But you haven't!" he crowed. "Your women are as good as dead! You can't get to them! If you walk up to the door, you'll blow up. If you bring in a helicopter, the vibrations will make some of my explosives detonate. BOOM! The entire cabin will go up in the biggest blast you've ever seen. It's going to rain body parts! There's nothing you can do to stop it. To stop *me*. I've still won!"

He laughed again. Even as Rex grabbed his shirt and wrenched him to his feet, he didn't stop his insane laughter.

It wasn't until Rex punched him in the face again that the sound stopped.

"I'll take care of the trash. You get your women," Rex said as he turned, shoving Ryan in front of him and fading back into the forest, with three of his men following.

JJ turned back at the cabin. It was almost a serene sight. All it needed was some smoke rising from the fireplace. But instead, all he saw was danger.

"What's the plan?" Eagle asked.

For the first time in his life, JJ had no idea. Ryan may or may not have been bluffing about the chopper. The force of the wind from the blades *could* set off particularly sensitive explosives . . . but he'd already demonstrated one of his devices for the women, clearly without causing a mass explosion. He was either lying about their sensitivity or perhaps lying about the number of bombs buried. Regardless, JJ wasn't willing to risk their women's lives on a guess.

They couldn't drive or walk up to the cabin, for fear of potentially setting one off. They could call in specialists, or bomb robots, but it would take too long for them to get there. They had no idea if Ryan had rigged a timer to any of those bombs.

"I don't know," JJ finally admitted in a whisper.

He turned to his team and saw the same look of frustration and despair on their faces that he assumed was on his own.

"What if we used the trees? Climbed them and jumped onto the roof? We could tear through the roof to get inside," Gramps offered.

"Then what?" Ryder asked. "I'm sure the women are motivated to get out, but June just had a baby."

"What if the chopper stayed high, so the downdraft wasn't strong enough to set anything off?" Arrow asked.

"Maybe," Blake said skeptically, "but the wind is picking up. Anyone on the end of a line would be whipped around like a ball in a pinball machine."

"A crane? It could lift someone over to the cabin," Cole offered.

255

"Or an explosives K9?" Gray suggested.

"There's not enough time," Cal whispered, sounding broken.

JJ stared at the cabin. There had to be *some* way to get the women, and baby Max, out of the cabin without setting off the explosives around and under the building. But at the moment, there were far too many unknowns for his liking.

The thought that Ryan might win after all made him want to throw up.

Then he heard April's voice calling his name. "Jack?"

He jolted slightly at the sound and had actually taken a step toward the cabin before he felt a strong hand grab his arm, holding him back. Shit. Yeah. He couldn't risk getting any closer because no one knew how far back Ryan had set the explosives.

"I'm here!" he said.

"Who are all those people?" she asked.

JJ wanted to smile at such a normal question. "My friends. They came to help."

"Oh, okay. And the big guy with the tattoos who took Ryan away? Are we sure he's good? Ryan won't escape?"

"Ryan won't escape," Ro reassured her from somewhere behind JJ.

"Rex and his teammates will take care of him, don't worry," he called out. He couldn't see her, only hear her, and the sound of her voice made his heart hurt even more. If he and his friends didn't think of something, pronto, she could be lost to him forever.

"Cal, June had her baby. Max is perfect! Ten toes, ten fingers, and lungs that work extremely well."

"I heard," Cal said.

"He's beautiful," April told him.

"Of course he is. June is his mother," Cal responded, his tone shaky.

"Right, so . . . it's very nice to meet you, Jack's friends," April said. "When can we get out of here?"

JJ frowned and took a step closer, even though he was pushing his luck. His toes brushed against the disturbed dirt a couple of dozen yards out from the cabin. He crouched down and studied the area. "We're workin' on it, sweetheart."

There was a pause, as if she was digesting his words. Then, proving how smart his woman was, she said, "You can't get us out."

"I didn't say that," JJ protested.

"We aren't stupid," she said a little huffily. "We've been brainstorming in here ourselves to try to figure out how to help. And I have an idea."

JJ tensed. He had a feeling he wasn't going to like this. Not one bit.

"I can talk you through how to get to the door the same way we did. Ryan picked up the markers he used, the ones we stepped on to get here . . . but I think I remember where they were."

CHAPTER TWENTY-TWO

April felt as if she'd just run a mile or two. She was sweaty, and her heart was beating so hard it almost hurt. Part of it was the stress she'd felt while helping to deliver June's baby, but the other part was seeing Jack and the rest of the guys through the hole in the door. It was obvious they didn't have any idea how to get close to the cabin.

She didn't care about Ryan, what the big man and his friends might be doing to him; she was positive he wouldn't be a problem ever again. She should've felt remorse over his death, but she was having a hard time mustering any sympathetic feelings toward their kidnapper right about now.

She wanted out of this cabin. Wanted to feel Jack's arms around her. Wanted to get June and Max to the hospital to make sure they were both okay. Wanted to marry Jack. Wanted to go home. To Maine.

She saw Jack jerk in surprise when he heard her voice, and she smiled a little at that. He was obviously in "soldier" mode, intensely focused on the task at hand.

"I have an idea," she told him through the hole in the door. "I can talk you through how to get to the door the same way we did. Ryan picked up the markers he used, the ones we stepped on to get here . . . but I think I remember where they were."

"No," he said firmly, turning around to look at his team and the other men in the small clearing with him.

Disappointment slammed into April. It was true she wasn't a Special Forces soldier, but she could help, she had no doubt. Jack wasn't even considering it. It hurt.

She watched as his head dipped and he stared at the ground for a moment. Then a hand came up and massaged the back of his neck before he turned back toward the cabin.

"Where are you right now?" he asked.

Confused, April said, "The cabin."

The way his lips twitched in amusement was so familiar, it was painful. She'd seen him try to hold back his laughter about something she'd said so many times.

"Where in the cabin? Can you see me?"

"Oh! Yeah, there's a hole in the door." She stuck two fingers out of the small hole and wiggled them before putting her eye back up to it.

She saw most of the men, other than Chappy, Cal, and Bob, were grinning. She belatedly realized her actions probably looked a little obscene from their point of view.

"Right, the path that you took to get to the door, was it straight or zigzag or what?"

"Straight," she told him. Was he really going to let her guide him to the door? His trust felt good, *really* good—then just as suddenly, nervousness struck.

What was she doing? If she wasn't completely certain about the path, if she told him to step in the wrong direction, he could literally be blown to pieces right in front of her.

"Never mind!" she called out, completely panicked now. "I don't know what I was thinking! I can't do it."

"April!" June hissed from behind her. She turned to see her friend sitting up with her back against the hard wall, Max cuddled against her chest. They'd used the sheet to wrap him up, and only his little face was showing above the material. The blanket under her was stained with bodily fluids and blood, and the umbilical cord was still attached. There hadn't been anything they could use to cut it, and it was freaking all of them out. They needed a hospital. Immediately.

"What?" she asked belatedly.

"You can do it. I saw you studying the path as you walked to the cabin. Your mind was going a million miles an hour. If anyone can guide our men to us safely, it's you. We trust you."

Carlise and Marlowe nodded their agreement, and April couldn't help but notice that both women had a hand on their bellies, as if touching their unborn children.

The pressure was immense. Not only was she risking the lives of their men, she could end up killing her best friends and their children.

"April!" Jack called.

Taking a deep breath, she turned back to the hole in the door.

"Where exactly was the trailer backed up when you got out?" Jack asked.

Was she doing this? Her gaze went from the man she loved to the trees the trailer had been sitting between. She took a deep breath.

"See those trees to your right . . . wait, I mean my right, your left." She let out an exasperated breath. How could she tell him where to step if she couldn't even figure out left and right? "The ones that are kind of skinnier than the others around them? They're at around two o'clock in relation to the door."

Jack turned and immediately walked over to the trees she'd pointed out, Cal, Chappy, and Bob at his heels.

"These?" he asked.

"Yes."

"Okay, now what?"

She didn't say anything for a long moment.

It felt as if Jack was staring straight into her heart. She could see his focus even across the distance. "I trust you," he said.

He didn't yell the words. He said them calmly, and April heard the sincerity in his words.

"You'll need something to get the boards off the door," she told him.

He turned to some of the men standing nearby, and the small break gave her time to take a deep breath. Her hands were shaking, but she clasped them together and turned her attention to the ground in front of the cabin. Twenty-five markers. She'd counted them. As if she was right back in that moment, walking on those pink circles, she saw them as clear as day.

"Okay, I've got a hammer. Where should I go?"

April blinked. "Where in the world did you get a hammer?"

One of the men near him laughed. "We're a resourceful bunch!" he yelled out.

Whatever. If they wanted to carry a whole toolbox around with them, she wasn't going to complain.

"You need something to mark your trail," she told him. "Ryan used bright-pink circles made of paper or something, but he picked them up to hide the path."

"Right, smart."

All the men started looking around them for something they could use to mark the path to the cabin. One of them suddenly pulled his shirt over his head and began using a knife to cut it into pieces. Before long, he'd handed a fistful of jagged strips of material to Jack.

"All right, hon, talk to me. Tell me how to get to you."

April felt a hand on her shoulder and turned to see Marlowe standing there.

"Breathe, April."

Realizing she'd been holding her breath, April let it out with a whoosh. "I love you guys. So much," she said.

"We love you too. Now hurry up. I'm hungry," Carlise told her from where she was sitting next to June.

April smiled, hearing the teasing in her friend's voice. They were all stressed to the max and wanted nothing more than to get out of this damn cabin . . . and take a shower. April felt grubby and disgusting, but that was the least of their worries right now.

Nodding, and more grateful than she could say that Marlowe didn't move away from her side, April peered back through the door.

"From the trees, walk forward until your toes are at the edge of where the grass ends and the dirt begins." Jack did as she directed. "Now step forward. No!" she immediately yelled as he was about to step down. He froze with his foot in the air.

"Move your foot back a little."

"Here?" he asked, moving his foot.

"Yes, that's better. I remember the steps being comfortable for me. Which means you'll probably think they're too close together as you're walking."

Jack nodded, and as a bead of sweat rolled down April's temple, he put his foot down.

When nothing happened, when the earth didn't blow up around him, she let out a shaky breath. "Okay, see that tiny patch of grass several inches in front of your right foot?"

Jack nodded again.

"Put your left foot in front of that, so your heel is right at the edge."

He stepped forward where she told him to, then turned and lifted his right foot a fraction of an inch and placed a piece of fabric under his boot.

"Okay, now move a little to your"—she hesitated, making sure she had the direction right before continuing—"left. There's a small branch sticking out of the ground. Put your right foot next to it."

Slowly—ever so slowly—April guided Jack closer and closer to the cabin. With each step he took, she got more confident in her directions. With every step, there was some kind of landmark. They'd seemed so inconsequential at the time, she'd barely noticed them when she'd made the journey herself. She was too focused on the pink circles. But when her friends crossed the minefield, she'd watched more carefully and realized each circle was next to some sort of natural marker.

When Jack was just three steps away from the door, April looked at the path and panicked. She didn't see any kind of rock, stick, or anything else that would give any indication of where he could step next.

"I'm almost there. Where next, April?" Jack said calmly.

But looking at his face, April could see he was anything but relaxed. He had sweat trickling from his temples, even though it definitely wasn't warm enough outside to sweat. His hands were clenched and his brow furrowed.

"I don't know!" she said, a sob escaping, surprising the hell out of her.

Marlowe tightened her grip on her shoulder, but April couldn't take her gaze from Jack. Out of the corner of her eye, she could see the rest of the men standing stock still by the trees where Jack had started his perilous journey. They looked just as tense as she felt.

Jack was so close and yet still so far away.

"April? Look at me," he ordered.

"I am," she choked out. He was blurry because of the tears in her eyes, but she refused to lift her head away from the hole in the door.

"I admit when you told me on the phone that you could help, I dismissed it. How could you help a bunch of Special Forces soldiers? I agreed just to make you feel better—but I was an idiot. You are literally the smartest person I've ever met. Who else would be able to do this? Lead me through a *literal* minefield to reach you?

"Two more steps, sweetheart. Then I'll get this door open, get us out of here, and you can marry me."

April huffed out a laugh. "With everything going on, that's what you're thinking about?"

"Damn straight," Jack said seriously. "I waited too long to ask you out, and I almost lost you. If you think I'm waiting an extra minute to put my ring on your finger, you're wrong."

"You have a ring?" she asked in surprise.

He looked a little sheepish then. "Well, no. It was a figure of speech."

April actually grinned. She backed away just long enough to wipe her eyes on her sleeve, then brought her face back up to the door. She glanced at the dirt at his feet, and—just like that—something clicked. "See that rock that looks like an arrow?"

Looking down, Jack nodded.

"Step right on it. I didn't see it until Ryan picked up the pink circle, so that means it was directly on top of it."

Jack did as she said. With his long legs, he was close enough to skip the last step and jump to the small landing outside the door, but he looked at the door as if waiting for her to tell him what to do.

"You can jump to the door now," she said in confusion.

"I could," he agreed. "But it's a little too far for *you* to step comfortably. One more, sweetheart."

Even though he couldn't see her, April nodded. "The dirt a few inches from the step is a different color than the soil around it. Darker. Step there."

He did, not forgetting to turn around and put a piece of fabric over the arrow-shaped rock.

April let out her breath in a whoosh and fell to her knees, sitting back on her heels.

"You did it," Marlowe said in awe.

"I knew you could," June said. "You're the most observant person I know."

"April? Step away from the door," Jack said from so close.

She immediately stood and shuffled backward toward June and Carlise. Marlowe had an arm around her waist, and all four stared at the door as they heard Jack working to remove the boards Ryan had nailed across.

Then he was there. Standing in the doorway, looking larger than life.

April threw herself at him, hitting him so hard he took a step backward on the minuscule front stoop to stay upright. The feel of his arms around her was better than anything she could remember in a very long time.

"Jack!" she croaked. His tight embrace almost hurt, but she didn't complain.

They stood there for a long moment before she felt arms go around her and Jack. Marlowe had joined them. Then Carlise was there too. The four of them stood just inside the door in a grateful and joyful embrace. Jack adjusted to hug the three of them, and April fell in love with him even more than she already was in that moment.

"I wish I could join the lovefest," June said with a sniff behind them.

April wasn't surprised when Jack gently disentangled himself from her and their friends to walk over to June. He knelt on the floor and gently hugged her. Then he put a hand on little Max's head and said, "Hey, Max. I'm your uncle Jack, and I'm gonna be your favorite."

Everyone laughed tearfully.

Finally, Jack stood with a smile on his face and said, "How about we get out—" He froze suddenly, his gaze locked on April. He stalked toward her with a look so scary, she was alarmed.

"What? What's wrong?" she asked.

"Your face. He hit you," Jack growled.

April blew out a breath. "Jeez, Jack, you scared me! I thought something was wrong."

"It is! He *hit* you," he repeated.

"Yes, but he's dead . . . right? I mean, that's what the big scary guy with the tattoos and his friends were going to do, wasn't it?"

Jack studied her for a moment, running his fingers over her face with a featherlight touch. "Yeah. Does that bother you?"

"No," April said flatly. "He kidnapped us. Locked us in a trailer. If I wanted to eat, I had to choke down his leftover hamburger, and for water, I had to suck on his gross contaminated ice. He didn't care that June was in labor and kept threatening to shoot her unborn baby. Then he put us in here with the goal of blowing us up. Why the hell would I care if he died?"

He looked pissed all over again. "Right. So, feel like getting out of here?"

"Yes! Please yes," Marlowe breathed.

Jack turned back to June. "I'm thinking you're first," he said.

April nodded in approval. If he'd even suggested she be the first to leave, she would've been disappointed. She should've known better.

He gently picked up June and Max and turned to the door. "Wait here," he said.

"Why?" April asked in confusion.

Jack didn't answer for a long moment before he took a deep breath. "I don't know. I just . . . I can't . . ."

April put her hand on his arm and leaned up to kiss his cheek. "You made it across okay. We will too. Now that we've got the markers."

"Be careful," he said. Then looked at Carlise and Marlowe. "Your husbands will kick my ass if anything happens to you. If you're scared, Chappy and Bob will come for you."

"I'm sure they would," Marlowe told him. "But I'm not willing to be in this stupid cabin a minute longer than necessary. Lead the way."

"Can you see where to step while holding her?" Carlise asked.

"Yes," Jack said confidently, making April relax a fraction.

She still held her breath as he took the first step out of the cabin. She gestured for Marlowe to follow behind him but held her back a moment. "Wait."

"Why?"

"Put some distance between you . . . just in case." She hated saying the words, but she couldn't banish the vision of something going wrong and everyone getting hurt or killed because they were following too closely together.

Marlowe nodded and waited until Jack, June, and Max were half-way across the clearing.

"Okay. Piece of cake," April said.

In response, Marlowe, hugged her hard, then pressed her lips together, held her hands out to her sides, and started the dangerous trek.

"April?" Carlise said as they watched Marlowe traverse the path.

"Yeah?" she said, glancing at her friend. To her surprise and alarm, Carlise's eyes were filled with tears.

"I'm so glad you were here."

April threw her arms around her, and Carlise returned the fierce hug. "Me too," she told her.

"I mean it," Carlise mumbled into her shoulder. "Without you . . . I don't think the rest of us would've fared so well. You kept us calm, you got us food, water, and blankets, you did most of the work with Max. Hell, you even found a way out of this hellhole without anyone getting blown up."

"Don't speak so soon," April quipped.

She felt more than heard Carlise's laugh against her. Her friend raised her head and stared at her. "I mean it. You're the reason we're almost home."

But April shook her head. "We're going home because we worked together. Because we're married—or almost married, in my case—to honorable men who would do whatever it takes to keep us safe. We're lucky, in all the ways that count."

"Yes, we are."

"Carlise! April! Are you guys all right?" Chappy called out impatiently.

April wiped the tears off her friend's cheeks. "Your man is worried. Go on. And whatever you do, don't trip."

"Shut up," Carlise muttered. "Although this would be easier if I wasn't so damn pregnant."

April agreed with her one hundred percent but didn't say anything out loud as her friend stepped into the dirt. She held her breath as Carlise very carefully picked her way across the yard.

April waited until she was all the way across, until Chappy snatched her up in his arms and fell to his knees with Carlise in his lap. She could feel the relief and love from all the way across the clearing.

"Your turn, April," Jack called. He'd passed June and Max off to Cal, who was nowhere to be seen. But since half the men who'd arrived with Jack and his team were also gone, she assumed they were busy getting her to a hospital.

Taking a breath, April turned to look at the empty cabin behind her. The plastic tubs were on their sides. There were empty water bottles strewn around the floor, as well as the soiled blanket. The floorboards were cracked and the windows still boarded shut.

And somehow, it felt as if April was leaving a part of herself in this run-down little building. She'd been terrified, for herself and her friends, but she felt stronger for having this awful experience. She didn't want to repeat it, ever, and probably would never feel the urge to vacation in a remote cabin in the middle of the mountains, but she was proud of herself.

Turning to the door, and Jack, she took a deep breath and stepped on the first piece of fabric.

The walk across the dirt didn't seem to take nearly as long as it had when she'd first arrived, or while she'd watched her friends and Jack do it minutes earlier.

And when she got to the end, Jack was there. He grabbed her and hauled her against his chest, much as Chappy had done to Carlise. April smiled against him. Even smelly, and badly in need of a shower, food, and two gallons of water, she'd never felt better.

CHAPTER
TWENTY-THREE

"Can I watch it again?" April asked.

JJ shook his head and put his phone back in his pocket.

She pouted at him.

"You've watched that video twelve times already," he told her, something she knew.

"I know, but it's so fascinating! And, I have to admit, *satisfying* to see the cabin go up like it did."

While JJ, Bob, Chappy, and Cal had ridden in the chopper with their women to the hospital, the rest of the guys had stayed behind. They'd taken Ryan's body and put it in the cabin, using the path April had amazingly laid out for them, then used the remote detonator they'd found in Ryan's pocket to blow up the cabin, not willing to wait and see if he'd set any timers.

They'd given the place a wide berth before blowing it up, which was a good thing, because the resulting explosion set off all the bombs and IEDs Ryan had planted. The fireball had risen high in the sky, and it was truly an impressive sight.

Luckily, because of all the land Ryan had cleared around the cabin, there wasn't much danger of starting a huge forest fire, though the nearest trees got hit by bomb shrapnel.

It all worked out well enough, and with Tex's assistance handling the local authorities, the story had been tweaked enough to keep the women out of the media. Officially, a man had attempted to kidnap four women, and his plan had been foiled when he'd gotten caught in his own trap and died in the resulting explosion. The narrative had been accepted at face value.

JJ didn't get the chance to thank the men of Ace Security, Silverstone, or the Mountain Mercenaries in person. He'd been too focused on getting to the hospital with April and the other women, but he'd emailed each group. And received a return email from Rex this morning with the footage of the explosion.

April, Carlise, and Marlowe had been checked out at a hospital in Denver and released the same day. June and little Max were kept a few days to make sure everything was all right, with Cal by her side and everyone else in a nearby hotel, refusing to leave without them.

But now they were all back in Maine. A little more aware of their surroundings and more grateful than ever for their friends.

The women had visited Cal and June's house every day since, not able to go a single one without seeing each other. Their men didn't object, not in the least. Whatever they needed to heal, they'd give them without question.

As for JJ, he'd done as he promised and gotten April in front of a justice of the peace as soon as he could. The day they'd gotten back to Newton, he'd brought her straight to the municipal building, purchased a license, and married her immediately after. He'd never been so glad Maine didn't have a waiting period as he was then. He still needed to get her a ring, but she didn't seem the least bit concerned about that.

He'd spent their wedding night checking every inch of her body for any bruises he might've missed before, kissing them better. The bruise on her cheek and her black eye were fading, which was a relief. Every time JJ saw them, he wanted to go back in time and kill Ryan himself.

Rex didn't detail how Ryan had died in the email he'd sent with the video, but he'd told Tex. Ryan didn't have an easy death. Tex, in turn, had given him the details, but JJ would never share them with April. She didn't need to have that kind of thing on her conscience. And even though she wasn't upset that Ryan was no longer living, she'd be horrified if she knew exactly how the man had died.

But JJ was satisfied, as was his team. They'd suffered not only at the hands of his brother but at Ryan's when their women had been taken. JJ never wanted to experience anything like those few days again.

"Pleeeease?" April begged, looking up at him and batting her eyelashes.

"No," he said. "I have other plans for you."

"Yeah?" she asked with interest.

"Yup." JJ waited a beat. "It's inventory day at the office."

April burst out laughing and smacked him on the shoulder. "You're mean!"

"Me? You were the one bitching the other week about having no idea where we stood with office supplies or how much oil was left for the chain saws. And now that we've had the first snow of the season, I thought we could lock ourselves in the back office and . . . count."

"Is that what we're calling it now?" April asked with a seductive smile.

JJ smirked.

"You know we have a perfectly good bed here. And it's comfortable."

"Oh, you don't want to go to the office?" he asked. "Do I need to take you back to the doctor? You *always* want to work."

April's smile died. "That was before. Now, I want to live life to its fullest. I don't want to work as much. I spent way too much time there, trying to avoid you and the thought that you didn't want to be with me."

"I wanted you," JJ said, grabbing her around the waist and picking her up in one fluid motion.

She squealed a little and clung to his neck. "Jack! Put me down!"

He strode toward their bedroom and dropped her on the bed. "There, you're down."

To his delight, his wife stretched sensuously and put her arms over her head.

"Yes, I am," she agreed.

JJ was straddling her in a heartbeat. He caged her in with his body and held her arms down by the wrists. "I love you," he said.

"I love you too."

"Is it too much?"

"What?" she asked.

"Me," he said simply.

"Never. I love your intensity. Your protectiveness. Your desire to 'scorch the earth,' as you put it, to show everyone what will happen if they touch me."

JJ closed his eyes in relief.

"You might be a scary, badass former military stud to a lot of people, but to me, you'll always be my lumberjack."

JJ opened his eyes and smiled down at her. "Yeah?"

"Yes. And speaking of which, I have an idea for a new advertising campaign. It involves you standing with one leg on a tree stump, wearing a red-and-black flannel shirt, and an axe over your shoulder."

"We don't use axes," he told her.

"I know, but a chain saw wouldn't have the same feel. So you'll do it?" she pushed.

"No way in hell," JJ said with a straight face.

"Damn. Well, it was worth a shot."

JJ shook his head. April kept him on his toes, and he wouldn't have it any other way. He didn't tell her that if she pushed a little harder, he'd pose however she wanted. Hell, she could've asked him to stand there butt-ass naked with an axe, and he would've done it if it made her happy.

For April, he was a marshmallow lumberjack. To everyone else, he was a coldhearted bastard who glared at anyone who came too close to his woman.

"Jack?"

"Yeah, sweetheart."

"Thank you for coming for me."

"I'll always come for you," he told her.

She stared at him for a beat, then she smiled, then started laughing hysterically.

Shaking his head, JJ let her get it out of her system before asking, "What was that about?"

"You'll always *come* for me?"

JJ rolled his eyes. His woman was a dork. But he loved her anyway. No, he loved her because of it.

Lately, she'd been using humor to try to deflect attention from herself. When she had nightmares, she tried to brush them off. When she had flashbacks, or when she saw anyone towing a trailer, she tensed, then immediately made a joke, usually at her own expense. JJ hated it, but he understood her need to gain control over her fears.

He didn't exactly regret showing her the video of the cabin exploding, but it might bring some of those fears back to the surface. That it could've been her and her friends inside the cabin when it blew. He planned to distract her from asking to watch it again, and he knew just how to do it.

"Keep your hands there," he ordered, squeezing her wrists to emphasize his point. He felt her squirm under him and knew she was on the same page.

"Bossy," she muttered but didn't move when he let go to slide down her body. He kissed her belly through her shirt, then teased the hem before slipping his hands under the material. He palmed her tits through her bra. She moaned and arched her back.

"You like that?" he asked.

"You know I do. Stop teasing," she scolded.

"But it's so much fun," he said before moving his hands out from under her shirt. He grabbed hold of the elastic pants she wore and roughly yanked them just below her ass.

She giggled as she writhed and tried to help as much as possible without moving her arms from over her head. Then she was lying under him, naked from the waist down.

JJ leaned down and inhaled deeply. He'd never get tired of this. Of her. He licked between her folds and was immediately rewarded by her legs parting and her heels digging into his back.

No more words were spoken as he got to work pleasuring his wife.

His *wife*.

JJ had gotten to the point in his life when he thought he'd never find someone to spend the rest of his days with. True, he wasn't exactly old at thirty-nine, but he'd just assumed any chance he might've had was in the past. April scared the hell out of him from the moment they met because he could instantly imagine himself sitting beside her when they were old and decrepit.

He'd made mistakes in his life, the worst of which was letting his own fears and insecurities get the better of him. But she was his now, in every way, and he wasn't going to let even one day go by without her knowing how much she meant to him.

April clutched his hair as he nearly went into a frenzy, eating her out. He couldn't find it in him to complain; he loved the way she tugged on his hair, letting him know exactly how good he was making her feel. The harder she pulled, the more intense her pleasure.

As soon as her orgasm began to peak, JJ got to his knees and fumbled with the fastening of his jeans. Cursing himself for not getting naked before starting this, he sighed in relief as he pulled out his rock-hard cock. Looking down, he saw April smiling up at him lazily, her arms still over her head.

"Ready?" he asked, not wanting to do anything without her permission.

In reply, she reached down and stroked him once, then pulled him forward by his dick, notching him between her legs.

In one smooth move, JJ buried himself deep in his wife's pussy.

They both inhaled sharply. He would never get enough of this. She felt amazing. He moved slowly at first but eventually gained speed until he was hammering in and out of her just the way she loved the most.

Her hand snaked between them and began to rub her clit, and almost immediately he felt her inner muscles tighten around him.

It wasn't long before he was following her over the cliff. He was still dressed, and she still wore her bra and shirt, but neither cared when he collapsed on top of her. Her hands slipped under his shirt, and she ran her fingernails gently over his back.

"Okay, inventory can wait," he muttered.

April laughed, and he felt it everywhere. Especially around his cock.

"Love you, Jackson Justice."

"Love *you*, April Justice."

EPILOGUE

Ten Years Later

Chappy/Carlise

"The house is too quiet. I don't like it," Carlise said with a sigh as she snuggled into her husband.

He chuckled. "I thought you'd been looking forward to coming to the cabin for some alone time."

"I was. I am. I just . . . I don't know . . . I miss them."

Chappy smiled. He knew exactly what she meant, but he was loving the time with his wife without their four energetic kids underfoot.

Atlas was ten, and Chappy swore he'd come out of the womb talking. The kid never shut up, but he was hilarious, so Chappy didn't really mind. Jasper was the opposite of his brother. He always had a book in his hand and was perfectly content to find a quiet corner to sit where he wouldn't be bothered while reading . . . which meant Atlas was, in fact, constantly bothering him and making him mad.

Will was six and a good mix of the first two. He was always up for going outside and playing with Atlas, but he also liked to sit by himself and put together a Lego set.

All three boys had one thing in common, though—they were extremely protective of their baby sister, Ivy, who'd just turned two.

Chappy supposed they'd learned that from their dad and their three equally protective uncles. Ivy was going to be spoiled rotten, because her brothers were constantly bringing her toys when she cried, they fought over who got to help her at mealtimes, and all three wanted to carry her around or sit with her when they watched TV.

"Do you think they're all right?" Carlise asked with a small frown.

"Yes, they're fine," Chappy said firmly. They'd been at the cabin for two days, and while he was also a little worried about their children, he had no doubt they were safe. They would've been notified immediately if they weren't. He needed to get Carlise's mind off her worries.

"I'm thinking maybe we should talk to Bob and see if we can get him to rig up a small ropes course up here."

Carlise straightened and stared at him in shock. "What?"

"Yeah, you know, maybe some pole jumps or high wires."

"No," she said flatly.

"Come on," Chappy cajoled. "You know how much Atlas and Will love going with Uncle Bob to the ropes course."

"You have got to be kidding me. Atlas would sneak out in the middle of the night to do that crap. I worry about him enough when he's up here. That he'll get lost while he's out playing in the woods."

Chappy couldn't hold the smile back any longer.

Carlise glared at him, then smacked his shoulder. "You're kidding. That was mean, Riggs."

He gathered her back up against him and kissed the top of her head. "I know. Sorry."

"No, you aren't," she complained. "But I love you anyway."

"I love you back." Chappy got serious. "You've made me the happiest man in the world," he told her. "The day you found me in the middle of that storm was the luckiest of my life."

"You mean when Baxter led me to you," she corrected.

They both looked to the corner of the cabin, to the old dog sleeping on a fluffy dog bed. Probably sensing they were talking about him, he lifted his head and looked at them as if to ask, "What?"

"He certainly doesn't look anything like he did that day. Remember how skinny he was?" Chappy asked.

Carlise nodded. "I still wonder where he came from."

"Doesn't matter where he came from. It only matters where he is now."

"With us. Safe. Remember that time he woke us when Atlas had gotten completely wrapped up in his blankets and couldn't breathe?" Carlise asked.

"Of course I do. Or when we couldn't find Will after he'd wandered off, and when we *did* find him, Baxter had planted himself in front of him and wouldn't let him move?" Chappy reminisced.

"Or when he just lay there and let Ivy smear mud all over him?"

The memories of their beloved dog came faster now, Carlise and Chappy grinning.

"How about when Baxter stuck his nose into Will's playpen and didn't bite or even whimper when Will pulled out every single one of his whiskers?"

"Or when we all were on that walk and we startled that moose? Baxter immediately rushed in front of us and growled and barked, giving us time to back away before the moose attacked."

"He's been the best dog," Carlise said with a sigh.

"He has," Chappy agreed.

As if tired just hearing about his own exploits, Baxter put his head back down on the bed and closed his eyes.

"Why can't dogs live forever?" she asked.

Chappy hugged her tighter. "I don't know. But it sucks."

Baxter had started showing his age lately. He didn't stray far from the cabin when they visited, and he slept more than he was awake. He still followed the kids around when they weren't in school, and he kept a very close eye on Ivy as she toddled around the house, but it was more than obvious he was nearing the end of his life. They didn't know how old he was when he came to them, but the ten years since wasn't enough.

"This has been a good mini vacation, but I think I'll be ready to head home tomorrow," Carlise said.

"Me too," Chappy agreed.

"I do love this cabin, though. Even if it's quite a bit bigger than it was when we met," Carlise said with a smile.

Chappy looked around proudly. He and his friends had worked hard to expand the cabin, making it big enough to hold his large family. They came up here regularly, even in the winter. Some of the best memories of his married life were here.

"You hungry?" he asked.

"Nope. Those fish tacos you made tonight were more than enough. It's not as if I need to eat any more," she said, patting her belly.

His wife had gained some weight over the years, but that just meant there was more of her to love. And Chappy loved every inch. It didn't matter what the scale said when she stepped on it. She was the best wife, mother, and friend he could ever ask for.

"Well . . . I am," Chappy replied.

"Oh. Well, let me move, and you can go find something to munch on," Carlise said as she attempted to shift away from him.

But Chappy tightened his grip. "I've got something here already that I want to eat."

Carlise giggled and rolled her eyes. "You know that was corny as hell, right?" she asked.

He smiled. "Well, since my children aren't around to hear me, I figured I might as well make sure my wife knows I desire her just as much now as I did when we were stranded here all those years ago."

"I think she knows," she said with a grin.

"So . . . you want to feed me?" Chappy asked with a lift of a brow.

Carlise looked at her watch. "Going to bed at seven-thirty . . . oh, you know how to spoil a girl."

He laughed, loving his woman more than he could express. He scooted out from under her and stood, holding out his hand. Carlise took it, and he helped her to her feet. He didn't move, though, simply held her against him as he stared at her beautiful face.

"What?" Carlise asked.

"I just . . . I'm happy," Chappy said.

"I'm glad."

"No, I mean . . . I've been happy for the last decade. I just wanted to make sure you truly understand that it's because of you."

"I feel the same," Carlise told him, lifting her arms and putting them around his neck.

Chappy lowered his head to kiss her, only to feel an insistent nudge against his leg. Glancing down, he saw Baxter beside them, looking impatient.

"The kids might not be here, but we're still interrupted," he said with an exaggerated sigh.

Carlise giggled again. "I'll let him out."

"I'll go with you. All right, boy, even though you were just out there, I'll let you out for one last pee. Make it quick, though, would ya?"

The three of them walked to the door, and to Chappy's surprise, as soon as it opened, Baxter ran out into the dark forest.

"What the heck? I haven't seen him move that fast in a long time," Carlise said. "I hope there's not a bear or a moose out there."

Chappy hoped that too. Bax was too old to be going up against large predators. There used to be a time when he could take them on without any issues, too fast and agile for them to catch, but those days were long gone.

Their loyal companion was in the woods much longer than usual, and just when Chappy was beginning to worry and wonder if he should go out and see if he could find him, they heard something off to the right.

Looking across the front porch, Chappy gaped at the sight that greeted him.

Baxter had returned . . . with a friend. An emaciated and extremely pathetic-looking brown-and-white Lab mix was at his side. And she was limping.

"Holy crap, Riggs! Look at her!"

He already was. And he couldn't help but smile. He walked off the porch and crouched down. "Who'd you find, boy? A friend?"

Baxter came right to his side, but the other dog hung back, clearly not sure about him.

When Bax saw his companion hadn't come forward, he went back to her, licked her snout, then made a low noise in his throat. This time when he walked toward Chappy, the Lab mix came with him.

"It's okay, girl, you're safe now. We've got food, water, and a nice soft place for you to sleep."

Chappy felt more than heard Carlise approach. She went to her knees beside him and held out a hand for the new dog to sniff.

To the surprise of both of them, the dog walked straight up to Carlise and laid her head in her lap.

"Holy shit, she likes me, Riggs!"

"Of course she does," Chappy told his wife. He leaned forward and rested his forehead on Baxter's. "Thanks for bringing her to us," he told his loyal companion softly.

"Think she'll come inside? I don't think I could just leave her on the porch like I did with Bax."

"Let's try it."

Surprising them again, the newcomer came inside without too much trepidation. She drank half a bowl of water and snarfed down the food they put out for her. It was obvious she was starving and neglected. Then, as if she'd done it every day of her life, she followed Baxter over to his bed and snuggled next to him and immediately fell asleep.

"Looks like we have another dog," Carlise said with satisfaction. "The kids are going to be so excited."

Chappy nodded, but deep down, he had a strange feeling he knew what this meant. Baxter wasn't going to be with them much longer, and he didn't want to leave them alone. He'd found someone to take his place.

It broke his heart, but Chappy was still full with love and gratitude for his old friend.

Without a word, he took his wife's hand and walked toward their bedroom. He shut off the lights as he went, and they got ready for bed without a word.

Proving she was on the same page, once they were under the covers, she snuggled into him and said, "I hate that Baxter will be leaving us soon, but it's so like him to bring us another stray. He really is magical."

Chappy nodded. Then he rolled over, making sure not to squish Carlise as he did. He propped himself above her. "I love you, Mrs. Chapman."

"Love you too."

"For the record . . . our kids aren't here."

"Duh," she said with a laugh.

"I'm just making sure you know that you can be as loud as you want."

She giggled. "Yeah? You gonna do something to *make* me get loud?"

"Damn straight," Chappy told her as he began to slide down her body.

They were going to have a hectic day tomorrow. They had to pick up their brood, introduce the new member of their family to the kids, take her to the vet to have that leg looked at, and get her settled into her new home. Not to mention the usual chaos involved in keeping everyone entertained and fed.

For now, though, Chappy had his wife to himself, and he was going to take full advantage of every second.

❡

June/Cal

"Stop fidgeting," Cal said. "You look beautiful."

"I can't help it. I'm nervous," she retorted as she tugged at the bodice of the beautiful gown she was wearing. It had been custom made for her by Giorgio Armani, and Cal had to pinch himself to make sure he wasn't dreaming.

The woman at his side belonged to *him*, and he couldn't be more proud. She'd given him two beautiful children, and he fell deeper in love with her with every day that passed.

"Don't be nervous. You know how much you're loved here."

They were currently in Liechtenstein for another royal wedding. Cal tried to come back to his home country at least once a year, now that they had kids, and another cousin getting married was a great excuse. More than seeing his homeland and relatives, he loved seeing how the people of Liechtenstein were drawn to June.

She could do no wrong, which Cal knew was both a blessing and a curse. They were lucky enough to enjoy a quiet existence back in Maine, without reporters camped out on their doorstep. Their kids—Maximilian, who was ten, and Georgina, who'd just turned five—could live a normal life, free of paparazzi. They were of royal descent but would never have to worry about the politics of their father's ancestral country or know what it meant to be constantly photographed.

"Does my hair look okay?" June asked as she brought a hand up to her head.

Cal grabbed it before she could touch the updo the hairdresser had painstakingly put together. He kissed her palm and kept her hand in his as he said, "Of course it does. You're going to outshine the bride, love."

Cal wasn't surprised when June rolled her eyes. "Whatever," she said. "No one's going to even notice me with all the other beautiful people around here."

She was wrong. So wrong, it wasn't even funny, but Cal simply smiled. He knew better than to correct her. One, it would just make her even more nervous and self-conscious to know the press and the onlookers were just as excited to see *her* as they were the bride and groom and the rest of the royal family.

"Come on, let's get going. We don't want to be late," Cal said.

He pulled June along next to him, and they got into the Rolls-Royce waiting to whisk them to the church where the wedding was taking place. The same church where they'd gotten married eight years ago. Max had been two, and their entire crew had flown to Europe on one of the royal family's private jets.

Unlike their civil ceremony, when June was in the hospital after being shot, the Liechtenstein wedding had been a lavish formal affair, just as today's would be . . . but of course, June and their friends had put their own unique stamp on their ceremony. Cal couldn't remember it without smiling.

As they neared the church, they had to stop because of traffic. Cars were lined up, waiting to let the guests out, each of whom stopped and posed for the media.

After about ten minutes, June sighed. "This is taking too long," she complained.

"You want to walk?" Cal asked, knowing his wife better than anyone in the world.

"Yes!" she said with a huge grin.

Cal leaned forward and told their driver they'd walk the rest of the way, and the man simply smiled. He was used to Princess Juniper's "quirks."

Cal scooted over, exited, and held out a hand to June. She grabbed it, and he helped her stand. He didn't worry about her walking in heels and hurting her feet, because she'd insisted on wearing a pair of sneakers under her fancy dress.

Cal already knew what was going to happen, so he wasn't surprised in the least when his wife stopped to talk to a little girl standing behind the safety barrier. June didn't speak any German, but that didn't seem to make a difference to either woman or child. They spoke with smiles and gestures, and when June blew the girl a kiss, Cal knew she'd just made the child's day.

She continued stopping to greet people as they made their way toward the church. She didn't see the crowds lining the walkway as subjects, just potential friends. It sometimes drove Cal nuts, because he knew better than most that literally anyone could be out to hurt a member of the royal family, but he could no sooner stop his wife from greeting the citizens than he could stop a hurricane.

So he stood back and indulged June. And secretly, he loved seeing her like this—being exactly who she was, real and kind and down to earth. This was why she was so beloved in his country.

By the time they reached the steps to the church, June's hairdo was a little skewed and she was dewy with sweat, but the smile on her face was genuine, making her more beautiful than the most perfectly coiffed and made-up woman there.

She also had a handful of flowers given to her by strangers they'd passed.

"That was fun," she whispered as she placed her arm in Cal's. He smiled at her adoringly . . . and later, he'd realize this was the exact moment the picture that was plastered all over the internet was taken.

But of course, right then, all he could do was look down at his wife with love. She went up on her tiptoes to kiss him, but never would've reached if he didn't lean in to meet her. Such a public display of affection was normally not done, but his June didn't care about protocol.

Just as they were about to enter the church, someone yelled out, "Where are Prince Max and Princess Gina?"

Internally, Cal sighed. They could've ignored just about any other question, but June couldn't resist talking about their kids. She turned to the man, who was standing next to a video camera. Obviously he was a reporter, but June didn't care.

"We left them at home this time," she said with an apologetic smile. "We thought Liechtenstein could do with a break from the little heathens."

Everyone around them laughed. Their kids were adorable, but they definitely weren't what Cal would call disciplined.

"We love Max and Gina!" a woman called out in English, making June smile even wider.

A few other people called out some things in German, how cute their kids were, how June and Cal were such good parents, how the kids were so friendly.

"Next time," June said with a small wave at the camera, then tightened her hold on Cal and headed for the doors of the church. When they were far enough away that no one could overhear them, June whispered, "Were they saying that Max was an unruly American and Gina was as far from a princess as possible?"

"You know they weren't," Cal said.

"They wouldn't have been wrong," she said with a shrug.

Cal could hear the rumble of voices in the nave of the church, which let him know the wedding hadn't started yet. No one would have blinked if he and June were late. They weren't exactly known as rule followers. He hadn't seen his parents yet, and they'd have scolded him for any tardiness, but since he was a grown-ass man in his forties, he didn't care.

He pushed June toward a door that he knew led to a small closet holding cleaning supplies and other odds and ends. Thankfully, it was unlocked, and Cal put a hand on the small of June's back as he encouraged her to enter. He turned on the dim overhead light and put his back against the door as he grinned down at her.

June rolled her eyes. "What are you doing?"

"I need some alone time with my wife," he informed her.

"You had plenty of that last night," she retorted.

"Yeah, but you had to get up at the ass crack of dawn to get ready. I didn't get my morning cuddles."

"You sound as pathetic as Gina," she said with a laugh.

"Do you care?" he asked, pulling her close.

"Not in the least," she assured him.

Cal looked down at the woman in his arms and wondered how in the world he'd managed to convince her to love him. Not only that, but she'd given him two children, and she still seemed just as in love with him as the day they'd said their marriage vows.

"What? You look so serious," she said with a small frown.

"I could've lost you."

June shook her head. "You didn't."

"When you were lying on that floor, bleeding from gunshots . . . I didn't know."

"Know what?" she whispered.

"How *much* I would've lost if you hadn't been strong enough to survive. You. Our kids. My country loving you almost as much as I do . . . and it scares me. And when you had Max without me in that cabin that could've blown up . . . so many things could've gone wrong."

June petted his chest. "But they didn't. I'm here. You're here. Max and Gina are here. We're fine."

Cal took a deep breath and nodded. "Yeah, we are."

"Shouldn't we be out there mingling? Hobnobbing with the king and queen? Talking to your parents?" she asked.

"Probably." But Cal didn't move.

"So?"

"I have a better idea," he told her . . . then began to gather up her dress.

"Cal! No! Don't wrinkle me!" June protested with a little laugh.

"Oh, I won't," he said, going to his knees and lifting her skirt over his head.

Her protest was muffled by what seemed like miles of material, and it was dark under there, but Cal knew his way around his wife's body and didn't need any light. His finger went to the hem of her panties, and he slowly pulled them over her hips.

He felt her hands grip his shoulders, and he smiled before leaning in. He paused for a moment to inhale, never getting enough of his woman's scent. How turned on she got for him. Even after a decade and two kids, he could still make her wet, which made him feel like a superhero.

It didn't take long to get her off. She was primed and ready, like always. He held her up as she shook in his arms, and he did his best to lick her clean before regretfully pulling her underwear back into place. Then he fought his way out of the material before reemerging and smiling up at her from his place on his knees.

She immediately burst out laughing. "Oh my God, Cal, there's no way you can go outside looking like that! Your hair is completely mussed, your lips are swollen, and you have some . . ." Her hand brushed against his cheek, even as she blushed bright red.

He could feel her juices on his cheeks. He always got a little carried away when he went down on her, wanting to bathe in her scent. Without thought, he turned his head to wipe his cheek on his shoulder.

"No! Don't—! Darn it, Cal. Now you've stained your tux."

Cal didn't care. He got to his feet and pulled his wife into his arms even as he was lowering his head. He kissed her. Long and hard. He wanted nothing more than to drag her out of this closet and back to their bed in the royal palace. But he needed to do his duty.

Taking a deep breath, he brushed his fingers over her flushed cheek. "I love you," he said.

"I love you too . . . most of the time. But I have a feeling when we get out there, everyone's gonna know exactly what we were doing in this closet."

"Do you care?" he asked with a tilt of his head. "Because if you do, I'll go out first, make sure no one is around, then take you back to the palace if that's what you want."

"What? No! We can't leave, Cal," she scolded. "That would be rude."

Again, Cal didn't care.

June nervously shifted in his arms, then brought up a hand and brushed her thumb over his lips. "You have my lipstick on you. Do I look okay?"

"You're beautiful." And she was. Smudged makeup, hair about to fall from the dramatic updo, and her upper chest flushed from her orgasm. He couldn't love her more.

June sighed. "I guess it's just one more thing for people to shake their heads about when it comes to us. Come on, let's get this over with."

This time it was June who tugged on his hand and pulled him out of the closet. They scared the few people who were standing in the foyer, and Cal smirked at the blush that deepened on June's face. But she'd learned over the years not to make excuses for the actions of her friends, her children, or her husband. She simply smiled at everyone, then held her head high as she headed for the entrance to the nave.

Cal heard a whispered comment about what a lucky man Prince Redmon was, and he couldn't agree more. He *was* a lucky man. Luckier than any one man had a right to be.

≈

Marlowe/Bob

"Why are there so many stuffed animals, hair doodads, and so much damn glitter in this house?" Bob grumbled as he made his way toward Marlowe, who was on their couch. She wore one of his oversize T-shirts, an old pair of sweatpants, and her hair piled on her head. They'd just finished dinner—comprised of artichokes, oysters, and Doritos. The first two because they didn't get to eat them when their daughters were home, and the third just because.

"Because we have a nine-year-old and a seven-year-old who love anything glittery and are girly-girls all the way through," Marlowe informed him with a laugh.

"Why couldn't we have had a boy first, like Chappy and Cal?"

"Don't look at me, it's your sperm that decided the gender of our kids," Marlowe told him.

They'd had many conversations like this, so she couldn't be all that surprised by his grumbling.

"I know," he sighed.

"Just wait until they're teenagers. When Violet's makeup is all over the bathroom and her hair is clogging the shower, and Kienna is hanging out with her friends in her band and they're shaking the neighborhood with their music."

"I'm not going to survive," Bob said dramatically as he fell onto the couch next to her.

Marlowe giggled and straddled his lap, draping herself over him as he sat boneless beneath her.

"You will," she told him. "Besides, I have something to tell you that will take your mind off our daughters being teenagers."

"What's that?" Bob asked, not able to keep his hands off his wife. She fit against him perfectly, and one of her favorite things to do was snuggle into him like she had when they were running from the authorities in Thailand.

"I'm pregnant."

Bob blinked, thinking he'd misheard her. He laughed. "Not funny, Punky."

"I'm not kidding. I'm about six weeks along, so it's still early, but this time next year, we'll be knee deep in dirty diapers once more."

"Holy crap, you're serious!" Bob said, sitting up and holding Marlowe tightly against him so she didn't fall backward. "What . . . how . . ."

She laughed. "Well, as to the how, when you make love to your wife without a condom and she's taking fertility drugs, that's kind of what's supposed to happen."

"I know, but I thought . . . it's been so long. I guess I just assumed it wasn't meant to be."

Marlowe shrugged. "Me too. But surprise! It happened."

Bob suddenly stood, ignoring his wife's screech. He'd never drop her, never let any harm come to her when he was there. He carried her through the mess of the living room, past the shoes in the middle of the hallway, up the stairs—which had odds and ends waiting for someone to carry them to various rooms—past their daughters' bedroom doors and straight to the master.

He crossed to the bed, still holding Marlowe tight, then he fell backward onto the mattress with his wife on top of him. Staring up at her, seeing how relaxed she was and how happy, Bob felt gratitude swell within him.

She sat up, and his hand immediately went to her belly to stroke the soft skin. "Pregnant," he breathed. They'd always wanted three kids, but after Kienna was born, no matter how often they'd tried, Marlowe hadn't gotten pregnant again. They'd done everything. Their last resort was the fertility treatments, and when nothing had happened for another year, they'd both assumed that was it.

But now she was pregnant. Finally.

Bob took a deep breath and closed his eyes, overcome with emotion. When he had himself under control, he opened his eyes and found his wife staring down at him with love shining in her gaze.

"Off," he muttered as he pulled on her shirt. Bob needed to see her. See where his baby was forming deep within her. Intellectually, he knew she wouldn't look any different than she had a few hours earlier, when he'd made love to her on the kitchen table, but he couldn't stop himself from needing to see every inch.

She laughed and indulged him as she stripped off the shirt. She went a step further and leaned to the side to kick off the sweats. She clearly hadn't put her underwear back on after the kitchen escapade, and Bob made a mental note to find where they'd ended up before their daughters came home the next day.

When she was naked as the day she was born, she straddled him again. She'd come a long way from the too-skinny woman whose periods had stopped because of malnutrition a decade ago. She was curvy now, having kept some of the weight she'd gained from being pregnant, and it looked positively gorgeous on her.

Bob's hands went to her legs, and his thumbs caressed her inner thighs for a moment before sweeping up to her hips, then to her belly.

He ran his hands reverently over her stomach before sitting up. He braced Marlowe as he lay her back and hovered over her.

"I need you," he growled.

"I'm yours," she said without hesitation.

Bob stripped in record time, having the presence of mind to make sure Marlowe was ready to take him before he pushed his cock deep inside her body.

"This one's gonna be a boy, I can feel it," he murmured.

Marlowe laughed under him as she stroked his arms. "I think it's too late to do anything about the gender at this point."

"Whatever," he said as he began to gently thrust in and out of his wife.

Bob wouldn't last nearly long enough, not with the thought that he'd once again knocked up Marlowe threatening to overwhelm him. He couldn't wait to see her pregnant again. She was so damn beautiful with her rounded belly. He loved everything about her pregnancies. Her weird cravings, how she got even lustier, her need to nest . . . he even loved her up-and-down moods. One second she'd be in love with everyone, and the next she was crying hysterically.

"More!" she demanded, squeezing his butt and trying to force him to take her harder. He should've known she was pregnant again, before she'd even told him. She'd been a lot more forceful in bed lately, just like she had when she was carrying Violet and then Kienna. To be fair, it had been seven years since the last one, but still.

"I love you," he told her as he gazed at her lovely face.

"I'd love you more if you moved faster and harder," she panted.

Laughing, Bob did as ordered.

After he'd filled her with the biggest load of come he could remember spewing in a long time, Bob turned onto his back and brought his wife with him. This was still her favorite way of resting, using him as a pillow.

She was boneless against him, and he stroked her back lazily. Their house was a mess, there wasn't much food left in the fridge and they had to get to the store, the lawn needed mowing, they'd given away the last of the baby things they'd been holding on to months ago . . . but Bob didn't care about any of that. *This* was the most important thing. Holding his wife.

He kissed her temple. "Love you."

"Shhhh," she mumbled. "Too loud."

Bob grinned, and shushed.

~

April/JJ

"Can you tell us the story about Aunt June's wedding again? Please, Aunt April? Pleeeeease?" Atlas begged dramatically.

April grinned as she stared at the little faces gazing up at her. Having all eight of their nieces and nephews over at the same time was exhausting, but she loved every minute of it . . . especially how quiet the house seemed when they were all picked up.

She hadn't lied all those years ago, she'd never wanted children of her own, but she adored spoiling her friends' heathens.

The children ranged in ages from ten to two. Little Ivy was already sound asleep in her crib, but the other seven were awake and wired from the sugar they'd eaten and the excitement of being at Aunt April and Uncle Jack's house.

And she had absolutely no problem telling the story of when they'd all flown over to Liechtenstein for June and Cal's wedding. It was one of her favorite memories ever.

"All right, but after story time, you all have to promise to lie down and go to sleep. We've had an exciting day, but tomorrow your parents are coming to pick you up, and if you're all cranky and exhausted because I let you stay up until three in the morning, you'll never get to come back," April warned.

Everyone giggled. The thought of staying up that late wasn't something they could imagine. Neither was not being allowed to come visit Aunt April and Uncle Jack.

"We promise!" Atlas said, enthusiastically making an X over his heart.

"Yeah, we will!" Max added.

"Mommy's not going to say we can't come over," Violet said solemnly. "She and Daddy like their alone time too much."

"Yeah, they get to smooch without us complaining," Kienna said.

All the kids made gagging sounds at the thought of their parents kissing.

April chuckled and couldn't help but look over at Jack. He was sitting on the floor on a beanbag, holding Gina in his lap. The little girl was half-asleep and leaning against Jack's chest as she sucked a thumb and held on to a stuffed walrus. The thing was hideous, but she'd carried it around with her since she was old enough to move.

Jack gave April a small smile. He looked tired as well, but they wouldn't trade being around these kids for anything in the world. And knowing it gave their friends some time to themselves was a bonus.

"All right," April said. "Once upon a time, there was a girl who had a very mean stepsister and stepmother. They made her do all the chores by herself and didn't let her leave the house, and they didn't give her any money. But there was a handsome prince from a land across the big ocean who visited the house and saw the girl. He helped her escape, and they came to Maine."

"And she got shotted!" Will said excitedly.

The kids had heard June and Cal's story so often, they knew it by heart.

"It's not shotted," Max said with an air of superiority. "It's *shot*. And hush, you're ruining the story!"

"Whatever," Will said with a roll of his eyes.

"You're right, Will," April said, continuing. "The girl—her name was June—was shot by a bad man who worked for her horrid stepfamily."

"But she didn't die," Kienna said, leaning forward as she spoke. She was sitting on the bottom of a bunk bed, listening intently.

"No, she did not," April said with a smile. "She lived, and she and the prince got married in a small, quiet ceremony and lived happily ever after."

"Aunt April," Jasper whined. "Tell it right!"

April laughed. "Right, sorry. The boy and girl *did* get married in a quiet little ceremony, but since the boy was a prince, the people in his country wanted a big fancy wedding. So after June and the prince had their first child—"

"Me! That's me!" Max said proudly.

"Yup," April agreed. "After they had you and you were old enough to travel more comfortably, when you were around Ivy's age, they packed a bag and got into a fancy private plane with six of their very best friends and flew across the ocean to have a huge wedding ceremony in the prince's country.

"The day arrived, and the girl wore a beautiful dress. Her train was so long, four people had to hold it to help her walk around. The prince looked very official in his tuxedo and all the medals he'd earned while being a soldier. The church was packed with people who'd come from all over the world to witness the marriage of the prince and the girl."

April looked around the room and found everyone's gaze glued to her. She loved this part of the story; it brought back so many awesome memories of that trip eight years ago.

"The prince was standing at the front of the church, waiting for his princess to walk down the aisle. His tuxedo didn't have any wrinkles, his hair was perfect, and he looked as handsome as the girl-turned-princess had ever seen. She began to walk toward him—when suddenly there was a loud scream behind her!

"Everyone gasped, afraid that maybe someone was there to hurt the princess or the prince, or maybe even king and queen! But instead, a little boy appeared from behind the princess. He was completely naked and crying hysterically. He yelled, 'Daddy!' and toddled down the aisle toward the prince.

"He didn't care that he wasn't wearing any clothes or that there were hundreds of people staring at him. All he wanted was his daddy. The prince knelt down and held out his arms, and the little boy, naked and, for some reason, soaking wet—which the prince didn't realize until he picked him up—ran straight into his arms.

"At first, all the people watching weren't sure what to do. The room was so quiet, you could hear a pin drop. Even the princess stood frozen at the end of the aisle. Her face got really red, and everyone could see she was embarrassed.

"Then another little voice yelled something, and *another* small body pushed his way past the princess. It was a second small boy. Also naked. Also crying. He looked around for a moment, then ran down the aisle toward his mother, who was standing in the front row of all the seats."

"We were wet because we were hot and it was stuffy in the church and we took off our clothes to play in the water in that fancy fountain. Then when the babysitter tried to get us to put our clothes on, we ran because she was totally scary," Max explained, defending their actions.

"That's right. You got scared because the very *nice* lady who was babysitting was just a little freaked out," April said with a small smile.

Max turned to Atlas and gave him a high five. The boys *loved* this story. They weren't embarrassed that they'd interrupted a royal wedding by running naked in front of all the guests. April had a feeling they might care when they got older, but for the moment, they simply loved being such a huge part of the story.

"Keep going!" Jasper said impatiently.

"Right, sorry," April apologized with a grin. "As I said, the entire church was completely silent as everyone was in shock. The two boys were still crying, and to add to the chaos, a little girl held in the arms of one of the princess's friends, also in the front row, began to cry because she heard the *boys* crying.

"The girl in the beautiful dress panicked, thinking she'd ruined the entire wedding. That everyone in attendance and all the people who lived in the prince's land would hate her. But then . . . someone giggled. It was muffled, but clearly a chuckle. Then another joined in. Soon, the giggles turned to outright laughter. It started in the front rows, where June's best friends were standing. And the sound spread. Before she knew what was happening, everyone in the church was laughing.

"And the prince did something no prince in the history of the land had ever done before. He stepped off the platform at the front of the church and walked down the aisle toward the girl. When he reached her, he leaned down and gave her a kiss. By now, his tuxedo, which had been pristine, was damp from the boy he was holding. His hair had been mussed by little fingers. But he didn't seem to care. Neither did his princess.

"He took her by the hand and led her all the way up the aisle to the front. He stopped at the first row to hand off the little boy to one of his friends, but his son refused. Not only that, but the other naked little boy held up his arms, wanting to join them.

"The princess gave her bouquet of flowers to one of her friends and took the second little boy in her arms. He immediately stopped crying and laid his head on her shoulder. And that's how the prince's country fell in love with the new princess. The marriage ceremony went on, with the prince and the princess holding naked little boys while promising to love each other for the rest of their lives."

April smiled at the memory. The wedding was anything but traditional, and while June had been terrified she'd be kicked out of Liechtenstein and never invited back, the opposite came true. The citizens loved how unruffled and kind she was, and the pictures from their wedding were still widely circulated every year on their anniversary.

The ball after the ceremony had been so much fun. The people they'd met were friendly and welcoming, and all the fears June had before the wedding were put to rest. Carlise, Marlowe, June, and April had found time to huddle at one point and simply enjoy being together, safe, happy, and healthy, and a photographer had caught that moment as well.

The picture was currently framed and on the wall downstairs. None of their faces could be seen clearly, as they were literally standing in a circle with their arms around each other's shoulders, but it was one of April's favorite pictures ever . . . maybe except for the one she and Jack had taken on the day they'd gotten married. She had a black eye and a bruise on her cheek, and Jack looked almost mean because he was still so worked up over the fact that she and the others had been kidnapped and almost blown up. But when April looked at it, all she saw was love.

"All right, story time is over. Time for all of you munchkins to go to sleep," she declared as she stood.

There were moans and groans from all the kids, but they headed to their beds—if they weren't already in them. Jack and April went around the room, doling out good night kisses and tucking everyone in.

By the time they headed to their own room, April was exhausted.

"Tired?" Jack asked as he put his arm around her waist and pulled her into his side.

"That's an understatement. You think they'll sleep through the night?"

"No way in hell," Jack said with a small laugh.

"How many do you think we'll end up with in our bed?"

"Definitely Gina. Maybe Will. Ivy will probably wake up and get everyone else up as well. We could end up with an impromptu tea party at three a.m."

April groaned. When they got to their room, Jack made sure to leave the door open, so any of the kids who woke up in the middle of the night and wanted to crawl into their aunt April and uncle Jack's bed knew they'd be welcome. He led April to their king-size bed and tugged her into him where they stood.

April immediately snuggled close, resting her head against his shoulder.

"This weekend has been awesome," Jack said after a moment.

April nodded. "Exhausting, but awesome," she agreed. Picking up her head, she looked up at her husband. "You don't mind?"

"I'm not sure what exactly you're asking, but the answer is no. Always no. If you enjoy what we do, then no, I don't mind."

April wanted to melt into his arms. This man was her everything. He wasn't perfect. He was still way too protective, but he worked his ass off, he made her feel like the most important woman in the world, and he loved her more with each day that passed . . . just as she did him.

"I was asking if you minded having all the kids at the same time," she clarified.

"No way. It's crazy, terrifying, and we'll sleep for a week once they're gone, but they're all really good kids. And knowing it gives our friends a break for a few days feels good."

"Yeah," April agreed.

"And . . . we get to give them back, so I get my wife, and our bed, all to myself when they leave."

April huffed out a laugh at that. Then got serious. "Jack?"

"Yeah, sweetheart?"

"I love you."

"I know."

She smacked his chest lightly.

He grinned. "I love you too," he echoed. "Thank you for giving this messed-up lumberjack a second chance."

"*My* lumberjack," April insisted.

"Yours," Jack agreed, then lowered his head to kiss her.

The affectionate gesture quickly heated up. April moaned in protest when he pulled away.

"Later," Jack vowed. "The second the last of the heathens is picked up, we're coming back to our room . . . you'll get naked and crawl under the covers . . . I'll join you and pull you into my arms . . . and we'll sleep for eight hours straight."

April burst out laughing. He wasn't wrong.

"*Then*, I'll show my wife how much I love and adore her. Your patience with the kids is never ending, and I love how good you are with them. They couldn't ask for a better aunt."

"I'm going to hold you to that," April threatened. "I want to show my husband how awesome he is and how proud I am that you didn't lose your cool when we went to the park and they all ran in eight different directions."

Jack shuddered. "Lord, that was awful. I couldn't keep my eye on them all at the same time. One of them could've been snatched up, and I might not have seen it. Let's not ever do that again. Or if we do, they're all wearing those trackers Tex sent us."

The infamous Tex had sent trackers to the guys after the women had all been kidnapped and had gifted a new one with each child born.

April smiled up at him. "They were fine. No one was more than thirty feet from us at any point. And they know they're to stay with their assigned buddy at all times."

They'd all taught the children everything they could about staying safe and about the dangers in the world—without scaring them to death. When they were out and about, everyone had a buddy they were required to stay with at all times, no matter what. So far the system had worked.

April leaned up and kissed Jack before running a hand over her face tiredly.

"Go on, get ready for bed," he said, physically turning her toward the bathroom.

April nodded. She grabbed the oversize T-shirt she still wore to bed and disappeared into the bathroom.

~

Thirty minutes later, JJ held his lightly snoring wife as he stared at the ceiling and counted his blessings. He was just as tired as April, but he couldn't sleep. He listened to the sounds the house made as he tried to relax. Nothing was out of the ordinary. The eight precious souls in the huge attic space, which he and April had turned into a large bedroom with four bunk beds and a crib, were safe.

He adored his friends' children. They were funny, kind, sarcastic, and smart, and the love JJ had for them was almost overwhelming. He and April were blessed to be such a large part of their lives.

Life in Maine had gotten better and better. Jack's Lumber was thriving. The ropes course they'd set up had been a huge hit right out of the gate. They were busy year round with tourists and locals, and organizations and businesses wanting to have trust-building and bonding trips with their employees.

They'd cut way back on leading groups on the Appalachian Trail. Between their families, Jack's Lumber, and the ropes course they all helped with, there simply weren't enough hours in the day.

But something no one was willing to sacrifice was time spent with friends. The number of picnics, girls' nights out, guys' nights in, movie nights, and semiquiet evenings at one of their houses, just visiting while the children played, were plentiful.

JJ was just as close to Chappy, Cal, and Bob as he'd been all those years ago, when they'd played a game of chance to determine their future. Who would've guessed they'd be where they were now? Not him.

April shifted in her sleep, tightening her grip on him as she did.

JJ sighed. *This.* This was what he'd longed for all those years after hiring April but had been too chicken to pursue. And he'd never let her go now. The kids would grow up and get on with their lives, but he'd still be here with April. Loving her as much as he could. He didn't know any other way to love her but fiercely. He still had the occasional nightmare about her being kidnapped, but with the passing of time, they'd lessened significantly.

A sound caught Jack's attention, and he lifted his head to look toward the door. Six-year-old Will was standing there, looking unsure.

"You okay?" JJ asked softly.

Will nodded. "I can't sleep."

"Come here, buddy," he said, holding out a hand.

Will quickly crossed the room and crawled onto the bed. He snuggled into JJ's other side and sighed. A minute or two passed before he held up a little fist and said, "On the count of three."

JJ grinned and curled his fingers into a fist on the hand that was around April's back, as she lay against him. "One, two, three," he said, flattening his hand to signify a piece of paper.

Will's index and middle fingers were spread into scissors.

"I won!" the little boy said happily.

JJ couldn't stop smiling. "So you did. Good job."

He'd taught all his nephews and nieces how to play rock paper scissors over the years. They could literally play the game for hours. It was as annoying as it was endearing. Luckily, Will seemed content with the one round, because he put his head on Jack's shoulder and immediately fell into a deep sleep.

As he and April had discussed, JJ had a feeling by the time morning came, there would be several more little bodies in their bed, taking up every nook and cranny. But he didn't mind, and he knew April didn't either. They'd have their house and bed back soon enough, and while it would seem a little empty, it would be a relief too. The best thing about being an uncle was being able to give the kids back to their parents. But he wouldn't trade the time he got to spend with them for anything.

"Jack?" April murmured.

"Yeah?" he whispered.

"Love you."

JJ closed his eyes and let his wife's words sink into his soul. Yeah, he was blessed. After the life he'd led, the chances he'd taken, the danger he'd faced, he was thankful for everything he had.

"Love you too," he said, kissing the top of his wife's head.

He concentrated hard once more on the noises around him, making sure all was as it should be, before allowing himself to completely relax . . . then shut his eyes and slept.

ABOUT THE AUTHOR

Susan Stoker is a *New York Times, USA Today*, and *Wall Street Journal* bestselling author whose series include Badge of Honor: Texas Heroes, SEAL of Protection, and Delta Force Heroes. Married to a retired US Army noncommissioned officer, Stoker has lived all over the country—from Missouri, California, and Colorado to Texas and Tennessee—and currently lives in the wilds of Maine. A true believer in happily ever after, Stoker enjoys writing novels in which romance turns to love. To learn more about the author and her work, visit her website, www.stokeraces.com, or find her on Facebook at www.facebook.com/authorsusanstoker.

Connect with Susan Online

Susan's Facebook Profile and Page

www.facebook.com/authorsstoker

www.facebook.com/authorsusanstoker

Follow Susan on Instagram

www.instagram.com/authorsusanstoker

Find Susan's Books on Goodreads

www.goodreads.com/susanstoker

Email

susan@stokeraces.com

Website

www.stokeraces.com